OBSTACLES TO YOUNG LOVE

David Nobbs was born in Orpington and educated at Marlborough, Cambridge and in the Royal Corps of Signals, where he reached the lofty rank of Signalman. His first job was as a reporter on the *Sheffield Star*, and his first break as a comedy writer came on the iconic satire show *That Was The Week, That Was*, hosted by David Frost. Later he wrote for *The Frost Report* and *The Two Ronnies* and provided material for many top comedians including Les Dawson, Ken Dodd, Tommy Cooper, Frankie Howerd and Dick Emery. But David is probably best known for his two TV hit series *A Bit of a Do* and for *The Fall and Rise of Reginald Perrin*, with Leonard Rossiter, now revived in a contemporary version written by David with Simon Nye and starring Martin Clunes. He lives in North Yorkshire with his second wife, Susan. He has four stepchildren, eight grand-stepchildren and one great-grand-stepchild.

DAVID NOBBS

Obstacles to Young Love

HARPER

This novel is entirely a work of fiction.
The names, characters and incidents portrayed in it are
the work of the author's imagination. Any resemblance to
actual persons, living or dead, events or localities is
entirely coincidental.

Harper
An imprint of HarperCollins*Publishers*
77–85 Fulham Palace Road,
Hammersmith, London W6 8JB

www.harpercollins.co.uk

A Paperback Original 2010
1

A catalogue record for this book
is available from the British Library

ISBN: 978 0 00 728628 7

Set in Meridien by Palimpsest Book Production Limited,
Grangemouth, Stirlingshire

Printed and bound in Great Britain by
Clays Ltd, St Ives plc

In memory of Father John Medcalf

Acknowledgements

Above all, I must thank Lynne Drew, not only for the enthusiasm with which she has taken me on at HarperCollins, but also for her wise and constructive editing. Thanks go also to my wife Susan and my agents, Jonathan and Ann Clowes, for their unfailing faith and support.

I am deeply grateful to Mike Gadd, of Boston Spa, who gave me invaluable and enlightening information on the art and craft of taxidermy. Further valuable assistance was given by Christine Giles and Keith Pettitt. I would also like to thank my good friend, David Lines, who read my first drafts and gave me great advice and encouragement.

In the early decades of my long writing career, in a supposedly more generous world, acknowledgements weren't made as widely as they are today. I want to mention two people who contributed so much in those days – my first wife, Mary, who was such a guide and support in the years of struggle, and Geoffrey Strachan, who published and edited several of my books with judgement, generosity and humour.

PART ONE

Obstacles to Young Love

1978

Three mighty obstacles threaten the burgeoning love of child-hood sweethearts Timothy Pickering and Naomi Walls. They are Steven Venables, a dead curlew, and God.

God it is who comes between them in Earls Court.

'I don't feel like it tonight, Naomi.'

She has turned towards him, sweet in her slenderness in the sagging bed beneath the print of old Whitstable. She has run her hand down his cheek and over his chin. Their rough-ness has pleased her. 'You'll need to shave again tomorrow,' she has said. And he has stiffened, not in the manner of the night before but in a shrinking way that has shocked her to her core, and she in the eighteenth year of her life has for the first time been forced to ask the question that has been asked a billion times before by women of their men, 'What's wrong?' And it is this that has drawn from him, like a wasp sting from a plump arm, the grudging admission, 'I don't feel like it tonight, Naomi.'

'You felt like it last night.' Naomi knows that her riposte is not worthy of her.

'Last night was last night.' Timothy is aware that *his* riposte is abysmal. He has spoken it sullenly, and his awareness of

3

its inadequacy makes him feel more sullen still. He is also seventeen years old, and unaware of so much, including his own good looks. When he wakes in the mornings he feels awkward, clumsy, raw, shy, ignorant. He does not feel handsome.

They are now miles apart, their naked bodies only touching because the exhausted, abused bed sags so much that it's impossible not to roll towards the middle.

'We shouldn't have done any of it,' he says. They are speaking in little more than whispers. It's a cheap hotel, and the soundproofing is almost non-existent. 'We shouldn't have come.'

'No use regretting it now. We did come.'

She is aware of the double entendre. He isn't. His thoughts are a million miles from sex.

'We've had a great time,' she says. 'Whether we should have done it or not, why spoil it now? Why go home with our tails between our legs?'

She touches his tail between his legs. It's as soft as an underdone egg.

'Please don't.'

'Timothy!' It's both a rebuke and a wail of anguish. 'If you're tired, that's all right. It's been a long day and you must have . . .' She wants to say 'really knackered yourself last night' but there are some words that you can't easily say to Timothy and she comes out with the much less felicitous, ridiculously formal, '. . . taken a lot out of yourself last night.' And put some of it into me, she thinks, shocking herself and realising for the first time that there might be quite a gulf between them.

'It's not that,' he exclaims, his manhood threatened. 'It's just . . . it's wrong.'

'It wasn't wrong yesterday.'

'It was. We just forgot it was.'

4

'I actually thought it was fantastic. I thought it was as good as being Juliet in front of four hundred kids.'

'Well, it was better than being Romeo. I hated every ruddy minute of that.'

'I know you did.'

Everyone at Coningsfield Grammar had expected that Naomi would be Juliet in the school play, but Mr Prentice chose Timothy as Romeo on a whim. Most people, and especially Mark Cosgrove and his mother, had assumed Mark Cosgrove would be Romeo. His mother has not forgiven Mr Prentice. Indeed, she has left her husband for him, run away with him, and embarked on the task of making the rest of his life miserable.

Mr Prentice's whim wasn't exactly a success, but it wasn't a catastrophe either. Timothy hadn't possessed the skills to play Romeo well, but the combination of his gawkiness, his intensity and those dark good looks of which he was so unaware moved the audience quite remarkably. The school hall became Verona.

Mr Prentice had cast them both in small parts in the previous year's play, Peter Shaffer's *The Royal Hunt of the Sun*, but they hadn't taken much notice of each other. Now, though, he told them, 'Feel. Feel. Feel. Feel the excitement of young love in the face of the world's hostility. Feel the emotion. Feel the sexuality.' They felt it. Mr Prentice, yes and Shakespeare too, must share some of the blame for what happened, for their falling in love, pretending to their parents that they were going on a school trip to Paris, and ending up in a sagging bed with thin, exhausted pillows in Earls Court.

'Don't you fancy me any more?'

'Oh, Naomi!'

She is almost as disgusted by her question as he is. He doesn't say, 'Of course I do,' and she doesn't blame him.

There's a silence, quite a long silence, but she knows that he is going to speak and that he is only silent because he's wondering how to begin, so she doesn't break it. A motor-bike roars boastfully past. Naomi thinks of all the grown-up things that they have done in London. They've been to see foreign films, films with subtitles, films that don't ever reach Coningsfield. They've eaten in restaurants. Well, no, only in one restaurant actually. The Pasticceria Amalfi, a cheery Italian place in Old Compton Street. It had all the easy surface friendliness of Italy. They have been frightened by London, aware of their vast ignorance of the world. They have been frightened by Soho, which they have imagined to be humming with wickedness behind the grime. They have felt very vulnerable, cowed by the vastness of London, and, despite that vastness, they have felt disturbingly visible, expecting at any moment to be spotted by someone who knows their parents. On the first day of their visit they saw some cheery young people entering the Amalfi, and were emboldened to follow in their slipstream. It turned out to be safe and warm. They have eaten there on all three days of that long, lovely, disturbing weekend.

At last Timothy speaks.

'It was when that funny old woman came up to us at breakfast. I thought she was going to accuse us.'

'Well, so did I.'

'I just felt so guilty. Didn't you?'

'No. I felt a bit afraid that I was going to be shouted at, that's all. Well, yes, I have been feeling guilty about lying to Mum and Dad and taking their money. But not about the sex. We're not in the Middle Ages.'

Timothy hasn't the words to explain how he feels. No, it isn't just about the sex – and even he knows that to say that the sex was wrong sounds horribly prim and proper and old-fashioned even for a Coningsfield boy – but the sex is the cause of the deception, and the deception makes him feel awful in the pit of his stomach. It's taking away all the memory of the joy, and after all they are in the middle of confirmation classes and what's the point of all that if they don't take it seriously?

But all he can find in himself to say is, 'What would the Reverend Bideford say if he knew? What would Mr Cattermole say?'

'I don't care what they say. It's what we say that matters. Mr Cattermole's a lech, anyway.'

'It's what our parents would say.'

He has touched a nerve. Naomi's father is an elder in the church. Her mother teaches at Sunday School. They are quietly, unshowily devout. Naomi is going to confirmation classes because it pleases them, and she likes to please them, and because Timothy is going. Timothy's reasons are much more complex, and much less understood. His relationship with God makes him feel that he has a place in the scheme of things, that he is important, that there is a point to being alive in a house full of death. Obeying a moral code gives him a reason to avoid what frightens him. His religion tells him what is good for him. It's the nearest he's ever come to a mother. And now, because of Romeo and Juliet, because of Shakespeare, because of Mr Prentice, he's in love, he's told terrible lies, he's received money under false pretences, there are more lies still to be told, he's truly wretched.

If only they could talk. In the distance some drunks are trying to sing. In room eight the silence is deep.

He reaches out with a shy hand, traces the inside of her right thigh with one finger, feels the stubborn softness of his prick, and turns away slightly lest she feel it too.

'Maybe we should get married,' he says at last.

'We can't. We're still at school.'

'Well . . . engaged, then.'

7

She's quite excited, but she isn't going to show it. Besides, it's absurd.

'Don't you want to get engaged?' he persists.

'I don't know.' It sounds feeble, but it's the truth. There's nothing else she could possibly say.

'I thought you loved me.'

'I do, but we're still at school.'

'I don't see what that's got to do with it.'

Nor does she, but she isn't going to agree. It becomes a long silence, too long, and the longer a silence lasts, the harder it is to break it. She thinks about what he did to her and what he let her do to him barely seventeen hours ago. How could he take this attitude so soon after that? She wants to talk about it, reflect on it, remember it together, as would seem natural. But it doesn't seem natural. It was so much easier to do than to talk about. She finds that she can't actually use the words that would describe the actions. Words could make what was beautiful sound dirty. She takes refuge in formality.

'Don't tell me you didn't enjoy the fellatio,' she says.

'Which film was that?'

'Oh, Timothy! Fellatio's . . . what I did to you this morning.'

'Sorry. I thought he was an Italian film director. You're always going on about films and film people that I've never heard of, showing me up.'

'I don't do it to show you up. I have to be interested in films. I've decided that I'm going to be an actress.'

Of all the times to drop this bombshell. Of all the times.

The train journey home is not a happy one. Timothy stares resolutely out of the window, as if the answer to their problems is going to be found out there.

'You won't find the answer in some passing farmyard.'

'Farmyards don't pass. We pass them.'

'I know that, you cretin.'

'You won't get far as an actress if you use the language so sloppily.'

'Don't be stupid. We don't make it up. It gets written. By writers.'

'I know that. I was Romeo, after all.'

He continues to pretend to be very interested in the singularly dreary countryside through which they are rattling.

'Nobody could be that interested in pylons.'

'What?'

'You're pretending you're looking at things. You're not. You're just eaten up by jealousy.'

They aren't speaking too loudly. There's a nun in a seat across the corridor.

'I'm not jealous.' Now it begins to pour out of him. 'I'm not jealous. I'm just astounded. You're religious.'

'What's that got to do with it?'

'Actors are all immoral. The men are all as bent as West End Lane.'

'What's West End Lane?'

'I don't know. It's a road somewhere, I suppose, and I suppose it must be as bent as actors. It's what my dad always says, anyway. And I expect the girls are all thespians.'

'Thespians means actors.' She can't keep a sliver of scorn out of her voice. 'You mean lesbians.'

'You see.'

'What?'

'I don't know anything about it. You do. We'll drift apart.'

'We won't drift apart. We don't need to drift apart. I love you, Timothy.'

'Good on you, lass,' says the ticket collector, arriving at Naomi's shoulder like a steamer appearing out of the fog. 'That's what I like to hear. Tickets, please.'

They show him their tickets.

'I'm frightened,' says Timothy softly.

Naomi recognises the truth of this and touches him on the arm. The ticket inspector sees the gesture and smiles. The nun can't find her ticket and blushes.

'You'll be a huge success. You'll go and live in London.'

'I needn't. I can come home between jobs.'

There's a problem with the nun's ticket. The nun blushes again. Her face is smooth, serene, almost aggressively serene. Yet how she blushes.

'Besides, you could come to London. You can stuff animals in London, can't you?'

'I'll be working for my dad. He hates London. He has a name for it. "The smoke".'

Naomi wants to tell him that everyone calls it 'The Smoke', but she judges it to be unwise.

'Anyway, we don't stuff animals. That shows that *you're* ignorant too. We're just ignorant about different things.'

The business with the nun is sorted, but the ticket inspector turns to have a word with them. They both know that he does this because he fancies Naomi.

'Ticket for the wrong train. Had to let her off,' he says in a conspiratorial whisper. 'Drive me up the wall they do. Always say they're so unworldly that they don't understand the ticketing restrictions. Same thing last week with a monk. Let him off too. Must be becoming a habit.'

Naomi recognises that this is a joke and laughs politely. Timothy doesn't.

'It was a joke, lad. Monk, habit. A joke,' says the ticket inspector.

It is now Timothy's turn to blush.

'He's not good enough for you,' says the ticket inspector with a jovial, hateful wink.

What a journey this is for blushing. Now it's Naomi's turn. She blazes with embarrassment and anger. The ticket inspector

10

looks from one to the other, realises he's put his foot in it, and digs the hole that he has made.

'I think I've put my foot in it,' he says, as he departs.

'You see,' says Timothy miserably. 'That's what everyone'll say.'

'Bollocks,' says Naomi more loudly than she intended.

Timothy looks shocked. The nun buries herself in her book.

'Quiet. She'll hear,' says Timothy.

'You're always so worried what people will think. She isn't listening. She isn't interested in us. She's reading her devotions or whatever it is they have to read.'

'You'll spend five months filming in Caracas.'

'If I do, I'll dream of you.'

'You won't. You'll fall for Nigel Havers.'

'I won't fall for Nigel Havers. God, how many pylons are there in Britain?'

'You shouldn't use God's name in vain.'

'That wasn't God's name. It was just an expression. I love you. I really do.'

'You do now, but when you're famous . . .'

'I won't be famous and if I am it won't change me. *"She comes in the shop and she's just like one of us," says attractive olive-skinned assistant Val Pogson.'*

'What?'

'It's what they say about nice actresses who haven't let their fame go to their heads. *She enjoys the glamour of filming in exotic places, but she's always thrilled to get back to her modest terrace home in Battersea and her taxidermist husband.'*

'You won't want children.'

She is silent for just a moment.

'I can't say I've thought about it, but . . . I think I'd really love to have your child. Honestly, Timothy.'

He leans across and kisses her. His tongue explores her mouth. He didn't mean to do this, but he can't help it.

11

The nun develops a sudden interest in pylons.

Let them be happy in their kisses. They have no idea of the storm that is about to break over their heads.

Timothy's steps never quicken as he approaches number ninety-six, but today they slow even more than usual. His father is not an unkindly man, he does his best, but it is not a happy house for Timothy. It's a square, stone, Victorian house on the gentle hill that takes the dual carriageway out of town in what was once one of the better areas of Coningsfield, but it's an area that's blighted by traffic and is slowly going down. Number ninety-four is a B & B called Ascot House. Number ninety-eight is lived in by an old man, Mr Lewis, and his wife, Mrs Taylor. Well, this is how Mr Lewis introduces them to people, on the increasingly rare occasions when he needs to introduce them. Timothy laughs because as the years pass and their health declines, Mr Lewis walks further and further behind Mrs Taylor on trips to the shops that are becoming slower and more hazardous by the month. Timothy's father, Roly, rebukes his only son for laughing at the elderly.

Timothy walks past the shaved lawn of Ascot House – 'Quality outside is the harbinger of quality inside, in the world of the B & B,' says the proprietress, Miss de Beauvoir, whose real name is Mrs Smith. In fact, she says this all too frequently. Her remark does not impress Timothy. He has been inside.

The lawn of number ninety-six is long and dotted with dandelions and docks. Last month, after a good rain, a post was hammered into the ground, and a board was hammered onto the post, bearing a message that alarmed Timothy. It says, 'R. Pickering and Son – Taxidermists'. Timothy's heart does not swell with pride as his legs lead him leadenly past it. He has been Romeo on stage and in life. Now he is again the only son of a taxidermist whose wife ran off with a plumber when Timothy was two and has never so much as sent him a birthday card since. 'A plumber!' his dad occasionally says, shaking his head in disbelief, as if the man's occupation is a greater blow to his self-esteem than his wife's abandonment of him.

As Timothy sees the board, he recalls that moment a month ago when he came home from school and first saw it. As he stared at it, the front door squeaked open – his dad wasn't exactly generous with anything, and that included WD40 – and his dad stood there, smiling.

'I'm taking you into the business, son of mine. You're ready now.'

Timothy had found nothing to say.

'Aren't you going to thank me?'

'Yes, Dad. Sorry, Dad. Thank you.'

'You're welcome.'

Timothy was too young to realise that by this his dad was trying as best he could to say, 'I love you, son.'

They had gone inside and his father had made a pot of tea and produced a couple of scones – a rare treat, but treats came with strings at number ninety-six, and the string was that his future was going to be discussed, or rather announced, and fixed for eternity. Timothy liked Marmite on his scones: he had described the clash between sweet and sour as 'orgasmic' but that was before his weekend with Naomi. On this occasion he hadn't dared get Marmite. His father disapproved. 'Marmite on scones? What travesty is this?'

'Well, lad, I saw you on stage and I'll say this, you were good. Our Timothy, the product of my very own seed, playing Romeo, who'd have thought it?' His father had his very own, idiosyncratic way of expressing himself. 'As I say, you were good, but . . . but, Timothy, you weren't that good. You are not an actor. The boards are not in your blood. The curtain has fallen on your brief career.'

13

'No, Dad, I know, I agree, I don't want to be an actor.'

'Good. Good. That's good. So what can you do? You're not stupid, but . . . but, Timothy. We don't want you ending up *a plumber* now, do we? Some say taxidermy is a dying art. Not so, my boy. Not so. More tea?'

'Thanks.'

Timothy had never thought of not being a taxidermist, but only because it had never occurred to him that he was ever going to be one. His ambitions stretched only to avoiding certain careers. He didn't want to be an actor, or a plumber, or a dentist, or a lavatory cleaner, or a teacher, or a racing driver. He expected that, being neither brilliant nor thick, he would go to one of the lesser universities, and if that didn't work out there was always Coningsfield Polytechnic. In the course of his prolonged studies he might or might not discover his vocation, which might or might not be the Church. He'd had no idea that he would suddenly, even urgently, need to make a decision as to his future. He was therefore unprepared to make a decision. Therefore he made no decision. And so, on that dark afternoon in that dark house, he realised that he didn't want to be a taxidermist five minutes after he had become one.

Later, when he looked back on that afternoon, he realised that there was no way he could have made a decision, because there was no way he could have told his lonely old father, with his failing eyesight and his sad, short marriage, that he was not going to join him and support him in his business.

'I have a steady trade, good contacts with most zoos, sources of supply from some of the great shooting estates of Old England. I've done well.'

'You certainly have, Dad.'

'It's not riches. Riches don't last. The Good Lord knows

14

that. But it's steady. Very steady. The Pickerings are steady people, Timothy, and you, you too are, I think, steady.'

'I hope so, Dad.'

'Is plumbing steady? No, it isn't. Three warm winters on the trot and they're knackered. But the world will always need taxidermists. Youngsters aren't going into it. Youngsters don't see further than the ends of their noses. That Naomi! Juliet! You can bet your bottom drawer she'll be wanting to be a film star, off to London before the frost gets into the parsnips. I'd take money on it if gambling wasn't a sin. No, as a taxidermist, boy, you'll be able to clean up very nicely.'

Timothy has not told his dad that he has walked out with Naomi. He has certainly not told him that he has been to London with her, fucked her, gone down on her, been sucked by her. In some ways Timothy and his father are alike, but with regard to Naomi there is a gulf between them that makes the Gulf of Mexico look like a village duck pond.

Timothy has time to recall this conversation in its entirety because he is walking up the garden path very slowly indeed. The house is dark. There is not a room in it, including the smallest room, that does not contain at least one dead animal or bird. In the smallest room it is, naturally, the smallest creature, a mouse that died of heart failure when startled by the Ascot House cat. There is stained glass round the front door, only slightly cracked. The floors are a monument to the past glories of linoleum. When he opens the front door Timothy feels that he is stepping back fifty years.

At last, though, he can delay the moment no longer. Earls Court, the Amalfi, the whole of London fades away. The door squeaks slowly open, he smells the slightly stale, utterly masculine linoleum and lavatory cleaner smell of his home and there, in the dim, narrow hall, at the bottom of the creaky stairs, stands his father, staring at him, glaring at him, pulling his braces forward and then letting them fall back onto his grimy ketchup-stained shirt with a savagery that sends a chill through Timothy's whole body.

His father comes forward and punches him in the face. Timothy staggers back, crashes into the little table by the door, falls to the ground. The dead fox that was on the table, his father's pride and joy, the one that the customers first see on arrival, falls onto Timothy's face. He hates the feel of the dead fox. He screams, grabs it and flings it off him. He cowers, expecting to be hit again. Then he thinks of Naomi and how he would hate her to see him cowering, and he glares at his father and tries to stand, but it's as though his legs are made of rubber, he falls again.

He looks up at his father who no longer seems angry.

'Naomi's mother met the French teacher in Stead and Simpson's,' says his father. 'A most unfortunate encounter.'

In that moment Timothy realises how naive it was of them to have thought that they could get away with it, and with his recognition of his naivety and of Naomi's naivety the whole long weekend seems to be stripped of all its joy and beauty and become a tawdry episode involving two very young schoolchildren who thought they were grown up. He hates this. He barely listens to his father. He can guess the details anyway. Naomi had told her parents the French teacher was taking a school trip to Paris. But the French teacher is not in Paris, she is in Stead and Simpson's in Coningsfield. Naomi's mother wonders where Naomi can be. The French teacher knows, from her friend Mr Prentice, that Naomi and Timothy are seeing each other. It might be a good idea to phone Mr Pickering. Mr Pickering tells her that his son has gone to France on a school trip.

Roly Pickering bends over, holds out his hand to his son,

16

and pulls him gently to his feet. He kisses the top of his son's head.

'I'm sorry I hit you,' he says. 'You're all I have.'

Naomi walks from the station to the bus station, where she catches the number twenty-eight Pouters End bus. She sits upstairs and gazes out over her home town, seeing it and not seeing it, loving it and despising it. So much has happened since she took this journey in the opposite direction just three days ago. At moments she feels too adult to be contained here, to go back to school and hockey and maths and confirmation classes, and then she feels a wave of regret for her disappearing childhood. So many wonderful things happened in London, yet in the end the joy went out of it like a pricked . . . she is going to think 'balloon', but she had been Juliet in Shakespeare and clichés just won't do. Like a shocked prick. And she feels shocked to be thinking about pricks, and in particular Timothy's prick, on the twenty-eight bus, in her home town. But the sex had been a revelation, and it was sex born of love, and she just can't think of any of it as in any way smutty or dirty or degrading. She holds her legs tightly together, as if the beautiful memory of it might slide out from between them. And then an earthquake of loneliness cracks her body and she shudders with the fear of the days without Timothy beside her in bed. She thinks about his lovely sullen darkness, his rough stubble, his occasional devastating shy smile. She loves him. She thinks about praying to God to arrange for her to leave school and live with him and marry him. But God would be too busy and people just didn't pray on the twenty-eight bus and in any case she isn't certain . . . no, she isn't yet ready to admit to herself that she has doubts about the existence of God. That's too frightening. That would make home life too difficult.

She is thinking so many things that she almost forgets to get off the bus at Cragley Road. She rings the bell and lugs her case down the stairs in a rush, trips, almost falls, almost tumbles out of the bus into the cool of the autumn evening.

She gazes up the hill towards the big houses of the old textile magnates in Upper Cragley Road, but her path takes her down past the pleasant detached but less impressive houses of Lower Cragley Road. It's still posh enough to have only names on the houses, though, the numbers being a secret known only to the beleaguered postmen.

L'Ancresse. A pleasant 1930s house with simple lines and a square bay window in the lounge. It had been Laburnum Villa but her parents had renamed it after their favourite bay in Guernsey, where they used to take their seaside holidays. Unlike Timothy, Naomi has always hurried happily to the warmth, safety and sheer good spirits of her family home, but today . . . today she cannot believe that it is sitting there so calm, so quiet, so sure of itself, as if nothing has changed in the three days since she was last there, and of course, inside the house, now that her elder brothers have fled the nest, nothing will have changed.

And she realises, with a flash of horror, that she has forgotten to make any preparations for the questions that she will be asked about Paris. And hers is a family that asks about everything, shares everything, demands that you share everything.

She stands stock still beside the old English rose bush which is still in glorious flower. Well, it's too late now. She marches to the front door, gets her key from her handbag, and opens the door, which does not squeak. There is no shortage of everyday essentials in the Walls household, and that includes WD40.

18

The house is quiet, strangely quiet, but Naomi is too nervous to notice this. Besides, she is not actually always very sensitive to atmosphere. Her teachers at drama school will soon be working on this.

'Hello!' she calls out. 'I'm back. *Je suis retournée.*'

Her mother and her father emerge slowly from the kitchen and the study respectively. Her mother is smiling. Naomi does not notice that the smile is strained. Her father is not smiling. There is nothing unusual about this. He is not a smiler.

Her mother kisses her, and says, 'So. How was Paris? Come through and tell us.'

Her father does not kiss her. There is nothing unusual in this. He is not a kisser.

The evening sun is slanting across the kitchen, lighting up the oranges in the Japanese bowl. There's a smell that Naomi recognises and loves, yet today, for the first time, it seems to smell of the past. It's a shepherd's pie, browning in the oven.

She doesn't know where to begin.

'It was lovely,' she says.

'What did you see?' asks her father. Naomi is too terrified to notice that he is being a schoolmaster now, not a father.

'Er . . . well, the Champs Élysées. Notre Dame.' She thinks hard, desperately. 'Les Halles.'

There is silence. She has run out of sights.

'Not a lot, in three days.'

Her father's voice is quietly, regretfully merciless. Her mother is moved to try to rescue her daughter, even though she knows that the rescue will itself make matters worse.

'So, what about the food?' she asks brightly, but as she pauses her mouth continues to work in that way she has that reveals her inner tension. 'The French are famous for

19

their food, aren't they? Where did they take you to eat? Nice bistros?'

Naomi's heart is beating like the wings of a trapped moth. Her throat is dry.

'Yes. Exactly. Nice bistros.'

She is afraid that she will blush. She strives so hard not to blush. Her brain is whirring and she even considers the possibility of confessing.

'One of them was called the Blue Oyster.'

'What a strange name,' says her mother.

'Surely you remember it in French,' says her father.

'*L'huître bleu*.' The girl's a fighter.

'And what did you have? Let's hear all about it.'

Her mother's chattiness is terrible for Naomi.

'Er . . . not oysters. Miss Malmaison had oysters, and so did two of the girls. Sammy Foster'll eat anything. I just had steak and chips.'

'Oh, dear,' says her mother, falsely bright. 'I was so hoping to hear details of really local Parisian dishes that I might make.'

Her mother, whose name is Penny – well, it's Penelope, but nobody ever uses that – is known for good plain cooking. She teaches domestic science and sometimes takes Sunday School at church.

'I quite thought I might have something new to teach my girls.'

Naomi knows that she has to get away from the question of food. The only food she can think of is the food at the Amalfi, and she hasn't the wit, in her anxiety, to say that they went to an Italian restaurant. Besides, the food at the Amalfi is a secret between her and her lover.

Inspiration strikes.

'We went to the Louvre. We saw the *Mona Lisa*.'

'Ah,' says her father. His name is William. He teaches Classics

20

and he's going bald. There is not necessarily any connection between these two facts. 'What did you think of her?'

Naomi dredges up something that she has read somewhere.

'She's a lot smaller than I expected.'

'That's strange,' says her father. 'Since you clearly read that somewhere, it's odd that you should not have expected it.'

'What?' She is confused.

'You haven't been to Paris, Naomi, so you must have read that.'

His voice is not cruel. His message is devastating, so he would have no need to be cruel, even if he was capable of it. His voice is pained, and that is worse than cruelty to Naomi.

She is free to blush now. All the blushes that she has fought come pouring out. Her cheeks blaze.

'I met Miss Malmaison in Stead and Simpson's,' says her mother quietly.

Naomi is amazed to find that it's a relief to be found out. She will lie about it no more. In fact, she will never tell another lie in her life, even if she should live to be a hundred. She promises that now in a quick newsflash to God, who does exist after all, it seems.

'I went to London with Timothy Pickering,' she says. 'We had sex together and I love him.'

She bursts into tears. Her mother comes to her and lets her fall into her arms. Her father wishes he was on his boat in the middle of the ocean.

'We're engaged,' sobs Naomi.

She feels as if she is nine, going on thirty-two.

'I'm so happy,' she wails.

Her sobs begin to subside.

'It's all right,' she mumbles into her mother's blouse. 'We know it's a sin, and we've both apologised to God, but, oh Mum, oh Dad, I'm sorry, but it was so lovely.'

She bursts into tears again. She sobs and sobs. Her nose runs. Her eyes water. Her body shakes.

Her mother, still holding her, looks across at William. Just for a moment there is the old rapport between the two, they both want to laugh but realise that it is not appropriate. Then the shutters come down and her father is paralysed by embarrassment and bewilderment. He can deal with life's personal crises in the poems of Catullus, but not in the cosy kitchen of L'Ancresse, where the knives and forks and the National Trust mats are on the formica-topped table and the shepherd's pie will be done to a turn in ten minutes.

In her mother's eyes there is shock, sadness, love, compassion, fear, pain and – yes, it's unmistakable even to William – a touch of pride.

Timothy, in goal for Germany against the might of England, at Wembley Stadium, just behind the abattoir, tries to concentrate but can only think of tomorrow. Tomorrow scares him.

Barnes squares the ball to Keegan, who shoots. He scuffs his shot slightly, but Timothy is slow to move and it dribbles just inside his left-hand post. Well, no, there isn't actually a post. It dribbles just inside the left-hand school blazer.

'What's wrong with you today, cabbage-bonce?' cries Keegan (Tommo). 'You're all over the placc.'

'It's Naomi's eighteenth tomorrow and I'm scared,' he admits.

'Are you really engaged?'

'Yep.'

It's Timothy's ability at sport that has saved him from the mockery that would otherwise be the lot of an awkward, shy only child whose father is a taxidermist and whose mother ran off with a plumber when he was two. Football, cricket, boxing, darts, shove halfpenny, he can do them all. But his engagement is also gaining him a bit of grudging extra respect. The others have all done it with girls, or say they have, but none of them are engaged. They are children. Timothy is a man. He must remember that, and not be scared about tomorrow.

Barnes (Steven Venables) has the ball on the left wing, he tears down the field, he's a tornado, his trickery and ball control leave three dog turds, an empty bottle of Tizer and a used condom helpless in his wake. He sends in a curling, tempting centre. It hangs in the air. Brooking (Dave Kent) rises gloriously to meet it, remembers how big and heavy the ball is, and hesitates for just a moment. The ball passes within inches of his sweaty forehead. Steven and Tommo shout their derision.

'Try heading your dad's oranges,' yells Tommo. 'They won't hurt.'

'He couldn't head a tomato,' cries Steven scornfully. Steven Venables does scorn well.

Dave Kent doesn't mind their mockery. It washes off him like water off a carrot's back. Mockery is his lot. Being happy to be mocked is his salvation. Tommo intends to be a gynaecologist because he likes women's bodies. Steven intends to become a banker because he likes money and is confident enough not to worry about the rhyming slang. Steven oozes confidence. Dave is quite confident too, but only because he knows he'll never be anything but a greengrocer, and, luckily, he doesn't want to be anything but a greengrocer.

'Come on, English swine. You can't beat me,' shouts Timothy.

And they can't. The shots rain in. He dives, sprawls, climbs, hurls himself to left and right, grabs the ball, punches it, tips it round the post (Tommo's manky blazer). He cannot be beaten.

If he remains unbeaten until they tire of it and go home, everything will go brilliantly tomorrow.

Then Tommo is bearing down on him, getting closer, which way will his shot go? Timothy hesitates for just a second, Tommo twists his heavy but surprisingly lithe body one way, slips the ball the other way. Timothy twists, flings himself towards the ball, touches it but cannot stop it.

'Goal!' cries Tommo. He whirls around the waste ground, turns with his arms outstretched towards the fans packed into the great Abattoir Stand in their thousands. 'King Kev is unstoppable,' he cries. His suicide is still many years away.

Stupid though he knows it is, Timothy cannot help thinking that failing to save Tommo's shot is a bad omen for tomorrow.

Sniffy Arkwright is scurrying towards them on his splay feet, which might as well carry a health warning, so unsuitable are they for football. Coningsfield Grammar isn't nickname territory, by and large, but Sniffy has always been Sniffy and nobody even knows his Christian name. Besides, his voice, hard though he tries to conceal it, reveals with every sentence that he belongs in the world of nicknames and is at Coningsfield Grammar by mistake. He's sniffing out the possibility of a game, his eagerness to join in setting up waves of instinctive resistance. The fun is over.

'We're just going,' says Timothy.

Sniffy Arkwright isn't surprised. People are always just going when he approaches. And, since this is what life is like, he doesn't resent it.

As they walk away, Sniffy following like an exhausted dog, Steven says, 'It must be awful to be engaged and not be allowed to do it.'

'Awful,' echoes Dave, who is much given to echoing.

'I couldn't stop myself if I was with Naomi. Christ almighty,' says Steven.

'Careful,' says Tommo. 'Timothy thinks Christ is almighty.'

They climb the gate at the end of the waste ground,

and drop down into the ginnel that runs behind the new industrial estate down to the stinking river. Sniffy still follows, even though he has no idea where they are going or why.

Suddenly Timothy can hold his secret in no longer.

'We did it when we went to London that time when we were supposed to be in Paris,' he says. 'We did it four times in one night *and* we did other things.'

'Yes, and I'm the Archbishop of Canterbury,' says Tommo.

Timothy suddenly longs most desperately for Naomi's body. He will pray for strength when he gets home. He will pray for strength and patience, and he will ask God to make sure that Naomi likes the very special present that he is giving her for her eighteenth birthday.

Timothy walks slowly down Lower Cragley Road, clutching his brown paper parcel. He is deeply ashamed of its inelegance. Of course a dead curlew is not an easy thing to wrap, the beak has proved a nightmare, but he still feels that he should have done better. The paper is crumpled. Pieces of tape hang from it like plasters left too long unchanged on cuts and warts. He has never been a dab hand at wrapping presents. Paper is never obedient under his fingers. Tape never sticks properly. String simply refuses to be tied. God knows what struggles he will have in his slow mastery of the art of taxidermy. Well, God knows everything, or so Timothy thinks.

'It'll just be a quiet little supper party,' Naomi's mother Penny has told him. 'Just us and you and Naomi's best friend Isobel, and her brothers and their girlfriends. That's all. She's having her own party on Saturday.'

Timothy likes Naomi's mother and he quite likes her father but is utterly tongue-tied in his presence. He has good reason to be wary of Isobel, and the thought of meeting both of

Naomi's brothers and their girlfriends for the first time all at once terrifies him. Oh, please, please, God, if you love me, as you say you do, move the clocks on and let it all have happened already.

God does not respond. Maybe Wednesday is his busy night. Timothy has to force himself to turn right into the garden of L'Ancresse. He has forgotten that yesterday he was a man. He is in psychological short trousers today.

He rings the bell. The door opens and Naomi stands before him in all her assumed purity. She is dressed in white, and has a pink bow in her hair.

He kisses her awkwardly, mumbles, 'Happy Birthday,' and thrusts the parcel rather too firmly towards her. She fumbles for it and almost drops it.

'You squashed my breasts,' she says.

'Sorry.'

A bad start. Don't panic, though.

'What on earth is it?' she says, examining it with, it has to be said, an element of disbelief.

'Open it,' he says.

He has hopes of getting this bit over in private, but his hopes are dashed.

'Not yet,' she says. 'We're having presents later.'

He has spent ages getting ready. He has brushed his hair five times. He's wearing his best suit, which is also his only suit. Luckily, he is unaware that his tie clashes with his shirt. Unfortunately, he has no colour sense, and unfortunately, he has no sense that he has no colour sense.

Naomi leads him into the living room. A log fire is burning brightly. The family stand in front of it like a firing squad. Above them is a painting of a heavily reefed sloop in high seas off Harwich. On the chaise longue in the bay window there is a pile of elegantly shaped presents, all wrapped in attractive gift paper, most of them tied with gossamer knots.

Naomi places Timothy's parcel on top of the pile. It sits there like a deformed weathervane.

'We'll have the presents after supper,' explains Naomi.

Introductions are made. Timothy meets Naomi's elder brother Julian and his fiancée Teresa. Julian is solid and smiling. Shaking hands with him is like holding a sweaty sea bass. Teresa is tall, cool and beaky. Her handshake is wristy and malevolent. They both look at Timothy as if he is an interruption. He then meets Naomi's other brother Clive and his girlfriend, who turns out to be a boyfriend, named Antoine. Clive is slight, boyish, wry. He presses Timothy's hand sympathetically. Antoine is tall and good-looking in a rather stately way. He is wearing a thick bottle-green corduroy suit and is the only man in the room without a tie. His handshake is brisk. Timothy runs his hand down his trousers in an involuntary gesture of shock. He has never shaken hands with a homosexual before.

Timothy also shakes hands very warily with Isobel. No one else in the room, and certainly not Naomi, knows that Isobel once leant across and pinched his prick with savage envy during geography. He has never felt quite the same about glacial moraines since. Or indeed about Isobel. Perhaps it's the name, he thinks. Isobel is not a suitable name for a child. You'd have to spend the first thirty years of your life waiting to grow into it.

He feels very uneasy. He's sure that his suit is badly cut. He worries that, even though he has chewed so much gum that his jaw aches, his breath may be tainted by fear. He is certain that he is unshapely, drab, ugly, the human equivalent of his parcel, which will sit on top of the pile on the chaise longue like a stinging rebuke all evening. If only he knew, if only Naomi could tell him, that, while her engagement to a taxidermist's son who has helped her lose her virginity in a cheap hotel in Earls Court is not the stuff of

27

her parents' dreams, it is as nothing compared to their first meeting with Antoine this evening. They'd had no idea that Clive's girlfriend was a boyfriend. They'd not been told that he was French. They'd had not the slightest inkling that he was a struggling artist with no money who sometimes rode a bicycle over pools of paint to achieve his unruly effects. In the Undesirable Partner Stakes, Timothy is an also-ran.

And all the time, the badly wrapped curlew sits there, impossible to ignore.

'What on earth can it be?' asks Julian.

'Something with a spout?' suggests Teresa.

'A teapot, perhaps. Though why should Timothy give Naomi a teapot? Unless . . .' Clive smiles. 'Unless they are about to set up home together. Has a date been fixed?'

'Hardly. They're very young,' says Naomi's father hastily.

Naomi looks across at Timothy and smiles uneasily. Something about her smile worries him, but he soon forgets it because he has a far greater worry. He's terrified that someone will successfully guess the parcel's secret.

Luckily, before this can happen, they are called in to supper, which is served in the rather bare dining room. It smells of not being used often enough. The oblong table is simply laid, with the usual National Trust mats and no table-cloth. The meal, too, is simple – melon, roast chicken and trifle. Naomi's parents do not have sophisticated tastes. But the melon will be juicy, the chicken tasty, the trifle first rate. There is also wine – a rarity at the Walls table. Only white, no red. Timothy refuses to try it. Julian takes a sip, looks at Teresa, then at the label, and nods. Antoine comments, in his almost showily immaculate English, that if he painted blue nuns the bourgeoisie would have kittens. Timothy remembers the nun on the train and catches Naomi's eye. She smiles. There is a brief moment of complicity across the table. But then she turns to talk to Clive. It is clear that she adores Clive.

Timothy is sitting between Julian and Antoine. He wishes that he was next to Naomi, but he understands that her brothers must have that privilege. He's relieved that he's not next to Isobel. The vicious little cow might squeeze his balls in mid-trifle. He sometimes wonders if Naomi is a good judge of character.

Julian turns to him with the air of a man dispensing charity, but his words are bombs that will explode if Timothy understands the subtext.

'I have to say, and this will probably amaze you, that in the whole of my life I have never met a taxidermist,' he says, smiling deceptively.

'Oh. Well, perhaps you could come and meet my dad some time,' says Timothy.

'An offer it would be hard to refuse,' says Julian. 'Tell me, I'm intrigued, is your house full of stuffed birds and animals or does your father see as much as he can stand of them during his working hours?'

Timothy understands enough to realise that this is one person who will not go into raptures of delight at the unveiling of the curlew.

'We don't actually stuff them,' he says rather stiffly. 'That's a popular misconception.'

'I sit corrected. I apologise for my ignorance,' says Julian stuffily, and turns away.

Antoine turns to Timothy and asks him if he's ever been to France.

'No,' says Timothy. He knows that his reply is short to the point of being brusque. He tries desperately to think of something to embellish it, but he is hopelessly incapable of dealing with Antoine. 'Never,' he says.

'Do you like art?' asks Antoine.

'Oh, yes. My dad says what we do is a kind of art.'

'Are there any particular artists that you admire?'

'I like Peter Scott,' offers Timothy after some thought.

'I do not know this Peter Scott,' says Antoine.

'He does birds. Geese. Ducks. That sort of thing.'

'I see.'

'They look, you know, just . . . er . . .'

'Just like real live birds, ducks, geese?'

'Yes. Exactly.'

'Oh, dear.'

Timothy feels humiliated, but Antoine continues.

'When we get to know you all, Clive and I will take you under our wing. We'll go to exhibitions. We'll show you true art. Good art. Great art. Oh, and bad art. That's always fun too.'

Timothy finds the prospect daunting. He isn't ready for this. He'd almost prefer humiliation. It's easier to deal with. Less emotionally demanding. He finds himself staring at a painting on the wall above the hostess trolley. It shows a ketch beating up the Deben towards a stormy sunset.

Antoine knows what he is thinking.

'No,' he says. 'Not good.'

'Bad?' ventures Timothy.

'No. Not bad. But what use is "not bad"? Not bad is no use. Why are all the paintings in this house pictures of boats?'

'Naomi's father sails.'

'And her mother?'

'No.'

'Oh. That's bad.'

'Well, I think she gets sick. Very sick.'

'No, no. I don't mean it's bad that she doesn't sail. I mean it's bad that all the pictures are of boats when she doesn't sail.'

The conversation stops there. Antoine is perfectly happy for it to stop but Timothy thinks that it's entirely his fault.

Now Penny calls across the table to Antoine and asks him questions about France, about his background, about his painting. Then she looks across at her husband, seeking help.

William, who has been staring wistfully at the schooner that is bowling along up the Solent above the bulky Victorian sideboard handed down from his family and impossible to sell until they're all dead, gives Penny a slight nod, turns to Antoine, and says, 'I believe quite a large proportion of people in French cities live in flats and apartments.'

'Yes,' says Antoine, as if it has been just the question he was expecting. 'Probably more than here, I think. We do not all see the need to own a house. We are not quite such a nation of gardeners.'

'Yes. So I've heard,' says William. 'I sometimes think only our gardens save us from mass outbreaks of insanity. You must have other escapes.'

Antoine doesn't rise to this.

'How did you and Clive meet?' asks Penny brightly, oh, so brightly.

'On the train,' says Clive. 'I was going back to college. I'd popped up to Edinburgh to see an exhibition. And there was this impossibly handsome man strolling sexily down the carriage. Naturally I followed him.'

There is a brief silence. Naomi cannot believe how bravely her parents are taking this. If only she'd known, maybe she and Timothy could have been honest with them. Too late now.

'Your food is very different from ours, isn't it?' continues Penny remorselessly.

'They eat frogs' legs,' says Isobel savagely. It is the only thing she says during the entire meal.

'We eat all sorts of other things as well,' says Antoine. 'You should try our cassoulet.'

Poor Timothy. He can think of nothing to say. He assumes that what he is hearing is sparkling repartee. He hasn't the experience to realise that this is one of the most stilted conversations he'll ever hear. He feels out of his depth. He wants to talk to Naomi, but she is sailing down memory lane with her brothers and he has the feeling that she has forgotten she has a fiancé. And all the time his present sits there, in the lounge, waiting. He clings to the thought that, because it has been so wretchedly tied up, it will be all the more of a sensation when it is revealed. But he is not entirely convinced. How slowly time passes. That wretched ketch seems to have been sailing towards that bloody sunset (he apologises to God for his language) for hours, and they still aren't onto the trifle.

Julian gets to his feet.

'We must have a toast,' he announces. 'Is there any more wine? Everyone must have wine.'

'Oh, sorry,' says William. 'We aren't wine people, I'm afraid.'

He goes out and comes back with another, differently shaped bottle.

'It's not the same, I'm afraid,' he says.

'That's a relief,' says Julian.

'Oh, Lord, wasn't it good? Sorry. Maybe this'll be better. Not doing my job, eh? Out of touch.'

Julian opens the bottle and makes no comment.

Antoine says. 'I'd be on safer ground painting black towers.'

'Right,' says Julian. 'All got a drop?'

'Timothy hasn't,' says Antoine.

'I don't drink,' protests Timothy.

'Got to have a drop to toast our Naomi,' insists Clive.

Antoine fills a quarter of a glass with wine and hands it to Timothy.

'Right. The toast. To my dear sister on her eighteenth birthday. How pretty you are, Naomi. Hasn't she grown pretty, Clive?'

'Every inch a Juliet.'

'To our lovely sister Naomi. Happy birthday,' say the brothers in unison.

'To Naomi,' they all cry, raising their glasses.

Timothy takes a sip and almost chokes, but it doesn't taste too bad, it's reasonably sweet and warm, he can't think what all the fuss is about.

Clive leads them into singing 'Happy Birthday to You'.

William moves his lips but he is so embarrassed that no sounds emerge, Antoine doesn't know the words, Penny sings too loudly to drown the silence, Julian growls like a stag in rut, Isobel performs as if she's in an opera but goes too fast and gets ahead of everybody else, Teresa smiles blankly, coolly, beakily, and Timothy succumbs to his choking fit and turns purple. It cannot by any stretch of the imagination be described as a musical triumph, and, after they have all sat down, there is another moment of silence.

Naomi stands.

'I think I should make a speech,' she says.

There are cheers and cries of 'Hurrah'. William hunches himself against further embarrassment and dreams of sailing sweetly into St Peter Port harbour on the evening breeze.

'Thank you all for coming,' says his daughter. 'Thanks for the lovely chicken, Mum, it was really great, and for the wine, Dad, very nice. It's really great to have my best friend Isobel here, and I'm thrilled that my dear brothers could make it, and it's really great to meet their partners. But above all it's great to have my fiancé here tonight. I'm really looking forward to that intriguingly shaped present. I'm sure he's got me something really great.'

There is warm applause.

'And now a great English delicacy – trifle,' Penny tells Antoine.

'I'm enchanted,' says Antoine.

Three people have seconds, and all the while Timothy's tension grows.

As at last they leave the dining room, Timothy finds himself walking just in front of Julian and Teresa, who have not been able to discuss matters with each other during the meal.

'All right?' whispers Julian.

'Just about,' comes Teresa's answering whisper, 'for one who's been completely ignored because they're all fawning over the Frog poofter to show they aren't prejudiced, and if that girl had said "really great" once more I'd have thrown up.'

Timothy is surprised by this, but he supposes that it's impossible to please everyone.

He has decided that he hates Julian, so he is slightly discomfited when Julian whispers, '"That girl", as you call her, is my lovely sister. What did I ever see in you?'

But now they are in the lounge and he can hear no more.

Even now it isn't time for the presents. There's coffee first.

'Now. The presents,' says Naomi at last. 'I can't wait another moment. Julian?'

Nobody knows quite why it has always been Julian who hands out the parcels, but the family sees no reason to change its traditions now.

'Er . . . just before Julian plays his part in what is obviously some cosy family ritual that I know nothing about,' says Teresa, 'I've got a bit of a headache. I'm off to bed if nobody minds.'

Nobody minds, nobody would miss Teresa if she jumped off a cliff, and that now includes Julian. But there is a little awkward feeling in the room, which affects everyone except Timothy.

When Julian had told his parents that he was bringing Teresa, there had been a brief discussion between Penny and William. They had both agreed that Julian and Teresa should not sleep together under their roof. Penny had thought that William should tell them. William had hoped that Penny would.

'You've so much more rapport,' he had said.

'And why is that?' she had retorted. 'Because you don't try, and because you sail for a month every August and miss most of our holidays.'

This had shocked William, who had felt that after eleven years of silence on the matter the sore had healed. He had immediately agreed to tackle the issue.

He had felt awkward talking on the phone to Julian about this. He always felt rather awkward talking on the phone, he always felt rather awkward talking to Julian, and he always felt very awkward talking about anything relating to sex.

'Julian, old chap, how are you? Look, it's like this. Um . . . bit of a problem over the . . . um . . . the sleeping arrangements. You'll probably think we're desperately old-fashioned, and probably we are, but there it is, and I *am* an elder in the church and your mother does teach at the Sunday School and we . . . what you do in your lives is up to you, you're adults, but . . . um . . . I'm afraid we can't condone sex before . . . um . . . before . . . um . . . marriage under our roof. I mean, sex under our roof, not marriage. I'm sorry, old thing, but that's all there is to it. If Teresa comes, you must share a bed with Clive like old times . . . nice, eh, memories of camping, memories of Guernsey, happy times? . . . you are still there, are you? . . . Oh, good . . . and Teresa will just have to muck in with Clive's girlfriend and hope they get on. Or, I mean, one lot could go to a B & B, we have recommendations.' He had realised that this sounded a bit dry, so had added, 'But we hope you'll stay. Be nice to have all the family under one roof.'

He had been so exhausted, after the emotional challenge of the longest speech he had made in his life outside weddings, classrooms and yachts, that he had entirely forgotten that the job was only half done and that he hadn't rung Clive.

Julian and Teresa had agreed, Teresa very reluctantly, and then Clive had turned up with Antoine. Clearly Teresa couldn't sleep with Antoine. That would solve nothing.

Penny had given William a bit of an ear-bashing for not phoning Clive to discuss the arrangements. 'Never face more awkward moments than you have to, do you?'

'I just assumed Clive would fall in with the plans. How was I to know his partner was a . . .' He had pulled back from using a derogatory term.

There had been talk of trying the B & Bs, but time had been short and in the end Naomi's parents had agreed that the two couples could sleep together.

'But we agree under duress,' William had said. 'And . . . er . . .' He had looked even more embarrassed than usual. 'I don't think I need to say more, but . . .'

'But you will,' Julian had interrupted.

'Yes. Yes, I will. I think and hope that I can trust all four of you to respect our family home and not . . . um . . . try any . . . um . . . funny business.'

Teresa had looked furious, but had said nothing. Antoine had looked amused, but had said nothing.

Clive had said, 'Please don't stay awake all night listening, Dad, especially to us, wondering what we get up to, as if you didn't know. After all, even Catullus did it.'

'I find that attitude unhelpful, frankly, Clive. If you had told us in the first place that Antoine was a man, none of this need have happened.'

'If I had told you Antoine was a man, it would have suggested that I thought it something I needed to apologise about. Let's leave it there, shall we, Dad?'

They had left it there. Only now, as Teresa leaves the room, is there any need to think about the matter and recall how difficult the early part of the evening has been.

'Right,' says Julian brightly, to show that he isn't upset by Teresa's departure. 'The presents.'

He picks up Timothy's misshapen offering and carries it over to Naomi as if it might explode.

She begins to tear at the paper, but the parcel proves almost as difficult to unwrap as it was to wrap.

If you have a dead curlew handy, try wrapping it and then unwrapping it bit by bit. It will not reveal the secret of its identity easily. For quite a while nobody can tell what on earth it is. Everybody feels the tension, but nobody more than Timothy.

At last the curlew is fully revealed, its magnificent curved beak, its barred grey-brown plumage, and its eyes. Its eyes look out at the group, sharp, inquisitive, dead. Naomi holds the dead curlew in her hands. She goes cold all over. She is in shock. She hates the lifeless feel of its feathers in her fingers. She heard a curlew trill one morning on the moors and thought that she had never heard a more beautiful sound. She hates it dead. Hates it.

She cannot tell Timothy this.

There is silence in the room.

'It's a curlew,' explains Timothy.

'Yes, I know,' says Naomi. 'I've seen them. But not dead.'

'We didn't kill it,' says Timothy. 'It crashed into a greenhouse up beyond Tangley Ghyll. It's mine. My very first effort. I did it for you. Dad let me.'

'I didn't realise,' says Naomi.

She is staring at Timothy. He doesn't know why. He wishes

she wouldn't stare at him. But she has to, for fear that she will catch someone else's eye. Anyone's eye. If she does, she'll succumb to hysterics.

'Thank you,' she says. 'Thank you, darling.' Saying 'darling' makes her feel about eighty, but she doesn't know what else to call him. 'It's . . . it's lovely, Timothy.'

She puts the curlew down on an occasional table. She feels so much better now that she's no longer holding it. She moves back and surveys it.

'Really lovely,' she says. 'Oh, Timothy. You did all that for me.'

She goes over to him and hugs him.

He beams.

'Was it dreadfully horrid, doing it? You know, putting your fingers up it and . . . whatever it is you do. Was it awful?'

'You don't put your fingers up it. There is no up to put your fingers up. You build a form, with papier mâché, and wire to hold the legs and beak and stuff. It's like sculpture. You don't stuff a bird, because you put the skin on at the end, over what you've built. It's an art. It's what I do. It's what I'm going to do with my life. It's my job. Of course it wasn't horrid.'

'I didn't realise,' she says again, weakly. 'Well, thank you.' And she kisses him on the cheek.

'Well . . . follow that,' says Julian, strolling over to the pile of presents.

'A most original present and a most personal gift,' says Antoine firmly to Naomi. 'And Timothy, as a fellow artist I would love to come and see your father's workshop.' He looks at the curlew critically. 'Not at all a bad first effort, Timothy.'

'Thank you,' says Timothy. 'My dad says if you've done it really well its eye will follow you wherever you move.'

Naomi tries to hide her horror at this prospect.

*   *   *

38

Naomi and Timothy are only a few feet away from each other in the great, dark, solemn church. Only Darren Pont, Lindsay East and Sally Lever are between them. All the others in the class, except for Sally Lever, are younger than Naomi and Timothy, who have both rather enjoyed setting an example, and pretending to be mature.

With its fine hammer roof and fifteenth-century font cover, the church is one of only two buildings in Coningsfield to merit a complimentary mention in Pevsner, and the other has now gone to make room for a monstrously ugly multi-storey car park whose entrances and exits snake so sharply that few motorists venture into it. The Poles have rebuilt their major cities in all their historical glory, but this is England.

Naomi is not thinking about Poles or the hammer roof. She is thinking of the hammering of her heart. Why does it hammer so? Could it be because she has realised that she and Timothy are poles apart?

She has a pit in her stomach and several moths are flying round there, trying to escape. She is uncomfortably aware of Timothy. She loves him, of course. She is supposed to be going to marry him. But . . . there is that distance between them.

It's the curlew. How could he give her such a dreadful thing? How could there be such a chasm between their sensi-bilities? She keeps it in a cupboard, so that she never has to look at its reproachful eye following her round the room saying, 'Why did you humiliate me in this way?' but she is still aware that it is there, in her home, polluting it. She tells Timothy that she keeps it in her bedroom beside her photo-graph of him. This means that, when he calls round, she has to bring it out in her gloved hands and put it there, in case he pops upstairs and peeps, to see how his proud creation sits, how fine it looks, how happy Naomi must be to wake up from her beauty sleep and see it there, reminding her of him.

It isn't just the curlew. It's God. Timothy looks so fervent, so exalted. She cannot feel either fervent or exalted. Why is she here? Because her parents are Christians, her father is an elder, her mother teaches at Sunday School, she sings hymns in school assembly, she prays in school assembly, she writes 'C of E' on forms, she tells the careers officer she is C of E. To write 'agnostic', to keep her lips clamped during hymns, to keep her head defiantly unbowed during prayers, to upset her parents, what a burden that would be. No, when it comes to religion, the playing field is not level. Oh, there is so much more than just Darren Pont, Lindsay East and Sally Lever between them. Will today bring them closer together? Once they have eaten the body of Christ and drunk the blood of Christ, will they be able to reignite their love?

She recalls the last time he had visited L'Ancresse, a week or so ago. She had felt obliged to take him up to her room, to show him the curlew that she had taken out of the cupboard that morning.

'There it is,' she had said, hating herself. 'In pride of place.'

'Who's that?'

His eye had fallen on a sepia photograph, beautifully framed, sitting in the centre of her dressing table. It showed a very handsome young man, with perfect features and a trim moustache. She had found that she didn't want to tell him, which had surprised her. He was her secret, her harmless secret.

'Just . . . a family friend,' she had said evasively.

She thinks about her evasion now. Her desire to evade seems significant to her. She tries to concentrate on the Bishop's words, spoken with such uninspired solemnity.

'To the end that Confirmation may be ministered to the more edifying of such as shall receive it . . .'

40

What a strange way to put it. Nice to be thought of among the more edifying, but still . . . odd.

More words, but she isn't listening. A dreadful truth has assailed her. It isn't just God and the curlew. It's Steven Venables. He's asked her out. She finds him attractive. He's so self-contained, so confident, so sure of himself. If she went out with him, he would tell her where he was taking her. Timothy asks her where she wants to go. And then says, 'Are you sure?' and they fuss about it till she doesn't know where she wants to go any more.

'. . . which order is very convenient to be observed; to the end, that children, being now come to the years of discretion . . .'

Discretion, is that what I've come to, it doesn't seem like it to me, thinks Naomi. I'm light years away from discretion.

'. . . and having learned what their godfathers and godmothers promised for them in Baptism . . .'

Auntie Flo is my godmother, but who the hell is my godfather? Oops, language, Naomi. I should be scared, using the word 'hell' in my thoughts in church, in the presence of the Bishop. But I'm not. Hell, hell, hell. Not frightening, because there is no hell except the one we humans make.

She's drifted away from the Bishop's words again. He really is a very dull bishop. Concentrate, Naomi.

'. . . may themselves, with their own mouth and consent, openly before the Church, ratify and confirm the same; and also promise, that by the grace of God, they will ever-more endeavour themselves faithfully to observe such things, as they, by their own confession, have assented unto.'

She looks across at Timothy. He looks swollen with good intentions, of consenting, of ratifying, of confirming, of evermore endeavouring, of faithfulness and of assenting unto.

41

Now the candidates for confirmation move forward towards the altar. They become more than a congregation now. They become active participants in the ceremony.

'Our help is in the Name of the Lord,' says the Bishop.

'Who hath made heaven and earth,' cry Timothy, Darren, Lindsay, Sally and all the others except Naomi.

'Blessed be the Name of the Lord,' exclaims the Bishop.

'Henceforth, world without end,' whispers Naomi, trying to join in, knowing that her feelings towards Timothy and God are inextricably and perhaps senselessly joined together on this oh, so solemn day. In a few moments she will be confirmed. It's too late now to do anything about it.

'Lord, hear our prayer,' thunders the Bishop.

'And let our cry come unto thee.' Naomi can hear Timothy's voice above all the others. She senses that he feels nearer to God than the others, and therefore further away from her.

'Almighty and everliving God, who hast vouchsafed to regenerate these thy servants by Water and the Holy Ghost . . .' the Bishop finds extra reserves of solemnity, 'and hast given unto them forgiveness of all their sins . . .'

No longer to have to be ashamed of those three nights in Earls Court, especially the second one, and all those lies to Mum and Dad, but what's the point of forgiveness if you can't forgive yourself?

'. . . Strengthen them, we beseech thee, O Lord, with the Holy Ghost, the Comforter; and daily increase in them thy manifold gifts of grace . . .'

Steven Venables has a sister called Grace.

'. . . the spirit of wisdom and understanding . . .'

The dentist thinks I may be going to have a bit of trouble from a wisdom tooth.

'. . . the spirit of counsel and ghostly strength, the spirit of knowledge and true godliness . . .'

The abstract words plop meaninglessly into Naomi's abstracted brain.

'. . . and fill them, O Lord, with the spirit of thy holy fear, now and for ever. Amen.'

The word 'fear' horrifies Naomi. She gasps so loudly that Darren Pont turns to look at her in amazement. The fear of God. It crystallises all her doubts in a second.

They are kneeling before the Bishop now, and he begins to lay his hand upon the head of every one of them, saying, 'Defend, O Lord . . .'

She can't go through with it.

She must. It's too late.

She can't. It's never too late.

She doesn't.

She stands, turns, runs from the church, flees, flees from the Bishop, from God, from Timothy.

'. . . this thy child with Thy heavenly . . .' In his astonishment the Bishop hesitates for just a moment, then recovers. '. . . grace, that he may continue thine for ever . . .'

Timothy sees Naomi go, he wants to follow, he wants to rush out and say, 'Naomi, my darling, what's wrong? Don't cry.' For he knows that she is crying. 'I am with you. God is with you.'

But he doesn't. He has come so far and he wants to be confirmed. He is exalted. The ritual is both exhilarating and comforting. He cannot let down his godparents, dear Uncle Percy Pickering and Auntie May Treadwell, whom he has neglected so shamelessly. He wishes to enter this hallowed world, in which the sons of taxidermists are equal to dukes in the eyes of God.

He will see her afterwards, when he is fully with God and is therefore able to help her better. That makes sense.

He is troubled, but the shared solemnity begins to comfort him, it's so exciting to share the ritual and be as one not

43

only with God but also with Darren Pont, Lindsay East, Sally Lever and all the other confirmees.

If he had followed her, maybe their lives would have been very different.

She walks slowly past Ascot House, where Miss de Beauvoir (Mrs Smith) is deadheading roses. She tries to smile at Miss de Beauvoir, but her face is stiff with tension. She opens the gate of number ninety-six. It squeaks. Supplies of WD40 have still not been replenished. She passes the notice with its unwelcome message, '*R. Pickering and Son – Taxidermists*'. She walks slowly, fearfully up the gravel drive, past the lawn that is so lank and studded with weeds. Weeds are beginning to force their way through the gravel on the path.

In her anxious state she can't decide whether to ring the bell or rap the knocker. Juliet, reduced to this. She really does consider running away, writing a letter. It's her last chance.

She presses the bell. She doesn't hear it ring. She presses again. Again, she doesn't hear it ring. Well, it's their fault if their bell doesn't ring. Call it a business, R. Pickering and Son? Can't maintain a lawn or a gravel path, can't be bothered to make sure the bell rings, what sort of business is this? She would be well within her rights to run away.

But she doesn't. To tell the truth, she has such happy memories of those three nights in Earls Court, especially the second one, that she doesn't want to run away.

So she tries the knocker. Sharply. Three times. Rat tat tat.

Roly Pickering comes to the door, shirtsleeves rolled up, hair unwashed, morning gunge still in the corners of his bloodshot eyes.

'Naomi!' He smiles a careful welcome. 'How's tricks, then, eh, Naomi?'

He casts a very quick look down towards her crotch. He always does this. She doesn't mind. It's irrelevant, and sad. His face approaches hers, slowing down, like a train nearing the buffers. He makes gentle contact with her cheek, apologetically, mournfully.

'Is Timothy in?'

'He most certainly is. You've caught us in mid-squirrel, he really is shaping up, but he'll be thrilled to see you.'

Wrong.

'Could I have a word with him?'

'Course you can. Let's go and find him.'

They walk up the stairs, Roly leading the way. At the top of the stairs, a moose regards them balefully.

'All the way from Canada,' says Roly Pickering. 'That's the kind of business my boy's inheriting.'

Naomi can think of nothing to say. Her legs are weak. She feels sick. She finds herself being led up another flight of narrower, rickety stairs, past two jays and a sparrowhawk in glass cases.

By the door to the workshop there is a peregrine falcon in full flight, about to catch a goldfinch.

'Look at that,' says Timothy's father. 'See those rocks. I climbed Gormley Crag to take an impression of the cliff face, so that those rocks would be authentic. They say pride's a sin, but I'm proud of that. Couldn't bear to let it go. Couldn't sell it. It wings its way straight to my heart, every time I clap eyes on it.'

Naomi realises that Timothy's father is incapable of doing anything as ordinary as seeing something. He has to clap eyes on it. She feels guilty about this thought. Timothy has told her that before many years have passed his father will not be able to clap eyes on anything any more. But oh, how she wishes he'd be quiet.

Roly opens the workshop door, which squeaks.

45

'Young lass to see you, Timothy my lad,' he says with dreadful good cheer.

Timothy smiles. It's the smile of a proud, professional young man interrupted in his work.

His father points to an assembly of three sculptured forms with wire sticking out of them.

'Going to be three puffins,' he says. 'Just waiting for them to come from Iceland.'

Timothy sees the horror on Naomi's face.

'They're pests there,' he says. 'They cull them. We don't use anything that has been killed illegally.'

'They're made of brand new stuff,' says Roly Pickering proudly. 'Rigid polyurethane foam. Far more flexible and workable than papier mâché.'

Naomi doesn't want to know. Not now of all days.

But Roly Pickering is unstoppable. Now he is showing her the large board to the right of the tiny window. Here hang the many tools of his trade – wire cutters, bolt cutters, pliers, scissors, and sinister things that she doesn't recognise. The words 'Scalpel, nurse' float inappropriately into her mind.

'I didn't realise.'

She can see how elaborate the work is, how clever. It is indeed an art, as Timothy had claimed. Her curlew didn't feel stiff because of rigor mortis, as she had believed, but because it was solid, a sculpture, the feathers spread over the sculpted form so neatly that she should have been proud of Timothy. But it's too late. She was wrong when she thought that it is never too late. It's almost always too late.

His father opens a series of small drawers. They are full of eyes, foxes' eyes, badgers' eyes, jays' eyes, stags' eyes.

'All from Germany,' he says. 'We get all our eyes from Germany.'

They aren't frightening. They're like buttons. And yet . . . the eyes of her curlew had sparkled with alertness. She

46

appreciates now what a miracle of skill her curlew is, what an illusion it is. It's not a dead bird, it's a work of art.

'I didn't realise,' she repeats feebly, and then she pulls herself together. 'Mr Pickering, can I see Timothy in private?'

Timothy suddenly looks serious. Has he an intimation?

'Yes, of course. You could use the office. Crowded, but clean.'

Timothy looks at her questioningly, then leads the way down the narrow stairs to the landing.

'He uses one of the bedrooms. We never have guests,' says Timothy. 'Nobody ever comes.'

This door squeaks too. Naomi just wouldn't be able to stand it. If she lived here, the first thing she'd do would be to invest in a huge supply of WD40. If she lived here. She surprises herself even thinking it.

They enter a small room with a desk piled high with unruly invoices and calendars from zoos. There's an unwelcoming hard wooden chair of the most basic kind, and a black leather chair which desperately needs a taxidermist's skill to patch up its bursting insides. A dead badger lies on the wide windowsill, which needs painting.

Naomi chooses the hard chair. It wobbles. The right-hand rear leg is wonky.

'Sit down, Timothy.'

It's a command.

He has gone white. He sits down. He knows. He's not quite such an innocent, after all.

'I'm really sorry, Timothy.'

His mouth opens but no sound emerges.

'I can't marry you.'

'Naomi!' He may have known but the confirmation of it destroys him. He cowers. 'What?'

'I'm sorry. I don't love you.'

'You said you did!'

'I did, and now I don't. I've . . . there's someone else.'

Timothy crumples. He bursts into tears. He is pathetic. Tears stream down his face and he whimpers like a dog. She despises him and sympathises with him and hates herself and loves Steven all at the same time.

'Don't be so pathetic.'

She doesn't mean to be cruel, but she hates the scene, the horrid room, the badger judgemental even in death, her former lover sobbing like a baby. She is repulsed. What a good move she is making in freeing herself from this wretch, and yet . . . and yet . . . she still recalls those three nights, especially the second one, and she cannot leave him while he is like this.

She goes over and stands by the chair, holds her hand out, touches his wet cheek. His sobs slowly subside.

'I'm sorry,' he says. 'It's the shock.'

'I know. Timothy, I've got to tell you.' She swallows. She longs for a pint of cool water. 'It's Steven.'

'Steven! No!' It's a scream of fury, and she's pleased to hear it, after all this whimpering. 'Not Steven!'

'I know.'

'He's . . . he's . . . he's not even nice, Naomi.'

'I know. I know.'

'Do you love him?'

'I don't know.'

He clutches at this.

'Well, then. You loved me. You said you did. Give it another go. I'll be different. I promise. I can. I promise.'

'It isn't a case of your being different. It's just . . . it hasn't worked.'

'It's the curlew, isn't it?'

'No. I wouldn't break it off over a present.'

'I knew you didn't like it. I just couldn't accept the fact. I fooled myself.'

'I do like it. I understand it now. I thought all its old insides were still there, liver and kidneys and things, preserved. I can appreciate it now. It will always be one of my most treasured possessions.'

She took it to the municipal dump yesterday. And this is the young lady who promised God only a few months ago that she would never tell a lie if she lived to be a hundred. But she doesn't believe in God any more, and besides, she has learned already that it isn't always bad to tell lies.

'Is it . . . religion?'

'Well . . . it hasn't helped.'

'I'll never ever try to convert you. I promise.'

'You mean it, but Christians always do try. They can't help it. And you will. You won't be able to help yourself.'

'I won't. I promise. Naomi, I'll do anything. Anything you want.'

'That's just silly. Don't be silly. I don't want to remember you as silly. Who knows . . . one day . . .' No! She curses herself for saying this. She needs to be totally definite.

She picks the badger up. Now that she understands a bit about taxidermy she feels no fear of it. It isn't a dead badger. It's a badger brought to eternal life by art. She turns it round so that it won't see the last embers of their love, and lowers it onto the windowsill with the respect its life deserves.

'One last kiss,' she says.

'I can't bear this.'

'Yes, you can.'

They hold each other, hug each other. She kisses his wet cheek. He moves his mouth towards her, but she turns her mouth away.

'Thank you for having the courage to come and tell me,' he mumbles.

'Thank you for loving me,' she says.

She breaks away, goes to the door, turns, gives him a

painful smile, and leaves. A moment later, he hears the squeak of the front door.

Tears stream down his face, but he doesn't crumple. He walks over to the badger, picks it up, turns it round, and lays it down again almost as gently as she had. There is no reason for his father ever to know any of the details of what happened.

PART TWO

The Other Side of the World
1982

They climb for well over an hour, high into the parched hills. At last they see a crowd of people standing outside a simple house. The best man claps Simon warmly on the shoulder and beams at Naomi. They shake hands with all the guests, even with some tiny toddlers. Everyone smiles. These are real mestizo people, a mixture of Spanish and Indian.

They say – translated by Paul, of course – that they are very grateful to Simon and Naomi for having honoured them with their presence on this great day. Simon and Naomi look instinctively for mockery. There is none. These people's hard lives leave no room for mockery.

Paul – Padre Pablo to his parishioners – is Simon's uncle. He has been a parish priest in Peru for thirteen years, and has invited them to visit before he returns to England next month. He found the climb difficult. He likes his rum and is somewhat overweight. Simon and Naomi, however, have no problems with the altitude. They are fit. After all, it was at Simon's gym that they met.

The little house is no more than a small barn. It's built of mud reinforced by lines of stones. The roof is tiled. Paul explains that one day it will be a two-storey house, but

Naomi wonders if the second floor will ever become more than an intention.

There's no toilet, no running water, no electric light, and no possibility of their ever having those things.

Normally the only decoration on the walls is a small mat, rather like the mat Naomi bought on a reed island in Lake Titicaca. Hers told the story of the life of the woman who wove it. She will give it to her mother, who will love it. She thinks for a moment of her mother, and is suddenly homesick for L'Ancresse.

Today, the house has been turned into a church, and there are decorations hanging from the beams, pictures of buses, condors, rabbits, pumas, a fish, a dog and some dancers. There is a table covered by a white cloth, and a simple homemade shrine to the Virgin. The simplicity overwhelms Naomi. She's afraid that she will burst into tears. Hastily, she pretends that she's an actress in a film, that she's being directed by John Huston, that he has told her that if she cries she will never work for him again.

Round the walls on two sides of the dirt floor are low benches. A cloth covers one of the benches.

'The cloth is there for our privileged, first-world arses to park themselves on,' explains Father Paul with a gleam.

Padre Pablo dons a long, beautiful white robe and stole, and the ceremony begins. Naomi and Simon feel extraordinarily privileged to be able to witness the wedding of Marcelina Mosquiera Teatino and Alberto Cerquin Chuqchukan. Paul has explained that they had a natural wedding many years ago, when they worshipped the Sun God, but now they have converted to Catholicism. They've had eight children, three of whom have died. 'It's par for the course in these parts, I'm afraid.'

Naomi feels so happy for them in their happiness, and yet so sad, for she is convinced that they are deluded, and she cannot think it good to be deluded. Yet she realises that her reactions are more suited to Coningsfield than to the village of Tartar Chico, high above the Cajamarca Valley in the mighty Andes.

The service is very simple. One woman breastfeeds throughout. A dog drifts in, decides that there's nothing for him, and wanders out. Paul's voice is low and warm and kind. The groom repeats his vows strongly. The bride repeats hers shyly, almost inaudibly. Some things are the same the world over. Father Paul puts the stole over them both, and they take communion. Their intense pride is heartbreaking. There is absolute silence in this simple home. Naomi feels the desperate heat of the faith that is warming this cold room. Again, she fears that she may cry. She fights the emotion by becoming a government inspector, directed by Stanley Kubrick, who will bully her if she breaks down.

After the ceremony, everyone goes outside. A vast pot of boiled maize appears, and they offer some to Paul, Simon and Naomi.

'We must accept,' says Father Paul. 'It would be a great insult not to.'

The three of them go back inside, but the other guests don't follow. Naomi lowers her privileged, much-admired, occasionally kissed, first-world backside onto the cloth that saves it from coming into contact with the hard, rough bench beneath.

Paul explains that nobody will eat until they have eaten.

'You may hate it, Naomi, but it has to be like this. I tried to change it, and it didn't work. Believing that all men are equal is one of the privileges enjoyed by those who are more equal than others. These people have incontrovertible evidence to the contrary.'

A tray, with a cloth on it, is brought in. On it are two

vast bowls of maize, one with one spoon, one with two. Married people eat out of the same bowl. It is the custom.

A bowl of sauce is brought. Paul warns that it will be very fiery.

'These people wouldn't be so poor if they were allowed to practise birth control,' says Naomi.

'Naomi!' hisses Simon. 'This is not the time.'

'No, no. Feel free to say what you think, my friends,' says Paul, 'but say it casually, as if we're discussing the weather. Don't let these good people see that we are arguing. They would be very upset.'

'I don't know that I'm up to that,' says Naomi.

'Really? I thought you'd just left drama school,' says Simon. 'I thought you were a fully fledged actress now.'

The remark hits Naomi just as she is experiencing her first taste of the sauce. The fire burns right down her throat. She can't breathe.

'That wasn't very nice, Simon,' she gasps.

'Children, please. We're on show. Don't spoil their day,' warns Paul again.

The maize is palatable, if not exciting.

'This will be their permanent diet,' Paul tells them. 'Ten years ago, there'd probably have been a little meat. Not now, even for a wedding. These people are cut off from everything except the effects of recession. Prices for their pathetic little crops remain stable, while inflation rises.' His voice remains calm, he is smiling, only his eyes show his anger. 'And these are the people with whom, in markets and railway stations, tourists think it clever to haggle.'

Paul's little history lesson defuses the situation, but Naomi is still shocked by the tartness in Simon's remark about her. It seems as if in the tension and embarrassment of the occasion some deeper, less pleasant aspect of his personality has been revealed.

The sauce is fearsome, but in tiny quantities, worked very thinly into the maize, it makes a tolerable meal – if you don't have to eat it every day.

Their bowls hardly seem to empty, and there is a whole wedding reception out there, waiting patiently. Patience is sprinkled over this land like a condiment.

'In Cajamarca,' Paul continues, 'there's a room called El Cuarto del Rescarte – the Ransom Chamber. After he'd been defeated and captured by Pizarro and his little band of conquistadores in 1532, Atahualpa realised how greedy for gold the Spaniards were.'

Naomi thinks back to Peter Shaffer's play, and wonders, briefly, what Timothy is doing at this moment.

'So Atahualpa offered to fill a large room with gold and silver in exchange for his release. But Pizarro had no intention of releasing him. Realising this, Atahualpa tried to escape. Pizarro wanted to keep him alive, but was overruled. He was led out into the Plaza de Armas, to be burnt at the stake. He accepted baptism, and the sentence was commuted to strangulation.'

Naomi winces and mutters, 'Fear. Always fear,' through a mouthful of recalcitrant maize.

'I took an American economist to the Ransom Chamber a few years ago,' continues Father Paul. 'He looked at it in deep awe, and said, in tones of wonderment, "I've always been telling my students that inflation began in this room in Cajamarca, and now I'm here." I really think he was almost on the point of having an orgasm about inflation.'

'Have you ever had an orgasm, Paul?'

Naomi says this to shock Simon. She is sorry to have to shock Padre Pablo, but there is something about Simon today that makes her really want to shock him.

Simon is shocked, but Paul isn't, not remotely. He smiles, and replies very casually, so that the waiting guests might think he was saying, 'Jolly good maize, this,' or, 'Pity England didn't qualify for the World Cup finals.'

'Hundreds,' he gleams. 'Not that I've kept count. Nobody ever pretended that celibacy was easy, or that priests are sexless freaks. Each time I have one I remind myself that if I hadn't taken Holy Vows I might be doing it with a beautiful woman and not just with my veined old hand.'

A small child enters with a bowl, a child much too small to realise that they are superior beings who eat alone and undisturbed. Several appalled adults rush in and remove the child, who doesn't cry. They learn to accept life's restrictions at an early age in this land.

'Actually, Naomi, I have grave doubts about celibacy. It's too difficult except for saints. And it separates us from our parishioners and makes us less able to understand their problems.' He smiles at her and there is naughtiness in those deep, understanding eyes. 'Besides, you remind me of what I have missed.'

Simon raises his eyebrows in surprise but Naomi knows that there is no lechery in the remark, and accepts the compliment gracefully.

At last Paul thinks that they have eaten enough, even though their bowls are far from empty. They mime their delight, and the fullness of their stomachs, and there is laughter.

They shake hands again with every single person, and every adult thanks them for coming.

And every adult is glad that they are going.

They walk down the great hills in silence.

That afternoon, in the warm sunshine, Naomi, Simon, Paul and Greta sit in the garden of the Parish House, the Parroquia. Greta is German. She's training to be a nun. She is of medium height and slim, with straight, sandy hair. She has a disappointed face and strikingly good legs.

The Parish House is on the little main square of the village of Baños del Inca. On the other side of the square are the hot baths. The water in the streams round the village is so hot that every morning Simon has to collect a bucket of hot water from one of them, carry it home and mix it with at least the same amount of cold, before he can shave with it. Simon and Naomi go over to the public baths every morning, and have a hot bath together in a space big enough for a football team. Twice they've made love in the hot baths. It's their delayed honeymoon, after all. But today for the first time Naomi doesn't feel that it's quite like a honeymoon. Today for the first time Naomi is not in paradise. Today for the first time she cannot be content with small talk.

'You Catholics are so caring about the poor,' she says. Simon glares but she takes no notice. 'How much better their lives might be if there weren't so many of them.'

'To which of them would you deny the joy and excitement of existence?'

'That's nonsense, Paul. A person doesn't exist until they're conceived. Birth control doesn't deny any actual person life. It just makes life better for those who are conceived. The arguments for birth control are overwhelming. How can you not see it?'

Simon thinks how young she looks. She hopes his uncle will forgive her because of this.

'Of course I think about these things,' says Paul. 'And I'm not unsympathetic to your views. I'm what they sometimes call a worker priest, Naomi, and as such not always entirely popular with my superiors. I have to tread carefully, but I can assure you, I and many others of my kind turn a blind eye.'

'For . . .' She is going to say, 'For God's sake,' but she stops. Simon smiles to himself as he witnesses the battle between her passion and her manners. 'Sorry, Paul, but I just don't think a blind eye's enough,' she says quietly. 'The message needs to be shouted from the rooftops.'

Paul smiles. Suddenly he looks weary. Perhaps he has faced enough of the world's poverty.

Greta, who has listened intently, moving her gaze back and forth like a spectator at Wimbledon, crosses her legs. Her skirt is tight and the stretched material makes just the faintest rasp. Simon turns to look at her legs, and Naomi notices, recalling suddenly how Timothy had only ever had eyes for her.

She hasn't given a thought to Timothy for months, and now she's thought of him twice in one day.

She wonders where he is.

She would be shocked if she knew. He is also on his honey-moon, and he is also in Peru. He was married eight days ago, in Coningsfield, in the church where he was confirmed and from which Naomi ran so dramatically. Tommo, who failed to get into medical school and so had little hope of becoming a gynaecologist, was his best man, and was surpris-ingly nervous when making his speech. Dave Kent managed an afternoon off from his dad's greengrocer's. Steven Venables was amazed to be invited, but Timothy explained that Christians believe in forgiveness. He suggested Peru for their honeymoon. Peter Shaffer's play had given him an interest in the country, and Maggie hadn't needed much persuasion. She wasn't one for lying around on beaches. Her naked body was known only to her and her Maker, and she was having a bit of difficulty in letting even Timothy in on the secret.

And now here they are on a train from Puno to Cusco. The train has run along the shore to the head of Lake Titicaca, which died gently in a salt-bed of mud and reeds. There were wading birds everywhere, including egrets and birds that looked like a South American species of curlew. Timothy thought briefly about Naomi's curlew. He wondered if she still kept it on display. He wondered who the handsome young man in the photograph in her room had been, and why she had refused to tell the truth about him. He wondered if she ever thought of him, of *Romeo and Juliet*, of their nights is Earls Court. But it was only a passing thought. He has long ago recovered from his Naomi-itis. In all probability he will never see her again.

They have found the great Andean Altiplano breathtakingly lovely. The emptiness of the land, the great wide skies, the bare hills, the thatched adobe villages, the silver ribbon of river in the plain.

There have been cheese sandwiches for elevenses. A three-course lunch of avocado, beef stew and a banana has been served throughout the train. As they ate, the train had still been in sunshine, but dark clouds had sat on the high peaks like cowboys' hats. And one lone cowboy had stood in the empty land, miles from anywhere, and watched the train go by just as every passenger had been eating a banana. Timothy has wondered if the man had ever seen a trainload of people all eating bananas before, and what he had thought of it. But he hasn't mentioned it to Maggie. It wasn't the sort of thing that interested her.

Now the train is descending into the valley of the Vilcanota, which becomes the Upper Urubamba, which becomes the Lower Urubamba, which becomes the Vilcanota again. Anyway, they are all tributaries of the mighty Amazon. Timothy and Maggie are going to visit the Amazon before they return home. Well, Roly Pickering is not too well, and his eyesight is bad. One day quite soon the board in the garden of number ninety-six will state '*T. Pickering – Taxidermist*', and then Timothy is going to be busy. They may never get another chance.

More cheese sandwiches appear throughout the train.

The countryside is much more fertile now. There are pictur-esque, tightly grouped villages, huddled against the hostility of the world. There are eucalyptus trees in abundance. And all the way the river rushes with them.

Twilight falls. The train stops. Somebody gives them the unwelcome news that on this very train last week, forty-six people were killed by bandits.

The delay is interminable. It's now dark outside, and the lights inside are dim and unencouraging. More cheese sand-wiches appear. An American further up the carriage calls out that they will not be allowed to move until all the cheese sandwiches have been eaten. The laughter is distinctly hyster-ical. Maggie doesn't laugh. Timothy suddenly realises that she almost never laughs. Not that he wants her to. They are dedicated to seriousness. They face life sternly, hand in hand.

An American lady wants to go to the toilet but is told that the door at the end of the carriage is locked, so that thugs can't get at them. This locked door will hardly save them from bandits, though. It has a huge glass pane running almost its entire length. Or appears to have. When the conductor steps right through it, they realise that there is no glass.

'Don't worry,' says the conductor. 'We have armed guards protecting you.'

This does not reassure them.

Suddenly, stubby fingers scrabble at a window. Timothy's heart almost stops. Goose pimples run right down his back. He holds out his hand to comfort his bride. Are they to die after eight days of wedlock?

But Maggie doesn't need comforting. She's facing her Maker with a grim face, set in the granite of her courage. She is a sight to discourage all but the most desperate of bandits.

But the stubby fingers do not belong to a bandit. Somebody manages to hoist the owner of the fingers up until she can see into the train. The fingers belong to a short, stubby Indian lady. She is possibly the world's unluckiest seller of cheese sandwiches.

There is laughter throughout the crowded, tense carriage. Timothy and Maggie are outraged by the cruelty of the laughter, but even Timothy cannot avoid a slight amused tremor. He looks out of the window, lest Maggie spots it.

The explanation for the delay turns out to be extremely banal. The engine has broken down.

Naomi sits in the bar of the Hotel de Turismo in Cajamarca. She has been buying little knick-knacks for her friends at drama school. Simon wants her to get presents for his friends too. He's happy to pay but can't be bothered to look. It's just one more little stain discovered on the shining surface of his perfection.

The bar has dim lights, bare tables and one other customer. He smiles at her.

'May I join you?' he asks politely.

'I'm expecting my husband,' she says hurriedly.

'Oh no, I am not trying to . . . I am German. I am a travel agent. I am on a fact-finding mission to improve services to my clients.'

'Well . . . fine . . . I hope I can help.'

He moves over to her table, bringing his beer. He is tall, stiff, flaxen-haired, quite good-looking in a rather inanimate way. He looks like a well-made waxwork of himself.

'The North of Peru is neglected,' he begins. It's his idea of introductory small talk. 'But it is much more interesting than the South. Most of the South is very overrated. Lake Titicaca, for instance, is very boring. Don't go there.'

'We've been there.'

'What did you think of the Chullpas of Sillustani?'

She has never heard of them. What are they? People?

63

Liked him, hated her? 'I . . . er . . . I haven't actually heard of the Chullpas of Sillustani.'

He jerks his head upward like a frightened thoroughbred. He is astounded. He is contemptuous.

'What?? But they are the most interesting of all the funerary towers in which the Aymara buried their nobles.'

'We didn't actually see any funerary towers,' she admits.

'What? But the funerary towers are the only thing of interest in the whole area around Lake Titicaca.'

'We missed them.'

He is shocked, but he rallies.

'You didn't get a boat to one of the reed islands, did you? They are tourist traps.'

'We did.'

Her coffee arrives, with three slices of sweet apple on a separate saucer. There has been some little extra gift everywhere they have been in Peru.

'But not the first island? That is a complete sham.'

'We went to the first island.'

'But you didn't buy a mat?' he asks with dimishing hope. 'Those mats are phoney. The women tell you that they represent, in pictures, their life story. They do not.'

'We bought a mat.'

He is silent. This is too difficult for him to bear.

Where is Simon? He should be here by now.

She begins to talk non-stop. It's the only way to avoid being lectured by him. She talks about Cusco, about the poverty she has seen: an old woman asleep on a pavement beside her wares, which consisted entirely of spring onions; a little boy selling cigarettes one by one; a sweet, pale girl, aged about nine, trying to make a sale in a café, holding out her complete stock on a tray – two toilet rolls. She contrasts these scenes with a description of a treasure she saw in the magnificent La Merced church in the city. It was a representation of the sun, with topazes, emeralds and pearl mermaids, and, at its shining centre, fifteen hundred diamonds.

'These contrasts are all too easy to make,' says the German dismissively.

'But true and obscene just the same.'

He shrugs. He is not pleased. Where is Simon?

He asks her where they are going next.

'We're going on a bit of a farewell tour with Simon's uncle, who is a priest, and then Simon and I hope to be off to the Amazon.'

'Don't. It is a very boring river.' He pauses. 'But if you do go, don't go to Iquitos. It is a very boring town.' He pauses again. 'But if you do go to Iquitos, don't go on a trip to any of the jungle lodges. They are a real waste of time.' He pauses again. Naomi glances out of the window, and an icy blast runs through her veins. She barely hears the last piece of the travel agent's advice. 'But if you do go to a jungle lodge, don't go to the first one. That is a very boring lodge.'

Simon has walked into view with Greta. He kisses her cheek. She walks on, he turns and approaches the hotel.

He orders drinks – a beer for himself, an Inca Cola for Naomi. The German refuses the offer of a beer and says that he has to go. Even when he has gone, Simon doesn't mention Greta.

'Had a nice time with Greta?'

Naomi doesn't like this new sound in her voice. She wishes she could swallow the words back.

'What do you mean? I met her, that's all. We walked a bit.'

'Do you usually kiss nuns you hardly know?'

'Yes, I'm the secret nun kisser of Basingstoke. I give myself ten points per nun, and fifty for a Mother Superior. No, of course I don't. But she showed me one or two things and I was grateful and . . . I kissed her.'

'You fancy her.'

'I do not. What the fuck is all this? What's got into you?'

Doubt. That's what's got into her. Not a very serious doubt. Just the very slightest dent in her conviction that she has done the right thing in marrying him.

A minibus collects Naomi and Simon from their hotel in Iquitos at nine twenty-five. Already, the heat and humidity are stifling.

There are three other passengers on the bus – Timothy, Maggie and the German travel agent.

Naomi is stunned. So is Timothy.

So is the German travel agent.

'What are you doing in Iquitos?' he says. 'I told you not to come here. It is too hot, the hotels are too expensive, the town is dull, and it closes at weekends.'

At first, Naomi and Timothy are too shocked to speak. At last Naomi says, 'What are you doing in Peru?'

'I'm on my honeymoon. This is Maggie.'

These words, spoken so innocently, are bullets that fly straight to Naomi's heart. She is astounded to find that this is so, utterly unprepared for her sudden yearning for Timothy's body beside her in a sagging bed.

'You?' he asks.

'The same. This is Simon.'

Introductions and explanations follow. Timothy's eyes are making a desperate appeal to Naomi, and she realises what it is. Don't mention our three nights together, especially the second one.

'So, this is a happy coincidence,' says the German travel agent.

'Happy, yes,' lies Naomi. 'Coincidence? Not entirely. We were both in a play about Peru at school. I think something of its magic touched us.'

The minibus turns off the road onto a wide track that leads down towards the river. It pulls up by a locked gate. The driver hoots several times, then gets out and bangs on the gate.

'Why are you going to the first jungle lodge?' asks the travel agent, almost angrily. 'I told you this was not interesting.'

'We only have time for one, and we did want to see the Amazon,' says Naomi lamely.

At last an elderly unshaven man, with a touch of the salt about him, shambles up and unlocks the gate.

The passengers proceed down a flight of steep wooden steps to a small pontoon alongside which lies a long, narrow, thatched boat. It seats about a hundred. They are the only five customers.

'Tourism has died here this year. It is because of the Falklands War. People are frightened. The Falklands are thousands of miles away. European people are idiots,' says the German travel agent.

The boat eases slowly out into the stream, and chugs off on its two-and-a-half-hour journey to the jungle lodge. Everybody wants to admire the scenery. Nobody wants to talk. There is going to be plenty of time for talking at the lodge.

Naomi links arms with Simon. She hopes he is unaware that she is doing this for Timothy and Maggie to see.

Outside the town they pass a great confusion of ships, shipbuilders' yards, half-finished boats, abandoned boats, rubbish dumps, timber yards, and rusty cargo vessels.

Three tankers, the *Tupa*, the *Rio June* and the *Alamo*, are moored at a large petroleum installation. They're all registered at Manaus.

Naomi gives a little sigh.

'Something wrong?' asks Simon.

'Not at all.' If only he was better at understanding her

thought processes. 'The registrations on ships excite me. All the way from Manaus. Suddenly the Amazon all makes sense. I mean, wouldn't you be excited if you saw a ship registered at Valparaiso?'

Simon smiles and oh my God it's the smile of someone attempting to pacify a child. How will they get through their night in the lodge with Timothy so close? This is devastating. Only a week ago, Simon was Mr Perfection. Julian had told her that he had wandering eyes, that he loved his own body, hence all that keep fit. Always quick to see the worst in anyone, Julian. He'll have a very successful career as a lawyer.

They meet thatched boats coming upstream, heavily laden, mainly with bananas. People in canoes are hauling in their nets. And all the while there is the rainforest on both banks, punctuated by small villages of thatched houses on stilts. One village looks very much like another. One house looks very much like another. One stilt looks very much like another.

'I told you,' says the travel agent. 'It is a very boring river.'

'And how very brown it is. How very, very brown,' says Naomi in a Noel Coward voice.

There is a question she has to ask of the German.

'You say Iquitos is boring. You say the Amazon's boring. You say the first jungle lodge is boring. Why are you here?'

He snorts like a horse approaching a jump which frightens it.

'For research for my clients. My clients demand these places. They are cowards.'

They see two large kingfishers. How beautiful they are. Simon, give him credit, loves birds. She points to them, and he smiles and squeezes her arm. Maybe things will still be all right. She certainly doesn't want Julian to be proved right. It's his hobby.

68

'Beautiful,' he murmurs.

Yes. Beautiful. But Maggie is so ugly. How can Timothy possibly fancy somebody so ugly?

A lady with a bright pink parasol rides in a canoe towards the green grass and well-tended fields of yet another thatched village. She carries more of an aura of Henley than of the jungle.

Ugly is putting it far too strongly. She has to admit that. The nose is a little too wide, but not horrendously so. The lips, though on the thick side, are reasonably shapely. Some people probably find bushy eyebrows attractive.

Maggie's skin, though white and lifeless, is not much marked. Except for the mole on the right cheek, of course. But the mole is really quite small and it's only when the sun strikes it that you can see the two thin hairs that are attached to it. Naomi turns now, and sees them in the sunshine. No, to her regret, they aren't horrendous.

She is appalled by her feelings. What sort of woman is she?

A big diving bird with a white head and a long, forked tail is hunting for food. Vultures and large hawks wheel slowly overhead. They see a small tern with a black head, birds like sand martins, birds like sooty chubby swallows.

Simon shakes his head. 'If only we'd brought a bird book.'

'Never mind. They're lovely.'

They kiss. It becomes quite a long kiss. Their tongues are two snakes mating.

Naomi turns round, hoping that Timothy and Maggie will have seen, but they are busy looking out over the water and Maggie is making notes. Only the travel agent has noticed, and he looks very wistful.

'Maggie?' asks Naomi, feeling strange to be actually talking to her and addressing her by name.

'Yes?'

'Can you identify any of these birds?'

'Sorry? What birds?'

How could a taxidermist fall for a girl who didn't like birds? Maybe taxidermists only like dead birds. Naomi is comforted by this thought.

No, Simon is great. What does it matter if he isn't interested in the registrations of ships? They will watch birds together, jog together, do yoga together, do Pilates together, ride bicycles together, use rowing machines together, make babies together. Life will be good.

Babies? Where did that thought come from? How would that square up with her career?

They swing round to nose upstream to a little landing stage. They step out into a Turkish bath, and walk slowly to the thatched lodge.

The five of them go for lunch in the large, thatched dining room, which seats a hundred. They had assumed that they would be joining other visitors, but they are the only five.

'I suppose . . . er . . . maybe the four of us should share a table,' suggests Timothy.

'It would be awfully British not to,' says Naomi.

'I think we have to, really,' says Maggie.

What a charming way of putting things she has, thinks Naomi.

The travel agent has gone straight to another table and is already sitting down. He is immaculate in shorts and sneakers.

'What about the Kraut?' hisses Simon.

Naomi glares at him.

'He looks happy enough,' she whispers.

'I suspect he's a bit of a bore,' whispers Timothy.

That's rich from someone married to Maggie, thinks Naomi.

The German is aware of what they are hissing and whispering. They might just as well have talked normally.

'No, I am fine,' he says. 'I am used to my own company. You will have much to catch up on.'

It's a buffet lunch, with fried fish, fried rice, spicy kidney beans, French beans, tomato and avocado.

'So, how are things, Naomi?' asks Timothy.

'Yes, fine. Really good, thanks. Yes, really good. Simon and I got married eight months ago. He runs the gym where I go.'

'Oh. So you'll both be pretty fit.'

Naomi reminds herself that Timothy was never known for his sparkling repartee.

'Things didn't work out with Steven then?'

'No. You were right. He isn't very nice.'

'And how about work?'

'Well, I've only just left drama school, but I've got my first job.'

'Great!'

She realises that his enthusiasm is utterly genuine.

'We go into rehearsal the first day back.'

'Oh, I'm thrilled for you.' The sullen look leaves his face and he smiles with boyish excitement. Naomi had forgotten how handsome he was.

'Yes, that's really good news,' says Maggie, and Naomi has to admit to herself that she sounds pretty genuine too.

'So what's the part?' asks Timothy. 'Not Juliet?'

'No. Sadly I have to learn my lines. It's an Ayckbourn play.'

'A what?'

'You must have heard of Alan Ayckbourn, Timothy. He writes comedies. He's very famous and very good.'

'I've heard of him, of course,' says Maggie. Naomi puts the 'of course' into the debit column of her newly opened mental 'Is Maggie nice?' ledger. 'But I'm afraid we're really rather serious in our theatrical tastes.' Debit. 'I wish I'd seen your Juliet. People still talk about it.' Credit. No, double credit.

'This food's good, isn't it?' says Simon, just so as not to be left out really.

'I suppose it is,' says Maggie. 'I'm afraid I'm one of those people who get talking and thinking and forget to taste what they've eaten and suddenly find it's all gone and wish they'd concentrated on it a bit more.' Debit. 'But it's difficult. I have a lot of responsibilities in my life.' Debit. They're piling up.

'Maggie teaches RE at Coningsfield Grammar.' Debit. Massive debit. Oh, Timothy, you should have gone for somebody who brings light into your shady life. No. Don't think like that. He's happy. He's in love. It's touching to see. Fucking irritating as well, though.

'Food's good, isn't it,' Simon calls out to the travel agent, in the hope that he won't feel left out. Naomi is pleased. It reminds her that there are pleasant sides to his personality.

'Very palatable. Did you know that until fifteen years ago, Peru was a net exporter of rice. Now it imports. Why? Because the Velasques government broke up the haciendas and gave the land to the peasants. When it's theirs, they don't expect to get their fingers dirty any more.'

They are glad they didn't invite him to join them, on the whole.

'So, how about you, Timothy? How's the taxidermy going?' asks Naomi.

'Oh, very well. Very well. Dad's leaving it to me more and more.'

'How is he?'

'Oh, he's very well, but his eyesight's failing.'

'Give him my best wishes.'

'I will. He'll be pleased. He really liked you. He was . . .' Timothy stops. Naomi knows he was going to say that his

72

father was upset they split up. So does Maggie. 'He really likes you too, of course, Maggie,' continues Timothy unwisely. He turns to Naomi. 'The first day back will be exciting for both of us. You'll be meeting all the other actors and rehearsing for your play. I'll be going to Kilmarnock Zoo to collect a tiger that lost its will to live.'

'I'd lose my will to live if I was in Kilmarnock Zoo,' says Simon.

'I hate zoos,' says Maggie. Credit. 'And if you think that puts me in a difficult position over taxidermy, it doesn't. Timothy's the most ethical person I know. He would never have anything healthy and happy killed to further his business.' Easy to mock, but, actually, rather reluctantly, credit.

After lunch, they have a walk in the jungle. Their guide, Basilio, is young, even boyish, and quite small. He takes his terrier with him, which gives it the feel of a Sunday walk in the park rather than an intrepid voyage of discovery. He shows them an achiote tree, picks a fruit from it and opens it up to demonstrate how the Indians paint their faces red. He thinks he hears rain.

'We are not having the jungle walk cancelled,' hisses the German. 'I will not accept short measure.'

The rain holds off. They see many kinds of trees, and some ants, but no animals. Basilio apologises for the lack of animal life. There are too many people here. Clearly, to see the animals of the jungle you have to go where you aren't.

The skies darken. The trees murmur their indignation at the increasing wind, and begin to shake anxiously. The walk ends forty minutes early.

'Short measure,' whispers the travel agent.

The next item on the agenda is a nocturnal canoe trip. It gets dark early here.

'They will try to cancel it because of the rain,' says their new friend. 'We must insist. I will not accept short measure.'

But the rain stops. They go to the creek and climb into a canoe. Their guide for the trip is Basilio. They drift down the creek beneath the mudbanks, in the dark. They hear the noises of the jungle – crickets, more crickets, and then . . . Can it be? It is. More crickets. They also see the tail of a young anaconda. Well, they're told that it's the tail of a young anaconda, and choose to believe it. They hear a bullfrog. And more crickets. Suddenly the moon shines brightly. Basilio explains that it is now too light for alligators. Presumably, you can only see them when it's too dark to see them. They are beginning to get the hang of this jungle travel.

The trip is abandoned.

'Short measure,' whispers the travel agent.

They invite him to join their table for the candlelit dinner. He is delighted.

They sit right in the middle of the huge, empty, candlelit room. Dinner is served by Basilio. It begins with a beetroot salad.

Their German friend asks Naomi and Simon where they have been since he last met them.

'We went to Chiclayo,' says Naomi.

'Ah! What did you think of the Bruning Museum?'

'The what?'

'The Bruning Museum at Lambayeque.'

'We didn't go there.'

'But it's a marvellous museum, and the wacas between there and Chiclayo are also very interesting.'

'We missed the wacas.'

'But there is nothing else to see around Chiclayo.'

'We went with Simon's uncle, who is a parish priest, for him to say farewell to some Canadian nuns. We liked Chiclayo, its stubby cathedral covered in vultures, its friendliness, names like the Bang Bang Amusement Arcade. We spent a lovely evening in the nuns' Parish House. They didn't know how to mix gin and tonics, though. Either that, or there's a great shortage of tonic in Peru.'

Naomi is trying to get a reaction from Timothy and Maggie. Even a slight sniff of disapproval would do. But they are impervious. So very disappointing.

The beetroot salad is followed by soup with a fried egg in it, tasty highly spiced chicken with poor fried rice, and a fruit salad. With so few people there the meal is finished in under an hour. Never mind. That will give them all the more time to enjoy the promised traditional local cabaret in the bar.

The cabaret is an embarrassed Basilio with a guitar. He plays quite nicely. Timothy holds Maggie's hand. Not to be outdone, Naomi holds Simon's hand as if they are walking down the Ramblas in Barcelona and it's her wallet. The poor travel agent tries to look as if he is delighted to have no hand to hold.

Basilio doesn't play all that long, to be honest, and the four English visitors can't blame him, but the German whispers, 'Short measure. Always short measure.'

Basilio now has a few words to say to them.

'Tomorrow we will visit an Indian village. They do not use money. They have nice things to buy, and you will need to barter. The best thing to use is cigarettes. They like cigarettes. If you want to buy things tomorrow, get some cigarettes at the bar tonight.'

Simon fetches more drinks – beer for him and the German, red wine for Naomi, bottled water for Timothy and Maggie. He also buys cigarettes.

'I will not spread this noxious weed,' says the German. 'I have fish hooks with me. Many fish hooks. I will barter with fish hooks.'

Timothy and Maggie also refuse to buy cigarettes. The travel agent offers to sell them some of his fish hooks.

'I don't think so, thank you very much,' says Timothy loftily. 'I don't honestly anticipate that there'll be anything we want to buy.'

By the time they have finished their drinks, the barman is asleep. It's almost ten o'clock.

Naomi has been wondering about Timothy's sex life. Maggie doesn't look sexy. Not that they will be likely to be having sex tonight. The chalets have single beds underneath mosquito nets. It's not conducive.

'I love your breasts,' whispers Simon from his single bed. 'I wish I was fondling and kissing them now. Imagine kissing hers. He's got a job on. They're enormous.'

'I must say they did remind me of some old English burial mounds I saw once in Dorset,' says Naomi.

'You're a terrible woman,' says Simon affectionately.

In the morning they're scheduled to walk to a village of the Yagua Indians. Basilio meets them outside the lodge. He bangs a big drum five times with a gong, explaining that this is an Indian method of communicating.

Their walk takes them about an hour. Animals seen amount to a slightly disappointing total of one iguana.

The German astounds them by saying, 'I know a German joke about the British.'

'Oh, do tell us,' says Naomi.

'There were two Englishmen who met at work.'

They wait to enjoy the rest of his joke, then realise, to their horror, that he has finished. They don't get it.

'They work at the same place, but they have never met, because one or the other of them was always on strike,' he explains. 'German jokes are subtle.'

After about three-quarters of an hour the little party cross a creek on a high bridge. They find themselves in a small village of thatched houses on stilts. There are two houses filled with people hiding. They can dimly see that they are wearing jeans and T-shirts. Basilio hurries them past these houses.

Waiting for them on a bench are four Yagua Indians, three men in grass skirts and a woman in a large green kerchief that doesn't quite hide her breasts, which look two decades past their suck-by date. It's difficult to say which group seems the more embarrassed by this travesty of tourism.

In front of them, on a wire, are rows of beads, necklaces adorned with alligator heads, and other delights.

The German decides to buy something, and the bartering begins, translated by Basilio.

'I give you two fish hooks.'

'Packet of cigarettes.'

'Four fish hooks.'

'Packet of cigarettes.'

It's the only currency they want, and they only want whole packets so they can sell them in town. Of course they use money. The German buys a packet off Simon, says, 'I can't think why they want this noxious weed,' and with the packet settles on a bracelet of alligator teeth. Who is it for? wonders Naomi.

Nobody else buys anything.

Naomi wonders if bartering with cigarettes is the derivation of the phrase, 'It costs a packet.' She must remember to find out when she gets home.

Home. Why does the word send a shiver through her? Is she no longer looking forward to home life with Simon?

There's some embarrassing fooling around with blow darts, and the charade is over. The travel agent, in generous mood, offers the villagers all his fish hooks. They don't want them. They use nets. He shows for the first time a softer side. He seems genuinely disappointed. Not hurt, just sad. Naomi

77

wonders if there is a woman in his life, or if the alligator teeth are for his mother.

The walk back is slow, as the heat and humidity rise. Naomi and Timothy find themselves walking side by side. Whether they have planned this or whether it's chance is not obvious even to them.

'I want to thank you for having the courage to come and tell me that dreadful day,' says Timothy. 'I think it really made a difference. Left me with a bit of self-respect.'

'I hope you got over it quickly.' But not too quickly, perhaps.

'I didn't. It took months.'

'How long after . . . me, did you meet Maggie?'

'Best part of two years.'

'And how are you now? Really happy? You seem it.'

'Oh, yes. Maggie's lovely. You? Everything all right?'

'Absolutely. Can't you tell?'

'Er . . . yes.' He hesitates. He wants to confess something. Naomi isn't sure if she wants to hear it. 'The . . . er . . . not everything is . . . I mean, it's different from you and me. It's . . .' His dark face colours slightly, and seems to swell with embarrassment. 'I mean, we do have sex. I mean, it *is* our honeymoon. But not . . .'

'Everything we did?'

'No. That was actually a bit special, Naomi.'

'Well, thank you, but . . . it was one night.'

'I know, but still it was a bit . . . you know. In fact, I can't believe what I did. I don't expect I'll ever do it again. It seems, somehow, with Maggie, you know, something we just wouldn't do.'

She wants to blurt out, 'Can't say I'm surprised,' but keeps it to herself.

'. . . Anyway, I suppose our relationship is more . . . spiritual.'

Why on earth is he telling her all this? He obviously needs to. She finds that very encouraging. This worries her. Why should she be encouraged by it?

'Talking about spirituality, how about you? Are you . . . do you still not believe?'

'No.'

'You don't not believe or you do not believe?'

'I don't believe.'

'I'm sorry.'

'Why should you be sorry?'

'I'm sorry?'

'Why the hell should you be sorry?'

'I wish you wouldn't be flippant about hell.'

'Oh, for God's sake.'

'And God.'

'Oh, Timothy. Loosen up.'

'I'm not good at that. Sorry, but what have I done wrong?'

'You've patronised me because I'm an atheist.'

'Oh, you're not even an agnostic any more. That's a bit arrogant, isn't it? Being so certain that you know.'

Naomi has never called herself an atheist before. She has believed that she is an agnostic. But she wants to make Timothy angry. She needs to make him angry.

'I don't believe this,' she says. 'I can't believe you people. What are you if not being so certain that you know? That's what pisses me off about you. You think I desperately want to believe and have failed. I don't particularly want not to believe, but it doesn't put me in some sad class of disappointed failures. The reason I don't believe is that I can find no evidence of a compassionate pattern in life, and it doesn't mean that I'm any more wicked than you or any less sodding spiritual than you. Oh, what a fucking good decision I made walking out on you, you fucking prig.'

She charges angrily after Simon, but he is disappearing at a fast sulk.

Soon they are back at another perilous narrow bridge, high above the piranhas. Ahead of them is the lodge. It has taken less than five minutes. They realise that the village is almost right opposite the lodge. The five bangs on the gong meant, 'There are only five of them. No need to try too hard.'

At the lodge, Simon is waiting with a face like the thunder that is beginning to threaten once again.

'Rather an argument, I see,' says Simon. 'Bit of tension.'

'So?'

'I didn't know you still cared enough about him to bother to be angry. I see that I was wrong.'

He is right, of course, which annoys her. She has been feeling pleased with herself for managing to end the meeting with Timothy angrily. It was sad for him, but necessary for her. She wished that she hadn't sworn, but the future would be difficult to bear if she'd ended on friendly terms with him.

After an early lunch they set off for the boat back. The German, who is staying for another night and is scheduled to have a four-hour jungle walk that afternoon, shames them by walking with them to their boat to see them off.

'I expect there will be a few more people on today's boat,' he says hopefully, 'and some of them will probably be taking the four-hour walk with me.'

As they watch today's thatched boat nosing towards the landing stage, he says a rather strange thing.

'Don't think too badly of Peru.'

Naomi likes him for that as much as for anything.

There are no tourists on the boat, none. He will be alone for his four-hour walk, alone for his second candlelit dinner, alone for Basilio's limited repertoire on the guitar all over again. Naomi's heart goes out to him, and she never even found out his name.

They shake hands with him, politely. His handshake is perfect, firm yet not too firm.

They enter the boat.

He stands on the landing stage, a stiff, erect figure, curiously forlorn and vulnerable.

The boat begins to move. He waves as if they are old friends whom he is going to miss. They wave back.

Just before he is out of earshot, they see him shout. A moment later, his words arrive over the brown water.

'I will insist on the full four hours. I will not accept short measure.'

Timothy and Maggie move to a seat near the front of the boat.

Naomi sits down quite far from them, in the middle of the boat.

Simon marches right to the back of the boat, and plonks himself defiantly into a seat. God, he'd be cross if he knew how young it makes him look, thinks Naomi.

The journey back, against the flow, takes longer than two and a half hours and feels as if it takes for ever. None of them would have wished not to see the Amazon, but none of them will ever go for a week's cruise on it. It just rolls on and on for ever, a slow, brown streak among the endless rainforests.

As they make their way off the boat to get onto the minibus back to their hotels, Timothy approaches Naomi.

'So,' he says, 'this is goodbye.'

'Yep. Sorry it ended in a row.'

'One last kiss:'

'It'll have to be a very quick, casual one. Simon's furious.'

'Really? Maggie won't mind at all. She hasn't got a sensitive bone in her whole body.'

He means it as a compliment.

At the last moment Naomi relents, holds her cheek against his, tries to put a real feeling of warmth and affection into it. After all, it will probably be the last kiss they ever have.

PART THREE

The Rocky Road to Seville
1991–1993

They're late. Lunch is ready. It's annoying.

William offers a second glass of sherry. This is very unusual, but they can't just sit around with empty glasses, waiting. It embarrasses him to have to do it, he's not a drinker, so he has to pass a little comment. 'It *is* New Year's Day, after all,' he says. When he's finished pouring he stops for a moment in front of the picture over the piano. It shows a Norfolk wherry sailing away from the staithe at Wells-Next-the-Sea. Naomi knows that, just for a moment, her father is sailing away from a staithe somewhere, and is happy. This worries her. She has become more sensitive to atmosphere over the years, and senses that something is afoot today. She feels uneasy, edgy, tense.

They're having curry, in the English style, quite hot but not fearsomely so, and sweetened with sultanas and slices of apple. On the side there will be mango chutney, slices of banana and finely minced coconut. The curry can be held quite easily in the Hostess trolley, but the rice may dry out. It's annoying that they are late.

'Where are they?' Penny cries.

'They'll have got utterly and totally arseholed last night,' says Julian. 'No discipline, artists.'

He's very grumpy today.

'Please, Julian, not in front of the child,' says his mother.

'I don't like that expression, "the child", Mum,' says Naomi. 'She does have a name.' The words are a rebuke, but Naomi speaks them very gently and without any hostility. Penny is tense today. There's that telltale working of her mouth when she isn't speaking.

'What's "arseholed"?' asks Emily.

'It's not a word you need to know, dear. It's a word silly lawyers who've never quite grown up and still want to shock their parents use. It means having too much to drink.'

'Dad used to get "arseholed" sometimes, didn't he? He still gets "arseholed" sometimes when he takes me out for a meal. He has a double gin and then a whole bottle of wine and then he drives me home.'

'Yes, yes, Emily. That's enough. And does he indeed? Right.'

'I prefer Dad when he isn't "arseholed". He's much nicer. I don't intend to get "arseholed" at all when I'm grown up.'

'Yes, Emily, thank you, good, I'm really glad, you stick to that, but we've had enough of that word, thank you.'

Emily is six. She isn't usually annoying, though sometimes she comes out with awkward things, the way children do. Once Auntie Constance, whom she doesn't like – you can't be made to like people just because they're your auntie – had said, 'You're as bright as a button, aren't you?' and Emily had drawn herself up to her full height, which at the time was two foot eleven, and said, 'I'm much brighter than a button, excuse me. I never saw a button do *anything* clever.' Pink spots had appeared on both of Auntie Constance's cheeks.

There's a welcome crunch of gravel.

'They're here!'

Relief sweeps over Penny's face. Emily dances up and

down. She loves Uncle Clive and Uncle Antoine. She takes them completely for granted and has never seen anything funny in their being two men together, but then she has no concept of the idea of a lover. Long may she not have.

But it's the delight on the faces of Penny and William that amazes Naomi. She hasn't realised how far they have travelled since they first met Antoine over twelve years ago, when she was eighteen. How embarrassed they had been in 1978. How affectionate they are in 1991. Clive and Antoine enter with beaming smiles and exciting parcels. The whole mood lifts. Well, no, not quite. Julian's mood doesn't lift. He never exchanged another word with Teresa after Naomi's eighteenth birthday supper, but to him Antoine will always be what Teresa called him, 'That Frog poofter.' On the surface it's prejudice, but deep down it's even sadder than prejudice. Deep down it's a defence mechanism against the sight of a man being so much more at ease with himself than he is.

There's a round of kissing in the French style, on both cheeks and slightly formal. Even William, not a natural kisser, manages to kiss both Clive and Antoine, and does it with a bit of panache. 'You've turned us all French now, Antoine,' he says with shy pride.

Clive and Antoine don't kiss Julian, though. His face is set in unkissable mode. His face is like a Pennine crag.

And almost immediately Antoine is on the floor, level with Emily, in front of the cosy, crackling winter fire.

'So, Emily, do you want me to help you with the jigsaw or do you want to finish it on your own?'

'Help me, please, Uncle Antoine.'

Naomi and Clive give each other a long, loving hug. Julian pours himself another sherry. Antoine finds a piece of sky. Emily squeals with delight. Penny's mouth moves anxiously. Something is up.

'What about the presents?' asks Emily from the floor.

'After lunch,' says Penny.

'Are you sure, Penny?' asks William.

'Well, no. Yes, now.'

Naomi realises that this exchange is meaningful. She just doesn't know what the meaning is.

'Julian,' she says.

'What?'

'The day you don't hand round the presents, this house won't be L'Ancresse any more.'

Julian pretends not to be pleased.

Clive and Antoine have brought lovely presents for everyone, they're really good at presents, and living in Paris does help, though how they get them all on the plane is a mystery. But things like weight restrictions don't matter to Antoine. He charms his way through.

In their turn, Clive and Antoine express great delight at the presents they have been given.

'Late night last night?' asks Julian.

'Yes,' says Clive. 'Good party. Francis Bacon was there.'

'Name dropper.'

'Excuse me, we hate name dropping,' says Antoine from the floor, where he has just found the piece that completes the funnel. 'I was saying so to Brigitte Bardot only yesterday.'

'Who's Brigitte Bardot?' asks Emily.

'A beautiful French actress who was better treated by animals than by people,' says Naomi.

'But that's not why we're late, Julian,' says Clive. 'We set off in good time. Had a problem with the ruddy car. Hire cars!'

'Right,' says Penny firmly, finding a suitable cue at last. 'Well, you're here anyway. Lunch.'

They take their seats at the table. The dining room smells even more of disuse now that all the children have left home. The table is plainly laid, as ever, but there are crackers.

'I know it's not Christmas,' says Penny, 'but Emily loves them.'

'Uncle Antoine loves them too,' says Emily.

They pull their crackers, with much laughter as Julian is left without any of the insides of either of the two crackers he's pulled, laughter which is killed stone dead when he says, 'You see. Can't even pull crackers.'

'I'm sorry. I'm not in the mood for paper hats,' he says, but Naomi says, 'Julian!' and she can wind this gruff, awkward brother of hers round her little finger. He puts on his paper hat – it's a bright yellow crown – without protest.

'What do you get if you cross a fish with two elephants?' reads out Clive.

'A very large bouillabaisse?' suggests Antoine.

'No. Swimming trunks.'

There is a loud, communal groan, but Emily laughs with delight.

Penny begins to serve the meal. She has made a special curry, not quite so hot, for Emily. Naomi waits for her to make some kind of disparaging remark to Antoine about the food. If only her mother had more self-confidence. The remark duly comes.

'It's only curry, I'm afraid, Antoine. Well, the food over Christmas has been rather rich and a bit bland, I mean, let's face it, turkey is bland, there's no getting away from it, so I thought it might make a nice change.'

'It's perfect, Penny. I like your curry. It's one thing we French are not good at.'

'Charming as ever, Antoine.' William beams as he says this, trying to show that he's not being sarcastic. But it doesn't quite work. Everything he says sounds at least faintly sarcastic. It's the schoolmaster in him.

'Antoine's charm is his weakness,' says Clive. 'You should see him in Paris. He makes Maurice Chevalier look like a yob.

People have to meet him at least five times before they realise he's sincere. It's held him back enormously in the art world.'

'How is business?' asks William.

'Not good. We struggle on. Couldn't do it without Clive's regular earning.'

Clive teaches English, and teaches it well. He has inherited his father's talent.

'He's a strange one, isn't he?' says Clive. 'The more way out his art gets – I mean, he's letting the cat walk over the paint now – the more he dresses like a bank manager.'

Clive is in jeans and an open-necked shirt. Antoine is wearing a suit and tie.

'Too many artists live their art instead of painting it,' says Antoine.

'What do you mean about the cat, Uncle Clive?' asks Emily, who loves cats.

'I slosh wet paint on a canvas and let her walk over it,' explains Antoine. 'The marks she makes become incorporated into the structure of the painting. She does it brilliantly. Sasha's very artistic. She's a natural. It's the element of chance in life that I need, you see. You can have too much composition. There is no composition in life. Sacha is therefore an essential element in my work, and doesn't she know it? She doesn't even mind too much when I have to use turps to wipe her feet.'

Emily laughs. She is so happy about the cat.

'I thought you were bringing your girlfriend, Julian,' says Clive.

'Just noticed, have you?'

'Well, no, I noticed when we arrived but I thought maybe she was in the bathroom or something. It was only when we were all sat down and there was no empty chair that I was sure. It's not easy, Julian, to broach the question of your love life with you. One usually finds one has touched on a sensitive spot.'

'Well, this time it's not sensitive at all, because it's good riddance.'

'Oh!'

'She was coming. We had a row in the station.'

'Terminal?'

'Yes. King's Cross.'

It's not often that Julian makes a joke, so everyone laughs a little too much at it, and then realises that it's rather heartless to laugh at his predicament, so they all stop laughing rather suddenly.

'But you're getting on all right with your partners at work, are you, Julian?' asks William.

Naomi has never seen her father taking such an active role in the conversation. Something is definitely up.

'Oh, yes,' replies Julian. 'Well, they're all men. I don't have problems with men.'

William goes round the table, pouring more wine. This is without precedent, not because he's mean, he isn't, but because he never even thinks about drink. But today he is drinking as well. Naomi's anxiety grows.

Penny offers seconds, again with, to Naomi's mind, an unnecessary verbal accompaniment. 'I didn't give you too much first time around, in case you all felt you'd been eating too much over the holiday period, or in case it was too hot for you. But I thought, you can always come back for more.'

Everyone comes back for more.

'It is very good, Penny. No more self-criticism, please,' says Antoine sternly.

Her father raises his glass. 'Well,' he says, 'I think we ought to drink to Naomi, and wish her good luck with her sitcom.'

He's ticking off the conversational boxes one by one, thinks

91

Naomi, smiling with a modesty that, sadly, is not false, as they toast the success of her upcoming sitcom, which goes into production in a couple of weeks and will be on the screens in April.

'Yes,' says her father. 'We're very proud of our little girl.'

'Dad, I'm thirty.'

'That's young. Only thirty, and a starring role in a sitcom.'

'What is this sitcom?' asks Clive.

'It's about a couple who keep having children. It's about how the mother has to do all the work. It's about the stresses of motherhood and of marriage, only it's funny.'

'Well, that sounds a good part,' says Julian encouragingly. Only on matters to do with Naomi does he brighten in the family these days. Naomi almost wishes that he wasn't so loyal to her. It makes it hard for her to criticise him for the rest of his unsatisfactory life.

'I don't play the mother,' says Naomi. 'I play the neighbour.'

'But you're regular,' says her father. 'You're in it every week. Aren't you?'

'Yes.'

'It's a start. You'll be back at the Coningsfield Grand. "Starring Naomi Walls from . . .". What's your series called?'

She doesn't want to tell them. She still hopes the title may change.

'It's not quite decided.'

'It's a pity you boys couldn't come over from Paris to see her in the touring production of *Antony and Cleopatra* at the Grand,' says her father. She has never known him anything like so talkative.

'She was wonderful,' admits her mother. 'She really was the Queen of Egypt. I couldn't believe it was my little girl.'

'Mum!'

'Well. I'm sorry, but it's the truth.'

'The drama group from the school went. And most of the teachers,' says her father.

'She's had her ups and downs,' says her mother. 'Her bits of bad luck. A broken foot when she was down to play a lady footballer. A play cancelled when the leading man dropped dead in the dress rehearsal. Casting directors, if I've got the title right, who couldn't recognise talent if they fell over it. But she's come through. She's going to be a star.'

'Mum!'

Naomi is deeply embarrassed, not least because Emily is believing it.

'Are you really, Mum? Are you really going to be a star?'

'We'll see, Emily. We'll see.'

'That's my girl,' says her father. 'Modest to a fault.'

No, Dad. I don't think so.

Over the apple pie and custard her father, who has undoubtedly drunk more wine than ever before, raises yet another new subject.

'Do you ever see Simon at all?'

'When he takes Emily and brings her back, on his days, if I can't avoid him.'

'Oh, dear. Still . . . still bitter, then?'

'Dad, he's Emily's father. I don't want to talk about him in front of her.'

'I was on the stairs when you talked about him to Felicity the other day,' says Emily. 'I heard what you said.'

'Oh, my Lord, what did I say? Or should I not know?'

'You said when you went away on holiday he was . . . I didn't really understand it 'cause I didn't know what it was, but you said something about he was a cornflakes adult.'

'What? Oh! Oh, yes. Oh, Lord. I said he used to look round in hotels even during breakfast to see if there were any girls he could try to seduce later that day. I described him as a cereal adulterer. Cereal as in cornflakes.'

'Yes, we did get it,' says Clive.

'I hope the jokes in your sitcom are better than that,' says Julian.

I hope so too. I ha'e me doots.

'What's an adulterer?' asks Emily.

'It's a childerer who's grown up,' says Antoine.

Emily giggles. Antoine can always make her giggle.

'No, what is it really?'

'It's a person who's married who goes off with someone else and spends time with them when he should be spending time with his wife,' says Naomi.

'Or husband, as the case may be,' says Julian.

'Was Dad an adulterer when he went to the gym then, 'cause he went to the gym nearly every day?'

Very probably he may have been, Emily, but we won't go into that.

'No. Not every time, Emily. Some of the times he was supposed to go to the gym. He works there.'

Emily is still a bit puzzled, but William leaps up, rubs his hands together, and says, 'Come on, Emily. I've got a job for you. Well, it's a game really.'

Immediately, Penny leaps up too and says, 'I'll make coffee. Coffee everyone?'

Emily, William and Penny all leave the room.

'What's going on?' asks Clive.

'I don't know,' says Naomi, 'but something is.'

Penny enters with a tray of cups but no coffee. William returns from the garden.

'I've got her collecting twenty different kinds of leaf,' he says. 'That should give us time. Sorry, everyone, I don't want to spoil your day, and it's a bad start to the year, but there's no way of telling you this except very directly, and there it is, but . . . well . . . the fact is . . . er . . .'

'I've got cancer,' says Penny.

94

There's a shocked silence. It's a remark that people hear all too often in their lives, but rarely when they are all wearing paper hats.

'How long have you known?' asks Clive.

'About a fortnight.'

'We didn't want to spoil Christmas, especially for Emily,' says William.

There's another moment of silence. Naomi can't bring herself to speak.

'What's the . . . er . . . the diagnosis?' asks Julian.

'Terminal, I'm afraid, Julian.'

Julian blushes, regretting his earlier joke, though there is no reason for him to.

'I don't believe that,' says Antoine. 'With a family like yours, and a medical service like yours – Coningsfield General has a good reputation, no . . . ?'

No. Everybody thinks it, but nobody says it.

'. . . And with a spirit like yours, I'm sure you can prove this diagnosis wrong. Come on. You are British. You are fighters.'

Emily enters with a bunch of leaves.

'Twenty-two different leaves,' she cries, with proud excitement.

Her innocence bruises their souls.

Maggie has been up since six o'clock, cleaning. She does two rooms every morning. There are fourteen rooms in the house if you include bathrooms and lavatories, so this means that she cleans each room once a week. That might not sound too bad, but this is no ordinary clean. This is a spring clean every week. Maggie has slowly become obsessive over the years. From her first waking moment – at six, with the alarm, meaning Timothy wakes up too and never drops off properly again – she is planning her battle against germs. It's May, a lovely spring morning, the first morning of the year on which none of the good people of Coningsfield, or indeed the bad people, of whom there are plenty, dream of being on the Algarve or in Southern Spain. Maggie goes round the house opening windows, letting the stale air out, but she doesn't have time to pause to breathe in the scents of yesterday's first mowing of the ragged lawn at number ninety-two and of the massed daffodils which are not yet quite dead all along the central reservation of the main road. Maggie never has time to smell the flowers.

Timothy reaches out sleepily and runs his hand gently over Naomi's soft, sleepy, still-slender body. His prick is as stiff as a dead curlew. But this can't go on. It's wrong. It's an invasion of her privacy, even though she will never know. He drags himself out of bed, kneels at the side of the bed, and prays to God to save him from his desires. O Lord, I know it's wrong. And, as you know, because I've told you, which of course I didn't really need to do, because you know everything, I must not covet my neighbour's wife or Simon Prendergast's wife. Prendergast. How can his precious Naomi now be Mrs Prendergast, which is what he assumes she still is. Oh, blow. He's lost his place in his prayer. Where was I, Lord? The Lord doesn't prompt him. Maybe Tuesday mornings are busy. Oh, yes. Not coveting her. Please, O Lord, give me the strength to have only clean thoughts, for I am ashamed of my wickedness.

He wishes he could just get dressed and go next door straight away, past the board which actually still says 'R. Pickering and Son – Taxidermists', for they are keeping up the pretence that his father still takes a major part in the work. Yes, they are living in Ascot House, formerly a B & B run by Miss de Beauvoir (Mrs Smith). Charlie Smith ran off eighteen years ago after falling head over heels for a physiotherapist. This has long been a sore point with Timothy's father, who regards it as less disgraceful than being abandoned for a plumber. Mrs Smith decided that Mrs Smith was no sort of name for the owner of a B & B with pretensions towards being select (she hated the word 'posh'), and became Miss de Beauvoir. She sold up five years ago. 'I'm getting out while the going's good. Mrs Percival at the Mount has been forced to take in people sent by social workers. She'll end up with immigrants, you mark my words. I'd hate to be young. What chance have the young got of running select B & Bs?'

But first there's the kids to be got ready. Sam is seven and Liam five. Why on earth did they call him Liam? Everyone will think he's Irish. Oh, well, too late now, and he doesn't seem to mind. Liam is cheeky, a bright spark, freckly, could almost be mistaken for Irish. Sam is dark like his father, serious like his father, showing real promise at his lessons, like his father. Maybe in his case the promise can come to fulfilment. His teachers think Sam could be clever. He isn't as quick as little Liam, but there's a solidity there, an understanding of all his subjects, which is rare in a boy so young. Timothy in truth doesn't know either of his boys very well; he loves them, of course, loves them utterly in their good and bad moments alike, but he leaves them mainly to their mother; he isn't awfully good with smaller children, his time will come when they are stronger and they can play football properly together and play card games and board games and go to visit beautiful places together. That is when his time will come, when he can show them the world.

He has to supervise their dressing and get their breakfast and make them eat it and make sure they clean their teeth because Maggie has been so busy cleaning that she only just has time to get herself dressed and tidied and ready for school.

At last she's ready and the kids are ready and she leaves

the house with them. It's a short walk across the park, and she passes the junior school on her way to the senior school where she still teaches, so it's all very convenient.

The most wonderful sound in the world is that bang of the front door closing. She has gone. The house is his. He knows he should go next door. He's got a fox to finish. But first he goes right round the house, opening the door of every room, savouring the emptiness of every room.

Now Timothy is at peace. Now he can face his work. At weekends and during the long, long school holidays he loves his work, it's an escape, but during the week he resents every moment that he cannot spend in his gloriously empty home.

He enters number ninety-six. The front door no longer squeaks. He has bought ample supplies of WD40.

He is surprised, as he is every morning, by the darkness of the house. Roly is standing in the cold vault of a kitchen, waiting. Whatever time Timothy enters in the morning, his father has had his breakfast and washed up and is standing in the kitchen, waiting.

'What are we doing today?'

The 'we' is royal, though Roly doesn't realise it.

'There's the fox to finish, and then I thought we might tackle Mrs Lewington's lurcher.'

'Righty ho. Anchors away.'

'Absolutely.'

Roly won't do much except fetch a few things that Timothy has deliberately left in the wrong place so that his father can fetch them and think he is useful. He can still see to move around the house, in which no piece of furniture has been moved for at least twelve years, but he can't see to do useful work any more. He has a blind stick for when he goes out on his own, but he never uses it, because he never goes out on his own. Maggie is a treasure, taking him to do all his shopping for the week at Tesco's every Saturday.

Timothy's spirits droop at the thought of Mrs Lewington's lurcher. He has tried to turn the business more in the direction of wild life taxidermy, but the location is against him. People knock on the door and buttonhole him in the street. 'He's seventeen, Mr Pickering. We've had him seventeen years. If Cecil hadn't been taken by the good Lord I know he'd want me to keep him. I'm going to put him where he always loved to sit, in his old basket, just to the left of the grate.' Timothy hates doing pets, asks three times the normal price, and the silly people accept the estimate without a tremor, in the hopelessness of their love.

'I'll be out for an hour or so late morning,' he hears himself say.

His father looks surprised, and so does he. He hadn't known he was going out. But suddenly the urge is irresistible.

'I'm sure there was nothing in the diary.'

His father can't actually read the diary any more, but he can see enough to know if a day is blank.

'No, it's not in the diary. It's just cropped up.'

It's not the sort of thing you can put in a diary. '12.15. Drive past Naomi's house. 12.20. Drive back past Naomi's house.'

For that is what he is going to do. It's something he has never done before, and it's a serious escalation of what could easily become an obsession. Maybe he needs an obsession too, to challenge Maggie. The thought of driving down Lower Cragley Road, past L'Ancresse, in both directions, excites him. It's naughty. It's dangerous. It's blissfully futile.

It's the sitcom what's done it, he thinks. Seeing her, every Thursday, on BBC1, in his lounge. Awful to see. *Nappy Ever After* is a stinker. A stinker full of jokes about stinking, as the critic in his paper gleefully pointed out. How many jokes can there be about potty training? Hundreds, according to the writers of *Nappy Ever After*. And what a dreary part. What miscasting. The neighbour! Always coming round to borrow sugar, but really to hear the latest gossip and to drool over the babies because her own life is so sterile. Naomi, sterile, drooling, using baby talk, silly. How dare they? He'd use a very naughty word to describe them if he wasn't religious. The humiliation of watching it. The impossibility of not watching it. No wonder his thoughts have turned to her.

The fox is finished all too soon and he has to make a start on the lurcher. At ten to twelve he can bear it no longer and breaks off.

'You'll be back for your sandwich?'

'Of course, Dad. Wouldn't miss my sandwich.'

'That's my boy.'

Roly makes them a sandwich every lunchtime. It's his task. Just occasionally Timothy has lunch with a client. 'Lunches with clients! I don't know! What's next? Buckingham Palace?' exclaims his father. But this is rare. Nineteen times out of twenty, his dad makes a sandwich for him. It's his task. It's his life.

'Well then, off you go, boy, if you're going. Chocks away.'

Timothy drives along the route of the twenty-eight bus. He's so excited that he has to take great care not to cause an accident, whether on the road or in his trousers, or both. This is madness. He knows it, and loves it.

He turns into Lower Cragley Road. Bliss. And nobody is following. He can drive really slowly.

There it is, across the road on his right as he slips slowly down the hill. L'Ancresse. Solid. Really rather attractive. Serene. So serene. There's the bay window of the lounge. That's where the curlew was, on top of the chaise longue. He wonders if she still has the curlew, if it's still in the house, or if she has taken it away with her. He wonders if she is still in their flat in . . . West Hampstead, was it? Strangely, it doesn't cross his mind that she might no longer be with Simon. When he watches her in *Nappy Ever After* he feels jealous of Simon, so Simon remains, in his eyes, a part of her life.

He wishes that he could go back and have her eighteenth birthday again because this time he wouldn't be nervous about the curlew, this time it would be simply the most wonderful evening of his life. But of course you can't go back.

But he can go back up Lower Cragley Road, and he does. It doesn't look as if there is anybody in L'Ancresse. It'll be quite safe.

There's no traffic at all this morning. Well, afternoon now, let's be pedantic. What a lovely day. Words come into his mind in Ken Dodd's voice. 'What a lovely day for looking up an old lover.' Careful. He doesn't want to sound like *Nappy Ever After*.

He becomes very bold and pulls up right outside the house. His heart is racing. Supposing she's there. She might be visiting. There's no sign of a car, but maybe she hasn't got a car. Actresses are probably funny that way. Maybe she can't afford a car.

He is safe. Nobody goes in or out. He should leave. It would be better to leave. But he doesn't.

He thinks about the last time he spoke to her, nine years ago, in Iquitos. He thinks about the last time he saw her in the flesh. A year ago, at the Coningsfield Grand, as Cleopatra. He'd had to go with Maggie. It had been a dreadful evening, because suddenly, seeing her on the stage, he had realised that he no longer adored Maggie, he had only been pretending to do so for a long time now, she had become obsessive about cleaning, she bravely tolerated occasional sex, it was her duty, and she lived for her thirty-four children, the two that were her own and the thirty-two that were her duty.

He had thought, as they had sat waiting for the curtain to go up – well, not the curtain exactly, he could remember every detail, they hadn't used a curtain – as they had waited for the lights to go down, he had realised that it would be very difficult for him to break away from Maggie, present himself at the stage door, and say, 'I'd like to see Miss Walls, please. I'm an old friend and I want to tell her how marvellous she was.'

But that had been the worst thing of all about that awful evening. She hadn't been marvellous. She hadn't been bad, of course she hadn't, in fact she'd been quite good, but it was no good being quite good, not as Cleopatra; she had never for one moment been the Queen of Egypt, she had been Naomi Walls bravely portraying the Queen of Egypt. The stillness, the power that she had shown as Juliet, it hadn't been there. Of course she was as good an actress as ever, you couldn't lose abilities like that; there must have been some other explanation, anything, a dislike of the actor playing Antony, an unsympathetic director whose vision had clashed with hers, an illness perhaps from which she had only just been recovering, or perhaps, even for the best of them, in long runs, there were performances where you'd got it, and performances where you hadn't. It had let his emotions off the hook about going round to see her, because he couldn't have gone if he couldn't have told her that she had been marvellous, but it had been terrible to witness. At the end, the applause had risen when Antony had come on for his solo bow. It hadn't dipped for her, but it hadn't risen further, and it should have done, and she had known it, and he had known that she had known it.

He drives on at last, up Lower Cragley Road, turns right, follows the route of the twenty-eight bus, drives round the new inner ring road, and up the hill and back to his dad's sandwich and Mrs Lewington's lurcher.

I won't do that again, he tells himself. That way madness lies.

When he has finished work, he asks his dad if he's organised for supper.

'Everything tickety-boo, boy. Worry you not.'

'Fine. See you tomorrow.'

'See you tomorrow.'

'Sleep well.'

'Sentiment reciprocated.'

'Bye, Dad.'

'Bye, son.'

He walks slowly back home, savouring for a moment the warmth of the late afternoon. He looks at the roses, which are beginning to bud nicely. He opens the front door with great reluctance, and finds himself in an empty house. This surprises him, but does not worry him. Anything may have happened.

He washes his hands, even though he washed them before he left number ninety-six. This evening he finds that he wishes he was a drinker – a moderate one, of course. But to reach for a beer now would be very pleasant, and he no longer has any disapproval of strong drink – in moderation, of course.

As the minutes pass he does begin to become slightly uneasy. He lolls in the rocking chair and tries to concentrate on the newspaper, but it's all bad news and he can't focus on it. He hurls the paper away in irritation.

There's a sharp rat-tat-tat on the front door, and suddenly he's very worried. Suddenly he knows that something is seriously wrong. He realises afterwards, long afterwards, when he can at last begin to think about it with detachment, that he was not at all surprised to see the policeman there.

The policeman is young, sweaty, nervous, wretched. He is clutching and unclutching his hands.

'I'm afraid there's been a terrible accident, sir. Your wife and the other boy are in shock and they're being treated at the General. I'm afraid . . . it was a car, sir, and it didn't stop. Right outside the park, sir, at . . .' He consults his note-book with trembling hands – even in his shock Timothy can see how ashamed the young man is of his trembling hands. '. . . Three forty-four p.m. this afternoon. I'm afraid, sir, your . . . I'm afraid your boy is dead. He died instantly, sir, there would have been no suffering. I hope in time that will—'

'Yes, but . . . which boy? Which boy, officer?'

The officer stares at him and a blush steals across his face. His embarrassment and misery and fury are terrible to behold.

Timothy is driven to the hospital. Which boy? Which boy? He dare not hope . . . hope that it isn't . . . which one, he can't say a name, he would never forgive himself if he said a name even to himself . . . oh, get me there, please, oh, which one, which one, I cannot grieve for either and I cannot escape grieving for both until . . . oh, which one, which one??

He is taken into a consulting room which has been made available. Maggie is sitting in a chair, ashen, staring. She has an untouched cup of tea at her side. Liam rushes towards him and hugs him, and bursts into tears, and Timothy . . . Timothy feels, just for a moment, only for a moment – but a moment is enough to haunt a man for a lifetime – a spasm of disappointment.

Sam's promise will never come to fulfilment. He will never show Sam the world.

Liam will find the world for himself. Sam was the one who would have needed showing.

He leads Liam over to Maggie. He bends and kisses her. Her eyes stare at him piteously.

'It was my fault,' she says.

'I thought it was a runaway car.'

'There were two cars. Boy racers. They just touched, touched each other for a moment. One of them lost control, mounted the pavement. Sam was on the outside. I should have been on the outside. It was my fault. It should be me that's dead.'

A nurse enters with some papers, which she puts on the consultant's desk. She looks out of the window, then turns towards them. She may be slightly surprised to see them there, but unexplained things often happen in the hospital.

She smiles brightly.

'What a lovely evening,' she says. 'First of the year. Does us all good to see the sun, doesn't it?'

'Do you speak English?'

'Only the bare rudiments, I'm afraid.'

'What is the name of that town?'

She knows its name. It's Boppard. But she needs to hear the woman speak. She needs to study her accent.

'That is Boppard.'

'Thank you. It's very pretty.'

'Oh, yes. Boppard is very, how do you say, my English, I have been to England many times, I have seen your Eastbourne and your West Bromwich and your Dorking, but I am rusty. Yes, Boppard is . . . picturesque, quaint.'

'You speak it very well.'

'You are too kind.' The German woman smiles. She has a very attractive smile. 'This is your first time in Germany?'

'Yes. I'm auditioning for a part in a new . . . what we in England call a sitcom.'

'I do not know this sitcom.'

'It's short for situation comedy. It's a series of half-hour television programmes recorded in front of an audience.'

105

'*Nächste station*, Boppard,' is announced over the public address as the large, crowded river boat noses in. It's ridiculous, but Naomi looks at the crowds politely and patiently queuing to get on and has an absurd hope that she might see their travel agent friend from the Amazon. There's not a chance, of course.

A quick burst of reverse from the engines, and the landfall is perfect. The captain must have done this several thousand times. Naomi wonders if he gets bored or if he pretends it's the *QE2*.

'You are an actress?'

'For my sins.'

Naomi wishes she hadn't made this singularly stupid reply. Especially when the woman takes her up on it.

'For your sins? I don't understand.'

'It means nothing. It's a silly phrase we English sometimes use, trying to be a bit self-deprecating . . . er . . . making it sound no big deal, trying to be modest.'

'Are you a star? Would I have heard of you?'

'Not a chance. My name is Naomi Walls.'

'You are right. Not a chance.'

They share a little laugh.

'And this sitcom, what is it about?'

Oh, Lord.

'It's . . . er . . . it's . . . it's . . . I mean I've only been told the . . . er . . . the bare rudiments . . .'

They share another little laugh. It's quite pleasant to share these little laughs in the sunshine with someone you will never see again. If only she hadn't committed herself to talking about the sitcom.

'. . . So all I know, from what they've told me, is that it's about a British shoemaker who falls in love with a German lady and moves to Germany where he makes . . .' She hesitates. It suddenly seems so unlikely.

106

'Friends?'

'Shoes. Well, friends as well, I hope. I haven't had the scripts yet.'

They lean over the rail, watching the people filing onto the ship, none of them flaxen-haired travel agents.

'And what is its name?'

Here we go.

'*Cobblers in Koblenz*.'

'I do not understand this *Cobblers in Koblenz*.'

'A person who makes shoes in Britain is known as a cobbler.'

'Ah. Now I understand. You say you are, what is the word – auditioning? – for a part. Do you know what part? Will you be German or English?'

'I think maybe I'll be German.'

'Ah. So you come to Germany to speak with Germans and listen to their accents. Which is why you speak to me, I think. I am your guinea fowl.'

'Guinea pig. It sounds awful when you put it that way.'

'Not at all. I am most gratified to be of assistance.'

New arrivals push in onto the rail to wave goodbye to friends on the shore as the boat begins to move off. The woman edges closer to Naomi. Their bodies are now touching. Naomi realises that this is no accident.

She hasn't really given the woman much of a look. She looks now. She isn't exactly attractive, but she's very well turned out. No, that's horses. Though there is something vaguely horsey about her. Handsome! That's it. She's a handsome woman. A handsome, well-dressed, German woman in her early forties, pressing her solid thigh against hers.

'You are travelling alone?'

'No. I've brought my mother.'

'Oh.'

107

'That's her, sitting on the open deck, just beyond the Greek Orthodox priest.'

'With the curly hair?'

'Yes.'

'She looks a nice person.'

'She is.'

'I . . . I live in Bingen It's a small town down the river. I suppose it wouldn't be possible . . . for you . . . this evening . . . to . . . I don't know if this is the correct phrase . . . give her the slip?'

'Of course it's the correct phrase. You speak English beautifully.'

'Thank you. I hope you don't mind this . . . suggestion. I have recently ended a long relationship. I am lonely. I don't know your . . . I search for the words . . .'

'No, you don't.'

'. . . Sexual proclivities. Do you think you can . . .'

'. . . Give my mother the slip? No. That curly hair is a wig. She is having chemotherapy. I can't risk hurting her.'

'I understand. Oh, well.'

'I have a daughter. Emily. She's seven. She's staying with her father for a long weekend. He has many faults, but he truly loves her. There. That's my family situation, complete, and it's not a situation comedy. Sorry.'

Naomi doesn't really know why she has said sorry. For explaining her situation? For forcing a reaction by telling this woman that her life is not a comedy? For not being able to give her mother the slip? She senses that if only for the sake of social propriety something more needs to be said, but she has no idea what. Luckily the German lady has.

'You are so lovely, Naomi Walls, in the early summer sun. This is so stupid, but when one is lonely one clutches at straws. You will understand if you are ever unfortunate enough to be lonely. I'm going to give you my card.'

108

She hands Naomi the card. Naomi puts it in her bag. She doesn't want to know this woman's name until later, in private.

'No, but seriously, if ever you find yourself anywhere near Bingen – maybe you will be on location nearby with your *Cobblers in Koblenz* – please phone. Please.'

'Of course I will. No, I will. But now I must go to her.'

'Of course.'

Naomi wanders back to her mother, sits between her and the Greek Orthodox priest.

'All right, Mum?'

'In heaven, darling. This scenery, it's so wonderful. It isn't real.'

There are lines of barges going up and downstream. On each bank there are busy roads and railways. The Rhine buzzes with the trappings of modern life. But the villages through which it passes, and the castles which look down on it, are medieval gems, and the endless rows of vines on the steep hills give the promise of equally endless pleasure. Soon they will have river trout for lunch, and maybe a glass of Riesling with it.

Naomi realises that her mother is crying.

'Mum!'

Penny blows her nose, angrily.

'Sorry. All right now.'

'Want to tell me?'

'It's just . . . this is so lovely. This is so kind of you. If only . . .'

'Yes?'

'If only . . . your father is a fine man, Naomi, a very kind man, a good man, you wouldn't find a better or a more considerate husband. I just wish that he'd taken me to more places. I'm going to die without knowing just how beautiful the world is.'

Naomi sighs.

'All that sailing got in the way,' she says.

'I'm not criticising, Naomi. Your father needs his sailing. He's . . . a slightly fragile bloom. He couldn't get by without his annual month of space.'

'He still could have taken you to places.'

'It's the way he was brought up. He's never quite got out of the shadow of his modest upbringing. He thinks he isn't quite good enough for nice hotels, quite sophisticated enough for posh restaurants. He's so proud of you, Naomi. Become a star, will you, for his sake?'

'I'll do my best.'

'That woman you were talking to. She . . . wanted something, didn't she?'

'Er . . . yes . . . she was wondering if we would be recording our series in Germany, if I get the part, and if . . . she could have tickets for the studio audience.'

'Naomi! Coningsfield isn't that far behind the times. She was one of those, wasn't she? I could tell.'

'She was a nice woman, Mum.'

'I didn't say she wasn't. You're kind. I loved the way you let her down so gently.'

'You see everything, don't you, Mum?'

Her mother sighs, and smiles wryly.

'Too much most of the time. But no, not everything.'

They slide up the mighty river, which is a trout stream compared to the Amazon, and Naomi is thinking, No, my mother doesn't see everything. She has no idea that, if I had been on my own, I would have seriously considered going to Bingen this evening.

Would she have gone?

She'll never know.

* * *

110

Tommo says he'll do everything, pick them all up, drive there, drive back, drop them all off. He's insistent.

He picks Timothy up first. Maggie answers the door. Tommo just doesn't know what to say to her about the tragedy, so says nothing.

'Few biscuits for you,' he says, handing her a large tin of their most upmarket selection.

Liam hurries along the passageway to see who it is, hesitates when he realises it's someone he doesn't know.

'Hello, young sir,' says Tommo, somewhat too brightly. Everyone speaks somewhat too brightly these days to Liam, who flinches. He is no longer so outgoing, or so cheeky. He's much easier to handle. 'Do you like biscuits, young man?' asks Tommo. 'I bet you do. All children like biscuits. Mine love them.'

Tommo blushes slightly. He has three children and feels that he has been tactless.

'Get your mummy to give you some biscuits,' continues Tommo. 'They're the best. They're the bestest biscuits ever.'

I do wish you'd shut up, thinks Liam.

'Timothy,' calls out Maggie. 'He's here.'

Timothy arrives, a little breathless, pulling a jacket on over his pullover.

'Sorry. Running a bit late. Bit of a snag with a muntjac,' he says.

'Where do you think we're going, Tim? The Arctic?' asks Tommo.

'Aren't we going up on the moors?'

'In my car. Which has heating. Into pubs. Which have fires. We aren't ramblers.'

Timothy is being taken on a pub crawl by his friends. It was Dave Kent's idea. 'We need to get him out of himself. Get him away from that woman.' There's a certain type of woman of whom Dave disapproves. They're called wives. He dislikes all wives, but Timothy's most of all, closely followed by his own.

Tommo cracks his fingers, a noise which Timothy loathes, it sets his teeth on edge. Maggie cannot believe how many little things irritate her husband these days. She would have thought that they would be of no consequence compared to the dark tragedy that has split their lives asunder. But grief is never logical.

Tommo sets off up the hill as if it's the final qualifying lap for the Coningsfield Grand Prix.

'Now then,' he says. What he means is, 'We're off on a pub crawl. Your first ever. But not your last. You've thought of pubs as wicked, haven't you? Dens of iniquity. They're the best of places. Warm, friendly sanctuaries where you can meet your fellow men from all walks of life, enjoy a spot of good cheer, maybe a pub game or two, and some excellent ale drawn by mine host, who is a card.' But Timothy knows all this, so there is no need to say it. And Timothy is dreading it all, so it's best not to say it. 'Now then,' does very nicely. So nicely that Timothy thinks it worth repeating.

'Now then,' he says. What he means is, 'I should be grateful to you for taking me out. I thought it would be good to get out of the house, but how can I possibly get out of the house, you well-meaning idiots? I carry the house with me wherever I go. My heart is split in two and your attempts to mend it are pathetic. How will I survive an evening of good cheer? How can you do this to me?' It would be silly to say all that. Offensive too. Ungrateful. 'Now then,' is so much better.

'This feller meets this bird in this pub,' says Tommo.

Timothy's heart sinks still further. He doesn't like jokes. His life's history is divided into two sections, Before and

112

After. Before the accident. After the accident. He liked humour Before, but not jokes. He likes them even less After.

'Motherly type, not in the first flush, but still a looker. And she looks a goer.'

Timothy's heart sinks further still. He doesn't like smut.

'"Do you fancy coming home with me," she says, "and having a bit of a threesome? Mother and daughter."'

Timothy's heart continues to sink. You would have thought it could sink no further, but it seems to have an infinite capacity for sinking. Threesomes are part of a world that he couldn't have coped with even Before.

'Well, he's over the moon. What an offer. So of course he goes.'

Pity. I'd be spared the joke if he didn't.

'They go into the house. She takes her coat off. He takes his coat off. She calls up the stairs, "We've got company. Put your teeth in, Mum."'

Timothy laughs, hoping that Tommo will be too insensitive to realise that there is no humour in his laugh. He laughs to be polite, to show that he recognises that the joke is over. And there is an element of genuine relief in his reaction. The punchline wasn't as revolting as he had feared.

'Nice one,' he says.

What else can he say?

'Belter,' says Tommo.

They pick Dave up next. His van is in the drive, white, dirty. On the side of the van is the legend, *Dave Kent. Garden of England – 66, East Street, Coningsfield.*

Timothy waits in the car. He hears Tommo say, 'Your lads like biscuits, Mrs Kent?'

Dave has dressed down, jeans and a T-shirt and a campaign jacket. He has four shops now, and has to take care still to seem like a simple greengrocer.

Dave squeezes Timothy affectionately, almost breaking his collar-bone.

'Got your drinking boots on?' he asks.

Timothy doesn't have the energy to reply. It occurs to him that he would quite like to be dead.

Tommo appears to be chasing the world 'Castlebridge Road to the Spelsby Roundabout' record. The suburbs of Coningsfield rarely witness such driving.

'This feller meets this bird in this pub,' says Tommo.

'Tommo's off,' says Dave proudly.

'Tim's heard it, but it's a belter,' says Tommo. Only Tommo ever calls Timothy Tim. 'Motherly type, not in the first . . .'

They will pick up Steven Venables last. This gives them a bit of time, after the joke, to discuss him, pool their knowledge, try to crack the mystery.

'What exactly does he do?' asks Dave.

'He was with some big firm in shipping,' says Tommo. 'Really big. Floats on the stock exchange. Anyway, he's lost his job. Sacked. Don't waste your sympathy, though. He got a pay-off. The best part of a million.'

'That's Steven,' says Dave, shaking his head in mystification.

Timothy says nothing. He will say nothing for as long as he can.

Tommo doesn't have to look at his bit of paper to check Steven's mother's number. It's the only house in the street with a Jaguar in the drive. Steven is back for two or three days to look after his mother while she has a minor operation, because, although he shows very little warmth to anyone else, he's good to his mother.

Tommo pulls up with a screech of brakes, and begins to get out of the car.

'You don't need to get out. The whole neighbourhood's heard,' says Dave.

'Want to give Mrs V some biscuits,' explains Tommo.

'Tommo's a sound type,' says Dave, while they wait in the car. It might not be the deepest analysis ever made of a man's character, but Timothy finds that there's not much to add. He's glad of this. He feels so very tired.

'Good old Tommo,' he says.

Steven bounces out of the house, his confidence untouched by the minor detail of his sacking. He's thinner than ever, though.

'Make sure he has some of them pies they have in those pubs,' his mother calls after them. 'They don't know how to feed them properly in that City of theirs. Look at him. I've a garden rake with more flesh on it. Oh, and thank you for the biccies, Tommo.'

'Pleasure, Mrs V,' calls out Tommo.

The tyres scream in protest as Tommo does the fastest U-turn in the history of the West – well, West Coningsfield, anyway.

'Sniffy gave me a bell,' says Steven meaningfully.

'Oh!' says Tommo, equally meaningfully.

People are often meaningful about Sniffy.

'Yep,' says Steven. 'Sniffing around. He must sense something. I wish I hadn't told him I was up, but I'm seeing him tomorrow. He obviously knows we'll be doing something tonight.'

'Why couldn't you just tell him?' asks Timothy, quite relieved at having thought of something to say.

Tommo, Dave and Steve look shocked.

'Sniffy wants to be in on everything,' explains Dave. 'Wouldn't be any kind of club if we let people like that in.'

'I didn't know it was a club,' says Timothy.

'It's an unstated club,' says Steven. 'Very exclusive.'

'What's the point of its being a club if it's unstated?' asks Timothy.

'To keep people like Sniffy out,' explains Dave.

'What's wrong with Sniffy?' persists Timothy. He doesn't really want to know, but the evening will be less awful if he occasionally finds things to say. If he's silent, they will all try to take him out of himself. He couldn't bear that. If they think he's fine, they may leave him in peace.

'Not a lot. Not really. I can take him,' says Steven. 'I mean, I'm seeing him tomorrow.'

'But he wants to be in on everything,' explains Dave for the second time.

'This evening's for you,' says Tommo.

Oh, hell. What a burden that is. Don't you think I have enough burdens, you idiots? Thank you for your evening. I don't want it.

'Wouldn't be for you if we asked all and sundry, would it?'

'We're the Gang of Four,' says Dave.

'Precisely. Can't have five in a gang of four,' says Steven.

There's a moment's silence in the speeding car. Timothy knows that he should say something, sound grateful for being included in the gang. He can't. He wants to get out, walk alone over the stark hills in the dark, never come back.

'This feller meets this bird in this pub,' says Tommo.

'Tommo's off,' says Steven with relief.

'Tim and Dave have heard it,' says Tommo, 'but it's a belter.'

After the joke, as they growl up onto the moors, Tommo, Dave and Steven begin on rugby songs. Tommo played wing three-quarter for Coningsfield Rovers for eleven years till his speed finally went. Even though he's still the life and soul of the party, even when there is no party, everyone agrees that just a little went out of him when he retired. 'Tommo's a lad.' 'You should have known him in his Rugby League days.'

Timothy feels that he has to join in, but there are bits in

116

the songs where you fall silent, traps for the ignorant, and he leaps into every one of these traps. Still, it amuses the others, and that's something.

First stop is the obscure Mill House in the hamlet of Bugginsby Far Bottom. The beer's drawn straight from the barrel. The landlord has a long face, and doesn't smile, but he's a card. The beer's wonderful. Tommo doesn't drink – 'Never do when I'm driving' – but Steven and Dave have two pints each. Timothy manages one. He isn't used to beer. The top quarter of the glass tastes a bit horrid, the middle quarter is better, the third quarter is really rather nice, the fourth quarter is a struggle as he has to hurry it.

He wants a pee.

'We don't pee till we get to the Lord Nelson,' says Tommo. 'Club rules.'

Luckily, the Lord Nelson in Osfinklethwaite is not far away. The landlord is small and has a gammy leg and a hump, but he's a card. The fire's lit, mixed coal and logs, even though it's June. The beer's wonderful. Steven and Dave have two more pints each. Timothy struggles with one. They initiate him into the skills and mysteries of fives and threes. 'The only domino game worth playing,' says Tommo.

Pretending to care which domino he should play is agony to Timothy, but it's preferable to conversation. He partners Tommo and they win the first game. Winning and not giving a damn is an unpleasant experience. 'Well played, Timothy,' says Steven. How much more cheering up can he take? Then they lose the next game, and losing is even worse, and that makes him feel deeply ashamed. Why should he care, what does it matter, what does any of it matter?

Tommo tells some quickies. 'This man rushes to the doctor's, bursts in. He says, "Doctor, doctor, I've got a domino stuck up my arse." The doctor says, "Don't you ever knock?"

Another man rushes to the doctor. He says, "Doctor, doctor, I've got a cricket ball stuck up my arse." The doctor says, "How's that?"' Timothy understands the jokes and knows when they are over. He laughs at the same thing as the others. Nobody watching would realise that he was a million miles away, separated from his friends by the very activities that were intended to bring them together.

The third port of call is the Black Swan at Cold Heptonwick.

'Hello,' says Sniffy. 'I thought I might meet you here.'

He shows no sign of resentment at his exclusion from the plans. He is affability itself. The pub is cheery. The beer is wonderful. The landlord is obese and not overly clean, but he's a card. Yet somehow, the evening is never quite the same to Tommo, Steven and Dave, and the only reason it doesn't get any worse for Timothy is that it couldn't.

They play more dominoes but, with five of them, one always has to stand down. Timothy struggles a bit with his third beer. It's beginning to dawn on him that the evening, whose end he has so longed for, is already more than half over, and that now he is dreading its end.

They are halfway to the Cross Keys at Fothergill-under-Snapsdon before any of them realise that Sniffy is in the car with them.

'Why shouldn't I be?'

'You've got your car.'

'I left it at the Black Swan. I'm over the limit. You can drive me home, can't you, and I thought, Steven, when we meet tomorrow you could bring me back and pick it up.'

Sniffy can get away with things like this. What can they do? They can't exclude him. He is already excluded.

The Cross Keys has changed hands. The new landlord is smart, polite and smiley, but he is not a card. It's quite full, but only with people eating. Timothy thinks that if he had come here Before he would have thought it quite nice, but

118

he doesn't understand. The others are appalled. They have seen a glimpse of the future. They are on borrowed time.

Timothy thinks that the drive back will give him time to sober up, but he starts to feel drunker and drunker. He wants the drive to go on for ever. He doesn't want to go home.

Tommo drops him at the gate. He doesn't want to have to think of something to say to Maggie again.

Timothy lurches to his front door. He's there all too soon. He hates his front door. It leads to his house.

'You're drunk, Timothy.'

'Not very.'

'You're disgusting. Go to bed.'

'All right. I am.'

'And don't wake Liam.'

As he passes Liam's bedroom, he hears the beginning of a scream, rapidly stifled. His son is dreaming.

He begins the long process of sobering up.

The gardens are quiet and peaceful. One or two of the early trees are just beginning to bud. A blackbird is singing. Spring is coming. Her mother will not live to see it.

Naomi walks slowly and quietly through the reception area. Silence reigns. The receptionist smiles. Smiles are the currency of communications here.

Death is everywhere, and death is usually violent. The news bulletins are studded with violent death. The world is not hurtling towards utopia. But in St Hilda's Hospice, death is not violent, and Naomi feels that it would be selfish to be too sad. She should be happy that, after a long, brave fight, her mother is ready to die, peacefully, in this peaceful place, surrounded by kind people who care about her. There are worse fates.

Penny is sitting in an armchair, by the window. Her smile as she sees Naomi is a smile of pure joy.

How frail she looks, but there is a new kind of beauty in her frailty. Her bone structure is fine. Naomi kisses her very delicately, for fear that she will fall to bits.

There can be no small talk between them now. No 'How are you?' and 'I'm fine.'

Her mother asks about her sitcom.

'So, Thursday week is the great day, eh?'

'Yes, Mum.'

'Nervous?'

'Always.'

'I'm sure you needn't be.'

She knows that it is unlikely but not impossible that her mother will live to see it. Should she lie? Should she let her mother die with the illusion that she is going to be a star? Supposing she lies and her mother does see it and realises that she has lied? It might seem that she has been patronising. That would be intolerable.

The truth. Always, the truth is better.

'Mum, the family silence over *Nappy Ever After* has been stultifying. It was awful, and everyone should have said so, because that would have got it over with, and there was no harm in saying it anyway, because it wasn't my fault that it was awful. It was a bad part in a bad comedy, and that was all there was to it. We made it into a mountain by our good manners. Did Dad ever watch it?'

Her mother laughs. It is a laugh full of affection for, and frustration with, her dear, dear imperfect William.

'I put the clock on him. He lasted eight minutes.'

'Oh, Lord.'

'No, that's good. Comedy on television embarrasses him. He only lasted four minutes of *Fawlty Towers*. Your poor father is so kind-hearted, and so easily made uncomfortable by cruelty or unhappiness or innuendo. He goes into his study and either works on his book or reads P.G. Wodehouse.'

'His book?'

'He's planning a History of Ancient Greece, for his retirement.'

'That's good.'

'Is it? I suspect half the Classics masters in England plan to write histories of Ancient Greece when they retire. The other half plan histories of the Roman Empire. So, tell me about *Cobblers in Koblenz*?'

The truth. Always, the truth is better.

She smiles, pushes her hand forward towards her mother's, to leave her mother with the actual gesture of holding it and faintly stroking it.

'First of all, I was called back in twice before they gave me the part. Mum, I have to tell you that I play a sex-mad German chiropodist with a foot fetish.'

Penny winces and smiles at the same time.

'Well, it sounds more entertaining than your last one.'

'Oh, I think it may be better than *Nappy Ever After*, but that doesn't mean it's good. First of all, there's the accent. They liked my reading but they didn't like my accent.'

'But you studied the accent.'

'I know. They said it was unlike everyone else's accents. They were all doing cod middle European. I had to do it too to sound like them. "Has anyone ever told you your foot is beautiful, Herr Beckenmeister?"'

Her mother laughs, then looks puzzled.

'His foot? Only one?'

'Yes. Injured in the war. No tragedy is so bad that it can't be laughed at in *Cobblers in Koblenz*. They told us they wanted to explore the tensions of living in a country that had been our enemy. They wanted to explore our similarities with the Germans and suggest that perhaps it was the French we should have been fighting. They said they wanted it to be a more thoughtful *Auf Wiedersehen, Pet*, a peacetime *'Allo 'Allo!*.

121

I'm afraid when I read the scripts I suggested that the title should be changed to either *Auf Wiedersehen, Comedy* or *Goodbye, Goodbye*. After I'd got the part, of course.'

'You're terrible.'

'I know. I can't help myself. Anyway, those were their ambitions, and what did they end up with? Every old joke in the book. All of them. "We won the war." "Well, we didn't do too badly. We came second." "Have you ever been to Dresden?" "Not by day." "Look at those retired shoemakers in that lorry. What a load of old cobblers." Even, and this is the killer, the English cobbler, Stan Ormerod, who has a dog, comes home to find dog turds all over the carpet. "What's happened?" "They think it's all Rover." Then they find the dog, dead. "It is now."'

'That's terrible. It's not even logical.'

'I know. It doesn't work on any level. And it's heartless. But I suppose some of it's not entirely unfunny, in an obvious way. Anyway, there is it, Mum. Sorry.'

'Naomi?'

A major change of tone.

'Yes, Mum?'

A certain wariness.

'Do you remember the woman you chatted to on the Rhine steamer?'

'Yes.'

'She gave you a card.'

'Yes.'

'Did you ever go and see her?'

'No. She said if I was ever near Bingen . . . Well, I never was.'

'Have you ever – I hope you don't think I'm being too nosy, but I want to know you before I go – have you ever – because we aren't as narrow as perhaps we were, not after Clive and Antoine who are so lovely – have you ever – I suppose I am a bit narrow still, well, we're church people and they are narrow, because I'm finding this a bit difficult to put, but have you ever . . . ?'

'Let me put you out of your misery, Mum. I've never had any lesbian experience whatsoever.'

'I want to say "good", but I don't know if it is good, because I think loneliness is the worst sexual experience there is.'

'Is loneliness a sexual experience?'

'Usually.'

The truth. Always, the truth is better.

'I think if you hadn't been there I might very well have gone to Bingen with her. But I also think I'm glad you were there.'

A smiling nurse brings Naomi a cup of tea. Like her mother, it's weaker than she would wish.

'Is there anyone?'

'Not at the moment.'

'Have you ever seen – what was his name? – the boy who played Romeo? The taxidermist's son.'

'Timothy. No. Well, we met in Peru. We were both on our honeymoons. I hated his wife. Why?'

'Your father said the other day that it was rather a pity you hadn't married *him*.'

'I didn't know he liked him.'

'You never do know with your father. But I think he only meant, "as opposed to Simon".'

'If I hadn't married Simon, we wouldn't have Emily.'

Naomi takes a sip of the weak tea. It's nauseatingly milky. She has three choices. To leave it, which is not an option, because the nurse is kind and does a difficult job. To drink it while it's still hot, which means it will have to be in smallish sips. To let it go cold, when it will taste even worse but can be drunk quickly.

She chooses the third option, not without commenting wryly to herself that it's absurd to worry over such trifles when in the presence of something as momentous as your mother's imminent death.

'You might have had other Emilies. Lovely children.'

'We cannot unmake this Emily. Retrospective wishful thinking is not an option.'

'Naomi?'

'Yes, Mum?'

'Do you believe that one day you and I will meet again, in a better place?'

The truth. Always, the truth is better.

No, Mum, I don't. I think that if I had not lost my faith before, I would be losing it now. How can any God with any love in him or compassion in him let this happen to you, let your lovely body be wracked by this awful disease, let my dear dear kind innocent father suffer so terribly, and allow so many dreadful people to go through their wicked lives unscathed. Free will is just a feeble excuse, an abrogation of all responsibility. I thought I was an agnostic. I surprised myself when I told Timothy, in Peru, that I was an atheist. I don't think now that I was. I think this, happening to you, is what has made me an atheist.

The truth is not always better.

Is there a form of words that I can use that will satisfy my conscience without upsetting my mother?

Perhaps there is. If I express it with enough conviction.

Well, I should be able to. I am an actress, after all.

Forget nosy neighbours coming round asking for sugar and sex-mad chiropodists with foot fetishes. Act properly for once.

'I certainly wish that we will.'

Not perfect, but her mother smiles.

Naomi holds her nose metaphorically, and downs her tea in two horrendous gulps.

A year ago today. How awful it is, though it makes no difference really. A year ago today he was still alive. A year ago today they were a happy family. Except neither Maggie nor Timothy has said that. And they weren't.

No mention of the fact was made at school today, because of Liam. It might seem unfair to Sam that it should not be mentioned at all, but Liam must come first, and small boys don't think in terms of this day last year, except for Christmas and birthdays.

Liam comes above everything. One of the many things they have never got round to in Ascot House is removing the telltale numbers from the bedroom doors. It still seems like a B & B upstairs. In fact, it was two months before they removed from their bedroom door Miss de Beauvoir's notice which said, '*Private. In case of emergency ring 294693*'. Sam had room number one, as the older, and Liam had room number two. The numbers remind Timothy every day of his feelings in that moment when he first saw that it was Sam who'd died. He so wants to move Liam to room number one. He could remove the numbers, of course, and indeed always intends to, but there's always something like a delivery of a dead pike that some self-important berk from the Coningsfield Angling Club wants preserved immediately because he's got visitors coming, and he doesn't get round to it, and anyway it wouldn't make any difference if he did, because they would still feel like rooms one and two.

They have put Liam to bed. He hasn't said a thing about the anniversary. They don't think he's aware of it. What do they do now? On the anniversary of something nice people drink champagne. What is the opposite of champagne? Arsenic?

They sit on either side of the coal-effect fire, which is lit up but not on; it's a warm day, though not as warm or as wonderful as that day. They sit in exhausted silence for perhaps two or three minutes. It seems longer.

'I can't believe it,' explodes Maggie at last. 'A whole year, and they've found nothing. Did no boy behave oddly that night? Have no tongues wagged? Has neither boy said a word to anyone? Have no parents noticed unexplained damage to either car? Did no garage make the connection? The police are pathetic. They didn't even try.'

'Leave it, Mags.'

'It's a conspiracy of silence. It's a cover-up.'

'We don't know that.'

'Whose side are you on?'

'I'm on our side, of course, but we have to move on. We have to—'

'Forget?'

'No. No, Mags, of course not. We have to rebuild our lives. Look to the future, not the past.'

'You sound like a politician.'

He feels that the insult is deserved, because he is saying things that he doesn't believe, he is saying them because he feels that he ought to believe them. Sometimes they do look, to outsiders, as if they *are* rebuilding their lives, because they have to seem to be doing so, for Liam's sake. There is laughter in their lives, for his sake. There is normality on the surface, for his sake. Everything is for his sake, and thank goodness it is.

'You're punishing yourself. You're hurting yourself. It's doing no good.'

'That . . . that murderer . . . driving around . . . scot-free.'

'Not a murderer, Mags. It was manslaughter at worst. Death by dangerous driving. Accidental. Terrible, horrendous, wicked, but accidental. I'm actually rather sorry for the young man.'

126

Maggie stares at him wildly.

'What did you say?'

Her voice is an iceberg, and Timothy is the *Titanic*.

'What did you say?' she repeats.

He remains calm.

'I said I'm actually rather sorry for the boy. He'll have to live with it for the rest of his life.'

She begins to shout. 'No, he sodding well won't. He'll have forgotten all about it, the callous little yob. He killed my son, who came out of my body, not yours I might point out.'

'No fault of mine. I'd have been happy to have him if I could.'

'Oh, shut up. Don't be so stupid, you horrid little man. He killed our son, and you forgive him.'

'I didn't say I forgive him.' He is also shouting now. 'I should forgive him, I call myself a Christian, but I don't, I can't. I said I was sorry for him. Listen to what I say, will you, woman?'

'I can't believe in any faith that forgives like that. It's madness.'

'I said I haven't forgiven.' He screams his frustration.

'I'm not talking about you. I'm talking about Christianity.'

The door opens. Liam appears, in his bright green pyjamas. They trail on the floor. He'll grow into them. If he lives. Nobody makes assumptions any more.

'Stop shouting,' he cries.

'We weren't shouting, darling. It was the television,' says Maggie.

'It's not on.'

'We switched it off because of all the shouting,' says Timothy. 'We hate shouting too.'

'You were shouting. I hate it when you shout.'

'We won't shout any more, darling. Kiss Daddy goodnight and I'll take you to bed.'

Liam looks very doubtful, then runs to his daddy, hugs him, turns away rapidly, and lets himself be led back upstairs.

Timothy sits and thinks. He turns off the light on the coal-effect fire. It was making the place look like a B & B.

They can't go on like this. They both had the thought that they must soldier on, for Liam's sake, and for their own. They can't continue to occupy this place with too many rooms, and with the dark presence of the dingy house next door always looming, the knowledge that there are dead animals just behind the chintzy wallpaper that had graced Miss de Beauvoir's select establishment. Dead animals next door. A dead son here. They should move. Or maybe they should part. Did he have the heart to suggest it?

Maggie returns.

'He's settled.'

'Good.'

'We can't go on like this.'

'No.'

There is just the slightest pause before she speaks, just the slightest softening in her tone.

'I'm leaving you, Timothy.'

'Oh.'

Why can he say nothing more? Why can he not acknowledge that it's what he has wanted and that he is relieved to have the decision taken out of his hands?

Because he's Christian and marriage is sacred? Does he really believe that? Because he can't admit failure? No, he's not as pathetic as that. Because he'll lose Liam, and without Liam there will be no need to even try to fight his grief?

'I really think it's best for us both. I can't go on working at that school, passing that spot. We remind each other of what we've lost every time we see each other.'

And then an extraordinary thing happens. At least Timothy thinks it's extraordinary. She smiles.

'Thank you for being such a good father,' she says.

'Me, a good father?'

He is utterly astonished.

'Specially since the . . . accident. Yes, you're right. I must drop all that. It's killing me. No, playing with Liam, taking him to the park, and having to go all the way to the other park, twenty minutes' driving every time. I know it doesn't come naturally to you but you've done it as well as you're capable of. Liam needs to get away too. A new school. A new town. Sell this place which is much too big for us, you move back next door – don't look like that, you can brighten it up. Your dad needs you. A new start, Timothy, for all three of us.'

Timothy sits there, wanting to agree, wanting to cry with relief, hating the thought that he can even contemplate feeling relief ever again, wanting a new start, believing that it is impossible to make a new start.

'I . . .'

Go on. It's not difficult.

'I agree.'

There. Done.

'I'll give in my notice tomorrow,' says Maggie. 'They won't be entirely surprised. I'll maybe look for jobs in Cornwall.'

'Cornwall??'

'Near my sister.'

He is aghast. He is drowning. Cornwall is a million miles away. He will never see Liam again. He will lose his other son.

'Don't look so worried, Timothy. There are trains and planes. You can see Liam whenever you want. You're a good man, Timothy.'

It's extraordinary. There is more affection for him in her tone than for . . . oh, months. Years.

She goes over to him, and kisses him.

'I love you,' she says.

He is reeling.

'Not in that way. I'm not made for marriage. I'll never have sex again. Wretched business. Wet sheets and a dry throat. What would you say to a bottle of wine?'

She mistakes his bewilderment for disapproval.

'Sorry. That's tactless. Nothing to celebrate.'

'No, I fancy a bottle too. We never do. If we can find one.'

They find a bottle. They can't remember where the corkscrew's kept, but they find that too eventually.

They stand in the huge kitchen where Miss de Beauvoir once cooked full English breakfasts and kippers for her guests, and where very little cooking now goes on. A house needs cooking, Timothy thinks, and that was one of our mistakes.

They raise their glasses to each other, feeling a little bewildered, extremely sad, but also, strangely, only slightly but mystifyingly excited.

'Do you get any consolation from that God of yours?' she asks.

'No,' he says after some thought. 'I don't think that's what I'm searching for.'

'What are you searching for – forgiveness?'

Yes, partly. For a spasm of disappointment that lasted all of twenty seconds, and I can never possibly mention that to Maggie.

'I'm not sure there's a great deal to forgive. I feel heartbroken, not guilty. Though I think I might start to feel guilty if I ever stopped feeling heartbroken. So I don't truly think there can ever be any happiness for me again.'

'We have to find some true happiness, Timothy. We have Liam.'

'*You* have Liam.'

'No, no. Oh no, Timothy. No.'

130

It's extraordinary. He has never seen her so animated.

'If we lived close together,' she says, 'there would be all the agony of sharing him, dividing up the week, trips to the zoo, endless difficult arrivals and even more difficult departures. Liam would live in a world of tension. If we live in Cornwall he will have a secure life there, a new school, a proper home. And you can come and visit any time you like for as long as you like. I promise you that, Timothy. Take him swimming, surfing, sailing. And he can come to visit you, holidays in Yorkshire, trips to the moors, outings to London, trips abroad. You can be the fun in his life, Timothy. I'll be the solidity. I don't have much talent for fun. So, for his sake, you need to learn how to have fun again. We'll have an easy divorce. On good terms. I'm not a horrid woman, Timothy.'

'Of course you aren't.'

They drink in silence for a while. They are as close as they have ever been, as they contemplate their separation.

'You should get married again, Timothy.'

He smiles. It is the first utterly genuine smile that he has managed in his life After.

'Hey! Slow down,' he says. 'Separated, divorced and engaged in one evening. Must be good wine, this.' He grows solemn again. 'I don't think I could dare to love ever again,' he says.

'You will. You must. Didn't you say your drinking chums wanted to take you to Majorca for a boys' weekend?'

'Ghastly thought. I couldn't stand it. Anyway, it's rather fallen through, luckily. Tommo pulled out. Needed at work. Apparently the world of biscuits is feeling the crunch. Steven's too busy in London, big new job, he's a rising star again. That leaves me and Dave. He's always up for getting away from his wife. I said I'd prefer Seville.'

'Why Seville?'

131

'Apparently it really is exceptionally beautiful. And very religious. Apparently the tapas bars are fantastic.'

'What's a tapas bar?'

'I don't know. Presumably a bar where they drink tapas.'

'What's a tapa?'

'I don't know. I live in Coningsfield.'

And with the mention of Coningsfield Timothy returns to reality. The beauty of Seville fades from his face. The glimpses of flamenco dancers disappear from his eyes. He has let himself down, thinking of these good things. He cannot believe that he has allowed himself to do so, even for a moment. He sighs deeply, and returns to his private hell.

'Get them off!' says the man with a smile, salt water dripping off him.

Naomi gives him an answering smile, trying to make it look genuine. She hasn't got much to get off. She has just raced Emily to the water's edge, and is standing there in her skimpy bikini, plucking up that little bit of courage which she still needs to find before she wades out into the sea.

The man turns round, a little anxiously.

'I have got it right, haven't I?' he asks. 'It is you.'

'Oh, yes,' she says. 'It's me all right. I looked in the mirror this morning to make sure, and there I was, me.'

Naomi wishes she hadn't said this. It sounds ungracious. So she gives him one of her very best smiles, and says, 'Thank you.'

The man gives her a thumbs-up, and calls out to someone, 'I was right. It is her.'

Emily, who picks up on everything, says, 'Don't you like being famous, Mum?'

'I'm not exactly famous, Emily, and I had hoped, when I started my career, that I'd be doing great work in Shakespeare and Chekhov and Pinter rather than being remembered for saying, 'Get them off,' in a rather silly sitcom.'

They stroll along the edge of the sea, swishing the water with their feet.

'I don't really get it why it's funny when you say, "Get them off," Mum.'

'Nor do I, really, but the joke is that people think I'm asking them to get their trousers off and all I'm meaning is the shoes and socks, so that I can do their feet. That's the little joke that is giving your mum her tiny slice of fame, Emily.'

'Let's swim.'

'Good idea.'

They are at L'Ancresse, the favourite beach of the Walls family on their summer holidays. There's a broad sweep of firm sand at low tide, sand perfect for playing cricket on, and beach tennis. Emily didn't know you could play tennis without rackets, and Naomi has shown her how to do it.

She worried a little that she might find her return to Guernsey sad, that it would all be spoilt, that her memories had exaggerated its charms, but all has been well. Emily has loved it, and they have already had six days of delicate pleasure together.

Delicate? Why? Because for Naomi all pleasure contains a slight fear of the moment when it will end, because all the pleasures adults get from their children are tainted by the fear of what will happen as they grow up and because, in this instance, there is always the possibility that her memories of her mother will turn suddenly to sorrow.

But they don't. Naomi has such happy memories of her. Her memories are so vivid that her mother has seemed to be with them this week as they've taken the boat to Herm, gathered shells on Shell Beach, explored rock pools at Cobo, drunk the beauty that Renoir loved at Moulin Huet, and

133

marvelled at the daily miracle of the sun. She has seen the anxious working of her mother's mouth, for her mother never truly relaxed, was always worrying whether Julian would behave, or Clive would stub his foot and cry, or Naomi would drown, or it would rain (which it never did in the memory). Now her mother is anxious no more. She is at peace. Her father, of course, has been absent from these memories. He'd never been with them in Guernsey; unless he popped into St Peter Port harbour on the tide and saw them for one night, he'd been away on his boat, in his space, which was why he had always seemed to be just a little bit of an outsider in the family. Now he is having to cope with his loneliness, having to learn to look after himself, although staff members and their wives are making sure that he is well fed and Mrs McGuire, the cleaner, comes in to do the ironing, lay out clean pants, matching socks and ties that go with shirts, to save him from sartorial howlers which would otherwise threaten his powers of discipline.

Emily is so at home in the water. She screams with pure joy, enjoying pleasure that is not delicate, for she doesn't even consider the possibility of its ending. She says, 'I love this sea, Mum. It does things. It goes in and out. It slides into rock pools. It knocks down my castles. That other sea, it just sat there.' The sea Emily talks about so contemptuously is the Mediterranean.

Naomi has hired two deckchairs and a wind break from the man at the kiosk. They don't really need the wind break today but it gives them a bit of privacy, makes them feel that a bit of the beach is theirs. After their swim they go back to their bit of the beach and rub themselves briskly with their towels so that they won't get goose pimples, and then they have their chocolate. A swim isn't a swim without chocolate afterwards. Then they have another game of beach tennis. Naomi wins. She had tried to let

Emily win once, and Emily had shouted, 'Don't toy with me.' And the adult expression had made her laugh, and Emily had stamped her foot and shouted, 'And don't laugh at me either,' which had only made her laugh all the more. Anyway, it makes a nice change to win because every day of every family holiday she had lost at everything to Clive and Julian. Not that they had been nasty to her. Clive was never nasty and Julian, who could be such a pain most of the time, had always been nice to her. The day after their mother's funeral, just before leaving, Julian had said, 'Story of my life. I've only ever met one woman pretty enough and nice enough for me to marry, and she has to be my bloody sister.'

'You're not concentrating, Mum.'

'Sorry.'

After the beach tennis Naomi begins to prepare their picnic. There have to be hard-boiled eggs and salt and pepper in foil to blow away in the wind, which had always upset Penny, though nobody had minded, it had been a tradition, after all. And there had always been sandwiches so that the children could take it in turns to shout, 'I hate the sand which is in the sandwiches.' And Guernsey Gâche, a kind of fruit bread. And an apple each.

While Naomi is preparing this feast which reminds her of all those other feasts, Emily thinks hard, then swallows, then says, 'Mum?'

'Yes?'

'You know Francesca?'

What's coming now?

'I know of Francesca. I don't know her.'

'She's nice.'

Naomi is horrified to find that she is not entirely pleased to hear this.

'Oh?'

135

'Yes. And Dad's much nicer now he's with her.'

Worse and worse.

'Oh, good.'

'He doesn't get arseholed any more.'

'I told you not to use that word.'

'Sorry. You know September?'

Here we go.

'Yes.'

'You know the first week of September?'

'Yes.'

'You know I don't go back to school till the second week?'

'Yes.'

Naomi swallows again. Am I such an ogre?

'They want me to go on holiday with them.'

'Do they? Oh.' Phrases to give her time to think, time to cope. 'That's nice of them.' You have to learn to let your children go from you a bit at a time, or they will go from you altogether and at once. Naomi knows this, but it doesn't make it any easier. 'And what do you think? Do you want to go?'

'Well, yes. I think it would be nice.'

It will actually be very convenient. She can make that trip to Seville that Clive and Antoine suggested. She can just fit it in before the filming begins for the second series of *Cobblers in Koblenz*.

'Well, then. Go.'

'Thanks, Mum.' Emily goes up to her and hugs her. 'I love you, Mum. I love you much more than I'll ever love them.'

Naomi is thrilled to hear this but at the same time devastated to realise how clearly an eight-year-old can see into her heart.

Suddenly, in the sunshine, Naomi realises that Emily is going to be devastatingly pretty. This fills her with pride, joy

136

and fear. What a lunchtime it is proving to be for contradictory emotions.

It isn't finished yet. While they eat their lunch in silence, because you have to concentrate on what you're eating if you're not to drop the tastiest titbits in the sand, Naomi thinks about the second series. The first series was condemned by the critics and pointedly ignored by her friends, but proved very popular with quite a large section of the public, far too many of whom had come up to her and said, 'Get them off.' You work hard at drama school, you attend countless auditions and recalls, you tour in tatty productions and stay in horrendous digs in towns that should have been razed to the ground, and when success comes it consists of people smiling fatuously and shouting, 'Get them off,' at you. But it's work, and she likes the cast, and they have fun, and she knows now that she isn't a great actress, so there's no point in taking it all too seriously.

After their picnic, they ignore the deckchairs and lie on the rugs that Naomi has brought. They stare up at the cloudless sky, and Emily asks the question that Naomi has been dreading, and preparing for, since March.

'Has Granny gone to heaven?'

The truth. Always, the truth is best.

Of course not. She's been burnt. How could she? It's over. She's gone. That's life. Or rather, it isn't.

'What do you think, Emily?'

'I think she has, because I think she was very good.'

I think that's claptrap. I don't want to hurt you, darling, but the human race has to face the fact that death is an end. We simply have to learn not to fear death, and to realise that the idea of heaven and hell is put about to keep us in order out of fear.

Is the truth always best? Naomi has found it so difficult to come to terms with the fact that she didn't tell her mum what she really believed.

'She was very good. Let's hope she went to heaven, shall we, darling?'

How can you hurt and shock an eight-year-old kid? But the lies really ought to end. We should all say what we truly believe at all times. But how can she?

'And when you die, you'll go to heaven too, because you're good too, aren't you?'

'I don't think I'm that good. Not as good as Granny. I have thoughts that are not good.'

'We all have thoughts that are not good, Mum. Thoughts don't matter. It's what we do that matters. And what you do is good. Mum?'

'Yes?'

'The only thing that bothers me is this.'

Naomi wants to smile at the word 'bother', which seems so adult. Eight-year-olds shouldn't be bothered.

'Granny was burnt. How would they have put her together again?'

'Even if you believe in heaven, darling, it doesn't mean that people are there like they are on earth. People who believe in heaven believe that it's your soul that goes there.'

'You don't know what Granny's soul looks like. How will you recognise her?'

Oh, Emily, Emily, how I wish that everyone was as intelligent as you. What a world we could have.

'I expect there's a way, darling. We'll find out at the time.'

Oh, Naomi, Naomi, what pain it is causing you to say these things.

'Mum?'

'Yes, darling.'

'I don't want to be cruel to Granny, but I hope she has to wait a very long time before she meets up with you.'

How can people abuse children and not kill themselves

the next day when they wake up and remember what they've done?

'Thank you, Emily.'

There's a break in her voice. She's going to burst into tears. She mustn't, mustn't, mustn't. Quick. Fetch the director. Trevor Nunn walks along the beach. No, not Trevor Nunn. He can be sentimental. Harold Pinter. Hi, Harold. Naomi, don't show your emotion. Bottle it. There must be no sentimentality. No indulgence. And, before you speak, pause. And then pause again.

Oh, thank you, Harold.

She is safe.

The city throbs with heat. The air dances with it. And, at two o'clock, it's not yet even lunchtime in Seville. Dave Kent has taken Timothy to the market in Triana, across the sluggish, mud-coloured Guadalquivir from the city centre. It's the second time they've been, and it's the last straw for Timothy.

On their first day they didn't visit the Cathedral or the Alcazar. They visited two markets and two supermarkets. 'I'm at the crossroads, vegetable-wise,' Dave had said. 'I need to smarten up my ideas. I need an intake of European sophistication.'

They had looked at huge red and green and orange peppers shining like traffic lights. Dave had looked in awe at wild mushrooms of strange, delicate shape. He had been particularly impressed by the aubergines, smooth, shining, as blackly purple as thunder clouds.

'Just look at the sheen on them, Timothy,' he'd said. 'It shows how healthy they are.'

'Isn't that horses?'

'Horses and aubergines. Same difference.'

On the second day Dave had hired a motorbike, and with Timothy at the back, with helmetless heads and a great wake of dust behind them, they had frazzled their way through the burning orange orchards.

Now, on the third morning, Timothy's thoughts had turned to the Cathedral, the Giralda, the Alcazar, the great sights of Seville.

'I'd just like to pop back to the market,' Dave had said. 'I just want to check on the way that feller'd strewn half watermelons among the veg. Not among the fruit. Among the *veg*. That was innovative, Timothy. That's the kind of forward thinking Coningsfield is crying out for.'

Timothy wondered for a moment if Dave had an ulterior motive in dragging him past endless fruit and vegetable stalls. Was this some kind of vegetable aversion therapy? But no. Dave wasn't clever enough for that. In fact, he wasn't clever enough for doing anything except selling fruit and vegetables. It was what made him such an easy travelling companion.

'I'll come with you,' Timothy had said reluctantly, 'if you promise to go and see the sights after that.'

Dave had promised, though not without a sigh of resignation.

Then, at the market, Dave had sampled the local nectarines – 'I'm not hungry, but it's research, i'n't it?' – and had spilt juice all down the front of his T-shirt. They'd gone back to their hotel to change, and now, at last, Timothy is edging Dave in the direction of the Giralda, the exquisite Moorish bell tower that guides the path of lost tourists all over the city.

Not that he really wants to see the Giralda. Or the Cathedral. Or the Alcazar. He knows that he will fail to be excited by their ravishing beauty, that he will believe that he will never be able to appreciate beauty again, that beauty will only heighten his despair by reminding him of how completely he is excluded from its pleasures, and that this will bring an uneasy comfort, a relief that his grief is so immutable and eternal.

No, he is only pulling Dave in the direction of those famous monuments because he knows that if he is forced to look at another pile of aubergines he'll be sick.

On their way they pass a small greengrocer's. Dave eyes it wistfully. Timothy pulls him past it. Dave takes a last lingering look at a pile of peaches that are almost bursting with uncontainable ripeness and vigour. He squares his shoulders, summons up his last reserves of energy, and follows in Timothy's wake, up the breathless furnace of the street, towards the Barrio Santa Cruz and the Giralda.

Naomi sits with Clive and Antoine outside a tapas bar on the shady side of the Calle Mateos Gago. At midnight, in this street that curves down to the Cathedral, the buzz of happy revellers is like the excitement of starlings settling down to roost, but now, at two o'clock in the afternoon after a long late lazy Spanish morning, things are more sedate.

She enjoys being in the company of gays. They are usually very polite and attentive, they don't cast furtive glances towards her crotch, she doesn't have to be on the defensive, and their presence deters heterosexual bores. But of all the gays she could possibly be with, her favourites are Clive and Antoine.

Clive is dressed in T-shirt, jeans and sandals, but even here in this heat Antoine hides his artistic identity behind smartly creased dark trousers and an immaculate white short-sleeved shirt. Looking at him, people would be unlikely to say, 'I bet that man's an artist. It wouldn't surprise me to find out that he paints large, brightly coloured pictures which boldly and energetically explore what he regards as the essential synergism between chance and design which, he believes, must inform art if it is not to wither back into representational sterility or collapse in a chaos of undefined forms.'

They have a bottle of local white wine, which they are drinking slowly, rolling the lovely cold liquid round their parched mouths before allowing it to slip down their throats.

Clive raises his glass.

'To the success of the second series of *Cobblers in Koblenz*.'

'To the success of the second series of *Cobblers in Koblenz*,' echoes Antoine.

Naomi raises her glass, drinks and grimaces.

'You don't like it? I think it's rather good,' says Clive.

'It wasn't the wine. I'm just not looking forward to the show. People love it, but I don't. And the critics slated it.'

'Join the anti-critics club,' says Antoine.

'The critics have a point, you know, Antoine,' says Clive. There's iron behind his gentle tone. He's grasping a nettle, seizing an unexpected chance.

'Oh?' says Antoine, exaggerating the tartness in his voice to show that he's not really offended. 'Pray explain.'

'This business of insisting that there's always an element of chance in everything you paint – he's getting small children in now to either start or finish the paintings, Naomi . . .'

'They love it.'

'That isn't the point, and you know it.'

'It's part of the point. What can be wrong in giving pleasure to children?'

Suddenly Clive is angry.

'If your art is a game to you, let's forget it,' he says.

'Of course it isn't. I'm teasing. You take it so seriously that I can't resist.'

'You're the artist. It's you who should be taking it seriously.'

'I do. I do.'

Naomi is happy to listen, though not happy to hear them disagreeing. Disagreement disturbs her. In her utopia everyone would agree about everything, and it wouldn't be boring, it would be heart-warming and exhilarating. This is one of the reasons why she finds it absurd to be at odds with so many people about religion.

She feels that she must intervene.

'So what was the point you said the critics had, Clive?' she asks gently.

'Oh, that he only has the one idea, this mixing up of chance and design. Why can't you do some paintings that are entirely planned and designed, entirely structured, Antoine?'

'Because I believe that our society is no longer structured. There are no clear forms in life any more. Everything is a battle between order and disorder. I have to be truthful.'

A horse, pulling four German tourists in a trap, clip-clops elegantly through the square in front of the cathedral.

'It's a bee in your bonnet,' says Clive.

'What does that mean? What is this bee in this bonnet?'

'It's a phrase. The bee is trapped in your bonnet, and cannot escape, so it will sting. So having a bee in your bonnet is bad.'

'I don't have a bee in my bonnet. I have an *idée fixe*, yes, but it doesn't sting.'

'It stings the critics, and they sting you in turn.'

'I can't help that. It might please a lot of people if art went back to the old certainties of form and composition and perspective, but it's simply not an option.'

'All right,' admits Clive. 'I just want you to make a bit more – oh, dirty word – money.'

Perhaps because she is made uneasy by Clive and Antoine's rumbling disagreement, civilised though it is, Naomi jumps at the opportunity of a link to a new subject, and reveals a secret that she has been intending to hide. Suddenly she wants to share it.

'I have a bit of a bee in *my* bonnet.'

'Oh?'

'Religion. I have this great desire to convert people.'

'Naomi!'

Clive is shocked.

'*From* religion. I want to convert them *from* religion.'

Clive is still shocked.

'Don't do it,' he says. 'Don't take that on.'

'Let this bee out of your bonnet now, Naomi,' says Antoine. 'No good will come of it if you don't.'

Timothy is utterly unaware that within five minutes his whole life could change. Within five minutes, if he steers Dave through the shady, airless, white lanes towards the Giralda, he will pass the tapas bar outside which Naomi is drinking white wine with Clive and Antoine. He will see Naomi, they will talk, they will discover that they are both free from emotional entanglements, and with his beloved childhood sweetheart he will learn to live and love again. It's a prospect to make a writer of fiction blush with shame at his facile use of coincidence. This is real life, however, and the prospect can only excite anyone with half a heart.

But Timothy stops, turns to Dave, and says, 'Do you mind if I pop into this church for a moment, Dave? On my own? I want a quiet moment.'

'No probs. Where will I see you?'

'Back here in quarter of an hour?'

'Fine. I'll have a quick San Miguel. Actually, I need to do a bit of thinking too. I've been all shook up, to be honest, with what I've seen. I'm behind the times. I've got to spice up me presentation.'

Dave now has seven shops in his Garden of England chain.

Timothy walks towards the Iglesia de Santa Maria La Blanca.

The chill of the church is a shock after the dry fever of the heat outside. Its roof is an elaborate pattern of swirls and whirls and whorls in stuccoed profusion. It's an old church, converted from a synagogue in 1392. On the north wall hangs a *Last Supper* by Murillo, as striking as one would expect from a citizen of this city of drama and extremes. But the church itself is surprisingly self-effacing. Timothy feels at ease here. He will be able to pray.

As he walks slowly towards the front of the church, he sees a very elderly woman going into a confessional. He wonders what sins she could possibly have had the energy to commit.

To his right a young man is shaking with silent sobs as he prays. Timothy can't bear to witness the severity of his grief, and hurries on. How can God have time for me and my insignificant troubles? he thinks.

But he doesn't leave. He finds an empty little side chapel, and there he kneels and prays.

'O Lord,' he says silently, but moving his lips in an attempt to feel more fervent. 'I'm not a Catholic. Well, you know that. If I was a Catholic, and if I was therefore going to confession, I would confess to one great sin. When I was told that my son was dead, I wasn't told which one, and when I saw that Liam was alive I felt a little stab of disappointment. I can't forget this. I'm reminded of it every time I see my son. So I have had to come to terms with it, and I have. I've done this by accepting that I am imperfect, that it would be inhuman and robotic, as a father of two children, not to love one more than the other. To love them equally, that seems a rather theoretical kind of love, perhaps a bit like your own love for all mankind. Which worries me a bit, to be honest. I mean, can you really love St Francis,

Jack the Ripper and Steven Venables equally? So I no longer feel guilty. I feel that it would have been a sin if I had not loved either of my sons. To love them both, but one a little more than the other, seems to me to be reasonable. And, if it is a sin, I hope I redeem it with my actions, for I make every effort to be a truly good father to the boy. I believe that what we do is far more important than what we think. Our acts are far more important than our motives.

'I'm just an ordinary, unsophisticated, Northern English taxidermist. I'm not particularly good at it, certainly nothing like as good as my dad, but I get by. So I don't know if I'm really clever enough to know how prayer works or how it's supposed to work. I mean, you can't hear every word that everyone who prays to you is saying. You aren't a great telephone exchange in the sky. So what do people expect when they pray? How can they expect you to answer? If I pray to win a football match, and one of my opponents also asks you to let him win the same football match, that would be putting you in an impossible position, so clearly that kind of prayer is simply wrong. But people must expect some kind of action or at least reaction from you, otherwise why would they pray? Clearly, if prayer is effective, you must be able to give some kind of answer to millions of people all virtually at the same time. And you must, in a sense, be all the Gods people believe in, because there surely can't actually be more than one God? So, unless all the other prayers made in the world are a waste of time, they must somehow come to you. Maybe you're a kind of electronic person or a person made out of waves or even of things that I don't know about or can't dream of, forces we don't yet know about. The owl sees at least two hundred times better than me. Maybe you can understand millions of things at the same time.

'I have a feeling that theologians and bishops would have

146

answers proving that what I think about prayer is very naive indeed, that I've missed the point, but if that is so then I have to say, I'm sorry, and hope that it's true that you love ordinary human beings as much as bishops and popes.

'All this may suggest to you that I'm having doubts, and, yes, I am. Lord, I want to ask you two things.

'The first, and the most important thing, is that I want help to overcome my grief. The thing is, a great part of me doesn't want to overcome it, but I know that I need to if I am to be a good father to Liam. Maggie has been true to her word – I've never liked her as much as I have since we parted, and I see Liam a lot. I know you know all this but somehow it doesn't work for me unless I tell you, even though I know I'm probably wasting my time. Anyway, Liam and I do quite a lot of things together, but my heart isn't truly in it, and children are very perceptive about hearts, and one day he will realise and I will lose him too. That prospect terrifies me.

'My second request is . . . I feel a bit self-conscious asking this. There's a story about all the diplomats in some country being asked what they wanted for Christmas. The English ambassador said, "A new camera." Then he heard that all the other ambassadors had asked for things like an end to poverty, world peace and fresh clean water for every human being on earth. Well, I feel a bit like him, because at this very moment people are praying for an end to war and poverty and cancer and earthquakes and all the other things that you have chosen to let us endure for reasons that I only dimly perceive, and I am asking you to help me meet a young woman whom I realise I love. You know her name, but I'll remind you. It's Naomi Walls. Or Naomi Prendergast, née Walls, but she still calls herself Naomi Walls for her work.

'I know that in the scheme of things this is a pretty trivial request, but I love her so much, and I am so sorry that we

147

messed up our first chance of happiness. I promise you this isn't some weird obsession – if she doesn't want me I will accept it happily, well, no, not happily, but you know what I mean. I'm not some kind of metaphysical stalker. I'm a man who has made a right old cock-up, if you'll excuse my French, of his personal life, and wants to put things right.

'I know you've got far more important matters to deal with, so I'll let you get on with them now, but I'd just point out one thing. If you grant me the second part of my wish, you'll also go a long way towards granting me my first wish, because with Naomi I am sure I could learn to have joy and fun again. And if you granted me both wishes, all my doubts would disappear and be as mist – well, no, you can see mist, but I'm thinking of that moment when the mist just disperses into nothingness. My doubts will disperse just like that.

'So really all my requests are tied in together, and so I don't think it's unreasonable or greedy of me to ask for so much. Thank you very much for listening to me. Amen.'

By the time Timothy and Dave reach the Calle Mateos Gago, Naomi has gone. The coincidence doesn't happen.

Their paths will cross very soon, however, and this time it won't be a coincidence.

PART FOUR

Get Stuffed

1995

It's a cold evening in West London, with flecks of rain on a north-westerly wind. The wind is creeping round the corner of the BBC Television Centre. Processions of cars, white vans, taxis, buses and lorries grind with agonising slowness in both directions along grimy, unlovely Wood Lane. It is not a scene, or an evening, to excite or warm a person. Yet Timothy is in a fever of anticipation, and a fire burns inside him.

No. It's too soon to be talking of fevers of anticipation, of fires burning inside Timothy. How could that be?

It is in the nature of our experience of existence that we see the world around us entirely from the viewpoint of our own eyes. This may seem obvious, trite, banal, self-evident, tautologous and worthy of many other uncomplimentary adjectives. Painters, sculptors, writers, actors, musicians show us the world through their eyes, but we can only see the world that they show us through their eyes through our own eyes.

Timothy is sitting in the back bar of the Wig and Mitre. It's the 'Happy Hour'.

No. It's too soon even to be talking of happy hours. The concept would have seemed indecent to the Timothy whom we last saw in Seville. So what has happened?

Nothing.

Except . . . Timothy has been thinking. He's quite good at that.

He has realised that, when he sees the world entirely through his own eyes, he is entitled to grieve, he is probably doomed to grieve, for his lost son for the rest of his life. He will also wallow in guilt. But if he makes a determined effort – and, my God, it has to be determined – to see the world through other people's eyes, everything changes.

He has already tried to see the world through Liam's eyes, and has realised that he must rediscover his capacity for joy, true joy. Young children can smell out insincerity. The older they get, the more insincerity they are faced with, and the more weary and blurred their instinct becomes. If he is incapable of true happiness, he will be unable to bring any joy to the life of his surviving son. He has to recover his spirits, for his son's sake.

'Oh, very convenient,' the cynic observes.

But there is also Roly. Timothy sees Liam from time to time, but he sees Roly almost every day. Roly is thrilled to have him back in number ninety-six. He has hated all his lonely suppers in that dark house. Timothy is by far the most important element in Roly's life. He has to be positive, for Roly. It's his obligation. It's his duty.

'Oh, brilliant,' cries the cynic in tones dripping with sarcasm. 'How very fortunate.'

But Timothy does not see any of this as convenient, or fortunate. His sorrow is his greatest friend, his lover, his indulgence. His first forays into true recovery are painful indeed. Every moment of pleasure is a challenge to his integrity. Every laugh is an outrage to his sensitivity. Sam is dead. He insults Sam by smiling. Yet he does no good to Sam by crying. By crying, he feeds only his self-esteem.

It's a deeply ironic and deeply sad fact – though, not being saints, we may permit ourselves to relish the rough justice of it just a little – that the most egotistical and selfish of people actually deny themselves much of the pleasure of life. They have fewer friends than the unselfish, receive fewer presents, are less well treated by the rest of the human race. In the sad world of the elderly there are many lonely old people who have never learned to give and are reaping a meagre and deserved harvest.

Luckily, Timothy is not, by the standards of society, very egotistical at all. He is not, in fact, a very self-conscious person. He worries about tiny matters: what to say at parties, how to tie parcels, which knife to use, whether he will remember his lines. He doesn't worry about the bigger pictures, no more worries about what people think of him, whether they like him, whether they will be convinced by his portrayal of Romeo. That, coupled with his good looks, is what attracted Naomi to him so strongly, in Coningsfield, in Earls Court, especially on the second night, and even in Iquitos.

Slowly, a step at a time, life returns to Timothy's soul. He swims with Liam as if they were dolphins, puts onto his father's dark table meals that taste of love.

It's a cold evening in West London, with flecks of rain on a north-westerly wind. The wind is creeping round the corner of the BBC Television Centre. Processions of cars, white vans, taxis, buses and lorries grind with agonising slowness in both directions along grimy, unlovely Wood Lane. It is not a scene, or an evening, to excite or warm a person. Yet Timothy is in a fever of anticipation, and a fire . . .

No. It's still too soon to be talking of fevers of anticipation, of fires burning inside him.

More than two years have passed since Timothy prayed so fervently in Seville. He has begun to learn to smile and laugh again. He has also, slowly, very gradually, learned how to drink. He has now been on no fewer than nine Pennine Piss-ups with

Tommo, Steve and Dave, and each one has become just a little less difficult than the last one. He has had to put on an act for his friends, and gradually it has begun to cease to be an act.

His gradual emergence into the world of alcohol has also led him into the habit of visiting the Wig and Mitre in Granary Lane twice a week after work, just for a couple of pints, and a third on rare occasions such as the upsetting affair of the angry coarse fisherman and the two large pike. The fisherman had been lucky enough to catch a nineteen-pound pike, which he had wanted stuffed, mounted and placed in a glass case.

'We don't stuff,' Timothy had explained. 'We model.'

'I don't care what it is you bloody well do. Just do it,' the man had said, revealing himself to be a coarse fisherman in two senses.

Timothy had thought of refusing, but it had been a quiet time and he'd needed the money. He'd begun the job straight away, sensing that this man would be quick to complain of delay. And then the man had caught a twenty-one-pound pike and wanted that done instead of the first one. Timothy had said that he was almost halfway through the first pike, so the man would have to pay for the time and materials involved. The man had refused. An altercation had taken place, the outcome of which need not concern us, and Timothy had felt justified in having a third pint. The pub was within walking distance, after all.

And there is another day, a hundred and thirty-eight days before his fever of anticipation in Wood Lane, on which he feels that a third pint is justified. Not only justified, needed. It has been a difficult day for him. He had the dream last night, for maybe the fourth or fifth time, he can't be sure. It is a very bad dream, and it did begin to occur shortly after Sam's death, but that has nothing to do with its subject matter. It's just one more thing that he has to deal with, and it's something that he finds it utterly impossible to admit to another human being.

154

He has taken his first pint and his evening paper to a far corner of the large bar. He still isn't a natural mixer. He has bought the paper, as always, from the seller with the squint on the corner rather than the good-looking one with the smug expression outside the hospital. These little things are important to him. He settles himself down for what he calls 'My own "Happy Hour"'. The pub itself runs a 'Happy Hour', during which spirits are half price, but Timothy's happiness lies not in the price of his drinks but in his being free from his father for an hour. He is not a saint. He truly loves his father, of course he does, his love for his father has played a great part in helping him to cope with his torment, but looking after a man who is now virtually blind is a responsibility and a tie. And his father has been a brilliant taxidermist, a master craftsman, more than a craftsman, an artist. Timothy is a plodder by comparison, competent enough, making a steady living, but not receiving reindeers to model from admiring Lapps and a shark sent all the way from Cornwall by taxi, as once happened to his father. And all the time, as he's worked, in the shadow of the dark house and the greater shadow of his father's reputation, he's been aware that at any moment he will hear the tap tap tap of his father's stick, and his father will enter the room, and say, with the curious archaic speech he increasingly favours, 'How goes it, esteemed product of my then less scrawny loins? Do you think perhaps that branch he's perched on should be a little higher in the case?' or, 'Greetings, thou to whom I bequeathed my business with such confidence. Making progress? Excellent. Um . . . is the face turned a little bit too much, do you think? Does it look just a little unnatural, a trifle forced? Only a thought, I may be wrong, I can't see, probably I should shut up.' And as Timothy had said to Tommo and Steve and Dave in the Mill House at Bugginsby Far Bottom, on one of their 'Pennine Piss-ups', 'He's always right. He's almost totally blind, and he's always right. Always. Every time. Never wrong. Never. Not once. Not that I mind. It doesn't irritate me. It doesn't get to me. I'm really cool about it.' Timothy cool? Come on.

Of course it did get to him, and that is why he so enjoys these moments on his own. And on this particular evening, he has opened the paper with a sigh of quiet delight, held it in front of his face to deter conversation, and drifted through its trivial delights. *'Councillor Arranged Building Contract for Cousin', 'Coningsfield Weather Girl Raises a Storm', 'Lost Goose Thinks City Dentist is His Father', 'Vandals Steal Bus Stop', 'Third Time Lucky for Sitcom Sexpot?'*

'Third Time Lucky for Sitcom Sexpot?'? Could it be? It has to be. His heart thuds against his chest. For a moment he thinks it's a heart attack. Then he realises that it's more serious than that. It's love.

He hardly dares read the article.

Lovely local actress Naomi Walls (33) is hoping that it will be a case of 'Third Time Lucky' when she takes a starring role in a brand new BBC sitcom, Get Stuffed.

The shapely Lower Cragley Road thespian has appeared in two sitcoms in recent years. Her first, Nappy Ever After, *lasted only one series and was what is known in media circles as 'A turkey'.*

Then she had a much more promising role as the sex-obsessed German chiropodist with a foot fetish in the Rhineland romp, Cobblers in Koblenz, *where she was known for her catchphrase, 'Get Them Off.' The show lasted two series and attracted good audiences but was cancelled by the new BBC comedy supremo, Gladys Mainspring, who said it was, 'Not my cup of tea.'*

Sexpot

*'I've not been too lucky in my comedy roles so far,' bubbly Naomi explained to me over a cappuccino in the Holiday Inn. '*Nappy Ever After *just didn't work, and I was embarrassed even to go to the supermarket or the hairdresser's.*

'Cobblers in Koblenz did much better, but it was hardly Shakespeare and I could understand the BBC's decision. I didn't really like people saying, 'Get Them Off' everywhere I went. My daughter Emily is ten and I don't want her growing up thinking her mother is just a sexpot.'

Naomi explained to me that she always tries to put her daughter first, especially in the years since her separation and divorce from her husband, Simon.

What?? Wow-ee. Hurrah. Timothy raises his glass carefully to his lips. He has to use both hands, he's shaking so much.

Now Naomi has a third chance to really hit the spot.

'I haven't seen the full scripts yet', she mused over her coffee, which she took without sugar. She is very weight-conscious.

Oh. Oh. Your slim body. The tops of your thighs, slender yet substantial. Steady on, Timothy. But oh oh oh, Naomi, my darling, my slim, slender sexpot. No, she doesn't like that word. Cool down, Timothy. There'll be someone else in her life. Read on and find out.

'But the scene I read for the audition was funny and touching, and that's the combination I respond to.'

Sex-sodden

'Of course I would like Emily to see me in great dramatic roles rather than in sex-sodden sitcoms, but I'm hoping that this one will have a bit more quality and less innuendo than Cobblers in Koblenz, *and you have to be realistic and take what you're given. Lots of my friends would die for a chance like this,' opined the level-headed former alumnus of Coningsfield Grammar School.*

So what is the new comedy about?

'I'm glad you asked me that,' Naomi smiled. 'It's about an area of life that many people know nothing about — taxidermy.'

What? But it's called *Get Stuffed*. Oh, Naomi, how could you do this to me? We don't stuff. We model. Don't those morons know anything? How could you take the part? Traitor.

Boyfriend

'Funnily enough I know a bit about taxidermy myself. I once had a boyfriend who was a taxidermist. I hope he won't be too upset if liberties are taken with the facts.'

'If?' They've been taken, they've sodding well been taken, and I only know the title. Oh, Naomi. Well, of course, you can't change the title. You hate it, but you can do nothing. I mustn't be unreasonable, mustn't blame you. Go on. Say something nice about me. He was a lovely lad. I often wonder about him. What a fool I was not to marry him.

The BBC tell us that the new series is about two rival taxidermists who don't get on and try to do each other down in increasingly hilarious ways. Naomi plays the daughter of one of the taxidermists.

Nothing more about me at all. 'I once had a boyfriend who was a taxidermist.' How flat is that? And two rival taxidermists, is that contrived or what? Oh, Naomi, Naomi.

Naomi hopes that the series will run and run and run, but she also hopes that she might get more dramatic roles in the future.

'Sitcoms are great, but I don't want to get typecast as a sitcom actress,' she explains.

Spoilt

I asked her if there was anyone in her life at the moment. She smiled – a little wistfully, I thought – and said, 'Not at the moment, no. I'll be very careful second time around. I wouldn't want a romantic entanglement unless it was absolutely right.'

Oh, Naomi. How wonderful. Oh, how right. Oh, my darling, where are you, how can I find you?

'I wonder if I could have a second cup of coffee?' she enquired politely. A well-mannered, level-headed girl, our Naomi. Not spoilt in the slightest. Coningsfield can be proud of her.

Thoughts whirr through Timothy's head like rampaging locusts. He drinks his second pint very quickly, and has a third.

'Thirsty today,' comments the barman, who has acne and boils on the back of his neck, probably, Timothy suspects, from too much wanking.

Thirsty? You spotty cretin. Not thirsty. Happy beyond belief.

'Absolutely. Very thirsty.'

He walks home in a trance, calls out to his father, 'Supper'll be just a few moments, Dad,' climbs the stairs to the upstairs lavatory, which has no lock – but his father is hardly likely to follow him upstairs and wouldn't be able to see what he was doing even if he did – and there, in the dark, watched only by an owl – but this one can't see even in the dark because it has been dead for twelve years – he takes off all his clothes, and all Naomi's clothes, and there, in that sagging bed, in that tiny lavatory, he loves her as she has never been loved before. After which, he has cottage pie with his Dad.

Oh, the attempts that he makes to get in contact with Naomi, and the fear he has of rejection. The letters that he writes to the *Coningsfield Evening Argus* and doesn't send. The times he drives down Lower Cragley Road and doesn't dare to stop and call at L'Ancresse. The times he drives *up* Lower Cragley Road and doesn't dare to stop and call at L'Ancressse. Many years have passed since he last saw her, and Naomi will be different. The newspaper said that she wasn't spoilt, but newspapers have stories to tell. He hasn't the courage to face another rejection.

And then the great thought comes to him. He can apply to the BBC and get a ticket for the show. He sends a personalised letter to the BBC's ticket department. No mention of Naomi, of course. They might take him for an obsessive. 'I am a taxidermist so I am particularly interested in the subject and would love to laugh at the many follies of my profession.' He doesn't know whether it makes a difference, but he gets a ticket. And now here he is, in Wood Lane.

It's a cold evening in West London, with flecks of rain on a north-westerly wind. The wind is creeping round the corner of the BBC Television Centre. Processions of cars, white vans, taxis, buses and lorries grind with agonising slowness in both directions along grimy, unlovely Wood Lane. It is not a scene, or an evening, to excite or warm a person. Yet Timothy is in a fever of anticipation, and a fire burns inside him. He takes his new leather coat off, for fear that he'll start sweating, and will be unpleasant to women before the night is out.

Well, not to women generally. Just to Naomi.

More people join the queue. He doesn't much like the look of them. Anoraks, he thinks. Nerds, he suspects. Not good enough for Naomi.

He's almost certain that he'll hang around at the end and ask to see her. In his dream he is not a brave man, but if he turns out not to be brave enough to do this he'll despise himself for ever. After all, there's no harm in it. This is the whole point. He is in no danger of rejection, because all he needs to say, at the beginning, is that he wanted to see the show, because of his interest in taxidermy.

At last they all file into the building, and through corridors, and into the studio. Stewards point them to their seats in an orderly manner. He's in luck. He's nowhere near the front. He doesn't want Naomi to see him, not till afterwards.

It's very exciting to sit in these seats, look up into the vast gantry above and see a bewildering array of technical equipment. It's even more exciting to look down on a floor crowded with five large cameras, with cables trailing everywhere, and beyond the cameras some scenery – he believes the technical term is 'sets', he's read that somewhere. One of the sets looks ever so slightly like his workshop, but not much, and a sudden fear grips him. What he sees is going to be a travesty of taxidermy.

A warm-up man comes on and starts telling jokes and getting them to shake hands with the person on their left. The person on his left has a handshake like a sweaty mullet. Timothy's tension grows. He has waited three thousand, three hundred and twelve hours for this moment. And there have not been many waking moments during those one hundred and ninety-eight thousand, seven hundred and twenty minutes – he has worked out the figures during the train journey – in which he hasn't thought of this evening that is now galloping so speedily and yet so slowly towards triumph or disaster, and he realises that he is much less able to face the twin prospects calmly than Kipling had been.

The cast are introduced one by one. The two taxidermists first. Matthew Cotherbridge, far too patrician to be a taxidermist, a luvvie if ever there was one, seriously miscast, thinks Timothy with a sinking heart. Then Francis Old, too weedy, a man of darkness, a man who looks like a dead mole, typecasting. Timothy's heart sinks further. And then their respective and respectable wives. And only then the son of one taxidermist and the daughter of the other, together.

There she is. In the flesh. So cruelly lovely. There isn't room in his body for his swelling heart.

He is amazed that this golden girl has only a shared entrance, half a round of applause. He is outraged, saddened, discouraged, made hopeful that she is not too much of a star, humiliated by proxy for the same reason.

And he knows. Knows before it starts what her role in

the series is. It's Romeo and Juliet with animals. Capulets and Montagues with stuffing jokes.

The actors take their places for the first scene. The tension suddenly rises, Timothy can feel the audience going stiff with it. Matthew Cotherbridge knows what to do, the old luvvie. He makes a deliberate mistake, and says, 'Oh, shit.' Everybody laughs.

'I've only said one line and I've cocked it up,' he tells the audience, and they love him for it. 'Back to the beginning,' he sighs, and he walks backwards very fast, rewinding himself, and the audience roars, and the tension is lifted, and the show begins.

Timothy cannot watch much of what follows. He sits with his eyes closed, thinking as he does so of the world his father now inhabits all the time.

The show is an insult to taxidermy. No research has been done. Taxidermists are figures of fun. He feels very insulted, all the more so because much of it is really quite funny, and both Matthew Cotherbridge and Francis Old are very expert. Matthew plays cod Scottish, Francis cod Welsh. They don't look like taxidermists, they don't act like taxidermists, but there's every chance that they'll be very popular. When the posher of the two wives, the Penelope Keith figure, only it isn't Penelope Keith unfortunately, says to the Welsh taxidermist, 'Gareth, please understand this. I do not want to be touched by a man whose fingers have spent half the afternoon up the backside of a singularly unprepossessing puma,' the audience laughs, and Timothy cringes and wants to cry out, 'Taxidermy is not like that.'

He finds it even harder to watch when Naomi comes on. The Romeo and Juliet bit isn't very funny, and the man playing the Romeo figure is very handsome, and Timothy simply can't bear to watch him kissing Naomi, which he does every time they're alone together. Naomi hasn't been

162

given any funny lines. She's a receptacle for kisses. It's very nearly unbearable, but he does bear it.

At last it's over. Matthew Cotherbridge tells the audience, 'You were marvellous. You were the true stars of the evening. Bless you. Can you come next week? And remember, if you liked the show, my name is Matthew Cotherbridge. If you didn't, it's Terry Wogan.'

The audience file out, smiling, happy, thinking it was good value, especially as they haven't had to pay. Timothy follows, heart racing, legs feeling terribly weak. They are approaching the exit door. He has to make a move soon. He can't just go.

He turns to the right and walks calmly, not too fast, not in any way suspiciously, along the dark passage at the back of the seats, then waits politely while the members of the audience stream out at the other side of the studio. One or two other people are also hanging around.

When almost all the audience have left, he walks, along with the other hangers-on, towards the door from which he had seen the actors enter and exit.

A young woman emerges.

'Excuse me,' he asks, his voice betraying his nervousness. 'I used to know Naomi Walls very well. Very well. Could you be very kind and tell her Timothy Pickering . . . no, say, her taxidermist friend is here . . . awfully sorry to be a nuisance.'

'You're a taxidermist?'

'Yes.'

'Really a taxidermist?'

'Yes'

'Fucking hell. Did you enjoy it?'

'It was amazing.'

The girl is happy and takes Timothy's words as praise. Her mood is ecstatic.

'Sorry to be a nuisance,' he repeats.

'Not a problem,' she says.

Timothy waits for what seems like twenty minutes, but is probably more like two. His heart is beating like the wings of an anxious hummingbird.

The girl reappears.

'She's coming,' she says.

Timothy so wants to ask her what Naomi's reaction was. But he doesn't, of course.

He waits for what seems like another twenty minutes, his heart thudding, his blood surging, his legs shaking. Then at last Naomi appears. He gasps with desire. He knows that the camera loves some actresses and they are a real disappointment in the flesh. Naomi is different. For some sad reason the silly camera doesn't like her very much, but in the flesh and up close she is as lovely as she was as Juliet.

She's smiling broadly. She is clearly delighted to see him, but is it any more than that?

'Timothy!' she says. 'How lovely.'

She kisses him on both cheeks, affectionately but formally. He longs to throw his arms round her, hug her to him, feel her soft flesh, search for her lips. He doesn't dare. He isn't sure. Fear assails him like drops of rain from a clear sky.

'No, this is fantastic,' she says. 'Is Maggie with you?'

He doesn't like this question. He wishes that she had instinctively known that Maggie and he had separated.

'Um . . . no.'

'You must come on up to the club and have a drink with us.'

Well, that's good. A fiasco can be ruled out.

Francis Old emerges from the bowels of the studio and joins them like a mole tunnelling into daylight. Naomi introduces them.

'A taxidermist! A real-life taxidermist! Oh, my God,' says Francis Old. 'How did we do, taxidermy-wise?'

164

'Well, you know, I suppose it wasn't all that accurate, but it is a comedy, after all,' says Timothy.

A tall dark girl joins them and is introduced as Melanie Cass-Wardrobe. Timothy is just about to say, 'That's an unusual name,' realises just in time and says, 'I thought the clothes were very good.' Before he's even finished the sentence he realises that he should have called them costumes, but she doesn't seem to mind. She's wearing black jeans and she has legs that go on for ever. She beams and says, 'Thank you!' as if surprised.

They walk to a lift, where there is quite a long wait. Timothy feels strange, almost disembodied. Words come from a long way away as if he is under water, yet certain words come at him sharply, and he finds himself analysing the minutiae of Naomi's responses to him. Pretty encouraging, on the whole. The words 'lovely' and 'fantastic' were used, although he suspects that in this environment, in the post-recording euphoria, if he'd said, 'You've got dog shit on your shoe,' she would have said, 'Dog shit! How lovely! That's fantastic!' Still, she did kiss him, and on both cheeks. But it was a bit formal. Anyway, he's been invited for a drink. That's definitely encouraging. Yet for some reason that he can't put his finger on, he is not overly encouraged.

In the lift he becomes aware that he has a huge erection. He studies a notice that gives details of the opening times of the various restaurants and cafeterias, and it slowly subsides.

Naomi smiles at him and shakes her head.

'I can't believe it,' she says.

All that trouble to make the erection subside, and it's back again.

They drift along a circular corridor, and turn into the entrance to the club. She signs him in, and while she does this the other two move on, and they have a brief moment when they're alone.

'So, did you enjoy it – really enjoy it?' she asks.

He decides to be honest, and to test the waters a bit.

'No.'

'Oh.'

'I hated seeing you being kissed by that bloke all the time.'

Halfway through this sentence, he wishes to abort it. He didn't want to show his true feelings yet. Naomi's eyes narrow slightly. She has recognised his admission of desire.

Her expression is not encouraging, but her words are.

'Not as much as I hate being kissed by him,' she says. 'He's got a horrible furry tongue and he goes further than he needs to. He's awful.'

Timothy's heart leaps like a twenty-two-pound salmon that has no idea that it will end up in a glass case. They stroll up to the bar in the huge club, which has two levels and vast long windows. It's dimly lit and not very full and there isn't much atmosphere, but he feels a delicious warm glow. His lips feel dry. He moistens them just a little with his gloriously unfurry tongue.

He offers Naomi a drink, but she says she's buying, but then Furry Tongue marches in and insists on buying for them both.

Matthew Cotherbridge discovers that Timothy's a taxidermist and he also says, 'Oh, my God.' 'We've been touched by real life,' he adds. 'How appalling.'

Timothy hears himself say, 'No, but I enjoyed it. It was funny.'

A rather short, chunky man joins the gaggle of self-congratulation at the bar, and is introduced as Colin by Francis Old.

'And this,' says Francis, 'is Timothy, and he's a taxidermist.'

Colin whistles and says, 'It's funny. You don't think of there actually being such people.'

This remark doesn't please Timothy, and Colin notices.

'Sorry,' he says. 'That must have sounded tactless.'

An intense pain passes through Timothy's overexcited balls. He wants to sit down.

'Are you all right?' asks Colin.

'Yes. Fine. Terrific.'

'Well, Mr Taxidermist, what did you think of the show? Really?'

Timothy is not going to rave to this man, or care about his feelings.

'I suppose it was OK,' he says. 'I think the script was a bit weak.'

Naomi comes over and joins them.

'Ah!' she says. 'So you've met our writer.'

Timothy closes his eyes in horror.

'Colin and I are going to be married.'

Timothy opens his eyes in horror. The blood in his veins turns to ice. His heart slips past his genitals. His prick shrivels. The pain in his balls gives a last, nostalgic spasm. His life is over. He smiles. How he smiles.

He recognises that Naomi made this horrendous announcement rather rapidly, getting it in before he could say anything he, or indeed any of them, might regret. And she said it very gently, so she is aware, to some extent at least, of how he feels towards her.

'Congratulations,' he says.

'Thank you!' says Naomi.

He is sorry that he has given her a clue to the intensity of his feelings.

'I hope you'll be very happy,' he lies.

'Thank you,' repeats Naomi.

But if he had given her no clue, her innocence of his feelings would have been a dagger plunged into his soul.

He kisses her on both cheeks.

He shouldn't have come. It's been yet another mistake, in a life of mistakes.

'Ah! Of course,' says Colin. 'I know who you are. The penny's dropped. You're Romeo.'

Timothy wonders what Colin means by 'of course'. He is shattered to learn that Naomi has talked to this man, this lazy writer, too lazy to find out anything about taxidermy, too lazy to grow beyond . . . oh . . . five foot seven; she has chatted to this short, thick, complacent tree trunk about him as Romeo, probably told him about their three nights in Earls Court, especially the second one. Possibly laughed at his lack of talent, well, maybe not, but for Colin to know anything about Naomi with Timothy is almost more than he can bear. But he has to bear it. He's still there.

His pride will not let him leave or show that he is hurt. He would rather be anywhere, even at home, asking his dad if he's ready for his cocoa yet, being kind and considerate to his blind dad, that would be a gas compared to this. Or he could be on the top of the cliffs at Beachy Head, contemplating . . . no, don't even think of that.

Sometimes one can drive for miles while thinking of something else, and suddenly realise to one's horror that one has driven through four roundabouts in perfect safety. Much of that evening in the BBC club is like that. Forty-five minutes pass by – he's always in touch with the time, it's one of his greatest virtues, or is it a vice? – between his learning of Naomi's engagement and the moment when they find themselves standing together on the edge of the slowly diminishing group of revellers, and she says, 'Let's sit down.' Afterwards, he can't remember a single word of the conversations he's had in the hectic group by the bar, can't remember who he's met, what he's drunk. Nothing remains.

They sit on the lower level of the bar, on a huge settee, hidden from the other members of the cast and production team.

'How long is it since the Amazon?' she asks.

'Thirteen years.' He doesn't tell her how many months, weeks, days, hours and minutes, although he knows.

'So, how are you?'

'Fine. I'm absolutely fine.'

'It's fun seeing you.'

Fun?

'Absolutely.'

'How's Maggie?'

Then he has to tell her his story. She's truly horrified, and he knows, and this is the worst part of it for him, that she is still the same old Naomi, she has not become spoilt by – well, not fame, but – whatever it is she has achieved. If she had become spoilt, then the whole world would have lost the real Naomi, and maybe he could cope. But only he has lost the real Naomi. This Colin, this second-rate writer, has won not some spoilt simulacrum of the old Naomi, but the real, wonderful, loving, caring, beautiful thing.

'Do you see much of Liam?'

'Yes. He lives with his mum in Cornwall, and it's all very amicable, she . . . isn't a sexy person, Naomi. And . . .'

'. . . You are. I know.'

He wishes she hadn't said this.

'He comes up to Yorkshire in the holidays and at half terms. Dad loves him. Dad's virtually completely blind now.'

'Oh, no!'

'He manages. He goes into a very nice home for three weeks every summer, and I go down to Cornwall, and Liam and I surf and water ski and have a hell of a time. I see quite a bit of Maggie then. We've got on well from the moment we stopped sleeping together.'

'Does he . . . I mean . . . how has . . .' She finds it hard to articulate it. '. . . Sam's death . . . affected him?'

'Well, this is the awful thing. I don't know. We've stopped talking about it. As if that'll make it go away. Every time I

169

see him I intend to talk to him about it. I just don't know how to. And the longer I don't, the harder it is.'

'It's not easy. Maybe it's best not to.'

'I don't think that, and nor do you.'

'No.'

'But on the whole he seems fine. Amazingly well-adjusted really.'

'And you?' she asks. 'How have you coped?'

'Not very well, except . . . I have coped. When I come home from Cornwall I get off the train, and I just don't want to go home. My father is there, needing me, waiting eagerly to see . . . sorry, to hear me. I walk, lugging my heavy case. I could get a taxi, but I walk. I want the weariness in my legs. I want the pain of the heavy case in first one hand and then the other. I just don't want to walk up the hill towards number ninety-six. But I do. I keep putting one foot in front of the other, one foot in front of the other, one foot in front of the other, and I get there. That's my life.'

'And you're getting there?'

'I think so, yes. I have to. Luckily Dad needs me.'

She nods, then pauses briefly, wanting to give breathing space before moving on from this sensitive area. 'So . . . ?'

She doesn't need to say any more. Her hesitation and her tone say it all.

'No. Not at the moment. I mean, I've been out with one or two, but you know . . . not like . . .'

'. . . Maggie.'

No! I wasn't going to say that. Not like the real thing. Not like you.

'I read about your daughter in the paper.'

'Oh, God. Not the *Argus*.'

'Yes.'

'Shit.'

'It was rather, wasn't it? But she sounds – Emily, was it? – great.'

'Emily, yes. She is great.'

The beauty in Naomi's eyes when she speaks of Emily . . . No. The lighting in the BBC club isn't quite good enough for him to see the beauty in her eyes. But he can imagine it, and that's just as bad.

'So what happened to Simon? I have to say – maybe I shouldn't – I didn't like him very much.'

'No, I don't think I did either.'

She laughs.

He wants to say, 'Why do you marry such unsuitable men?'

Something of the thought must have got through to her, because she says, 'Colin's great.'

'Good.'

'Simon is actually much improved. He's married again. Francesca must have something I lack. Or he's scared of her. He doesn't play around any more. He's very good with Emily and she's very fond of him and of Francesca.'

'Do you mind that at all?'

'Well, I did a bit and maybe I still do a bit but I can't really. It's so convenient. It's somewhere for Emily to go when I'm working.'

She lowers her voice just a touch, as if approaching sad or weighty matters.

'Do you still believe in God?'

'Oh, yes.'

She shakes her head.

'How can you after . . . ?'

'I know. Maybe I need to. Maybe I can't give up the hope that I'll see Sam again one day. Although . . .'

'What?'

'I do have doubts.'

'You do?' She's excited.

'Yes. I . . . I remember once, getting very emotional and lost and feeling very homesick, it was in Seville.'

'I've been to Seville. Remember Clive and Antoine? I went with them.'

'How are they?'

'Fine. Fairly poor, very happy. Like you. Or maybe you aren't poor.'

'Not very, no.'

'Sorry. I interrupted. You were talking about your doubts.'

'Oh, them.'

This conversation is so difficult, so painful. But I don't want it to end. Ever.

'Yes. I suddenly needed to pray. I went into this Catholic church. I prayed my heart out. I didn't get the experience I wanted. I wasn't moved as I had hoped. I had . . . I admit it . . . just for a while . . . I had . . .'

'You see. You say, "I have to admit it." As if it's a disgrace of some sort to have doubts. That's what's so unfair. It's intelligent to have doubts. How can it be something to be ashamed of? So say it. Come out with it. You had doubts. You don't still?'

'Not so much. I asked God to help me with my sorrow, to help me pull through. And he has.'

'How do you know it's him? How do you know it isn't your strength?'

I don't. I'm tired of this. Move on.

There is a gleam in her eye, though he can't see it very well. It might disturb him if he could. Maybe it's a pity that he can't. It would at least tell him that she is not quite his old Naomi of the three nights, especially the second one.

'Give me your address and I'll send you some stuff,' she says.

172

'Stuff? What sort of stuff?'

'Booklets. Books. Articles. Pamphlets. They'll show you you're not alone in having doubts. I just wish the world would stop thinking that doubts are bad.'

He doesn't want the pamphlets or books. He wants her to have the address so that she can write, 'I've made a terrible mistake. Please can we meet.' He wants to save her, not have her save him.

He writes it on the back of the outward half of his railway ticket.

'Oh, still the same place,' she says. 'I remembered the number. I just needed the postcode.'

'I've driven past L'Ancresse once or twice.'

'Really?'

She tells him about her mother. It shocks and saddens him. He longs to comfort her, to have been around and comforted her at the time. Then Colin breaks in.

'A few of us are going for an Indian. Are you coming, Timothy?'

I'd rather be captured by cannibals, basted with sunflower oil and roasted alive in a medium oven with three cloves of garlic shoved up my arse.

'Yes. I'll come.'

'Good. I'm glad,' says Naomi.

He has to go. It'll give him an hour and a half before he has to part from her.

It's all becoming a blur. He's in somebody's car, being driven somewhere. There is great difficulty in finding a parking place. They walk through the cold London night. It's raining properly now, steady, merciless rain driven on a gusty wind. The carload tumbles into an Indian restaurant, and there, at three tables pushed together, is another carload from the show.

Timothy finds himself sitting opposite Colin, and between

173

a grizzled man in his fifties and Melanie Cass-Wardrobe. He finds that he can't think of her except as double-barrelled.

None of the leading actors from the show are there.

'Eleven people,' says the grizzled man, who introduces himself as Nick Sampson-Lighting. 'Eleven sodding people. Where's all the fun gone? Where's the sociability gone? I remember studio nights, in the old days, there'd be thirty of us or more. Take over the restaurant we would. Now they go home, watch their figures, worry that if they come they'll get drunk and insult somebody important. In the good old days it's what you looked forward to, somebody important that you couldn't stand being insulted by somebody else you couldn't stand. What do you do?'

'I'm a taxidermist.'

'I didn't realise we had one. That's good. Very thorough.'

'Oh, I'm not on the show.'

'Oh, I see. I thought you meant you were an advisor. Taxidermy consultant – whatever your name is.'

'Timothy Pickering.'

'Good. Good name. Look good in the credits. Pity you aren't an advisor. They need one.' He lowers his voice. 'Fucking awful script. Don't think mine looks too bad on the credits, actually. *Lighting – Nick Sampson.* Of course, lighting lets the side down. *Director – Nick Sampson*, that would trip off the tongue. And I should have been made a director. Everybody says so. Or, better still, producer. *Producer – Nick Sampson*, because they do fuck all and the camera stays on the credit for ages. But no. They aren't looking to promote you any more. Unless you're useless. Can't promote old Nick – too good at his job. Bastards. This industry is now run by bastards. In the good old . . .'

Luckily the waiter comes at this moment and Timothy is able to break away and study the menu, although he knows what he's going to have. There are lots of specials here, things he's never heard of, but visits to Indian restaurants are moments of routine. He always has prawn puri and lamb dhansak on his monthly visit to the Taj Mahal in Coningsfield, between the off-licence and the betting shop, and he will have prawn puri and lamb dhansak here, for all their fancy London specials.

He turns towards Melanie, because talking is much more stimulating than listening to Nick.

'Do you like Indian food?' he asks.

'No. I loathe it. That's why I go to Indian restaurants. I'm a member of the Battersea Masochists' Society. In fact, I'm the secretary. Horrible job. Everyone wanted it – but I got it.'

'I'm sorry. It was a stupid thing to say.'

There is a pause between the two of them. Large amounts of bottled Indian beer and red wine appear, plus white wine for Colin.

Nick nudges Timothy hard with his elbow. Timothy, only moderately winded, turns towards him. Nick indicates Colin with a dismissive thumb.

'White wine. No wonder his scripts are so colourless. I knew a writer who in one day, on the same day, was sick in Yorkshire Television, Leeds City station, Manchester Piccadilly station and Granada Television. Writers were writers in those days.'

'It's absolutely fascinating hearing your tales of the olden days,' says Timothy, 'but you'll have to excuse me. I have an overwhelming desire for a woman. I'm going to talk to Melanie.'

He turns towards Melanie, who is now talking to the person on her other side. He touches her on the arm. He likes the feel of her arm. It's nice and fleshy. She's not unattractive.

She turns towards him, enquiringly.

'Sorry,' he says. 'I wanted to say something to you.'

'Well, fire away.'

He tries to think of something to say. 'How long have you been in wardrobe?' vies with 'Do you actually live in Battersea, then?' Neither remark strikes him as a winner. He remembers someone advising him that, if you didn't know what to say, there was often no harm in the truth.

'I didn't actually have anything to say,' he says. 'I'd just much rather talk to you than to Nick.'

'Listen to Nick, you mean.'

'Now I can't think of anything to say.'

'Do you really think I'm sitting next to you for your conversation?'

She leans towards him and runs her tongue round the inside of his ear so quickly that a moment afterwards he can't believe she's done it.

'How did you know Naomi?' she asks.

He tells her.

'That is so sweet,' she says.

He doesn't tell her of the three nights, especially the second one, but when she says, 'Did you . . . you know?' he says, 'What do you think?'

His prawn puri arrives, and just as he's taking his first mouthful she says, 'I've never done it with a taxidermist.'

He chokes.

'Too hot for you?'

'Yes, I think you may be.'

'I'm serious, Timothy. It is Timothy, isn't it?'

She starts to tell him about her relationship that has just ended, and how she's decided all she wants from now on is a bit of fun. Men dream of hearing such sentiments, and he has to hear them while the woman he loves is sitting across the table, deep in conversation with the man on her right. Timothy hears the dreaded word 'pamphlets' and begins to wonder if she's getting a bit obsessed, but nothing can take away his love for her. He can't tell her that she is the only person in the world for him, but it's inconceivable that she can stay with Colin for ever and one day he will want to say to her, 'You remember that Indian restaurant that night after I came to your show. God, it was agony, I was so in love with you,' and he doesn't want her to say, 'No, you weren't. You were all over Melanie Cass-Wardrobe and you went to bed with her. I know, because on the next show she said to me, "I can tick off 'taxidermist' now on my list of occupations I've cracked."'

He's listening just enough to avoid making a serious mistake in his replies, and of course he's sipping away at his Indian beer. The lamb dhansak arrives just as she finishes her sad tale of the ending of her affair, and she says, 'So, Timothy, am I going to be stuffed by a taxidermist tonight?' and he hears himself say, 'We don't stuff. We model.'

She looks at him in astonishment, then narrows her eyes and turns away.

Nick Sampson-Lighting has been waiting, and he pounces.

'I remember an after-show supper at which three marriages broke up,' he says. 'Three. Television was television in those days.'

'I come from a different world,' says Timothy. 'We don't have after-tiger piss-ups in taxidermy. We don't all go to the bar and tell each other how wonderful we are every time we mount a salmon.'

'You talk of tigers. That reminds me—'

'I'm sure it does.'

Even Nick in full flow can recognise this as a put-down, and he too turns away. Timothy is now entirely on his own. Naomi is still talking with passionate earnestness. Colin is sipping his white wine and smirking. Timothy is getting very full. He can hardly eat his lamb dhansak, hardly force the stuff down. Even the beer is unwelcome. He feels as if he's going to explode.

He explodes.

'Don't stare at me, you smug little bastard,' he says. 'You haven't a clue about taxidermy, have you? You've never even met a taxidermist before. You think we stuff things. We don't.' He is getting louder and louder, intoxicated by his own aggression. He doesn't care. 'We make forms, we cast clay to make mannequins, we use fibreglass, papier mâché, rigid polyurethane foam. We know how to sculpt, cast, mould, skin, tan and paint. It's a huge, complicated, deeply skilful process.'

He can see Naomi looking across at him with her mouth open. He wants to stop, but he can't. He doesn't want to alienate her, but he must.

'My dad was a great all-round craftsman. He was an artist. He had an international reputation. People sent him their dead puffins from Iceland, their dead reindeer from Lapland, their dead tigers from India, because they knew of him, they knew he would do a good job, they knew their birds and animals and fish would live on through his vision. Widowed old ladies brought him their poodles so that they could be given everlasting life. Children brought him blue tits and he helped them not to be afraid of death. He was well-known in the highly respected Guild of Taxidermists. In fact, I was told that he was known as the taxidermists' taxidermist.

'For some reason we're a laughing stock, but recently we've made a bit of progress in being taken seriously. Your show will set us back fifty years. I wouldn't mind if it was really funny. It isn't. It's not funny enough.

'And this is what I really can't forgive you for. You haven't even written a funny part for Naomi.' He shouldn't be saying this. There's no point in it. Yet he cannot stop. Not now. It's too late. 'She could do anything. That wonderful woman.

That wonderful actress. Anything. You've given her nothing. I . . .'

There is no point now in his avoiding telling the world that he loves her. There is no point. But he doesn't. He can't.

His speech has stunned the table. In fact, it's stunned the restaurant. The four Muslims at the table at the back are gawping. The rather drunken lovers behind them are gawping. The six men on a night out, whose laughter at the next table has been long, coarse and harsh, burst into applause. They've had a show, and they've enjoyed it.

Colin fumes. Naomi still looks astonished. Nick is silent, momentarily unable to remember any better moment from the halcyon days of the industry. Melanie Cass-Wardrobe looks at him in a new way, realising that there is nothing trivial in his rejection of her, they simply met on the wrong night.

'I'm sorry,' says Timothy. 'I'm sorry.'

Conversation resumes, uncertainly, uneasily, throughout the table and the restaurant. Timothy tries to chew a piece of lamb. He can't. It won't go down. He begins to sweat. He starts to feel icy cold. He feels dizzy, rather faint, colder still and colder. Sweat pours off him. The colder he feels, the more he sweats.

He's frightened. He turns away and hurries towards the gents. He wants to be alone. Nobody follows. They think he's drunk. They think he's rushing to be sick.

He just manages to get to the toilet before his legs give out. He falls forward, his head crashes into one of the urinals, and he slips onto the floor. He tries to stand, just manages it, just makes it to one of the two cubicles, collapses to the floor again. He scrambles to his feet, and sits on the bowl. The sweat is now streaming off him.

The door into the toilet area opens and Naomi appears. She looks extremely worried. Colin follows behind.

'Ring for an ambulance,' she calls.

Timothy tries to say no, but can't, can't get the word out.

Colin disappears.

Timothy tries to stand. His feet give away, he crumples to the floor. Naomi tries to hold him and can't.

He passes out.

He comes round. Naomi and Melanie are looking at him anxiously. Other people from the table are trying to peep in and see how he is. Dimly he hears Nick say, 'I knew a director who fainted seventeen times on one shoot, and he won a Bafta.'

He sits on the cold floor. His skin is clammy but no longer dripping. He doesn't feel quite so cold.

'I feel a bit better,' he says.

'Good,' says Naomi.

'That's good,' says Melanie.

There is just room in the crowded cubicle for them to bend down, one at either side of him, and take a hand. Naomi takes his right hand, Melanie his left. He sits there and lets his hands be stroked, one by the woman he wants, who doesn't want him, and one by the woman he doesn't want, who does want him.

Naomi gets a tissue and gently, oh, so gently, wipes some of the dried sweat from his forehead.

The paramedics arrive, the crowd disperses, and they soon have him on a stretcher.

They lead him out through the shocked restaurant. He's feeling much better now, and intends to have the last word.

He lifts his head just a little, so that he can see the remains of their table, the six cynical young men, the two drunken lovers, and the four Muslims.

'Don't have the lamb dhansak,' he says.

180

Second Time Around
1995–1999

It's hard to imagine a worse moment to start having what the medical profession calls 'vaso-vagal incidents' and the rest of us describe as 'panic attacks' than on the evening of one's first meeting for well over a decade with the woman one has loved, without always realising it, for the whole of one's adult life.

Of course, as he is carried out of the Indian restaurant on that fateful evening, Timothy believes, despite his show of spirit in saying, 'Don't have the lamb dhansak,' that he may be suffering from something far worse than a panic attack. He quite expects a diagnosis of serious heart problems, or even a brain tumour.

On his arrival at the hospital his blood pressure is so low that it can barely sustain life. They inject him with steroids before they even try to find him a bed.

The next day he is given exhaustive and exhausting tests. He's wheeled down long, draughty corridors and round endless steep corners by various porters. One of them looks so fragile that Timothy, much recovered after a night's sleep, feels like offering to change places with him. Another clearly has secret ambitions to become a leading figure in Formula

183

One. How they avoid a collision with a trolley carrying an unconscious woman from the operating theatre Timothy will never know. He sits in several lifts, his bare legs numb with cold, smiling at other people's tense visitors and at patients who look far more ill than he. He's X-rayed, photographed, injected and strapped to fearsome machines. He's moved slowly through tubes so narrow that it seems impossible for him not to become stuck. Twice he's taken past the double doors to a restaurant, from which there comes an odious smell of overcooked animal. He misses lunch, and is grateful. He's addressed as Timothy, Tim, Dear, Love, Pet, Darling, Mr Pickering and twice, rather alarmingly, Mr Townsend. He regularly waits for long periods, a cold wind blowing up his skimpy hospital nightshirt towards his shrivelled prick, outside doors that look extremely unlikely to open. And all the time he hopes, irrationally, to see Colin brought in on a stretcher, fighting for his life. And each time that he's returned to his ward, only to find that he's already late for somewhere else, he hopes to see Naomi there, anxiously waiting for him. Or even Melanie Cass-Wardrobe, with her legs that go on for ever.

At the end of this long day, aching and shivering and starving, craving nourishing food, he attacks a reconstituted and remorselessly grey meat and potato pie with ill-advised enthusiasm and is amazed that nobody in this great hospital has been able to detect something as simple as a bleeding heart.

'Oh, I forgot,' the fat, jolly nurse says just before she goes off duty. 'A young woman rang.'

'Was she called Naomi?'

'I think so.'

'You think so? Could she have been called Melanie?'

'No. I'd have remembered that because my sister's best friend is a Melanie and she's just emigrated to Tasmania only

184

yesterday, so I'd have thought of her. Because I met her once or twice for a drink on a Tuesday, because my sister and I always go out on a Tuesday. She's going to miss her. It hasn't sunk in yet.'

'Yes. Thank you.' Irritation shows in Timothy's voice, and the fat nurse's look reveals just for a moment that she is capable of being much less jolly. 'What did Naomi say?'

'What did she say now? I'm like working backwards, because I said, "He's fine today. They think it's just like a panic attack," sort of thing, so she must have asked how you were sort of thing.'

'Did she say anything, you know, when you told her I was fine? How did she react?'

'Oh, she was pleased. Very pleased. I can't remember exactly what she said, but, no, she was pleased. Oh, yeah, that's right. She said she'd like be sending you some pamphlets sort of thing.'

'Thank you. So, is that what I've had, then? Just a panic attack?'

'I'm not a doctor, darling, but I'd say so. Doctor may say something different tomorrow. Wouldn't think so, though. Night night.'

The nurse moves off, and Timothy feels a spasm of real depression. He wants love, not pamphlets.

The nurse may sense something of this, because she turns back and says, 'She sounded nice.'

'Oh, yes,' Timothy says gloomily. 'She is nice. Very nice.'

He spends a disturbed night listening to a man dying, and in the morning the registrar confirms what the nurse said. 'You had an emotional evening, I gather. A lot of stress, evidently. Deep feelings, I'm told. Too much to drink. Eating too late. Spicy food, hard to digest. You didn't treat your body well, and it felt it had had enough. It rebelled. It closed down. Let this be a lesson to you. Never forget it. Bodies have minds of their own. Nothing wrong with you. You can go home.'

He feels relieved but also, in a curious way, disappointed. It's as if he's been cheated of the central role in a drama. He's become a bit player in a hospital soap, much like Naomi last night in her sitcom.

Everything comes back to Naomi.

'Home. You can go home.'

The words he has longed for. The words he has dreaded.

Three days later, when he already feels that he has been back in his old life for half a century, a young woman calls at the . . . the what? Timothy is never quite sure what to call his place of business. 'The office' doesn't seem right, nor 'the surgery'. He tries 'the taxidermery', but that sounds ridiculous. What about his 'home'? But it doesn't feel like a home. He ends up simply referring to it as 'number ninety-six', unimaginative though that is.

The young woman is as tall as him. She has striking eyes, large and green, and her black, straight hair falls almost to her waist. What he notices above all, though, is how full her cheeks are. This makes her face seem very soft and he has a ridiculous desire to place his cheek against hers then and there.

Her name is Hannah.

'How much would you charge to stuff a salmon?' she asks. 'It's to be a surprise for my dad, if I can afford it.'

'We don't stuff,' says Timothy sniffily. 'We model.'

It's not a propitious first remark to make to the woman who will become one's second wife.

Naomi would not look back on her second wedding day as one of the highlights of her life. In fact, she wouldn't even look back on it as one of the highlights among her wedding days. She finds its scale embarrassingly small, and she isn't even entirely sure that she's marrying the right man.

Present in the rather cavernous registry office, dwarfed by rows of empty, unlovely chairs, even though thirty chairs have been tactfully removed and stacked in the basement, are just fifteen people. The registrar, of course, a brisk woman with enormous breasts and a bossy manner. Colin and Naomi, naturally, Naomi in green and purple and Colin looking constricted in a dark suit and bright red tie. Naomi's father, William, his face weatherbeaten from a month's sailing. Her daughter Emily, who had her eleventh birthday last week. Her brother Julian, unexpectedly unaccompanied. Clive and Antoine, hotfoot from Paris. Rosie, an acting friend of Naomi's, who played the wife of the cuckoo-clock maker in *Cobblers in Koblenz*. Glenda, the midwife in *Nappy Ever After* and Naomi's only other real thespian friend (and lesbian, as it happened). Colin's father, clothes shop owner Michael and his second wife Gloria. His brother Taylor, who was also his best man. His schoolfriend and fellow West Ham supporter Vince Cosgrove. And Lennie Welsh, a struggling stand-up comedian for whom Colin contributed occasional one-liners.

There is just one telegram. It's from Colin's first wife. It reads, '*Wishing you all the best. Hope the bitch gets food poisoning.*' This telegram is not read out.

Naomi has an uneasy feeling that this is unusual among weddings in that her family believe that, if she is not exactly marrying beneath her, she could and should have done better, and Colin's family feel exactly the same.

But if she has had any doubts about marrying Colin, she has kept them well hidden even from herself. They have been happy together, seeing films and plays, eating and drinking, and the sex has been good. *Get Stuffed*, although it has brought them together, is little more than a hack job, which will lead rapidly to better things. Colin has great respect for his own talent: there are great things in him, he will write wonderful drama series providing a host of rewarding roles for Naomi. Their writer – actor partnership will go down in theatrical legend. In time everyone will forget *Get Stuffed*.

And then, just after they have tied the knot in the dry registry office manner, just when they are about to show, in their affection and excitement, that deep down this actually is a great day in their lives, Naomi sees Timothy, sees him as he was at the BBC Television Centre, hears his words, 'I hated seeing you being kissed by that bloke all the time.' Regret sweeps over her. There is a great pit in her stomach and the rest of her body is sinking into it. It's as brief as an earthquake. And then it's over, it's gone, she's just standing there as normal in this prosaic room, she is making all the noises of delight, there are outbreaks of kissing on all sides, and everything is as it was before. Except that, after an earthquake, nothing is as it was before.

The reception is held in a little Italian restaurant round the corner from Colin and Naomi's flat. This is Colin's idea. It's what he wants. He hates formality, dreads convention, abhors solemnity and pomp. It isn't even a private room, just a large alcove to the side of the restaurant. Nor is the food particularly good. But the champagne and the wine flow, and the food is just good enough, and the waiters are very cheery. In fact, they are rather more cheery than the wedding guests. 'Lovely cannelloni for the lovely bride.' 'Oh, nice steak for the groom, give you energy, no?' 'Yes, quite possibly "no", actually,' says Colin. 'Oh, you English, you are like the table. You are reserved.' The waiter laughs uproariously.

People move places between courses, so that everyone gets a chance to talk to everyone else. It's a good idea, in theory, but in practice it means that just as tongues are loosening and subjects of mutual interest are being discovered, the relationship is nipped in the bud and you are saying,

'So where do you live?' to someone whose place of residence is of no possible interest to you.

Naomi chats to Colin's father and discovers many fascinating details about the difficulty of anticipating which colours will be in fashion when buying shirts for the new autumn season. She listens to his second wife's hope that Colin will not suffer from the same snoring problem that seems to assailed all the male members of the clan after the age of thirty. She sits beside Taylor for the main course and is rather dismayed to discover just how keen Colin is on football, a subject he has hitherto barely mentioned. For dessert she gets Vince on one side and sails with him into the unexplored waters of West Ham's defensive frailty. On the other side she has Emily, who says, 'I think this wedding has come a bit soon for you, Mum. You should have become a star first. Then you could have married in a castle and had all the other members of the National Theatre there.' Naomi asks her how she's getting on with Colin. Emily clams up and says, 'All right, thank you.' Naomi has heard Colin saying, 'You're quite tall, aren't you?' which is just the sort of remark children loathe, so she says, 'Give him time, darling,' which puzzles Emily.

Over the coffee and grappa Naomi sits next to Glenda, who says, 'Your brother kept putting his hand on my knee. I had to tell him I'm a lesbian. Didn't get another word out of him.'

As the party begins to break up, Antoine says, 'I haven't had a chance to have a word. Are you going to be happy, Naomi?'

When Clive says, 'I really hope this works out really well for you, I really do,' Naomi begins to get really worried.

Rosie kisses Naomi on both cheeks and says, 'Your brother kept putting his hand on my knee. I had to pretend I was a lesbian. He said, "Fuck me, what's wrong with that profession of yours?"'

Julian kisses Naomi and strokes her bum very briefly and says, 'Ah, well. I wouldn't think anybody who married my sister was good enough for her, but I think he could turn out be an improvement on Simon.'

Naomi holds her father in a determined hug. This is one day when he isn't going to get away with not being tactile. She says, 'Do you know you've got odd socks on?' He winces and says, 'I'm not actually very good at this widowhood caper.'

Afterwards, several of the guests agree that it was strange, but they can't remember the stand-up comedian making even one faintly amusing remark throughout the whole event.

The happy couple set off for a honeymoon in Majorca.

Timothy sits with Hannah in a cosy corner of the Happy Valley Chinese Restaurant. He is awash with jasmine tea and frustration. It is, after all, many years since that third night in Earls Court, when he told Naomi that sex outside marriage is wrong. He tries not to have regrets about the past, but how he has come to regret that.

He runs his hand up her thigh under the table. Her thighs and hips are broad. Plenty of kissing there.

She frowns.

'Timothy! Behave!' she says.

He wonders if she knows that when she is matronly it excites him even more. He doesn't know if he can stand much more of this.

More food arrives. They have ordered too much.

They always order too much.

This is their eleventh meal out, and their fifth at the Happy Valley. It's their favourite. They love the crispy duck and the jasmine tea. He still isn't a big drinker, despite the Pennine Piss-ups, and she is almost teetotal, so at restaurants of other nationalities they are never quite sure what to drink.

It's a Sunday evening, a quiet time in the Happy Valley. They have spent the whole day together. They have driven out to Troughton Hall, a stately home so large that there are rumours of the death of a small boy from starvation during a game of hide-and-seek. The paintings and tapestries and the Chippendale chairs and the Adam ceilings have exhausted Timothy, and then there has been the pain in his balls, which has built up through the long day till he could hardly stand up straight as the guide pointed out the Rubens in the Long Gallery. At the sight of the nude in the Rubens painting Timothy almost passed out. This can't go on.

After returning from the countryside, they called in at number ninety-six, and prepared Roly's tea together.

'Dad always comes first,' Timothy has told her.

He swings the lazy Susan round to bring the thin, delicate pancakes round towards him. He takes slices of the chilled cucumber and spring onion, spreads the luscious, spicy, sticky sauce, puts a few pieces of the crispy duck on top, rolls the pancake up, takes a bite and sees half the pancake's innards fall out onto his plate. Why can't he do it delicately, like her?

'I'd have thought a taxidermist ought to be able to stuff a pancake,' she says, smiling to show that this is just a gentle tease.

But he takes it seriously.

'I should never have become a taxidermist,' he says.

'You do all right, don't you?'

'Yes, but it's a struggle. I have no flair. You should have seen my dad in his heyday, Hannah.'

His naughty, barely controllable right hand is at it again, tracing the inside of her right thigh under the table.

'How old would Sam be now?' she asks.

If she had repeated, 'Timothy! Behave!' his hand might not have responded. But at the mention of Sam it has nowhere to go, and returns to its rightful place. He wonders if she deliberately uses Sam references to cool him down.

They'd been up on the moors when he had first mentioned Sam's death. The whole story had come pouring out. She had stroked his cheek as she listened in silence, and he had wondered if he could use her emotion to persuade her to have sex with him, there among the heather. But he had banished this shameful thought.

He doesn't reply to her question, because he can't remember to the exact year how old Sam would be now.

She doesn't seem to notice. Perhaps the question has done its job. He swings the lazy Susan back, and watches her assemble a quietly elegant pancake and eat it with natural grace.

'Sorry,' she says. 'I shouldn't have mentioned Sam. Wrong time.'

'There is no wrong time, Hannah. Some part of me on some level of consciousness is thinking about him at every minute of the day. For many reasons, as I've told you, I have had to learn to live with this and I manage it without too much difficulty.'

And slowly, so slowly, it becomes easier. A year is a long time. Each year it will become just a little easier.

But, goodness, how a bit of sex would help. Tonight? Any chance?

He does a little better with his next pancake.

Hannah is a believer. She goes to church quite regularly. The last few Sundays they have gone together. He has found himself praying to God to intervene and persuade her to make love to him, explain to her that as the twentieth century draws to a close certain of his rules can be sensibly relaxed. He has been aware that this is ridiculous, but he has continued to do it.

Today, because the weather was so unusually lovely for

Coningsfield, they have skipped church and driven out into the countryside. That, and the Rubens, have given a naughty feel to the day. Tonight, he can't help feeling, there is a chance.

Their only discussion about sex outside marriage took place a couple of weeks ago in the unlikely setting of the Pizza Hut. She told him that she thought sex outside marriage was wrong. He noticed that she said 'outside marriage' not 'before marriage'. He had no idea what she would say if he asked her to marry him.

Unfashionable though it might be in late twentieth-century Coningsfield, she felt that something would be lost for ever if they had casual sex together. He might have accepted this view more easily if what was being lost had included her virginity. But that had gone when she was fifteen with a boy called Ginger Wallace. 'He works at Asda now,' she had told him contemptuously, as if his job was his punishment for taking her virginity.

It just wasn't fair.

She looks at her watch and says, 'I must go and get my beauty sleep.'

There is no way in which he can interpret this remark as being promising.

'So early?' he says limply.

'We've a busy day tomorrow. I can't let Mr Finch down.'

Mr Finch is her boss at Amalgamated Plastics. She has described him as 'up and coming'. This is another remark that doesn't altogether thrill Timothy.

They walk out of the Happy Valley into the unhappy town. He holds her hand demurely as they stroll through the dying evening towards the taxi rank.

He knows better than to try any 'funny business', as she calls it, in the taxi. She knows a boy called Greg Watson who practically did it in the back of a taxi, and the driver lost concentration and hit a milk float. God works in a . . . etc.

He gets the taxi to stop a few doors away from her house in the Upper Cragley Road. Yes, her dad is richer than Naomi's.

They walk slowly up the hill. He turns to her, puts his arms round her shoulders, rests his cheek against her lusciously full one, turns his mouth towards hers, gently parts her lips, feels her willing tongue enter his mouth and slide itself along the jagged edge of his teeth. He hears her gasp. This is all so silly.

'Hannah?' he breathes. 'Will you marry me?'

He just misses the last bus, and he hasn't enough money for a taxi, and the pain in his exhausted balls is so acute that he can barely walk. But it isn't that which really worries him on his long, bent walk home.

What worries him most is that you should marry for love, not because you're desperate to get your end away.

The bee, how it buzzes. The bonnet, will it hold?

'I think that's dreadful,' says Naomi.

'Dreadful,' agrees Colin. 'Appalling defending. He was left completely unmarked.'

'I wasn't talking about that. I was talking about that striker. He crossed himself when he scored.'

'For God's sake, woman, you've no sense of proportion. What is it with women? We're one–nil down against a crap team of part-timers from some Balkan country that didn't exist until it fell off the edge of another Balkan country that nobody had ever heard of, and you go on about the scorer crossing himself.'

'It's you who've got no sense of proportion. It's serious. It's rude. It's arrogant.'

They are sitting in front of a television set in the rather

bare front room of their small house in a street that's coming up, round the corner from a street that's going down, just to the north of the Angel, Islington. They are watching football. Colin hid his love of football until she was safely hooked. It's one of the things she resents about him. Only slightly, of course. They are, after all, happily married. And he's good in bed, even though his penis isn't quite as large as Timothy's, as she is sometimes almost tempted to tell him, for, despite their happiness, he can be an irritating bloke at times.

He wants to watch the match. They've only got thirty-eight minutes left to equalise in, plus however many extra minutes the ref allows for injuries and delays, but unfortunately he's Greek, and liable to seek revenge for the theft of the Elgin Marbles. Nevertheless, he can't resist going back to their discussion.

'What's rude about crossing himself?'

'It's such an insult to the goalie. He's saying, "God's on my side, not yours."'

'It's harmless, isn't it?'

'I don't think so. Sportsmen are doing it all over the place. "I owe it all to God." "I'm dedicating my victory to God." "I prayed to God, and he answered my prayers." As if any kind of God could take sides. It's pathetic.'

'Anyway, leave it. I want to watch the football.'

'Oh, that's far more important, isn't it? I'd forgotten. Men have such a great sense of proportion. Unlike women. And please don't address me as "woman" again. I hate it. It's very rude.'

'Well, I agree with that. I'm sorry. But I was irritated. Can't I even watch the football in peace?'

How typical of him to chuck that little word 'even' in, suggesting this is just one more in a long line of unstated grievances, stoically borne.

Her irritation with him had begun before the match even

started. She'd said, 'I suppose you want to eat on our laps,' and he'd said, 'Plates might be easier.' She could have taken that from some people, but not from the man who was supposed to be writing funny lines for her. He'd been upstairs all day, writing the second series. If her jokes were going to be like that, what was the point? And he hadn't said a thing about the lasagne, which she'd thought was one of her best.

What is it about men and their game? She wants to continue the discussion. She so wishes that he'd understood. Well, no, he must have understood. She wishes he'd take it seriously. But she remains quiet. She's had her say.

But now the part-timers are on the attack again, and unfortunately another of them scores, and he crosses himself too.

'Bloody hell, another one's done it,' she exclaims.

'Oh, Naomi, shut up,' he yells. 'We're two–nil down.'

'Good.'

'I've worked bloody hard all day. Sodding hard. It's not always easy writing comedy, you know.'

'That's obvious.'

'Oh. I'm so sorry if I don't reach the high standards you'd like.'

'You do for the other actors. Not for me. You never give me anything funny.'

'Because you don't make it funny. You aren't funny.'

Suddenly this is serious. He looks appalled at what he has said, which makes her think it may be the truth, which makes it more serious still. He can't cope with this. She knows what he's going to say, and sure enough he does.

'I'm going to the pub.'

The pub, his crutch.

She hears the door slam.

She feels awful. They have only been married for a few

months, and it's come to this. What can she do? She really doesn't want to argue and fight. She hates arguing and fighting. But it would be ridiculously premature to give up on their marriage just yet.

The truth, she used to tell herself, always the truth. Now she has spoken the truth to Colin, and he, maybe, has spoken the truth to her. And these are truths that should never be spoken.

She thinks again, as she thinks so often, of how she wasn't able to tell, either to her mother or to Emily, the truth of what she felt about her mother's death. That failure hangs over her every day of her life.

The football is still on. She's simply forgotten to switch it off. And now, just as she's about to switch it off, luck takes a hand again, and gives her a chance.

She rings him on his mobile.

'They've got one back. It's two–one. You ought to come back and see the end.'

He does. He gives her a quick kiss and says, 'Thanks, darling.' That 'darling' is as near to an apology as she will ever get.

She gets him another beer, without being asked.

'Thanks, darling,' he says again.

He's actually rather moved by what she's done. He longs for them to be happy. He doesn't want to give up on a marriage that has barely begun. He senses that she's in a sexy mood. He thinks about suggesting they go to bed, there and then, or even rip their clothes off and do it on the carpet. In fact, he will suggest it.

Not yet though. There are only eleven minutes in which to get an equaliser. Surely even the most aroused of women can wait eleven minutes, plus whatever the Greek ref adds on?

*   *   *

197

Timothy would not look back on his second wedding day as one of the highlights of his life. In fact, he wouldn't even look back on it as one of the highlights among his wedding days. He finds its scale embarrassingly large, and he isn't even entirely sure that he's marrying the right woman.

This morning, of all mornings, he had the dream, his nightmare. He almost always does when he would particularly wish not to have it. Maybe the anxiety expressed in the dream is actually not anxiety about the subject of the dream. Maybe the dream is a metaphor for other anxieties, although, in that case, it's hard to see why it always takes exactly the same form.

Certainly he is particularly anxious this morning. He's used to a degree of gentle scorn, but even he is anxious not to be totally humiliated at his wedding. He had hoped for something quiet, in view of the fact that a church wedding was out of the question due to his status as a divorced man. He has reckoned, however, without Hannah's father. He's a stockbroker, and he's anxious for his stock to be well and truly broked on this great day.

Hannah's mother, Eileen, wants a quiet wedding. She doesn't want anyone else to share the shame of Hannah's choice. But Freddie has said to her, 'We have two choices, Eileen. We go hole in corner, or we brazen it out. And, to be fair, he's not a bad lad, as taxidermists go.' This is a strange remark, as Timothy is the only taxidermist he has ever met. He still hasn't even met Roly.

The wedding is taking place at Langenthwaite Castle, a luxury moated hotel, licensed to provide wines and spirits, hold weddings, and charge £350 a night for bed and breakfast. Unlike most moated castles, it was built in the nineteenth century.

Hannah is not a particularly gregarious girl, but she has quite a few friends, and they all have boyfriends. She also has two sisters and a brother, and they have partners. And then there are the aunts and uncles, the nephews and nieces, the cousins twice removed but still coming back. It's a large family, and it begins to mount up. And then there are Freddie's contacts. Freddie lives by his contacts, and has invited as many of them as can reasonably be persuaded to come. And there are Freddie and Eileen's bridge friends, and their golf friends, and Freddie's rugby league friends. Then there are the people from Amalgamated Plastics, notably Hannah's boss, the up-and-coming Mr Finch. Altogether, there'll be at least a hundred on the bride's side. Freddie is in denial over the minor detail that this is not a church wedding. The guests will be led to their seats, on the groom's side or the bride's side, by ushers in morning dress, which Freddie spelt as mourning dress in a letter to Timothy about the arrangements.

How can Timothy compete? There's his father, of course, and Liam, and Liam's friend, invited so that Liam has company. There are his godparents, Uncle Percy Pickering and Auntie May Treadwell. But his is not a family rich in relatives, and until now that has been regarded as a bit of a boon. There's Tommo and his wife, whose name Timothy can't remember. There's Dave Kent and his wife, whose name Timothy doesn't want to remember. There's Steven Venables and his partner – Steven's a real bonus, he's rich, and will soon be richer, because he's got a new job. Timothy can't quite remember what, but it's prestigious. Steven has promised to add a bit of tone by bringing the Porsche. And it's said that his partner is exotic, she's a circus artiste from Krakow who does amazing things on the trapeze, though it's doubtful if there will happen to be a trapeze handy at Langenthwaite Castle.

But who else? Surprising people will have to be roped in.

Roly can bring a couple of the friends he's made in the Home for the Blind during his summer stays. Well, he could invite more, but how many blind people can you have at a wedding without rendering it slightly ridiculous? Their old neighbour Miss de Beauvoir (Mrs Smith) is very touched to be invited, as are some of the people who've supplied dead birds, fish, animals and materials over the years, the manager of Big Cats at Kilmarnock Zoo, the Master of Foxhounds at Bradbury Flintstock, the sales manager of Guisethorpe Foam Products, Herr und Frau Müller from Lubeck, who have provided Timothy with so many of his bird and animal eyes over the years. Mr Prentice, his old drama teacher, made miserable for fifteen years by the mother of the boy he passed over for the part of Romeo and Mr Cattermole, his long-retired R.E. teacher, who has aged with spectacular suddenness since his retirement, are both astounded to be invited, along with their good ladies, but the invitation makes it clear that this is to be a lavish black tie affair, with a champagne reception and a four-course dinner, and then dancing, and carriages at one a.m.

'I smell money, Muriel, and I smell vulgarity,' says Mr Prentice. 'We'll not go.'

'I smell lots of champagne. We'll go,' says Muriel.

'One a.m., Hilda,' says Mr Cattermole. 'That brings back memories.'

'One a.m.!' says Hilda. 'You won't make eight thirty.'

Timothy even thinks of inviting Sniffy Arkwright, but he doesn't want everyone to know just how short of invitees he's been, so he doesn't.

In the final count the bride's guests outnumber the groom's by one hundred and fourteen to twenty-six, which, amazingly, is almost identical to Timothy's blood pressure as he was admitted to hospital four days before he met Hannah for the first time.

The wedding day dawns cool and breezy, but blessedly dry. Timothy is awake before six, and has only slept fitfully.

He has a bad attack of nerves. He dreads the whole event, its flamboyance and extravagance. All that long, endless, slow, tick-tock-tick-tock-of-clock morning he wonders if he is capable of going through with it. He also wonders if he is capable of not going through with it.

When would he break it off? How would he break it off? Tommo drives him to the castle, up the long drive towards its mighty medieval phoniness, over the drawbridge to his fate, looking, in his morning suit or mourning suit, like a penguin immortalised by an inexperienced taxidermist.

He walks into the spacious, high-vaulted Lancelot Room, done out like the church that it isn't. He walks slowly down the central aisle, Tommo at his side. Tommo would be a solid, bulky, reassuring presence, were it not for his eyes, which do not reassure because they are full of compassion.

His legs are not his own. He has no control over them. He's smiling at people, Liam so freckly, Mr Cattermole so frail, Miss de Beauvoir so select, Steven gleaming with confidence and self-satisfaction, his exotic partner looking very superior, but then you would expect a trapeze artist to be a bit above it all. He smiles at the massed ranks of golfers, bridge players, financial consultants, venture capitalists, bankers, wankers and their partners. How can he disappoint them? He cannot do it now. Later, perhaps? When the vicar asks for objections. Yes, vicar, I, the groom, object. I still love Naomi.

But there isn't a vicar. There's a registrar. Do registrars ask if there are any objections?

What does it matter? He isn't going to object.

Now the music blares out, beautiful, irresistible, enriched by cliché, strengthened by memory, powered by repetition. And Hannah, his bride to be, sails down the aisle of the Lancelot Room like one of the sloops in Naomi's father's pictures – no, don't think of Naomi! Think Hannah, Hannah, Hannah. She's like a swan, with her long, pale neck. Her father's smile

201

is fixed, he has never seen so fixed a smile. He would love to unfix her father's smile, shatter it into a thousand pieces, but how could he make Hannah cry?

Soon he is a married man, and Hannah is Hannah Pickering, and her mother is not losing a daughter, she's losing a daughter and her daughter's husband.

They file slowly out and into the elegant, flower-bedecked Guinevere Suite, its roof decked out like a marquee. Canapes under the canopy. The champagne flows. Even Liam has some. He's very solemn about it and says, 'Congratulations, Dad,' going very red and hating himself for going red, and Timothy says, 'Love you, son,' and is thrilled to find something he can say and mean.

'Always knew you had it in you,' says Mr Cattermole, his voice as frail as papyrus.

Dave Kent looks worried. He hates wives, and Timothy has another one, who seems very nice now, but you never know, she may well turn out to be as ghastly as the first one, relegating Dave's own wife to third place in the Horrendous Wives League.

Steven is thrilled. He likes seeing men get trapped. He introduces his partner, Vandra. She smiles superciliously. Her body is lean and wiry. Well, what would you expect from a trapeze artist? But is she really a trapeze artist? Timothy doesn't dare to ask, doesn't know how to ask. 'Incidentally, is your partner by any chance a trapeze artist?' sounds curiously naff.

He puts on a social face. He circulates. He does his bit, and thinks, If you do your bit as much as I'm doing, can it still be your bit? Doesn't it become your lot? Well, I know what my lot is now. Marriage to Hannah.

'Is Hannah pretty today?' asks his father, which is a curious way of putting it, but appropriate, because Hannah looks radiantly pretty some days and rather ordinary on others.

'Yes,' says Timothy. 'She's like a swan with her long, slender neck. Her cheeks are full like downy pillows, her mouth is wide and generous, and her eyes are big and green.' He begins to feel much better about things as he describes her.

'Thank you,' says Roly.

They move on to the King Arthur Room for the wedding breakfast. To the left of the great double doors is the seating plan. Timothy doesn't need to look at it. He will be at the Top Table. To the right of the doors a plaque announces that Coningsfield Rotary Club and Round Table meet here. How could they not?

Top tables are hell to Timothy. There's an awful lot of food. He can't taste it and he doesn't want it, but he's sitting next to the man who chose the menu, so he chews and chews with stoic dedication. He smiles a lot, and pleases his father-in-law by having a few drinks. He's a bit more worldly than I gave him credit for, thinks Freddie.

Mr Cattermole, who seventeen years ago still had enough life in him to be described as a lech by Naomi, doesn't even make it to eight thirty. He dies during the cheese, but he dies as he lived, quietly, unassumingly, suitably. In a corridor outside the Galahad Room, under a sign saying '*Reserved for Allied Dunbar*', to be precise, while trying to find the gents' toilet. But the Langenthwaite Castle staff really turn up trumps in this crisis. The matter is handled with total discretion. Hotel guests are told that he has fainted and is being taken to hospital as a precaution. In the King Arthur Room nobody knows anything about it, except for Mrs Cattermole, of course. The show must go on.

And the show does go on, and on, and on. The speeches are interminable, and deserve to be forgotten. Freddie tells stockbroker jokes, Tommo rambles amiably enough and makes one or two cracks about the world of biscuits, including the word 'hobnobbing' used to comic effect. Timothy doesn't try to make people laugh. He gives a brief account of his father's talents and fame, a very concise explanation of the dignity of taxidermy, and then just praises Hannah and says how lucky he is, and under the influence of his own words, believes it.

After that he is very tired. They repair to the Guinevere Suite, transformed into a night club. He has to dance a bit, of course, which is a shame, as he has two left feet, but Hannah has two right feet, so it sort of fits. On and on the wedding goes, slowly move the clocks this night. On and on go the congratulations, there are so many people to speak to, he has no idea who most of them are, he can't hear them, they can't hear him, why is the music always too loud? He feels that he doesn't want another drink for at least ten years. He hardly gets a chance to have a word with Hannah. And then he begins to feel unwell. He recognises the symptoms, the intense cold, the shivering, the sweat on his brow. He knows that he must look deathly pale. He struggles to make it to the gents' toilets, but he doesn't even make it to the edge of the room.

It's hard to imagine a worse moment to have one's second experience of what the medical profession calls 'vaso-vagal incidents' and the rest of us describe as 'panic attacks' than just before the end of one's second wedding reception. It's not the climax that Hannah had been anticipating, with, it has to be admitted, a mixture of hope and fear. Now she will have to wait to discover which emotion was the more justified.

Naomi knows that her attitude to churches is strange. She loves them, when she has them to herself, and can wander around and examine monuments to people who, unlike her, had faith. She loves the beauty of them, especially when they are not too dark. She just doesn't like them when services are being held in them, and she hates them when they are crowded, and the more fervent the worshippers are, the more she hates them. And she loathes organ music.

Today she has organ music, loud and, to her, empty. Today she has a modern Catholic church, a bare, unlovely shell of a place, but brimming with candles, incense, piety and emotion. Today she has to contend with a huge crowd of very religious people who are all deeply moved.

Naomi is deeply moved too. She hasn't met Padre Paul since her honeymoon in Peru, but she recognised a good man and has never forgotten him.

She is sitting beside Simon, and beyond Simon is his second wife, Francesca, who is slim beyond belief, a walking tribute to rowing machines, Pilates machines, cycling machines, treadmills and sun salutations.

The funeral is in Guildford. It's been a long journey from Coningsfield, and this evening she has to go all the way back again. She's upset that Colin wouldn't come. It would have helped. 'I never met him,' he'd said, 'and I've got to get on with the rewrites.' It made sense. He had deadline trouble with the third series of *Get Stuffed*. Yes, it made sense, but sometimes in a marriage you needed something more than sense. Naomi feels that Colin has failed her today.

She knows that Simon's uncle was a charismatic figure and a widely loved and respected priest, but she cannot believe how many priests file slowly in behind the coffin. There must be more than fifty of them, tall, short, thin, fat, but all looking as though they are in a trance. What are they really thinking? She cannot guess.

It's a strange experience, being an atheist in a congregation such as this. As the service rolls on, with intensity and dignity, it's very difficult not to be moved by it. This is not some hollow sham, some conventional ritual, but a deeply felt moment of shared admiration and values. Naomi shares the admiration, even shares some of the values, but she feels utterly excluded from whole parts of the experience. It's hard to hold on to the fact that you don't wish to be included, you are excluded of your own volition. It's hard not to feel that you are in some way a failed human being, inferior to those who have the faith. But it's also hard not to feel that you are a person who sees more clearly than others, who is more honest than others, who, far from being inferior, is actually superior. Naomi doesn't want to feel inferior or superior. Naomi feels very sad that Colin is not at her side today. She needs his help.

She wonders if she is the only person here who doesn't believe. There can't be many, but surely there must be a few? She looks round at the crowded pews. Some people have glistening eyes. Many seem to be in a kind of ecstasy of suffering. Some are calm and impassive. Are they atheists, or is that just their way? We reveal so little of how we feel.

There comes a part of the service in which individual members of the congregation can go forward and say their bit about Padre Pablo. Naomi likes this bit, it's refreshingly free from dogma and pretention and falsehood.

A Peruvian woman with a face so serene that you cannot tell her age walks quietly to the lectern, and delivers, in a low voice as clear as a mountain stream, one of the most beautiful – and shortest – speeches that Naomi has ever heard.

'We must all carry on Father Paul's work of comforting the afflicted and afflicting the comfortable.'

Naomi is excited. These words are a call to action. She is on her feet. She is walking towards the lectern. She looks back and sees shock and fear on the faces of Simon and Francesca. She glances across to the massed priests. She reaches the lectern. She realises that she has no idea why she is there. What is she going to say? What can she say? Why has she done this stupid thing?

She clings to the sides of the lectern. The silence is deep. People are expecting her to say something. She has to say something. She is terrified that if she doesn't speak quickly somebody will cry out. Supposing someone shouted, 'Get them off.'

The truth, not always but whenever possible.

'I'm an atheist,' she says.

There's a buzz of surprise, a murmur of cautious shock.

'I'm an atheist, but we are not as far away from each other as perhaps we think. My friends, my friends, I agree with that wonderful lady. What a mission in life – to comfort the afflicted and afflict the comfortable. You don't have to be religious to do that. Father Paul was a great man, he believed in the need for clean water above all things, and I'm so with him on that, and he did his best, he turned a blind eye to birth control, but, oh, turning a blind eye to birth control is not enough. We are destroying our planet.'

There are mutterings. What she has said is not appropriate to the situation. She hasn't meant to say it.

She stumbles back to her seat. She doesn't look at anybody. Her face is set. She tries not to look at Simon and Francesca, but a glance escapes. She sees that they are taking care to avoid her eye.

The next speaker makes no reference to her speech. The service rolls on. Naomi feels . . . well, what does she feel? That she was right to try, but somehow, it didn't come out right. How do you make sure that these things come out right?

She finds herself looking at the priests. She knows that celibacy is difficult. She knows that some priests do terrible things, particularly to, or with, small boys. She shocks herself

207

with a terrible thought. By the law of averages and statistical probability, there is likely to be one child abuser among those priests.

She tries to fight this ghastly, inappropriate thought, though what does it matter, since nobody will ever know that she is thinking it. But then it gets worse. She spots a particular priest, a fairly short, rather fat priest, with a look on his face that might be the height of piety but looks a bit more like smug self-satisfaction, and she thinks, He's the one.

She tries to forget this thought. She tries to think about Colin, about how he will react when he hears how she walked to the lectern and spoke. But she knows how he will react, and it isn't interesting. He'll say, 'Thank God I wasn't there.'

She tries to think about the Ivy. She doesn't need all the glamour of showbiz, award ceremonies and so on, but she would like, just once, to be taken to the Ivy, to see what it's like. Perhaps she can persuade Colin.

Thinking about Colin doesn't work. She pictures him wrestling with a scene involving her, trying to make her funny. She is coming, slowly, bit by frightening bit, to really believe that she is not funny. She finds herself looking at the priest again, and a shiver runs down her spine. He's the one.

How can men who profess faith do such dreadful things? Her anger slowly rises, contempt fills her gullet, she has to fight against the urge to go outside and throw up.

The service ends. The coffin is carried out, slowly. Behind it file the priests, so slowly, with such dignity, such calm, such an indivisible look of both sorrow and joy. Naomi's priest is right by her now, and as he passes, she says, very quietly, 'You dirty bastard.' She hasn't meant to say it, it has forced itself out through the turmoil of her soul.

She is horrified by what she has said. Appalled. She said

it so quietly that she hopes Simon and Francesca didn't hear. But she knows that the priest heard, because he turns to look at her, and on his face there is an expression of complete astonishment, utter bewilderment and absolutely no shame. Naomi knows, in an instant, to her horror, that she has got it terribly wrong.

Timothy feels the tension seeping into Hannah's body. It's horrid. It's as if she's slipping away from him into a private world from which he's banned. Suddenly his flesh against hers becomes very uncomfortable. He's not a selfish lover, he's too sensitive to try to force things, so he rolls off her on to his back, then reaches out with his hand to stroke her beautifully flat stomach, just at the very edge of her pubic hairs, very gently.

'What's wrong, sweetheart?'

The sex has been the best thing in their early married life. It has, in the rather coy words he used when asked about it by Tommo, 'surpassed expectations'.

'It's your dad. It makes me self-conscious thinking about him listening.'

'How do you know he's listening?'

'He says he doesn't sleep well.'

'Probably that means he wakes up early.'

'We don't know that. It may mean he takes ages to drop off.'

They are speaking in whispers.

The last bus to Gressingham Lane Top roars past up the hill.

'That bus would have woken him even if he was asleep before.'

'You went all tense before the bus, so that's irrelevant. Anyway, he's quite an old man. He probably can't hear very well.'

209

'When people are blind the other senses grow sharper to compensate. I bet he can hear your socks when you drop them on the carpet, which I wish you wouldn't do, now that I come to mention it. Couldn't you pile your dirty clothes neatly on a chair or take them to the laundry basket or something, not just drop them higgledy-piggledy all over the place? It's not nice.'

Timothy is beginning to realise that tidiness, cleanliness and hygiene may become issues in their marriage.

'I thought we were discussing our sex life, not my laundry.'

'We are, but I just thought I'd mention it while I thought of it. Sometimes you have to mention things when you think of them. I mean, dirty clothes just—'

'Yes, yes, I get your point.'

'There's no need to get irritated. He'll hear. Like he probably hears every gasp, every moan. Poor man, blind, alone, abandoned for a plumber over three decades ago, tossing in his empty bed, waiting for my cries of ecstasy.'

'Well, on that point, do you have to make quite so much noise?'

'Well, yes, I think I probably do.' Her thin, almost priggish dirty-socks voice has melted away. Now her tone is breathy, sexy, he can feel himself stiffening. 'I love my sex with my lovely man.'

He twists her right nipple very softly. She gives a tiny gasp, and gently removes his hand. They lie there, silent, close. She strokes his leg briefly, to show that she wasn't upset by his touching her nipple, she was just worried about making a noise.

'Timothy?'

This is said in yet another tone of whisper, a tone steeped in ulterior motive, a tone that sends a shiver of unease through him.

'Yes?' He wants to say, 'Yes, darling?' but her tone of voice makes the word 'darling' shrivel before he can release it.

'I'm very fond of your dad, as you know, very fond, but . . .'

His heart begins to flutter with anxiety. He decides not to say anything, to make her say it all.

'Well, I've been thinking.'

Evidently.

'He's been going to the Cadogan for three weeks every summer when you go to Cornwall, and you've said yourself that he's happy there, and that it's a very nice place.'

He remains silent. She is going to have to force the words out like the last bit of toothpaste from the tube.

'This house is very dark and gloomy, and you say the Cadogan's lovely and light and airy.'

What use is that to him when he's blind?

'And it's very close. We could visit every day, or bring him here every day.'

We could, but would we? Suddenly he sees her saying, 'Oh, does he have to come today? He comes every day.'

'I mean, it's not natural, a parent in the same house as a newly-wed couple.'

It's very natural. It happens all over the world, except among the rich and spoilt. It used to happen in this country all the time.

'I mean, I don't want to be mean. I am a Christian, after all.'

He has been beginning to think that she is more of a Christian than he is. But this doesn't seem very Christian, and she clearly realises this, which is why she has felt it necessary to mention it.

'Say something, Timothy.'

'I am not putting my father in a home.'

There is silence between them then, utter silence. Neither

211

moves a muscle. Now neither even thinks of giving the other an affectionate stroke of the hand. There are a hundred miles of tundra between his prick and her vagina.

'I was only exploring,' she says. 'Only thinking aloud. Only suggesting. Nothing more.'

'Drop it.'

She is unable to yet. After a minute or two of deep silence she speaks again.

'I love your father. I'm very fond of him. I like him a lot. I was only . . . trying out ideas.'

There is more silence between them.

'I won't mention it again.'

A car with a loose fan belt growls and squeaks up the hill.

'Ever.'

Cautiously, even timidly, her hand reaches out across the dry tundra, and touches him.

He thinks of refusing it, pushing it away. He doesn't. Some gestures can be very dangerous.

He clasps her hand, gently.

Colin is reluctant even to put one foot in front of the other as he trudges back from West Hampstead underground station towards their new home in Narcissus Road.

He tries to find the strength not to call in at the pub en route, but he knows that he will. Boy, how he needs his crutch after his meeting with the BBC about the fourth series of *Get Stuffed*.

But he isn't a weak man, he won't need to get even remotely drunk, it's just that one pint of bitter – well, maybe two, yes, two pints, top whack – will give him the energy of spirit and the fluency of tongue to enable him to break the news to Naomi in the best possible way. That's all. Because it isn't news that's going to be easy to break. As he sips his lonely pints – he doesn't know anyone yet in this pub, in fact, he doesn't think he wants to, he doesn't like it, he doesn't like anything about West Hampstead, except that they own their house now, they are no longer renting, they are on the ladder – he rehearses various ways of breaking the news. None of them please him, so he orders a third pint, just to give himself a bit more rehearsal time. It isn't cowardice, it's just that, as he knows as well as anyone, rehearsal time is vitally important.

The danger of ordering a fourth pint is that he might get past the point of no return, but he puts it to himself as 'one for the road'. Nobody has two for the road, so it will definitely be his final pint. Besides, if he were to need to break off for a pee in the middle of what is bound to be a very difficult scene, it would ruin everything. No, one more pint is the absolute limit. Even so, he can't avoid the feeling that it is weak of him to be having one for the road, but he feels that when the road in question is Narcissus Road it is probably justified.

He does leave after the fourth pint, walks only slightly unsteadily round the corner, and then turns again into Narcissus Road where the identical, detached brick houses look mean to him in both size and spirit. He realises in that instant, as he looks at his new home with horror, that it is to blame for his dilemma. If he hadn't got this substantial new mortgage, he would have told the BBC to stuff their *Get Stuffed*. But he was in no position to be brave. Nobody's brave unless they can afford to be.

The tiny hall smells of cauliflower cheese. In fact, the whole house smells of cauliflower cheese. Of all the meals that Naomi cooks, in her relatively limited, not in truth very inspired repertoire, cauliflower cheese is his least favourite. If only it had been a curry or spaghetti bolognese. But it wouldn't be, not today. It's a cauliflower cheese sort of day if ever there was one.

213

She looks at him anxiously as she doles out the unappetising mess, which has already been kept hot too long.

'You've been to the pub,' she says. 'Does that mean bad news? Does that mean the Ivy's off?'

She has got him to agree that, if the fourth series is commissioned, he will take her to the Ivy.

'Am I so predictable?'

Silly question, because he knows the answer.

'They've decided not to go ahead, haven't they?'

The good news first, although even the good news could be regarded by her as bad.

'They are going ahead. They said very nice things about the series. The ratings aren't sensational but they're steady, and the appreciation index has risen. They think it's probably got the legs for two more series. They said nice things about me. Well, fairly nice. They called me Mr Reliable. Well, fair enough, you and I know my best work is still to come.'

Do they? Naomi isn't as sure as she once was.

She pours the wine.

'It's Chardonnay. Sorry. Rosie brought it.'

'It's fine.'

He couldn't care less what he drinks tonight, provided he drinks something.

'So what's the problem? Why the pub? Why the haunted look?'

'They . . .' There's no easy way to put this to your wife. 'They want to lose the subplot.'

'What do they mean by the subplot?'

'I'm afraid they mean you. You and Furry Tongue. They think it isn't working.'

'It isn't. It's crap. We all know that.'

'Well, won't you be happier not having to do it, then?

You hate working with him. You've no confidence in the character. It'll be a release for you.'

It isn't a release. It's a body blow. It's the end.

'It's all my fault,' he says. 'I was inhibited writing it, the moment I'd fallen in love with you.'

'You said it was my fault.'

'I've never said that.'

'You have virtually. It was while you were watching that bloody football match of yours. I said that you never give me anything funny. You said, "Because you don't make it funny. You aren't funny."'

Marvellous, isn't it? She forgot to buy rice last week, so we have curry with mashed potato, but she remembers every word of the only truly disastrous remark I have ever made to her in the whole of our long, long marriage . . . God, it's almost a year now.

'So you just agreed to do the series but drop your own wife from it?'

'I could see the artistic sense of what they were suggesting.'

'Artistic sense? It's not a bad series, Colin, and for those who don't know anything about taxidermy it's probably the best I've been in, but it isn't *War and Peace*. You should have walked out.'

'I can't just walk out. I owe it to the others. I owe it to Matthew and Francis.'

He takes a large sip of the Chardonnay, forces some more of his glutinous supper into his reluctant mouth, and wonders whether he has the courage to tell her the real reason that he hasn't walked away from the project. There's a danger that telling her will diminish her respect for him and her faith in the existence of future projects that they can be involved in together. But it will probably go some way towards smoothing her ruffled feathers.

Oh, God. Smoothing her ruffled feathers. He's a writer and he thinks in clichés. I really am second-rate, he thinks.

He decides to tell her the truth, omitting the reference to his being second-rate.

'I'll tell you why I didn't walk out,' he says. 'I couldn't. I'd be too terrified. Terrified that I will never have another good idea, that I'm not ready yet to write this great novel that I feel I have in me. I'm haunted by an exchange I read about between Peter Cook and a journalist at a party. Peter Cook asked him what he was doing these days, and he said, "I'm writing a novel." "Really?" replied Peter Cook. "Neither am I."'

There is silence between them. They chew the increasingly unappetising cauliflower cheese. He feels the need to pee, but daren't break the mood. He has no idea what she will say next, how she will react. He realises how little he knows about women.

When she does react, he is delighted. She comes over to him and jumps on to his lap. He would be even more delighted if her weight didn't make his need to pee even more urgent. The absurd thought comes to him that he has never seen a single love scene of any kind in any film that has been interrupted because one of the characters needs to pee. Somehow, this puts his whole life into unflattering perspective. His is not a heroic story.

But he is thrilled by Naomi's generous reaction.

'My poor darling,' she says, and she kisses him warmly, forces open his mouth, explores it with her tongue, strokes the top of his head. 'My poor baby.'

She slips off his lap, gives him a final sweet little kiss on the cheek, and returns to her seat.

'It's the right decision,' she says. 'I have to admit it.'

He is awed by her generosity of spirit.

'I hope the series runs and runs and runs.'

'There won't be a series if I don't go and pee pretty damned rapido.'

When he returns she gives him one of her very broadest smiles, raises her glass and says, 'To other, happier, more successful collaborations, my darling.'

He raises his glass, clinks it with hers, and drinks.

He feels very sad. He hasn't told her the real reason that she is being written out, and it's a reason that makes it very unlikely that they will ever work together again.

The real reason is that there have been complaints about her behaviour. She keeps trying to convert people away from religion. She upsets people with the tone of her voice, which suggests that she thinks they must be halfwitted to believe. This lovely, radiant, beautiful, smiling, intelligent, passionate, compassionate woman is in danger of becoming a crashing rehearsal room bore. She is on the verge of being black-listed, by word of mouth if not by document.

But he is not the person to tell her. He is not brave enough.

He takes the dirty plates over to the sink, scrapes the unfinished food, cool now and congealing, into the waste bin, and looks out of the window at the darkening sky. Sometimes they see lovely sunsets from here, but tonight there is no sun, just cloud. Tonight the London sky is, as he might have expected it to be, a uniform, slightly grey white with just a hint of rather dirty yellow – just, in fact, the colour of cauli-flower cheese.

The Sancerre glows golden in the glasses.

'Impressive, eh?' says Tommo to his friends, as the asparagus soup is being poured into wide white plates with a silver ladle.

'Astounding,' says Steven Venables.

A large, over-varnished oak table fills the room. There are bulky, impressive oak chairs. The walls are panelled.

The windows are high. Portraits of men who have been big in biscuits hang on the walls.

There has been a choice of sherry, Madeira or gin and tonic. Tommo has chosen bottled water.

'I never drink at work,' he has explained. 'I find it takes the edge off that lovely first drink as the sun goes over the yardarm.'

Timothy realises that he isn't quite sure what a yardarm is.

Eight places are set round the immaculate table. There is a menu in every place. Today's luncheon – nothing as vulgar as mere lunch – will consist of asparagus soup, roast Welsh spring lamb with caper sauce, sticky toffee pudding, and English cheeses.

They will drink Sancerre, Fleurie, Sauternes and port.

This is surely a London club, or a senior combination room at Oxford or Cambridge?

No. It's the boardroom of Great Northern Biscuits, outside Coningsfield.

Tommo has invited 'the lads', as he calls them, to visit the factory, see the process of making biscuits, and have luncheon in the boardroom. There's a formal luncheon, with invited guests, on the second Thursday of every month. 'Suits, chaps, I'm afraid.'

'Lots of people are giving up the old traditions,' says Brian Anstruther, Head of Development, 'but tradition is at the heart of our style.'

'Tradition is the bedrock of our biscuits,' agrees Sir Walter Melrose, retired textile magnate, now lending his name to the boards of eight companies, and very valuable he is too, with his great talent for saying the right thing and having lunch.

'Even the women on the assembly lines get a glow of pride from the knowledge that we are keeping up the old standards,' says Simon Ellsworthy, Head of Sales.

'Don't you feel a need to keep up with the times?' asks Timothy, who feels obliged to take an interest out of politeness.

'Nice asparagus soup,' comments Dave Kent, whose suit is fifteen years behind the times and too tight over his paunch.

'Well, there are people here who wish to modernise,' says Tommo.

'The secret is to use at least some prime asparagus,' says Dave.

'And I mean, we do keep up with technological developments,' continues Tommo.

'You follow the trends or you find you've let the trends follow you,' says Watson Sinclair, Head of Marketing.

'In business the present is a staging post between the past and the future,' comments Sir Walter Melrose.

'Interesting,' said Steven Venables, whose suit is so sharp and well cut that Tommo almost purrs with pleasure every time he looks at it.

'It'll not be tasty if you just use the thin ones and the bottom of the stalks,' says Dave Kent. 'There's no way it can be.'

During the morning Tommo has shown them a vast vault of a room filled with assembly lines of biscuits, sliding along in what looks like a huge model railway designed by a deranged train spotter. They have seen the custard creams sliding creamlessly into a creaming machine and emerging proudly with their cream. They have seen lines of biscuits dropping with perfect timing into lines of boxes which are moving almost imperceptibly along low-level lines in these sweet and savoury sidings. Tommo has shown them the workings of the new computerised sales system. 'You want to know how many Garibaldis we sold to Belgium last year?' he demands of his three friends, none of whom have the slightest desire to know the answer. 'There we are, in a flash.'

'This is delicious,' says Timothy of the lamb with caper sauce.

'Unbelievable.' says Steven Venables, who seems to be speaking entirely in enigmatic adjectives.

By sticky toffee pudding time, voices are getting louder, and Tommo, who is sitting next to Timothy, takes the opportunity to return, in a low voice, to the subject of Timothy's new wife.

'How are things in the bed department?'

'Fine.'

Tommo detects the hint of reservation that Timothy cannot entirely conceal.

'But?'

'Well, the thing is . . .' Timothy lowers his voice even more. 'I feel I shouldn't be saying this, it's not fair to Hannah, but . . . we only do it on Tuesday evenings.'

'I see. No, I don't. What's the significance of Tuesday evenings?'

'Dad gets taken to the Cadogan. They play dominoes. He lives for his Braille fives and threes on Tuesday nights. Well, let's face it. He doesn't have a very exciting life.'

'You mean you can only have sex when he's out?'

'Hannah's very noisy.'

'I see.' Tommo gives Timothy a strange look. Timothy thinks he can detect elements of respect and wistfulness in it.

'But don't you find that if you're confined to Tuesday nights a certain element of surprise, of spontaneity, is missing?' Tommo lowers his voice still further. 'That sudden unexpected taking of her from behind in the kitchen while she's whisking the mayonnaise.'

'You flatter us, Tommo,' replies Timothy. 'Very few people make their own mayonnaise these days.'

Over the cheese – this is a mammoth meal, 'the lads' will

later fall asleep in the taxi, Watson Sinclair and Brian Anstruther will nod off in their offices, Sir Walter's snoring will get up his chauffeur's nose, and only Tommo will remain alert through the long reaches of the afternoon – Tommo says, 'Have you heard the one about the parrot on the *Titanic*?'

Timothy's heart sinks. What is it with Tommo and jokes? Why is he drawn to them like a spider to a bath?

'This passenger is on the *Titanic* with his parrot.'

Please, God, let it be clean. Let Tommo not let the side down.

'And there's this magician on the ship, and he's doing an act that night.'

Timothy is surprised to find himself speaking to God. It hasn't happened recently.

'And so the passenger goes up to the magician, and he says, "I'm coming to see your act tonight. Would it be all right if I brought my parrot with me?"'

Fatuous too. As if even God could get someone to change a punchline in mid-joke. There must be limits even to omnipotence.

'And the magician, who's a nice man, says, "Of course. Bring him along."'

Think of something else. Anything else. Think of Hannah. Lovely Hannah.

But he can still hear the words.

'So the passenger takes his parrot to the show, and the show begins. The magician does his first trick, and the parrot shouts out, "I know how you did it. You had another one hidden in your hat." The magician isn't very pleased, but he carries on.'

I didn't tell Tommo the main problem I have with Hannah.

'The magician does his second trick, and the parrot cries out, "I know how you did it. It had a false bottom."'

221

Hannah doesn't want children and I do. She's a career woman, and she kept it hidden from me until we were married. All that spirituality, it's a bit of a smokescreen concealing her ambition. She doesn't call it ambition, though. She calls it 'not letting Mr Finch down. He'd be lost without me.'

'The magician isn't very pleased, but he carries on with his third trick. The parrot cries out, "I know how you did it. You had the other one hidden up your arm."'

This isn't what I meant when I told myself to think of Hannah.

'And, at this moment, the ship hits an iceberg.'

But I so want a child. I want a half-brother or sister for Liam. I want a replacement for Sam, and a little child to care for, so that it will be easier to live without Sam. Oh, God, the punchline's coming.

'Well, the next morning, the magician is clinging to a plank of wood in the frozen ocean. And the parrot is clinging to another plank of wood. And the magician sees the parrot. And the parrot sees the magician. And the magician glares at the parrot. And the parrot looks at the magician. And the parrot says, "All right. I give up. What have you done with the ship?"'

It's clean. Good old Tommo. I needn't have worried. I needn't have thought about Hannah. Why do I worry about so much? Why do I worry about nothing? Why do I worry about everything?

And, in the way that worries have, because his worry over Tommo's joke disappears, all his other worries seem to disappear too. He's a reasonably successful taxidermist, married to an attractive young woman who loves him and enjoys sex, even if only on Tuesdays. If there are clouds on the horizon, they are tiny. He accepts another glass of port.

*   *   *

She's lying. Regularly. That's what hurts. He would never have thought it of her. She has always spoken of the importance of truth. Now she's become devious, secretive. Even Emily notices.

'Mum's changed,' she says.

'Well, I agree,' he says. 'She's not quite herself at the moment.'

There can only be one explanation. She's having an affair. That is something he would never have thought possible for her. He is devastated.

Of course the marriage has hit a rocky patch. It's hardly surprising, given the situation over *Get Stuffed*. The atmosphere in the house has not been good. Naomi has become convinced that she will never work again, that she is unemployable.

Day after day she has called out, 'I'm just taking Emily to school,' and then something like, 'I might shop for some shoes,' or 'I'm going to try to get in and have my feet done,' and then she would return home with Emily six or seven hours later and say, 'Sorry. I got held up,' or 'She couldn't fit me in till two thirty,' or 'I met Sandra Hardcastle in Boots and she said, "Do you fancy a sandwich?" – and she always ended up, 'So it wasn't worth coming home before I picked up Emily.' Once or twice she has even phoned and said, 'I've got a bit delayed. Can you pick Emily up?' and he couldn't say, 'I do have the scripts to finish, you know,' because the whole subject of the sitcom was taboo in the house. It had become an unmentionable, invisible wall that kept them apart from each other in their own home. Really Emily was old enough to go to and from school on her own, but this was a stage in her development that they both rather dreaded. She showed no sign of undue naughtiness, but in this world you expected something to erupt at any time and, the longer it didn't, the more you feared the time when it would.

Colin thought of hiring a private detective to follow Naomi and see where she went, but that seemed very dramatic, very clichéd, not to mention very expensive. He decided to follow her himself. A friend in publishing had told him that his work lacked 'the salt and pepper of experience'. He was writing too much and living too little. Well, tailing his own wife counted as experience. It might help him to kick-start that novel.

So, every morning, after she has driven off to the school, he gets into his car and drives to a spot from which he can see the school gates. He sees where she parks, and when she sets off after dropping Emily, he follows. He does this for two days, loses her both times, and goes back home to his four cups of coffee and his writer's block. On the third day he parks in a side street on the other side of the school, and follows her as she passes by the end of the road. He feels quite safe. She isn't the world's most careful driver and he's noticed that she very rarely looks in her mirror. The next two days he sees where she parks, watches her set off on foot, but by the time he's found a parking space she has disappeared. On both days her walk is taking her in the general direction of West Hampstead tube station, and so on the fifth morning, the Friday of his first week of stalking his own wife, he gambles.

He thinks it likely that she is going to the tube station. He feels that she wouldn't risk an affair in her own neck of the woods. He decides not to follow her to West Hampstead station. She's very likely to spot him if they're standing on the same platform, waiting for the same train. As soon as she is out of sight of Narcissus Road, he will leave the house in the opposite direction, and get on a train bound for the West End at Kilburn station, which is one station further away from Central London than West Hampstead station. Then he will get off at West Hampstead station, and await

224

her, hiding behind his newspaper, like any good spy. She will not be there yet, for she has to drop Emily at school and then park before she catches her train. He is working, of course, on the assumption that Naomi will be getting a train going towards Central London. But he thinks that this is a pretty safe assumption. She's no snob, but she just isn't Dollis Hill material. She isn't a Neasden type of girl.

So, the moment she has gone, he slips out of the house and walks rather fast to Kilburn tube station, only to be told that there's a twelve-minute wait 'due to the knock-on effects of an early-morning signal failure in the Baker Street area'. So that's no good. She will almost certainly catch the same train, and it will be very, very crowded due to the delays. She might get into his carriage and he might find her standing right by him.

So he doesn't get the train. He goes home, and spends a terrible weekend wondering, imagining her slender body next to some obscenely hairy chest. He has been embarrassed all his life by the smoothness of his chest. There's nothing wrong in a man having a smooth chest. It suits some men. But he feels that he is a man who should have a hairy chest, and hasn't.

On the Monday morning, she takes Emily to school. He walks very swiftly to Kilburn station, gets a train immediately, gets off at West Hampstead station, sits on a seat at the end of the platform furthest from the entrance and exit, hides behind his newspaper as planned, and waits. At West Hampstead underground station the platforms and trains are still actually above ground; the train burrows under London shortly after the station. Somehow, being in the open air makes him feel more secure, more in control, than if he was having to do all this hundreds of feet under the surface.

He considers again his belief that she will be travelling towards Central London. Much as he would like to imagine

225

Hairy Chest as living in Neasden because it's so convenient for Wembley Stadium, or choosing Dollis Hill because of the views (he presumes that there's a hill there), he knows it isn't likely. Hairy Chest's a city centre slicker, knows his way around. He'll be modern, trendy, he's where it's at, he isn't some end-of-the-line nerd with glasses. Colin's heart is pumping. He hates the thought of what he's going to find, but he hates the uncertainty even more.

There she is! Oh, God! She's quite a long way down the platform, but he can see her sense of purpose. This is a woman with a mission. She looks hungry. He knows what her mission is – to meet and get laid by a virile young man with a very hairy chest. It stands out a mile.

He hears the train approaching. He walks slowly towards his wife's part of the platform. This is really risky now. How foolish of him not to rely on a private detective, whom she wouldn't recognise. He has his story ready, of course, in case she does see him, but still, it will rather abort the whole exercise.

He's in luck. She gets into the far end of the next carriage, and he slips into the other end of it. The carriage is very crowded. They both have to stand. He hides behind his newspaper. He feels self-conscious, but then he realises that nobody is looking at him. People survive the torments of the rush hour on the underground by incarcerating themselves in their own world. They don't ever meet anyone else's eyes.

At each station he peers down the carriage. At the first one she doesn't get off. At the second he isn't quite sure. But no, at the third, he sees her.

She gets off at Oxford Street station, but he has difficulty getting out of his crowded doorway, and he loses her.

He goes home to his writer's block in a foul mood. This following your wife, this stalking business, isn't nearly as exciting as he'd hoped. He's not getting any material for his book. And it's far more difficult than you would suppose from all the books and films he's seen, in which the stalkee never turns round and the stalker never expects the stalkee to turn round. And as he wrestles with his writer's block he realises suddenly that he's come to hate his two fictional taxidermists. They are two albatrosses round his creative neck. He'd like to kill them off, stuff them – no, model them and paint them silver and leave them by the Thames near the London Eye, so that the hordes of tourists would think they were real live people standing stock-still and would put money into the caps on the ground in front of them, which he would empty at the end of the day.

The next day he takes another risk. He gambles that she's not changing trains at Oxford Street, but getting out. So he takes his train from Kilburn straight through West Hampstead, and gets off at Oxford Street. He goes up the escalator and stands near its top, hiding behind his paper, heart thudding.

There she is. He notes again her eager, hungry look, and suddenly he understands. It isn't just for the sex that she visits Hairy Chest. He takes her to the Ivy, the flash bastard. It's her revenge on him for not taking her there as promised, when the fourth series was commissioned. But how could he, how could they celebrate the commissioning of the fourth series, dwarfed as it was by the fact of her being written out of it?

He slips into the human stream behind her, follows her up the steps, sees her go eastwards along Oxford Street. She'll probably turn down Poland Street, Hairy Chest probably lives on the fringes of Soho, he's a musician, they'll smoke dope together, not too much, just enough to give an additional excitement to that lunch at the Ivy.

She enters a doorway, a vile, sinister doorway, a doorway

to filth. Colin is shocked to see her enter this doorway. Suddenly thoughts of the Ivy fade. He's got it all wrong. Hairy Chest inhabits the sordid underbelly of the city, lives on the grotty end of Oxford Street and – oh, God – probably has several sexually transmitted diseases.

He isn't quite sure what to do now. To tell the truth, he's a little frightened. Nothing good can happen behind doorways like that.

He decides to wait until she has had time to get into bed with Hairy Chest. He needs to catch her in flagrante delicto.

He crosses the road, so that if she should look out of the window – unlikely, she's gasping for it, but possible – she won't see him.

One more minute. He's pretty frightened now. He's not a man of action, he's a wordsmith. Hairy Chest could be violent. Those forearms are pretty muscular. Maybe he should just go home and ask her in the evening what she's been doing.

No. Be brave. Enter.

Just as he is about to enter, she comes out, along with five other people, three men and two women, all somewhat younger than her.

He can't believe his eyes. They're all carrying sandwich boards and large, heavy bags.

They set off westwards towards Oxford Circus.

He follows in their wake.

On one side of each of the six sandwich boards are the words, '*There is no God*' in large letters. On the other side, in even larger letters, the message reads, '*And it doesn't matter*'.

The six sandwich-board people each get a pile of pamphlets from their bag and start offering them to passers-by, smiling and saying, very politely, 'Please take one of these.' Some people smile and shake their heads. Others walk on without meeting their eyes. A few people do take pamphlets, which they examine briefly. Some of these people dump them in the nearest litter bin, others drop them onto the pavement, a few stuff them into their pockets, one or two even open briefcases and put them in with their other papers.

Colin follows Naomi for about a quarter of an hour, fascinated yet repelled. At first he feels relieved. She isn't having an affair with Hairy Chest. But then a wave of dismay sweeps away the relief. This nutter is his wife.

At last he feels that he has seen all he needs to.

He approaches Naomi, his heart pounding. He is hating this.

He taps her on the shoulder.

She turns, sees him. The blood drains from her face. She smiles – a little desperately, he feels.

'Naomi, Naomi, please stop this,' he implores.

She smiles rather sadly, tells him to meet her in Starbucks in half an hour, and hurries on to catch up with her five colleagues.

He walks the streets for what he hopes is half an hour – he doesn't wear a watch – but he still gets to Starbucks five minutes early. It's his first experience of this new chain, and it isn't his kind of place. It's so full that he has to sit downstairs, in unattractive gloom. His medium coffee is so large that he feels full before he even starts on it. He wishes he was an eighteenth-century writer in the coffee houses of Vienna. Oh, to be in Vienna in its heyday. Oh, to be anywhere in its heyday. Oh, to be anywhere but here.

Ten minutes pass. She isn't coming.

And then there she is, coming down the stairs, smiling and so pretty. She has an even larger coffee.

'Sorry I'm late,' she says. 'Chrissy, she's the very tall one, I don't know if you noticed her, but she's very pretty, she's really nice, she's half Danish though you wouldn't know it, she was trying to persuade me not to come. She thinks you'll persuade me not to go back.'

'Who are they?'

'They call themselves Atheists of Acton.'

He notes that she doesn't say, 'We call ourselves . . .' It gives him hope. He needs to play this very cool, very straight. Any mockery could be disastrous. He resists the temptation to smile at the mention of Atheists of Acton.

'"Atheists of Acton?"'

'Yeah. Jamie's actually the only one from Acton, he's the balding one, he's really nice, but he started it and it sounds snappy with the alliteration.'

This from a woman who has played the immortal words of Shakespeare, not to mention Colin Coppinger, thinks Colin.

'How did you find them?'

'On the internet.'

'You really . . .' He lowers his voice. A man who's just come in may be a BBC producer and if word of this gets around, Naomi will never work again '. . . want to go out on a limb with this anti-God business, don't you?'

'I don't want to. I have to. Mickey—'

'Matey lot, aren't you?'

Careful, Colin.

'Well, yes.'

'Is he really nice too?'

No. Don't.

'I suppose you're bound to mock.'

'Sorry. Listen . . . darling . . .' Damn. The endearment hasn't worked. It sounded like an afterthought.

She ignores it.

'Mickey, he articulated exactly what I've been thinking. "The world is living through a pivotal period. Science has given us the chance to create a truly secular society. We can all live together in secular unity, or the world can dissolve into hatred, persecution and terrorism."'

'Bit of an extreme choice, touch of simplification just possibly, but I do have . . . um . . . a certain sympathy with those views. But you can't achieve anything going round with Atheists of Acton, Agnostics of Aldershot or even Sceptics of Swindon.'

Careful, Colin. She's bridling.

'No, darling, but seriously, if you want to get that sort of message across, forget sandwich boards. They're all about sad men standing in the cold with dewdrops on the ends of their noses advertising Indian restaurants, and religious maniacs who fear that Staines and Guildford will turn into Sodom and Gomorrah announcing that *"The End of the World is Nigh"*.'

'Funny you should mention that. Carrie, sorry, but that's what she's called, and she's really nice too, sorry, but she is, she said maybe we ought to have a board that said, *"The End of the World isn't Actually all that Nigh at all"*, but then Jamie said that would make it sound as if we didn't believe in global warming, so Mickey said we ought to have a board that said, *"The End of the World is Nigh, but not for the Reasons that People Thought it was Nigh Before"*, and we had a bit of a laugh, so you see we don't take ourselves too seriously.'

'I never said you did.'

'No, but you thought it. So we settled for simplicity.'

'I'm really not making fun, and I'm sure they are very nice,' says Colin, 'but you are my wife and I am being rather neglected and I don't want you to do it and neither does Emily, and I think she feels rather neglected too, and you've done such a wonderful job with her so far, it would be a pity, well, a tragedy actually, to spoil it now. You're a sitcom star and if the press get hold of it they'll make fun of you. "Get Them Off." You'll never work again and it'll get Emily mocked at school. Honestly, darling.'

This 'darling' is a success, it attaches itself nicely to his preceding word. Colin longs to tell her that the publicity wouldn't do him much good either, but it would be a big mistake to mention this.

'I do love you,' he says. He isn't absolutely sure that he means it entirely, but he means it enough for it not to be classified as a lie.

'I love you too,' she says. He no longer has any idea whether she means it.

They hold hands. They make a pretty picture.

'I just wish you'd use other methods, darling,' he says. 'Better methods. That's all.'

Naomi squeezes his hand.

'All right,' she says. 'I will.'

Colin thinks that something has been achieved. He really does.

'Would you like some more coffee?' she asks.

'Possibly, in a fortnight,' he replies.

The sight of all the chairs and settees depresses him. He knows that they are necessary, because there will be times when large numbers of people need to sit down all at once, but they speak so loudly of the fact that this is not anyone's home, but *a* home. They are bulky, so that the residents of the home can be comfortable in them, and there is no way that so many chairs and settees can be arranged with elegance in so large a room.

'Now then, sole product of my under-used loins, how goes it at number ninety-six?'

Only some seven or eight people are in the room this somnolent afternoon, but Timothy is deeply embarrassed by Roly's rotund language, spoken, it seems to him, more loudly than is necessary, as if the Cadogan is a home for the deaf, not the blind.

'Not bad, Dad.'

Now he is embarrassed because his language seems so

232

shrivelled by comparison. He tells himself not to be embarrassed. No one in the room knows who he is. No one in the room can see him. Surely the fact of their blindness can protect him from the need to feel embarrassed?

Come on, boy. Don't be feeble, he tells himself, before his father can.

'But how are you, Dad?'

'I'm happy in this place, Timothy. It's right that I should be here. Nobody wants a gooseberry in their marital home, especially a blind gooseberry.'

'I wanted you to stay, Dad.' This in a much stronger voice. He has to accept the fact that this very personal conversation is being overheard by seven blind strangers – eight now, another has tip-tapped his way to one of the chairs.

'Don't blame Hannah, boy. She had the sense to see that it was not appropriate. Besides, I like the Cadogan. I have friends here. I'm in my element here. At number ninety-six I was a shadowy figure, surplus to requirements, a redundancy. Here I'm Roly, the retired taxidermist. Bit of a character, our Roly. Bit of an artist, too. Used to be one of the best taxidermists in the North of England. Not the most modest of men, but a bit of a card. Oh, yes. They don't make them like Roly Pickering any more. You see. Hannah's done me a favour, chucking me out.'

'Dad! She didn't chuck you out.'

'Not in so many words, no. Just lodged the thought in my mind, and it was a good thought, otherwise it wouldn't have lodged, would it? Don't get me wrong, Timothy. She's a nice girl. Big improvement on the Maggot.'

'I don't like you to call Maggie that.'

'Sorry. Something you inherited from your old man, unfortunately. The curse of the genes, eh, my son?'

'What?'

'Bad taste in women.'

'Dad!'

'Quite right. That's going too far. Nice girl. Best of the bunch.'

'I've only married twice, Dad. Pretty small bunch.'

'I was including Josie.'

Timothy believes that this may be the first time his father has ever mentioned his mother's name to him.

'Anyway, I can't talk. None of your wives will abandon you for a *plumber*. There's a limerick about a plumber.'

Next time, I'm going to see Dad in his room. I won't make this mistake again. In the meantime, courage, Timothy.

> 'There was a young plumber from Leigh
> Who was plumbing a maid by the sea.
> Said the maid, "Stop your plumbing,
> There's somebody coming."
> "I know," said the plumber. "It's me."'

'Very good, Dad. Very funny.'

Why should he worry that he's blushing, here? None of them can see that he's blushing.

'I console myself with the hope that your mother's love life was what one would expect of a plumber.'

Timothy has a sudden flash of inspiration.

'I know what you mean, Dad. Late on the job and leaves off halfway through.'

'Precisely. Well said, boy.' His father's voice drops a level, as if he is sparing his son more embarrassment, in recognition of his spirit. 'I used to listen for sounds of marital activity. Well, an old man in a big house, lonely, with nothing to do. Sorry. Anyway, I have to say, I didn't hear much, not after the first flush, anyway.'

The truth, Timothy. Don't be frightened of the truth. It won't bite you.

234

'Hannah is . . . well . . . noisy, Dad.'

'Is she, by Jove? She's a goer? You surprise me. Always thought she was religious.'

'I don't think the two are always mutually exclusive, Dad. So Hannah was embarrassed to . . . do it . . . when you were around.' Timothy lowers his voice. 'We used to make love on Tuesday evenings, when you were out.'

Roly Pickering slaps his thigh, and laughs. He finds this really funny. Timothy is a little hurt that his father finds it so very funny.

'Oh, my God. Oh, Timothy. That's rich. Oh dear, oh dear. I'd have gone out to play fives and threes every night if I'd known.'

His father blows his nose, wipes his eyes, and suddenly looks serious.

'You know the one you should have married. That one you ran off to London with.'

'Don't you think I don't know that?'

'It's a bit late to apologise now, but I'm sorry I hit you. Only time I ever hit another person. Didn't even hit your mother when she told me she was running off with a *plumber*. I want to say something about that. Do you know why I hit you?'

'Because I lied to you?'

'Got it in one, boy. Well said. Didn't mind about the sex. There was sex, was there?'

Timothy finds himself telling his father about the three nights he had with Naomi, especially the second one. Then he tells him, as perhaps he should have told him long ago, about the night when he went to see Naomi in her sitcom, and later, in the Indian restaurant, spoke up for his father and the art and craft of taxidermy. The room begins to fill up, for quite soon the call to supper will come, and life and mealtimes are indivisible here, here life is as it is for birds

235

and animals, a matter of eating and sleeping and trying to stay alive; people who once thought long and hard about the purpose of life feel that there is no purpose in worrying about whether it has a purpose now.

And at the end of it, there's a moment's true, peaceful, close silence between the two men, and then Roly says something he's never said before.

'I'm proud of you, boy.'

And then Timothy feels free to tell his father that the business, though sound enough, is nothing like what it was in the old days.

'You were an artist, Dad. I'm a craftsman.'

Roly drinks this compliment in silence.

'Hannah wants to make some changes to the house.'

'Quite right, too. Drag it into the twentieth century just before the century ends and you'll have another ruddy century to drag it into. Quite right, boy. Not a bad girl, on the whole. Doesn't want children, eh?'

'How do you know that?'

'Smelt it, son. The blind see things that others cannot see. Bit of a career woman on the QV, eh? Dare I mention the dreaded word "hypocrite"? She won't run off with a plumber. She'll run off with that boss of hers.'

'Dad!'

'That Mr Tit.'

'Finch.'

'Whatever. I could hear it in her eyes when she spoke of him.' Roly leans forward and touches his son's arm, affectionately. 'Said too much. Fault of those with too much time on their hands. May not happen like that. Probably won't. If it does, though, if it does, you go after that other one. That Naomi. One in a million, that one. Girl with sense. Couldn't understand why you didn't marry her. What came between you?'

'God, Dad.'

Roly digests this in silence.

'Suppertime. Time you were off. Timothy?'

'Yes, Dad.'

'We look forward to our meals here. Highlight of our lives. I've enjoyed your visit. Today, supper will be an anticlimax.'

'Wow! Thanks, Dad.'

'Come again soon.'

I will, thinks Timothy. And, do you know, I haven't felt at all embarrassed for the last hour. I completely forgot there was anyone else in the room. Maybe I won't bother to ask to see you in private, in your room, after all.

Where on earth is Naomi? It's past ten o'clock. Why hasn't she phoned? Colin is always slightly worried when she's gone out in her car. She's not the most reliable of drivers. And her car is a very old Ford Sierra, nearing the end of its safe life. They can't afford anything better. She has found no acting work since being written out of *Get Stuffed*, and Colin isn't confident about his future, he's clinging onto a dying sitcom. He suspects that this will be the final series, and he hasn't an idea in his head for what he'll write next.

The thought keeps going through his mind. If she was all right, and knowing that she was at least four hours later than expected, she would have phoned. Naomi is not an inconsiderate person. So something must have happened.

But even as he thinks this, he knows that he isn't sure that he truly knows Naomi any more. She has promised to try other methods, but can he trust her any more to keep her promises? There's a secretive, devious side to her now. He's unable to follow her to all the places that she goes to in her mind. Besides, he has realised that 'trying other methods' can mean anything she likes. The minor victory that he thought he had achieved in Starbucks may be a complete illusion.

He doesn't know what to do about Emily. She has school tomorrow and her bedtime is looming. She says she's done her homework, but he hasn't seen much evidence of it. The truth is that he doesn't know how to talk to her. He can see that she's worried, but he's helpless. She's always been so close to her mother. He minded that at first, he felt excluded, a gooseberry in his own household. But he's honest enough to realise that their closeness lets him off the hook, for he has no idea how he could be close to her. He's also happy, to a certain extent, that she gets on so well with her father and his second wife. Again, it lets him off the hook. It allows him to keep his distance, be pleasant to her, be good to her, help to bring her up as well as he can, but remain uninvolved. 'We'd better ask your mother,' that's the catchphrase in the sitcom of their life together.

This evening he suddenly knows that all this is not enough. This evening they both need to be close to each other. But neither of them can do it. The tick-tock of the grandfather clock that once stood in the hall in L'Ancresse usually sounds so mellow and reassuring. Tonight it is saying, 'Another two seconds gone, another two seconds gone, another two seconds gone.'

Emily's all right for the moment. She's watching television. No problem about that. She's no couch potato. She has no interest in organised sport, but she loves to be outside, enjoys walking even on her own, adores swimming in the sea, cycles enthusiastically whenever it's considered safe enough. No, he can leave her in front of the television with a clear conscience.

He goes back to his tiny study and sits again in front of episode five. He'll make one more effort to wrestle with the awkward scene in which one of the taxidermists is suspected of having sex with the other's wife. This scene contains the ninety-seventh stuffing joke of the series. Even when one couple went to Greece on holiday, there was no respite. They went to Paxos. And he has been painfully aware, ever since he met Timothy, that taxidermists don't stuff. The whole thing's a mess.

He has realised more than ever, during this long, anxious evening, that working on the series is no way to try to stop thinking about Naomi. Her absence from it is palpable. She is making more impact on him now that she's written out than she was when he was struggling to find ways to avoid her having to be kissed by her rival's son. He has never admitted to anybody that writing those scenes made him feel very jealous. Watching them, seeing that self-satisfied streak of egotistical piss sticking his snaky, conceited tongue into Naomi's mouth, was pretty unpleasant, but the real feeling of being cuckolded by a sitcom came to him not as he watched them, but as he wrote them. He hated them, but was drawn irresistibly towards them. Then, gradually, it had all changed. He had begun to want her to be kissed by him, because he needed to feel jealous, because otherwise he would feel nothing. He hadn't entirely understood this, he hadn't yet been aware that his love for Naomi was dying, but tonight, all these thoughts and half-thoughts are churning around somewhere near the edge of his consciousness, and still the clock ticks, and still Naomi doesn't appear.

He goes downstairs, stands by the door, watches Emily. She really is growing into a beautiful girl, now that she no longer has the braces on her teeth.

He wants to go up to her, and put his arms round her, and hug her. He wants to hold her close and comfort her. But can he, at the end of the twentieth century, the century in which innocence died? Can he? Might she not think he was making advances? Might she not twist her way out of his embraces? Might she not accuse him of attempted rape? He'd read about such things. Not Emily, surely? Not Emily. Not Naomi's little girl. And yet, how well does he know Emily? How well has he tried to get to know Emily? What does she really think of him? What is she thinking on this tense night?

He moves further into the room. Now he is standing some six feet away from her, yet he is continents away. She is a young girl, growing up and troubled, her hormones developing, her thoughts turning to . . . to what? Her thoughts are so far away from him that if she tried to transmit them to him, they would have to stop in Singapore to refuel.

And she is beautiful. What a gift. What a curse. Can he . . . can he be sure, can he be absolutely sure, totally sure, that if he kissed her . . . away, away, oh, Colin, you do not want to think these thoughts, but how can you unthink a thought that you have thought? . . . and maybe innocence has died in you too . . . can he be absolutely sure that he wouldn't . . . wouldn't . . . he can't frame the words, even to himself. He walks out of the room, quietly. She doesn't even know he's been there. He stands in the lounge and listens to the ticking of the clock. 'Another two seconds gone. Another two seconds gone.'

They are together in the house, and surely they can comfort each other? But no. There is no comfort to be had.

If Naomi is safe, if she's all right, he will never raise his voice to her again. They will make a new start. He hasn't been a bad man, just selfish and inadequate and insensitive, but he can be a good man, he will be, he will be a perfect husband.

Emily enters the room, and it's the schoolgirl, not the stepfather, who has the courage to raise the subject.

'Something's happened, hasn't it? Something bad.'

'We don't know that.'

'There's something wrong with Mum, isn't there?'

'I think perhaps there is, Emily.'

The impossible hug. It dominates the room. They both want it. They both fear it. And still the clock ticks.

'If there is, Emily, we'll sort it out.'

Emily doesn't reply.

Are they being hysterical? It's only a woman coming home late.

Very late.

'Don't you think you ought to try to get to bed? You've school tomorrow.'

'I'm not going to school if Mum's not back.'

'She will be.'

She gives a wan smile. She knows that his words are empty.

'Goodnight, Colin.'

'Goodnight, Emily.'

The hurried, perfunctory goodnight kiss, the contact of the two cheeks so thin it's almost imperceptible. The shadow of the hug that's not to be.

Two policemen bring her back in a Crimestoppers car. She's deathly pale, her hair is bedraggled, her eyes are staring, her cheekbones look very prominent. Suddenly Colin sees for the first time that she has become terribly thin. She is grey and gaunt.

Emily comes rushing down and hugs her, but the answering hug is mechanical, the love in it is but a memory of love past.

The story the police tell is not so terrible. The older one reads it out of his notebook, as if they're in court.

'We had complaints from the Warrender Estate that a woman had been knocking on doors and causing a nuisance. She was saying to householders, "My name is Naomi

241

Coppinger, née Walls. I have reason to believe that there is no God."'

'I didn't put it like that.'

'Please, madam, if you don't mind.'

'Let him finish, Naomi.'

'Thank you. "... to believe that there is no God, and I would like to come in and talk to you about it."'

'Exactly! I was being perfectly polite. What's wrong with that? I was enthusiastic. I was cheery. I told them that I was bringing good news.'

'She was forcing leaflets on people, and was excited in a manner that made people uneasy. They felt that she was ... well ...' The officer is embarrassed. '... not quite right.'

'Tell them what I said to you,' cries Naomi.

Her mother's shrillness alarms Emily, who moves towards Colin, as if for protection.

'Mrs Coppinger ...'

'I don't like that name.'

'Naomi, please!'

Colin speaks quite sharply. Emily looks anxiously from one to the other.

'Mrs Coppinger was telling people that she wanted to banish fear from the world, but her manner was making people afraid,' continued the officer. 'We decided that this amounted to causing a nuisance. We didn't want to charge her, she told us where she lived, and we decided that she was unfit to drive herself, and brought her home.'

'You don't stop the Jehovah's Witnesses,' says Naomi fiercely.

'That's different,' says the officer.

'What's different about it?'

'They have faith.'

'I have faith. Faith that I'm right. You see, the world's weighted against us.'

'Don't shout, Mum. I hate it when you shout.'

Emily grabs Colin's hand and huddles into him. He doesn't want this now. It's unnatural.

The officers look at each other uncertainly.

'Can you handle this situation if we leave her with you, sir?' the younger officer asks Colin.

'Of course I can,' says Colin. 'She's my wife. I love her.'

The words seem to have no effect on Naomi.

The officers give each other doubtful glances.

'Well, all right, sir,' says the older officer.

The three of them go to the window, to watch the officers drive away. A curtain across the road twitches as they walk to their car.

Colin tries to kiss Naomi but she backs away. All his good intentions melt away.

'You've got to stop this nonsense,' he shouts.

'You too,' she cries. 'You too. You're just like them all.'

She rushes out of the room.

'Where are you going?' he screams.

He hastens after her, trips, falls, cracks his head on an occasional table. Even as he falls he remembers a silly joke – 'What's an occasional table the rest of the time?' – but this is no time for jokes, he really ought to find another job, being a comedy writer is unhinging him. By the time he's scrambled to his feet she's out of the door. Emily is rushing to the door, screaming, 'Don't go, Mum.' Colin grabs Emily, holds her firmly, says, 'This is for grown-ups, sweetheart,' pushes her into a chair as gently as he can, hurries to the door, and hurls himself down the steps and onto the pavement, just in time to see Naomi driving off in his car, her pale face hunched over the steering wheel.

She turns right at the end of their road at such a speed that the tyres squeal their pain.

Colin has no car in which to give chase. He goes slowly

back into the house. Emily begins to cry. Colin puts out a hand towards her. She turns and runs upstairs. He picks up the phone to ring the police.

And Naomi drives on, furiously, determinedly, towards the M1.

The motorway isn't very busy at this time of the evening, and as she drives north, the traffic becomes slowly more sparse. Now it's mainly her and the juggernauts. Eddie Stobart. Norbert Dentressangle. Prestons of Potto. Kings of the road. Knights of the night. And Naomi among them. Faster, faster, faster, ninety, one hundred, a hundred and ten, overtaking them all, irresistible, unharmable, queen of all she surveys, fulfilling her destiny at last.

They all have missions – delivery of fridges, of parts for caravans, of a barely imaginable amount of chutney. But Naomi has the most important mission of them all.

PART SIX

A Glorious Summer's Day

1999

A man in hiking boots stops on the edge of the moor, takes off his knapsack, examines the sheep-cropped grass, selects a patch that looks innocent of sheep shit, and drops down onto his back. He stares up into the sky, which is entirely blue except for the vapour trail from one aeroplane. He can hear the drone of another aeroplane, a light aircraft. It's making that even, soft, slightly distant reverberation that planes make when the pressure is high and the weather settled. The noise reassures him, makes him feel calm.

The man puts his binoculars to his eyes, and peers up into the sky for several minutes. Then he lowers the binoculars, and rubs his eyes with his right hand. Then he just lies there for . . . oh, maybe a quarter of an hour. Then he looks up through the binoculars again, but this time he doesn't hold them so steadily; they are moving, following something. Then he lies on the ground again, perfectly still, he might even be asleep. After some ten minutes or so he stands up, slips the straps of his knapsack over his head, hitches the knapsack higher onto his shoulders, and looks down over the fertile valley below the moor, over the stone walls, the stone barns, the stone houses of this stony land, shimmering in the summer sun. Then he sets off up the hill.

On the face of it these forty or so minutes have not been very exhilarating. They have certainly not been what a film director would describe as 'action packed'. Yet in times to come Timothy will describe them as perhaps the most important forty minutes of his life and, even more surprisingly, as among the most exciting.

It's a skylark that he's watching through the binoculars, a skylark larking in the sky in the English countryside on a perfect summer morning. It's gloriously unaware that it's a cliché. Even through his strong binoculars he can hardly see this tiny bundle of feathers and bones, alone in the vast emptiness of the heavens, its little beak parted to emit sounds of astonishing power, amazing beauty, inspiring joy. There are people who say that it's merely marking out its territory, telling other skylarks that this is its patch. Presumably the same people would say that a Mozart sonata really means, 'This house in which I am composing this great music is mine, not yours, so there!'

Timothy feels overwhelmed by the emptiness of the sky. He knows, with absolute certainty, that there is no old man up there, with flowing white hair and a huge white beard, looking down on him out of wise, all-seeing eyes. He hasn't believed in that image for a long time. But now he realises that he believes in no image, no conscious or even unconscious force looking over him and looking after him in his struggles. The doubts that have been assailing him in recent years suddenly cease to be doubts and become certainties.

The bird sings on and on, remaining in the same spot, high above the grass, on swiftly fluttering wings. The bird seems tireless, but Timothy's eyes are growing tired and he lowers the binoculars. The hum of the light aircraft recedes, a motorbike startles him with its ugly savagery, and the bird sings on. He listens to its seemingly inexhaustible repertoire, its rolling, its whistling, its chirruping – why, it even throws in a passing imitation of the relatively feeble singing of the swallow, it does impressions, this bird. Why should it do impressions but for the joy of life and the love of existence?

Timothy thinks of Naomi, the lost songbird in his life, and a wave of regret shivers right through him. He can almost hear Naomi's voice, telling him that this bird sees no ultimate purpose in life, seeks no meaning, no pattern, is content to enjoy life's pleasures, the delights of the moment, the perfection of a fine summer's day, and to breed, so that another generation of skylarks can enjoy this fleeting pleasure in their turn, and, in their turn, pass it on. It knows nothing of eternity, of rewards for morality, its morality is the morality of the species, which puts the next generation ahead of its own.

A taxidermist is very conscious of death. No taxidermist is likely to believe that the morality of the natural world could go any way towards solving the problems of existence. It's a harsh world, full of inter-species carnage on a huge scale. Even skylarks kill insects and worms But he believes that this tiny bird is not frightened to die, indeed it may have no concept of death. None of this constitutes in itself an argument for there not being a God, but it does convince Timothy that if inability to believe in eternity, and in life after death, and in an overall purpose and design to our existence is a failing, then the whole of the natural world has that failing. To suggest that life without an overall purpose is futile is to condemn every mammal, every bird, every reptile, every insect – and, Prince Charles might add, every flower, every leaf, every branch, every twig – to a life of futility.

He knows now that he has long wanted to admit to himself

that he is not a believer, but that he has refused to admit it, because he has believed that life without belief will be more difficult, and that the inability to believe is due to some lack in himself. Now suddenly it occurs to him that it is the inability not to believe (there are still a lot of double negatives in his life) that hints at a lack of faith – faith in himself, faith in the human race.

He feels such a desire for Naomi that it almost burns him. He decides, there and then, that while it is unlikely that he will ever be able to see her again, let alone live with her and marry her, he really does want to leave Hannah. He is still fond of her, but she is slowly, perhaps unintentionally, stifling him. He must find the courage to do so. Why does he find courage so difficult? Look at that little bird, still singing its heart out. He peers again through the binoculars, can't find the bird for quite a while, locates it at last, watches it entranced, even blows it a little kiss, he loves it so much. Can he not find something of that bird's spirit?

He is very moved that this tiny bird can have achieved what the huge shock of Sam's death could not achieve. But he realises now that Sam's death may well have delayed this moment, this epiphany of disbelief, this miracle on the road from Damascus. He could not allow himself to believe that his loss and grief were without purpose. They had to have a meaning. Now he cannot think of any meaning that has a shred of dignity or value. Now he faces what he has tried to avoid. Sam has gone for ever, and for no purpose. It was an accident.

And then, as he watches, the bird begins to descend, still singing, wings still fluttering frantically, down and down it goes, he has a real job to keep track of it in the binoculars, and then, just before it reaches the ground it falls silent, it folds its wings, the job is done, the performance is over, it drops gently to earth, making a soft and perfect landing.

He recalls the prayer that he made in Seville, the doubts that he expressed then. He prayed to God to let him meet Naomi again. It didn't happen, until he went to see her himself. He asked for help in overcoming his grief. Well, to a great extent he has overcome it. But, as he lies there, above the hazy valley, he believes that God gave him no help, that he overcame it, to the extent that he has overcame it, by his own courage, his own powers of rational thought, his own need to relate to other people, by the sheer persistence of time's beating wings, and because of the brutal fact that there was no alternative. Because to have taken his own life would have brought undeserved sorrow to several people. Appallingly difficult though it would have been, it would have been too easy.

He doesn't know how the bird feels, but he is exhausted from just watching it. He lies back, and suddenly sees his house, number ninety-six, which has been so much updated now at Hannah's instigation and to her design. The avocado bathroom suite has sailed away in a skip, the birds and animals so proudly made by Roly in his heyday have been banished to the top floor, the cellar and the outhouses. The house has been modernised, lightened, feminised, sanitised. It has been done gradually, and he has found nothing to argue against at any stage. But, now that the job is completed, he sees that the atmosphere of the strange old house has been lost, its history has been destroyed, his father's life has been erased. It is now a house that tries to hide the fact that it is a place where a taxidermist conducts his business.

Taxidermy. The skylark has revealed another important fact to Timothy, a fact that really excites him on this perfect summer's day. He wants to work with live birds and animals, not dead ones.

This thought brings a brief surge of exhilaration, a joy

such as he has rarely felt. But soon the guilt floods in. The thought seems to him to be a betrayal of his father. The thought contains an implicit acceptance of the world's view of taxidermy as not quite a wholesome occupation for a man. The old joke. A dying art. Recently, he knows, he has become bored with all the work he is having to do to drum up business, all the little gifts he sends to influential men in zoos, to tempt them to point dead lions and cheetahs in his direction. And slowly, year by year, fewer dead animals are coming his way. Other taxidermists, men with more push, are getting the best.

Only the other day, when, as bad luck would have it, Hannah was in the house on her own, she had to take delivery, with great reluctance, of a dead wombat. She'd been ashamed to look the driver of the van in the eye.

'Why did you want a wombat?' she had asked him drily when he got home.

'They offered it. I've never done a wombat before. It's a new challenge.'

'Has anyone ordered a wombat?'

'No.'

'Does anyone around here want a wombat?'

'Not that I know of.'

'We need a new carpet for the dining room, you say we can't afford it, but you've bought a dead wombat.'

'It's business. That's different.'

'Is it going to be snapped up? Are wombats trendy? Are the young of today going to be known as the Wombat Generation? Is it the Chinese Year of the Wombat? Do half the children at the grammar school come from two-wombat homes?'

'Of course not.'

'It isn't very good business if nobody wants it.'

They had eaten their stir-fry in near silence that evening.

252

'Anything on the telly?' Hannah had asked.

'Shouldn't think so.'

'Fancy a game of Scrabble?'

'Sorry, no. I think I'd better unpack my wombat.'

He'd known better than to make sexual advances that night.

And then there were the phone calls late at night, not many but always at the wrong moment. The last one had come when Hannah was on the point of orgasm. She hadn't wanted him to answer it but at one a.m. it might have been an emergency. It had been drunks who'd looked up Yellow Pages and got confused. A slurred voice had said, 'We're outside the Lamb and Flag.'

He'd felt very angry, had been very naughty, had said, 'We're very busy tonight. We'll be there in three-quarters of an hour.'

And Hannah had rebuked him. 'That was cruel.'

He couldn't win with her.

A dying art. So unfair. It's a living art, giving life beyond death. Except that it isn't life. But look at Roly's best work and tell me its eyes don't follow you round the room. Oh, hell, that brings me back to the curlew. Oh, Naomi, Naomi, if only I could uncurlew my life and start again. Oh, Mr Finch, please stop being up and coming, it's about time you upped and came. Up and come into Hannah and enable me to leave her with a clear conscience. For I am off, off to pastures new, off to a completely different life. I have only been a taxidermist because my father was. I do not share his love for it. I do not share his talent for it. In my hands it *is* a dying art. That's why I get the wombats, and not the lions. It's a blow to my pride. Who ever heard of a pride of wombats? It's time to leave. I am now happy to take responsibility for my life, and no longer burden God with it. Oh, thank you, brave skylark.

253

The Timothy who stands up, on that perfect summer morning, is not the Timothy who laid himself down on the grass, barely forty minutes ago.

William Walls is a good man, but he has sailed through life on a following wind. There have been few white horses on the sea of his personal experience. There has always been a sense that he is in the family, but not of it. The fact that he went sailing every August and was therefore not part of all the family holidays that are so important to young children, had an effect on his relationship with the family throughout the other eleven months. He has been a slightly distant figure. He has faced other people's crises, of course. There's been no escaping them. Generations of schoolchildren remember his kindness to them at moments of personal difficulty. But he has never needed to face his own crises. He always had Penny to face them for him. Now Penny has gone, and a crisis is coming.

It's a lovely summer morning in East Anglia, just as it is on the moors outside Coningsfield. William's house is small and damp. It's built of uncompromising red brick. Like William with his family, it is in the countryside, but not of it. If there were fifty other similar houses around it, it would not look so odd, but on its own it almost shouts its angularity, its ugliness, its lack of grace. But to William it is paradise, because out of the guest bedroom, which doubles as his study, he can see the estuary, he can see the sailing boats and dream. Every wall is covered by the paintings of sailing boats that once adorned L'Ancresse.

William's friends at the school felt that he was making a big mistake in retiring to a house more than two hundred miles away from them. They didn't know, and would have been very hurt if they had known, that the distance was one of the great factors in his decision. 'Everyone's been so kind,' he had explained to Naomi once. 'So kind. It's killing me. They invite me to bridge suppers and pair me up with spinsters who are either spinsters because they have hairy legs or have hairy legs because they are spinsters, I can never quite decide which. Mrs Wynne-Ellison brings me what she calls "my legendary blancmange". "It slips down so easily, William. Even an old cynic like you will have no trouble swallowing it." Graham Coldcall rings me up to ask for help with *The Times* crossword, because Tilly Coldcall has told him to. I can hear him listening to my tone of voice to see if I'm depressed. Wally Hampsthwaite invites me to rugby matches, and won't take "no" for an answer. I sit there, in the freezing drizzle, with a force seven north-westerly blowing straight into my phizog, watching thirty-two excessively muscular legs straining against each other in the mud. Eighty minutes? More like eternity. Ghastly. Terence Pullman calls for me "on the off chance", takes me to the worst pub in Coningsfield and, over two pints of flat beer, which I can hardly force down, proves to me that he and I have nothing whatsoever in common. I haven't even got onto Dot Partridge. Oh, my goodness me, Naomi, Dot Partridge. Overflowing with concern. Unstoppable. Insists on doing my laundry. When she brings it back, she lays out sets of matching clothes to see me through the week.'

He had lowered his voice, and coloured slightly. Naomi knew that, for the first time in living memory, he was about to touch on the subject of sex.

'She's asking for it, Naomi. Begging for it. I'd rather go to bed with an anchor chain. It'd be softer.'

'You're cruel, Dad,' Naomi had said, and he had smiled wryly.

'I know,' he had said. 'I know. But you see, I have to be so nice to them all the time. Everyone says how nice I am. Everyone says what a gentleman I am. So I have to be. I am imprisoned by my reputation. They say this is a harsh world, Naomi, but I am slowly being strangled by kindness.'

This morning, William reaches the only kind of climax that is available to him now – a literary climax. He writes the last sentence of his description of the Battle of Salamis. It has been a bit of a purple passage. Maybe he will have to go back and tone it down. Maybe he will have to shorten it. He has reached page 543, and there are still several centuries to go in his History of Ancient Greece.

He goes to the window, and opens it. The air that drifts into the room is sweet and salty, warmed by the sun, cooled by the estuary. It's finer than any cocktail man has yet devised. William drinks it in. Enjoy it, William, then make your cheese sandwich – Wensleydale, your favourite – and enjoy that too, because, shortly after you have finished your sandwich, Colin will ring.

In some respects, William and Colin are similar. 'We'd better ask your mother,' the catchphrase in Colin's life, could have applied to William too. And they are both writers now. But William doesn't like Colin's writing. His tolerance of *Get Stuffed* is minimal. A 'friend' in inverted commas once asked him what he thought of it, and was delighted when he said, 'I lost interest during the second word of the title.' William cannot forgive Colin for putting Naomi into it, and then giving her nothing to do. He has never watched her, he couldn't bear it, but he has been told that she has nothing to get her teeth into.

There is a skylark in William's world too, but he barely notices it. Birds aren't boats. He goes downstairs and begins to make his cheese sandwich, at exactly the moment when Timothy is opening his knapsack to get out – you've guessed it – a cheese sandwich.

It would be hard to say which of the two cheese sandwiches is the more ungainly.

William finishes his cheese sandwich, makes himself a cup of tea, goes out into his minuscule and somewhat neglected garden, sits on the unscrubbed rustic bench at the edge of the scruffy lawn, sips, and thinks about the next chapter of his book.

For just a fraction of a second the phone is ringing in the Acropolis. Then William, realising that there were no phones in Ancient Greece, gets up and wanders, not very fast, into the house. He's too late. The phone stops just as he gets to it. He finishes his cup of tea, not hurrying – let the world wait – and only then does he check to see if there's a message on his answerphone. There is. He doesn't know whether to be pleased or sorry, but before he has heard twenty words he's sorry.

'Oh, hello, William. I hope you're well. It's Colin here. I'm . . . um . . . I'm afraid we've got a major problem with . . . um . . . with Naomi. Um . . . she's . . . um . . . well, look, I just think you need to ring me. Sorry about this. I'm . . . I'm on my way to see her, in the . . . well, perhaps I'd better not tell you anything until we can talk. I mean, everything's all right. I think. I'm . . . um . . . I'm on the platform at the station. I'm catching the train. I . . . um . . . I haven't got the car, because . . . well, that's sort of like part of the problem. Look, I'll explain when you ring. Anyway, not to worry, don't panic. It's not . . . well, I mean, it is serious, but . . . you know . . . things are going to be all right, but I think I should be with her and . . . um . . . maybe you'll think you should too, when you . . . when I've told you what . . . um . . . what it's all about. I mean, I don't know how you're fixed, obviously, but if you could. Anyway, give me a ring on my mobile and I'll explain, though I may not want to say too much if I'm on the train and people are listening, you know how it is on trains, and I mean, it is all a bit private. Anyway, this is much too long a message, so I'll stop now. And, as I say, I'll tell you more if you can ring me on my mobile, not my landline. Oh, heavens, you may not have the number. It's . . .'

Colin has given the number and rung off. William realises that he should have written the number down. He presses to save the message, then has an awful moment when he wonders if he's actually pressed to delete it. He dials the number again.

'Oh, hello, William. I . . .'

Thank goodness. He presses to save it again, goes upstairs to get a piece of paper and a pen, comes downstairs again, dials the answerphone again, and realises with a sinking heart that he has to listen to the whole ruddy message again. It encapsulates everything he dislikes about Colin, his lack of organisation, his long-windedness, his repetitious nature, the extraordinary lack of clarity and quality in his speech patterns. During the long reaches of that interminable message he takes refuge in his prejudice against Colin. It saves him from worrying about Naomi.

He writes down the number, hangs up, and hesitates. He doesn't want to ring Colin's number. He dreads what might have happened to Naomi. Then he plucks up his courage and dials. He is desperately nervous. His heart is racing. What on earth has happened to his darling?

His darling. How he has neglected her.

'Hello.'

'It's me, Colin.'

'Oh, thank goodness. Listen, William, don't worry—'

'You've said that. What's happened?'

'Naomi is in . . . it's not as bad as it sounds . . . hospital.'

'What? Why?'

'The police . . .'

'Police?'

'. . . brought her home last night.'

Colin tells him the story of the events of the previous evening, how Naomi had driven off in his car, how he and Emily had heard nothing all night.

'I managed to persuade her to go to school, I thought she'd be better off with her friends than just hanging around in the house waiting, and I honestly think she was glad to get away from me, quite honestly, and then half an hour or so ago I got a call from Clodsbury District Hospital.'

'Clodsbury?'

'I know. I know. She'd collapsed in the market area. Don't panic. She's going to be all right. As I say, she'd collapsed in the market area. There's a very big Muslim population in Clodsbury.'

'I know. I know. But what was she doing there?'

'It's this anti-God thing again. She was shouting at them not to believe in Muhammad.'

'Oh, my God. Well, no, that's not quite appropriate.'

'Apparently she was telling them that it's all nonsense that terrorists will be rewarded with unlimited virgins when they get to heaven.'

'Oh, my . . .'

'Exactly. She said that if it was true the people who were telling them this would be off to heaven themselves like a shot.'

'Oh, my . . .'

'Exactly.'

'How do you know all this?'

'I've spoken to the police. They were called to the market. They found she'd collapsed and they . . . they said they had reason to believe that the state of her mind was disturbed . . .'

'I'll say. Oh, Colin.'

'I know. I know. I'm really sorry to have to tell you all this. I realise that it's all been coming on. But I didn't notice. Anyway, the police got her straight into an ambulance . . .'

'You mean, they were sensible?'

'I know. I know. Hard to believe.'

'So what's wrong with her? Physically.'

'They aren't sure, but not a lot, they think. I mean, it doesn't look as if she'd slept and she was very weak and very dehydrated so she probably hasn't eaten or drunk anything.'

'Oh, dear.'

'Um . . . the thing is, the police are worried about . . . well, her mental state.'

'What?'

'I know.'

'I'll come up.'

'Will you? Oh, thank you, William.'

'Well, of course I will. I'm her bloody father.'

Colin has never heard William swear before.

'Oh, thank you, William. I'd be very grateful. I think she's going to need us both.'

'I'm sure. I'm sure. What about Emily?'

'Oh, my God.'

'What?'

'I've forgotten to do anything about her.'

'You've forgotten?'

'It's been a shock, William.'

'You forgot your daughter?'

'I know. Well, stepdaughter. Daughter-in-law. Step-daughter-in-law. God, I can't work out quite what she is.'

Imbecile.

'For Christ's sake, don't split hairs at a time like this. Ring that number at the school. They'll be able to arrange some-body for her to go and stay with, I'm sure.'

'Yeah, I'm sure they will. Thanks. Oh, William, I'm really sorry about that. You can tell what sort of a panic I've been in.'

'Yes, yes. Get off and ring them.'

'Will do. William, do you know where Clodsbury District Hospital is?'

'Is the name a bit of a hint? Could it possibly be in Clodsbury?'

No, William. Wrong time. Besides, you're not a schoolmaster any more. You've retired from sarcasm.

'No, what I mean is . . . do you have this new sat nav thing?'

No sense of humour. Bit of a drawback in a comedy writer.

'Of course I don't.'

'Will you drive?'

'Have to. The trains are diabolical in East Anglia. The roads, too. I'll be ages.'

'I'll phone you on your mobile with directions when I get to the hospital.'

'I don't have a mobile.'

'What?'

'I know. I know. Naomi tried to persuade me to have one. Julian bought me one. I couldn't make it work. I lost my temper with it and threw it into the Deben.'

'Into the what?'

Ignoramus.

'It's a river. Look, forget all this. Ring off and phone the school. I'll find my way to the hospital. I'm not senile, and I'll see you there.'

'Fine. I won't leave till you arrive.'

'Good. Thanks, Colin, for letting me know.'

'That's all right. See you, then.'

'Yep.'

'Oh. Bring some ID.'

'Well, I always do, but why?'

'They've got a police guard on her.'

'Haven't they got any serious crime to go to?'

261

'I know. Probably serious crime frightens them more than an unemployed sitcom artiste.'

'Right. I must get started.'

'Yes. Oh, and William?'

'Yes?'

'Thanks.'

'Oh, shut up and let me get started.'

'Sorry. Bye. And William?'

'What?'

'Thanks.'

Pillock.

William looks at the map and calculates that it's just over two hundred miles from front door to pillock. He makes himself another cheese sandwich for the journey – Wensleydale, his favourite – stuffs a few overnight things into a bag, and sets off.

When he returns home, Timothy soaks in a hot bath. He's rather addicted to hot baths, although it is a bit of a love-hate relationship.

As he soaps himself, he reflects on his momentous day on the moors. He feels a sense of power that is quite new to him. It began, he thinks, on his visit to the Cadogan, when he suddenly found that he was no longer embarrassed in front of all those blind people. He visits his father regularly, and on subsequent visits he has again felt free, or at least almost entirely free, from the inhibitions he has suffered throughout his life.

Today, he also feels free from the constraints of religion, and he doesn't feel it as a loss. He will not become a wicked person overnight.

He washes his hair, and lies there, steaming, thinking. It's only a few hours since he was watching, and listening to, that magnificent skylark. Magnificent, yes, but no more magnificent than every other skylark, whereas you would be lucky to meet two magnificent people in a year.

Timothy has decided what he wants to do with the rest of his working life. He wants to work with birds. He has no idea how to go about this, but the obvious thing to do is to approach the Royal Society for the Protection of Birds.

The window of the bathroom is open, letting in the warm, slightly oily air of the town on this lovely late afternoon.

He decides to be just a little bit naughty. Instead of rinsing his hair with clean water through the mobile shower attachment, he ducks his head into the bathwater and moves it from side to side until all the shampoo has gone out of it. Well, almost all, because there will now be diluted shampoo in the bathwater. Hannah had caught him doing this once.

'That is so filthy,' she had said. 'That is so disgusting. Why do you do these things when you know they upset me?'

His reply of, 'I didn't know you were going to come in at that moment,' hadn't appeased her.

'The bathwater's dirty. Now your hair's all dirty again,' she had said.

'Not as dirty as it was before,' he had argued. 'There was a whole bathtub of clean water there, so it's only a little dirty.'

'Oh, Timothy, you're incorrigible,' she had said.

He had known it was silly, but a reign of hygiene can do that to a man.

Anyway, Hannah isn't home yet, and he no longer believes that there is a God to witness his little foible. And, had there been, what arrogance, what hubris to believe that the God of all mankind would have time to turn away from war, famine, pestilence and poverty to frown at the sight of Timothy rinsing his hair by ducking his head into the bathwater rather than spraying it with clean water from the mobile shower attachment. Hannah won't be back for another hour at least. An hour of peace before . . . before he has to tell her.

She isn't a bad person. She hasn't stopped his father from coming to the house. It's just that he doesn't like the house as it is. She didn't intend that. Or did she? He doesn't know her any more. Did he ever?

He thinks of all the services they have been to together, with Coningsfield's mighty church dwarfing the congregation. He realises that for years he has prayed without really believing in the efficacy of prayer. And the sermons he has endured in his life. A few months ago, during a particularly dreary homily from a visiting parson, he had calculated, in his head, how much of his life he had spent listening to sermons. Say on average forty sermons a year from the age of five, that's thirty-four years, forty times thirty-four is . . . forty times thirty is four hundred plus four hundred plus four hundred, equals twelve hundred, plus four forties because it was thirty-four years, not thirty, so that makes it one thousand, three hundred and sixty. One thousand three hundred and sixty sermons of average length fifteen minutes, four sermons an hour, one thousand three hundred and sixty divided by four is . . . three hundred and forty. Three hundred and forty hours of his life listening to sermons. Well, some were longer, a few much longer. (The Rev. E.V.Wilmot!) Throw in the odd homily at christenings, weddings and funerals. Say three hundred and fifty. Three hundred and fifty hours of his life spent listening to men, mostly of advanced age and not excessive intellect, telling him how he should lead his life. He couldn't pretend that he regarded it as an economical use of time. Only the hymns still moved him. Oh, those hymns. So beguiling, so addictive. Some of them ought to have a certificate banning the under-fifteens from hearing them. Christian soldiers moving onward into a world where everything was bright and beautiful. Too, too simplistic and persuasive.

He soaks a little bit longer. He knows that he will regret it, but it's so wonderful to lie in hot water with the window open and hear the sounds of cars, buses, angry horns, lawn-mowers, strimmers, people being busy while he does nothing. And he can continue to do nothing for . . . well, almost an hour. And then, this new Timothy, this man who has cast off embarrassment, this man who has come to terms with the fact that he is in the wrong career and is determined to do something about it, this strong man in early middle age, this man who does not need the crutch of faith to find life a worth-while, even a joyous experience, this man will have no trouble in making a strong, simple, moving, generous, elegant speech, a speech of which any great political leader would be proud.

'Hannah, darling, I've something to say to you. Sit down,' says Timothy to the hot and cold taps and the unused mobile shower attachment which is draped round them, working the hot tap with his right foot as he does so, because the water is getting almost lukewarm. 'You may have guessed something of how I feel. You may not have done. I'm very fond of you still, but I no longer love you and maybe I never did love you quite enough. I am therefore unable to offer you the kind of happiness that you need and deserve. I no longer believe in God, and this would become a source of friction between us. You are ambitious, and I have none of the kind of ambition that you have. I'm not going to expand my taxidermy business, as you would like. I'm not going to take on assistants, as you would like. Maybe I would if I was as good as my father, but I'm not. I'm going to sell the busi-ness, and I'm going to apply for a job with the Royal Society for the Protection of Birds. My ambition is to do good work with birds, maybe become a warden at a bird reserve, maybe just be a helper.

'You're an attractive woman, and I have enjoyed making love to you, especially on those Tuesday nights when Dad was playing fives and threes. I suspect that you hold a candle, to use an old-fashioned phrase, for Mr Finch, who is up and coming. Maybe he has already upped and come. I think you are in love with him, though I don't think that you have necessarily realised this yet. How you square that with your religious beliefs, since he's a married man, is not for me to say. Let there be no critical thoughts at this difficult time. So, Hannah, our marriage will soon be over. I should not have married you, because I still love Naomi and always did, but I'm not sorry I did, we have had some good times, and I will always remember those. I hope that you and Mr Finch will be happy together, will eventually be free to marry, and will have a great life in which you will both be up and coming.'

Timothy knows, in his heart, that nobody speaks like that, and that he will never make that speech in that form. What he doesn't know is that he isn't going to make a speech at all, in any form.

At last he gets out of the bath, carefully, water streaming onto the floor, his last act of defiance against a strict hygienic regime. He feels so hot. The moment he moves, he can feel himself beginning to break out into a gentle sweat. He's going to need a bath. It's always like this, it's ridiculous, showers are so much better, especially in summer, but they are not for him; he doesn't like their brevity, he doesn't like having to wipe the shower down afterwards, he doesn't like stepping out of the warm cubicle into a bathroom which seems cold by comparison.

He puts his feet into his slippers. That's another act that would have made Hannah frown. 'You should put socks on before you put your clean feet into slippers that aren't as clean as them, otherwise you'll soon need to wash your feet

266

again.' That must have been at least a year ago, but he can hear her voice as if it was yesterday.

He wanders, slowly, enjoying his nakedness, up the narrow stairs to his workroom. He looks around it, calculating how much time his remaining commitments will take, how long it will be before he can begin his new career.

He has to sit down. His bath has exhausted him. It's knocked all the stuffing out of him. Suddenly he feels that he hasn't the energy to tell Hannah that it's over. But he must. He must.

He goes down to the bathroom, leans out of the window, feeling the cool onset of evening on his face and shoulders. Then he towels his hair, taking the edge off the wetness, and applies some leave-on conditioner.

He goes into their bedroom, looks a little sadly at the bed, and suddenly feels a surge of desire for Hannah. He glances at the alarm clock. He still just about has time to take advantage of his nakedness.

He leaps into the bed and starts to make love to Hannah for the last time. Oh, Hannah, Hannah, this is . . . it *is* a shame. I still . . . Oh, Hannah, you're still lovely. And then suddenly it's Naomi there in bed with him. No, no, Naomi. Not now. Go. Please go. Later. Please go. Your time will come. I hope. Oh, Hannah, Hannah, Hannah.

When it's over he feels sad, slightly repelled, vaguely ashamed. It has been like this lately, even when she's there in person.

He begins to dress, carefully choosing colours which match sufficiently well not to irritate Hannah. She must not be irritated this evening.

His new-found confidence is struggling. He feels a pit in his stomach as the moment of her return draws near. The sound of the front door is painful to him. His heart begins to race. How does the body understand so well what is going

267

on in the mind? And is he right to be doing this? After all, he does still seem to want her body. Should he abort the plan? No. Be brave. Or wait, do it later. Oh, God. No, no help there.

He goes into the lounge, which she calls the sitting room, because Mr Finch calls his lounge the sitting room. She enters. Her face is very pale. She is twisting her hands.

'There's no easy way of saying this, Timothy,' she says. 'I'd sort of half rehearsed a speech, but you deserve a bit better than a speech. I love Gerald. I'm . . . I'm going to go and live with him, Timothy.'

It's a total shock. He feels a disturbing sense of déjà vu. Is this his fate as an emotional being – to be constantly pre-empted?

'Oh, Timothy, I'm sorry,' she continues. 'And you can say, "Oh, that's rich. You're sorry. Well, why do it then?" Well, we can't help ourselves. It's rough on Helen – that's his wife – and it's wrong in the sight of God, I suppose, and Gerald is just as religious as me, and Helen isn't, so it's all, I don't know, ironic, maybe just messy.'

It's a shock, but it's what he wanted, or at least almost wanted, and Timothy husband of Hannah is a stronger and a better man than Timothy husband of Maggie. This time he feels no hurt pride.

'I don't feel happy about this, Timothy, but I don't think I need to feel too guilty. I don't believe you ever really loved me. Not like Gerald does. Sorry, perhaps that's insensitive. I'll remember you fondly, Timothy, especially . . . well, you know. I'm going now, there's no point in hanging about, is there, when your mind's made up, and we both hate farewells. I'll come and collect my things, we can arrange that at a mutually convenient time. Oh, Lord, "mutually convenient", that sounds like lawyers. You're a good man and a kind man and I won't make trouble and I know people say that and then do but I won't. Gerald's outside, waiting, which may not be exactly tactful, but there it is, it seemed best to get it over with.' She kisses him swiftly on the cheek, and he's pleased to detect a bit of a break in her voice as she says, 'Goodbye, Timothy. And good luck.'

And he doesn't say anything, not a word, because the only thing he can think of to say is, 'My speech would have been much better than yours,' and that is hardly appropriate.

He walks through the warm evening air to the Wig and Mitre in Granary Lane. He takes his pint into the beer garden. Romance is in the air this summer's night. Only Timothy is alone. But he doesn't feel sad. He feels light-headed, not quite rooted in reality, in an emotional limbo between happiness and sadness, relief and regret. An observer would not notice this. He would see a solid man reading an evening paper, eyes narrowed as the light fades, and drinking three pints of bitter in reflective silence.

He walks home slowly. The heat of the day still rises from the pavements. When he gets home he will have another bath and leave lots of water all over the floor. Further than that he cannot see.

Naomi awakes very slowly, from a deep darkness, a bottomless blackness, a dank pit. She finds it very difficult to open her eyes. A great weight is pressing down on both her eyes. She realises what the weight is. It's her eyelids. She has no idea where she is. She has only a faint idea who she is.

She stares at the only thing she can see without moving – and she cannot move, she is possessed of a tiredness that is in part a quite delicious languor and in part a horrible constriction.

The only thing she can see is a corner, a corner where three areas of grimy flaky white paint meet, and from which there hangs an intricate pattern of faintly shining filaments. It takes her a few moments to realise that this is a spider's web. Contract cleaning hasn't worked very well at Clodsbury District Hospital.

Slowly, so slowly, she begins the long, painful journey towards full consciousness. She is Naomi Coppinger, née Walls. She is in a bed. She wakes up in a bed every day. Why does it feel so very strange to wake up in this bed? Not just because she doesn't know where she is. That's happened before. Often during the tour of *Antony and Cleopatra* she woke up in some strange theatrical digs, not knowing where she was, her mouth acid from the cheap wine of a struggling theatre bar, in a bed that twanged when she turned to try to understand her surroundings.

She's an actress! Well, she was an actress. The knowledge of her unemployment gushes to the surface, and is most unwelcome.

She can't remember going to bed. That's why she feels so strange. The last thing she remembers is – and suddenly she's alarmed – two policemen walking towards her. Lots and lots of black people everywhere, women wearing veils, and two massive policemen with huge feet; she can't remember their faces, but she can still see the size of their feet. But why should policemen have been approaching her? Are they still here? She tries to sit up, but it's a huge effort, her limbs are strangely leaden.

Although she knows that she knows the man who is sitting at the side of the bed looking at her with deep concern and not a little fear, she has no idea who he is. He is at once utterly familiar and totally unidentifiable. This is very disconcerting.

She begins to remember. He's the man who keeps promising to take her to the Ivy and doesn't. That's not nice of him. Oh, he's her husband. Crikey. He's that Coppinger bloke.

What's his Christian name? Ought to know her husband's Christian name.

Why does the word 'Christian' alarm her so much, even in her thoughts?

Colin. That's it.

Oh, Lord, she doesn't want Colin to see her like this.

'You're awake!' says Colin, and a little imp deep inside Naomi sits up and thinks, You still have your talent for stating the obvious, then. Whatever's happened, that hasn't changed.

She senses that she should reply, that Colin is waiting for her to reply. She doesn't want to reply. She's worried about the mechanism of voice production. How does the connection between thinking and speaking work? It takes a huge effort, swimming in this lethargy, swimming against the tide of the approaching night, to even formulate the two words, 'Hello, Colin.' But she tries. She does it. Out come the words, 'Hello, Colin.'

First hurdle over. But why is everything so very difficult?

Colin looks across the bed, she follows his eyes and sees . . . her father! She recognises him instantly. Her dear, distant dad. Only he doesn't look so distant. He's smiling, and his smile is warm, radiant. He wipes a tear from his eye, and she thinks, I never saw my dad cry before, not even when Mummy died.

When Mummy died! All that comes back. She's waking up now, with difficulty, fighting the drugs, although of course she doesn't know that this is what she is fighting. She knows where she is now, though. She can see the drips attached to her arm. That's very alarming.

'Why am I in hospital?'

Her father puts his large, gnarled, yachtsman's hand into her tiny veined one, presses gently, and tells her, very softly, very carefully, all that he knows of what happened to her, culminating in her long drive to Clodsbury, and her

271

sensational appearance at a street market where she harangued a crowd of astonished Muslims, mostly veiled ladies who were busy doing their shopping.

'You tried to turn a large crowd of Islamic women into atheists, my darling.' There is concern and astonishment in her father's voice, but also . . . yes . . . respect.

She looks down, trying to see her body, but it's hidden beneath the sheets. She is suddenly terrified. Has she perhaps no legs? She can't feel them. But she can't feel the absence of legs. But do you feel the absence of legs at first or do the nerves continue to give you the illusion of having legs?

'How badly injured am I?'

'Why, bless you, you aren't injured at all, my darling.'

Her father, the least tactile of men, bends over and kisses the top of her head.

'But didn't they tear me limb from limb?'

'We aren't in some primitive corner of the world, where the white man is unknown. You were very weak, we don't believe you'd eaten for two days. They saw this and one of them rang for an ambulance on their mobile. You crashed to the ground, and somebody told the crowd not to move you. It's dangerous to move someone in those circumstances, so they didn't. They were really very good.'

'But my message, didn't it inflame them?'

'I get the impression they were just astonished. I imagine that you made quite a picture, my darling. A slight little girl, faint from hunger and exhaustion, shouting like a mighty wind.'

She squeezes her father's hand. It's so good to have him there. She's so lucky to have such a father.

'But . . . the police?'

'I think somebody sent for them too. I don't know why. Maybe they thought you needed protection.'

'They had enormous feet.'

'Anyway, they arranged for you to come here.'

'No, but both of them had enormous feet. I mean, that's a bit of a coincidence, isn't it? Unless that's the qualification for the police force. I certainly don't think it's intelligence.'

William and Colin exchange very brief concerned looks.

'Yes, darling, but I don't think we really need to worry too much about their feet, do we?'

'No, but I was thinking . . . I think you're right, I'd forgotten to eat, I think I might have been hallucinating a bit, and I wondered, did I just imagine they had such huge feet? I mean, really huge. Not just big. Massive.'

'I think perhaps you did, sweetheart. You've done all sorts of things, and we know why you've done them, but you did get rather carried away. It wasn't very sensible, was it, rushing off like that in my car, after spending all day knocking on people's doors. You hadn't eaten a thing. You hadn't slept for well over twenty-four hours. If you did . . . you know . . . see their feet, in your mind, as unnaturally large, well, it's understandable, and maybe it was a symbol of . . . of being frightened at seeing the police. Anyway, the thing is . . .' He presses his hand gently onto hers again. 'The thing is, the police were concerned for your . . . I'm sorry, darling, but you can understand their point of view . . . your mental state. They don't know you like we do. Now the police were very anxious to find out, when you woke up, how . . . how you were.'

'Whether I was mad, you mean?'

'No, no. No, just . . . still a bit disturbed. So, they left a man here, to see how you were. And he stayed until we came.'

'You saw him?'

'I had to show him my driving licence before he'd let me in. Though how that proved I was your father I don't know. Still, it's lucky they didn't ask for some sperm to analyse. They'd still be waiting.'

It crosses Naomi's mind that she never thought she'd live to hear her father use a word like 'sperm', but she has another worry on her mind.

'Did he have very big feet?'

'I didn't notice.'

'He can't have had, then. You'd have noticed. You couldn't not.'

'He might not have been one of the same two officers.'

'Of course. Silly of me. Sorry.'

'Try not to worry about the feet.'

'No, but it's not nice to think you may have hallucinated.'

'Well, it's over now.'

'Yes.'

She smiles. How her father loves to see that smile. It's pure Naomi.

'So he's gone, has he, the policeman? Now you're here. He's not worried any more?'

'Yes. He's not worried any more. He's plodded off on his big feet.'

They share a little laugh. How her father loves to hear that laugh. It's pure Naomi.

'But, because they are concerned, we've had to promise to look after you and take care of you until . . . while you get your strength back. So, for the time being, you're going to have to promise to do what we tell you and be a good girl . . . and not . . . you know . . .'

'What?'

'. . . try to save the world from religion. Will you promise that for us, Naomi?'

'Us?'

'Colin and me.'

'Oh.'

'Will you? For the time being at least.'

'Will I what? Sorry. I'm so tired.'

'Will you promise not to try to save the world from religion?'

'Oh. Yes. I promise.'

As the glorious summer day approaches its midnight end, Colin goes to the Clodsbury Hilton, which on first sight promises to be as good as it sounds, and books a twin room for himself and William. They'll take shifts, one of them sleeping, the other sitting in the hospital, until Naomi is fit to leave.

Naomi feels so very tired again, after the exertion of conversation and the trauma of memory. She snuggles back into the sheets and pillows, and lies there, waiting for sleep. But, even under sedation, sleep doesn't come straight away. She tries not to worry about the policemen's feet, and whether she has hallucinated. She reflects on everything that has happened. She thinks about her wanderings along unlovely Oxford Street with her sandwich board, and about her door-to-door visits on the even more unlovely Warrender Estate, and about her drive up the M1, overtaking all the juggernauts, touching at one stage a hundred and eighteen miles an hour. She's amazed now, that the old car managed it. She shudders at the thought of the speed, which had so exhilarated her at the time.

She sees all the faces of the astonished Muslim women, and they aren't frightening at all any more. It's curious. She knows that she has done all those things – she must have done them because she's been told that she has – but she can't really remember them. It's as if they've happened to someone else, or have just been a story.

Then she thinks about the evening's conversation, in the ward, beneath the spider's web, whose presence comforts her, though perhaps it should alarm her. But above all she thinks of her father, how much more wonderful he is than she has ever realised.

275

And then suddenly, a single word, a word of just two letters, courses through her like an electric shock.

'Us?'

She remembers being puzzled when her father said, 'Will you promise that for us, Naomi?' She hadn't known what he meant by us. She had forgotten Colin was there.

That isn't good.

PART SEVEN

Farewells

1999–2002

Naomi is going home today, and she's nervous. She doesn't know whether she wants to go home, especially as Emily is staying with Simon and Francesca for the summer holidays. That makes sense, of course, but sense isn't always what a person wants.

She has really enjoyed staying with her father, in his square, ugly, red-brick house beside the river. But it's time to leave. Tomorrow he will be going to his boat, to prepare for his annual cruise. It's been wonderful to spend two idle summer weeks with him, doing nothing, eating regular meals, going for long, leisurely walks and cycle rides, talking intermittently about her mother, about some of his pupils and their escapades, about ancient Greece and Rome. He has revealed to her a great secret – that he loves the poems of Catullus. He has read them to her, in the evenings, in Latin and in an English translation. She hasn't understood a word of the Latin, but she liked the sound of it, and it was amazing how sombre and classical and scholarly the poems sounded in Latin, and how rude and wild and immediate they sounded in English.

'"Lesbia, forever spitting fire at me, is never silent. And now if Lesbia fails to love me, I shall die. Why?

Do I know in truth her passion burns for me? Because I am like her,
   because I curse her endlessly. And still, O hear me gods
   I love her."
'Catullus gives a wonderful insight into the excesses of Rome, Naomi. Sexual excesses above all, often homosexual, sometimes cruel, then suddenly tender. Exhilarating, depraved, repulsive, joyous, never never dull. And the fact that they are in Latin gives them a patina of respectability, so that a retired Classics master, who is an elder in his church, and who has practised moderation in all his pleasures, can dream of being someone very different, and can enjoy the dream, safe in the knowledge that he would hate it if it were ever to become more than a dream.
'"O Cato listen, here's something so fantastic
   it deserves your laughter,
   laugh then as heartily as you love your Catullus:
'"I saw a boy and girl (the boy on top) so I fell,
   chiefly to please Dione,
   upon the boy and pierced him,
   held him to his duty with my rigid spearhead."
'How different from our life in the Lower Cragley Road. I received a parcel this morning, Naomi, a little gift from Mrs Wynne-Ellison. "We are thinking of you, in this lovely summer weather, and I can't resist sending you a jar of my legendary gooseberry chutney. Best ever this year, I think." Catullus delighted in rampant heterosexual and homosexual sex. I delight in gooseberry chutney. Naomi?'

This in a different voice, a lower register. Naomi had looked up.

'I love you.'

Naomi had tried hard to hide her shock. She hadn't heard her father say anything remotely like that, ever.

And now her father is driving her away from the wide

skies and the salt marshes towards the endless dispiriting suburbs of East London, and with every mile her nervousness grows. She has thought a great deal about what happened, what she has done, how unfair it has all been to Colin. There has even been a corner of her that accepted the gentle suggestion of her father's doctor that it was all a cry for help from a woman unhappy in marriage and deeply disappointed in her career. When she had told her father what Dr Pelham had said, he had been angry.

'I know my daughter better than that,' he had said, 'and I'll tell Pelham so next time I want a boil lanced. "Pelham," I will say. "She has more passion and sincerity in her left elbow than you have in your whole body."'

'Please don't. And why do you say "left elbow" rather than "little finger"?'

'I'm a writer now. I avoid clichés.'

'The cliché's actually better, Dad.'

He had smiled and then looked at her with penetrating seriousness. 'It still burns, doesn't it, my darling, your desire to lead us away from the promised land?' he had said.

'It still burns.'

'But you can't fight fanaticism with fanaticism. You need better, softer, gentler, more persuasive weapons.'

'I know.'

'You do, don't you? You do know? You won't do anything stupid?'

'No, Dad.' This just a trifle wearily. 'I won't do anything stupid.'

Now they are arriving at Narcissus Road. It's more than two years since she moved with Colin to West Hampstead, but she still doesn't have the feeling of coming home. The sight of this street of identical characterless houses depresses Naomi enormously. She longs to be back by the gentle East Anglian river. How mean the street looks.

She tries so hard not to be irritated by the heavy weather her father makes of reversing into a parking space that is only just large enough. She has long been aware that there are two Naomis: a patient, loving, considerate Naomi, and the Naomi of the motor car, a snarling tigress. She closes her eyes, tries to breathe slowly, calmly, thinks of her love for Emily, but that only makes her anxious too.

At last the job is done, though the car is still at an angle of at least five degrees from the pavement.

'I'll come in and see everything's all right,' says her father, and she's pleased. She dreads his departure.

Colin's out. The house is so quiet. And so small. It was never big, but surely it wasn't as small as this? Can you shrink a house?

There's a note on the kitchen table, and what a sad affair the kitchen table is.

The note is sadder still.

Dear Naomi,

This letter will come as a great shock, and, believe me, I don't enjoy writing it. I have decided that I can't cope with our marriage any more. I don't say that I don't love you, but I don't love you enough any more to be able to deal with the hard work that our marriage would inevitably be.

This isn't just to do with how you've behaved in the last few months, although it hasn't been easy, and I have to say that I think you have been very selfish. Well, that may be the wrong word, because you didn't think you were doing it for yourself and I do appreciate your point of view. Maybe I should just say that you have been very difficult to live with, and that goes for Emily as much as for me, and I think you need to think about that.

No, but it goes back further, and it's all to do with the fact of my writing that bloody sitcom with you in it. I was so pleased you were doing it when I first met you at that very

282

first read-through, but the moment the second series began I knew that the fact that I was in love with you inhibited my writing those scenes. It was a bad part because it wasn't really what the sitcom was about, and I was embarrassed to have you in such a bad part, and that made it even more difficult to write, so it became an even worse part.

I despise myself for not having the courage to tell you this face to face. I remember you telling me how you went to that taxidermist twit's place and told him you were leaving him, which on the evidence of his behaviour at the show that night was more than he deserved. I am not a brave person. That's why I was too shit scared about my career to stand up for my principles when they wanted me to write you out, even though because it was bad maybe I was doing you a favour by writing you out.

This is the third draft of this letter, well, I'm used to writing lots of drafts for the bloody Beeb, but I do want you to know I'm not taking writing it easily.

I just have the feeling, with great regret, that there just isn't enough left between us for us to be able to work on making the marriage work.

An unworthy thought flashes across Naomi's mind. This letter isn't very well written – for a writer.

There's also Emily. She's a great girl but I can't really relate to her. No doubt the fault is entirely mine.

As you know, I'm trying to write a novel, a really ambitious state of the nation novel, searingly satirical and passionate, and I will get round to it some time, but I need to eat so I have been working on an idea for a new sitcom set in a dentist's surgery, which I think is a very promising idea. I'm calling it 'Third Molar from the Left'. An independent company is very keen on it, no money yet, but it looks promising. If it comes off, I'll try to write a part in it for you.

*When we're not together, who knows, I may be able to write
funny lines for you.*

*I saw your brother Julian in the Ivy the other day, with a
very pretty girl. I was going to go up to him and say something, but they started having a row, and she stormed out. He
stayed on. I could see that they'd ordered the* poulet landaise
*I think it's called, which is for two. He sat there for ages
ploughing through it, valiantly trying to finish it, but
something about his face told me that it wouldn't be a very good
time to go up to him and chat. Also I wouldn't have known
what to say if he'd asked me about us. He did look over
towards us but I don't think he recognised me. People don't.
I've never kidded myself that I'm dripping with charisma.*

*Naomi, I still think you're great and a much better person
than me. One day you'll look back on this letter, and think,
'Thank God . . .' Oh, shit, I shouldn't have said that, but I'm
not going to tear this up and start a fourth draft. What I
mean is, you will look back and be glad to be free of your
wimpish second-rate writer husband, who so typically ran out
on you at your moment of greatest need.*

With love, apologies and happy memories.

Colin.

*P.S. Don't be mad about the Ivy. I know you always
wanted to go and I never took you, but I had to go, this was a
real business opportunity. Nothing came of it, but I wasn't to
know that.*

Naomi hands her father the letter. He sits down to read it.
She opens her meagre, unpromising pile of mail. She isn't
interested in a giant carpet sale. Her house is much too small
for a giant carpet. She can't afford to give to Guide Dogs for
the Blind or Amnesty International or the Home for Retired
Actors. Her inability to give to charity shames her.

Her father puts the letter down and looks at her with
compassion.

284

'Pillock,' he says at last. 'Sorry, Naomi, but he is.'

The fact that Colin is a pillock doesn't make Naomi welcome his decision. In fact, she wants to cry. But she's determined not to.

'Julian should never order any dish that's for two. Terribly risky,' she says with a brave smile.

Her father smiles back. She thinks what a lovely smile he has. What a pity he hasn't used it more.

'So, what's to be done?' he asks.

'I'll be fine. I'll survive.'

Her father stares at the ceiling, stands abruptly, goes to the window, looks out over Narcissus Road, with its rows of mean houses neatly parked in rows and its lines of cars, also neatly parked, with one exception. Naomi knows what he's seeing. The road is the River Crouch, where he keeps his beloved yawl. The cars are boats, gently swinging on their moorings. Her father is slipping past them towards foreign parts, under engine, just about to raise the mainsail.

'I'll take you home,' he says, in a voice suddenly hoarse.

'You can't. You're going sailing.'

'I won't go.'

'That's ridiculous. You always go.'

'Well, this year I won't. I can't abandon you.'

'Dad, I'm all right.'

He can't stop himself from giving her a doubting look.

'I am, Dad. I don't think I was ever mad, I think I was just . . . a bit obsessed . . . well, all right, a lot obsessed . . . but I'm fine now. I'll be all right. I promise.'

'I don't think I can do it, darling.'

He looks up at the ceiling and his lips move.

'What are you thinking?' Naomi asks, though she knows.

William looks slightly embarrassed.

'I was asking your mother for forgiveness. For going away for a month every year. For only knowing now that some things are more important than my pleasures. I've been a selfish man.'

'No, Dad.'

'Well . . . a bit. Quite a lot, actually.'

'Well, you're being very unselfish now.'

'Not really. I'm suggesting it – and it's actually more than a suggestion, I'm telling you, I'm not going sailing, my mind is made up – because if I did go, and anything happened to you while I was away, I wouldn't be able to live with myself, and I'm all I've got. You see. Not at all an unselfish motive.'

'I believe in judging people by their actions, not their motives, Dad.'

'Wise words, from a very special girl. Of course I can't go. I mean it, Naomi.'

Naomi gives him a searching look. He stares back, unafraid of meeting her eyes. She breaks away first. She knows now that he means it.

'Let's get back,' he says. 'I'll have to ring Carruthers and tell him the sailing's off.'

'Carruthers?'

'Ridley. But I always call him Carruthers. He's a Carruthers to me, last of that soon-to-be-extinct breed of Englishmen who shy away from the intimacy of friendship and call each other by their surnames. Anything you need to take?'

Naomi gathers a few things together, puts them in the car, locks the door of her unloved house, remembers, unlocks the door, rushes up the mean stairs, into the mean marital bedroom, opens the third drawer down of the chest of drawers, pulls out from among her knickers the sepia photograph of the handsome young man that Timothy had once seen all those years ago, but which she has always hidden from Simon and from Colin, hurries down the stairs, locks the door again, puts the photograph carefully on top of all the items piled onto the back seat of the car, and smiles apologetically at her father, who gives her an understanding smile in return.

She offers to drive.

'Wouldn't hear of it. No fit state.'

Yet that is the extraordinary thing. She is in a fit state.

William drives back rather faster than usual, which pleases Naomi. Curiously, under the circumstances, he is happy. He even hums once or twice, and two or three times, on straight stretches of road, he runs his left hand affectionately down her right arm. Naomi feels extraordinarily happy, and that is even more curious, under the circumstances.

The phone is ringing as they enter the house. Her father doesn't hurry, risks the caller ringing off, but the caller doesn't.

'Hello . . . Ridley! I was just going to ring you . . . What? How? When? . . .' He gives Naomi a thumbs-up and a very theatrical grin. What's going on? 'Oh, that's terrible . . . Well, what bad luck . . . Well, of course you can't.' He gives a tiny leap into the air. Naomi is nonplussed. 'I'm so sorry, Ridley . . . Well, no, you can't say that. You're not letting me down. How can you say you're letting me down? . . . Well, of course I'm disappointed.' He gives another thumbs-up. 'Dreadfully disappointed.' He puts his free hand to his nose and mimes elongating it furiously. 'Well, thank you so much for letting me know. And I really am sorry,. Truly sorry. I hope it mends very quickly.' He puts the phone down and does a little, hopelessly inelegant jig, then roars triumphantly, 'Ridley has broken his leg!'

Naomi stares at him.

'What?'

'In two places. Chelmsford and Colchester.'

He roars with laughter at his joke. Naomi is astounded. She's never seen him like this. He's like a naughty, over-excited child.

287

But now he sobers up.

'No. I mustn't laugh.'

But then the naughty, inappropriate delight steals over his face again.

'My sailing companion has fallen off a ladder. He cannot go sailing. Hallelujah!'

'I can see that this lets you off the hook about letting him down, but why are you so delighted?'

'Because I'm going to take you.'

Naomi stares at him again.

'I've never sailed in my life, Dad.'

'Well, we aren't going far, Only to Denmark. You'll come, won't you? You're a girl of spirit. You're *my* girl.'

'There's Emily.'

'Oh, blast. So there is. Lovely girl. Gem. Can't you phone? She may be perfectly happy with Simon and long name.'

'Francesca. Yes, I suppose I could phone. But, Dad, I'll be useless. No help.'

'We aren't going round Cape Horn. Do me the favour of believing that I am a highly competent sailor and a fully qualified captain of my ship.'

'I haven't got any clothes.'

'East Anglia is weighed down with yachting clothes. That's why it tilts. That's why it floods. Phone.'

Naomi phones.

'Oh, hello, Francesca. How's things? . . . Good. Brilliant. Look, Francesca, something's come up. Ridley – that's the man my father sails with, but he calls him Carruthers, I don't know why – has broken his leg . . . I don't know his Christian name. Maybe he hasn't got one. So, he can't go sailing with my dad. So my dad wants me to go . . . Well, tomorrow . . . About a month. I know it's impossible, but I thought I'd ask . . . Do you mean it? For a whole month? . . . Are you absolutely sure? . . . That's good to hear. But what about

Simon? . . . Are you sure? . . . Look, is . . . Thank you . . . Hi, Emily, are you having a good time? . . . Great. That's, that's just great . . . Oh, much better, thank you. No, I'm fine. Absolutely fine. One hundred per cent. Look, darling, it's a long story, but the man Grampa goes sailing with every August has broken his leg . . . Ridley, that's right, gosh, what a memory. And . . . no, I don't know what his Christian name is either . . . no, sweetheart, of course I'm not worried about calling it a Christian name, all that's over, I mean I still . . . but, no, it's over. But anyway, with Ridley with no Christian name not being able to go sailing, Grampa wants me to keep him company and go instead . . . Well, for about a month . . . Well, yes, I'd like to go, it would be fun, but I won't even dream of going if it would upset you staying on there another month . . . Are you sure? . . . Oh. Well, that's all right, then . . . Oh. Well, that's just great . . . Oh, do you think so? . . . Well, that's great, then. Terrific . . . Denmark . . . Of course I'll send cards. Lots of cards . . . Yes, with storks on, if I can find any . . . So, you'll be good, won't you? . . . I know you are . . . I'll try. I may be a bit frightened . . . I will . . . I love you too.'

She puts the phone down, very slowly. She turns towards her father.

'She's delighted,' she says.

'Good. Good.'

Her father is delighted too, and can't hide it.

'Absolutely delighted.'

'Good. That's good.'

'Thrilled.'

Her father is beginning to realise that it isn't actually all that good.

'She said, "I think the time and space will help you sort yourself out, Mum."'

William shakes his head in wonder at the precocity of

children. He smiles. Naomi tries to join in, but her smile is a sad little affair.

She bursts into tears.

A new millennium. A new start.

The auction takes place at the premises of Tankerley and Phipps, Coningsfield's leading auction house. Correction: Coningsfield's only auction house.

There are a few pieces of Pickering family furniture, mainly Georgian and Victorian and not of spectacular merit, but in the main the lots consist of the works of Roly Pickering, plus a few of Timothy's.

Timothy hasn't found it easy to tell his father that he's retiring from taxidermy, but he had felt confident that the tactful way in which he'd chosen to put it – that he has been far from his father's equal and unworthy to continue the family tradition – would flatter the old man. In the event he had felt that his father's acceptance – 'Take your point, son of mine. Take your point.' – was just a little too ready. A little gentle disagreement – 'No! Unworthy? You. Surely not?' – would perhaps have been a little more tactful on his father's part. Sometimes he felt that all the tact in the relationship went one way.

In fact, Roly was quite excited at the idea of his works coming under the hammer. 'I'm tickled pink. Tickled pink I am. I can't see them any more, so let the world see them. The Roly Pickering Collection goes under the hammer.' He would only be allowed to keep one item in his room at the Cadogan, which had strict regulations on ornaments due to Health and Safety and the cost of modern dusting, and Timothy would take his favourite piece, the three Icelandic puffins, as a memorial to his father's life and talents, but all the other items would be up for sale.

The various lots are on view from nine thirty, with the

sale commencing at ten thirty. Timothy arrives early. He's anxious. He hasn't slept well. He's had the dream, as he so often does before difficult events. It was really vivid, perhaps more vivid than ever, really upsetting. He's woken so bathed in sweat that he's needed a bath. There hasn't been time for one, he hasn't fancied a shower, so he's had to fall back on washing himself from head to foot in cold water. He feels better now, but still shaken. And stirred.

It has been decided that he and his father will split the profits of the sale equally, but it isn't this that worries him. What worries him is that his father's masterpieces won't meet their reserve. It will be awful if the poor, proud man is humiliated in public on this great day.

He's also worried that nobody will come. Then the humiliation will be his, for holding the event.

A few people drift in, a couple of collectors, the owner of a local gallery, a tourist who's forgotten his raincoat and will at least keep dry for a couple of hours, the retired piano teacher who goes to all the auctions and never buys anything, and a taxidermist from the other side of the Pennines, who encourages and discourages Timothy all at once by saying, 'Your father's a great man. A legend in taxidermy circles. His stuff'll sell. Lot of people want to get their hands on a Roly Pickering.' Timothy suddenly wishes he could withdraw the few items of his own making that he has entered.

A tall, thin woman in a shabby coat comes through the door, looks around nervously, then approaches Timothy.

'You're Timothy, aren't you?' she says.

Her eyes are bloodshot. Her complexion is blotchy. Her cheeks are hollow. Her hair is straggly and lifeless. She doesn't look well.

'Yes. Yes, I am,' he agrees cautiously.

'You don't know who I am, do you?'

A door creaks open in the barn of Timothy's heart. An icy wind blows in.

'You're my mother, aren't you?'

She nods apologetically.

'Yes. I'm Josie.'

He hasn't seen her since he was two. He can't have recognised her. Yet he knew. This shakes him, in his delicate post-dream state, more than somewhat.

'Why have you come?'

'I read of the sale.'

'You're not a collector, surely?'

'No. No.'

She has three teeth missing on the left-hand side of her mouth.

She colours slightly in the middle of both cheeks.

'I wanted to see you. I wanted to see how you've turned out.'

'I'm not a cake.'

Her remaining teeth are heavily stained by nicotine.

'I didn't know whether to come. Maybe I should go now I've seen you.'

Timothy is drawn to that gap every time she speaks.

'Well, yes, you could. I'm all present and correct. Two eyes, two ears, two arms, two legs. You can leave, reassured.'

She smiles sadly. That gap again.

'I'm not surprised you're a bit bitter,' she says.

'Well, no. I mean, any marriage can break up, but . . . just to walk out on your son when he was two. Never get in touch again. What do you think that did to my self-esteem?'

'It wasn't personal, Timothy. It was nothing to do with you.'

'Oh, great.'

He gets a whiff of stale gin and armpit. There is about his mother now the air of a woman struggling to run a doomed pub on her own, or spending her weekends alone with eighty cigarettes and a litre of gin in an unmade bed in a static caravan in a very unattractive caravan park in one of the less salubrious stretches of the Lincolnshire coast.

'I shouldn't have come.'

All this in very low voices. A couple of people are looking at them, wondering what this earnest conversation is all about.

'I'm what they used to call a bad lot. Didn't your father tell you?'

'The only thing he told me was that you ran off with a plumber. That upset him. He doesn't like plumbers.'

She tries to laugh. It comes out as a snort. She has a coughing fit. The cough sounds ominous. Timothy is frightened that he will start to feel pity for her.

'Your father's died, I take it.'

'Oh, no, no. No, he's fighting fit still.'

'Oh, Lord. Somehow I assumed he'd died.'

'Why?'

'Well, I suppose because of the sale. Besides, he's the dying type.'

'Is there one?'

'I think so.'

'And you aren't?'

'No.' Her smile is sad. 'I'm the type that should die, but doesn't. Doesn't eat, drinks too much, addicted to drugs, just had double pneumonia for the second time, still here, fuck it. Oh, sorry, sad to find how coarse your mother's become. Will he be coming?'

'Just try to keep him away.'

'I'd better go. I didn't realise he'd be still alive. I don't think he'll want to see me.'

'He won't be able to see you.'

'What do you mean?'

'He's blind.'

'Oh, no. Oh, I'm sorry. I *am* sorry about that. Well, in that case . . . maybe I could stay, watch, see how it goes, not speak to him, he'll never know I was there.'

'If you want to. It's of no account to me.'

'Tell him – it'll cheer him up a bit – the plumber soon ditched me.'

A rather dreadful thought strikes Timothy.

'Do I . . . ?'

'. . . have any half-brothers or sisters? No. You're safe from social embarrassments.'

'Oh, Mum.'

He closes his eyes for just a second.

'You wish you hadn't called me "Mum".'

'How do you know that? How did you know what I was thinking about brothers and sisters?'

She smiles even more sadly.

'I am your mum.'

'I won't sympathise. You didn't have to come.'

She follows his eyes. Roly has arrived, on the arm of a carer. Her mouth drops open slightly as she looks at him. He is looking straight at her and goose pimples run down Timothy's back. Can his father sense her? He even has the thought that maybe his father's eyesight has come back, from the shock, but even as he thinks it he knows that it's crazy, because he wouldn't have had the shock until his eyesight had come back.

His mother waits until his father has been seated, and then goes to sit as far away from him as she can, but behind him, so that she can observe him.

Tommo comes in. Good old Tommo. 'Got a business meeting at twelve,' he tells Timothy. 'Thought I'd pop in for a mo', lend a bit of moral support.' He glances towards the door, doesn't like what he sees. 'Oh, no. Well, I'm not going to sit with him.'

294

Tommo hurriedly goes off and sits down. Timothy looks towards the door and sees what Tommo saw. Sniffy Arkwright has arrived.

'Hello, Sniffy, what brings you here?' he asks, managing to sound pleased.

'Thought I might pick something up. I quite fancy something stuffed.'

'They aren't stuffed, Sniffy. They're modelled, as I told you.'

'Oh, yes. Sorry. My brain! Oh, there's Tommo. Great. I didn't think I'd find anyone to sit with.'

The auction begins, and it goes with a swing from the start.

'Lot one. Peregrine falcon and goldfinch at Gormley Crag. Who'll start me off for this splendid exhibit? Roly Pickering at his very best,' intones the auctioneer in his plummy voice. It goes for fourteen hundred pounds.

'Cheap at the price, for an R. Pickering,' comments the auctioneer.

A golden eagle fetches nine hundred. A wildebeest makes twelve hundred. Even a Victorian commode raises four hundred and fifty.

Sniffy bids for everything, but always pulls out well before things get dangerous.

'Lot twenty-three. One fox, with case. This is a T. Pickering, not an R. Pickering.' The first of Timothy's efforts goes for a rather shaming ninety pounds. Roly's show fox, from the table by the front door in the hall, fetches six hundred.

The unwanted wombat goes up in humiliating single-pound jumps. Sniffy pulls out at twelve pounds. It goes for seventeen.

A magnificent R. Pickering deer is sold to the gallery owner for twelve hundred and fifty pounds. A T. Pickering deer, really almost as magnificent, struggles to get to the hundred mark. Then Tommo suddenly bids a hundred and fifty.

'Two hundred pounds,' cries Timothy's mother.

There's a deep silence in the room now. Everyone is afraid to sneeze or twitch. Josie goes very pale. The auctioneer raises his gavel.

'Going, going . . .'

'Two hundred and ten,' says Tommo.

Timothy sees Josie giving a great sigh of relief. Absurdly, he feels relieved for her too.

Tommo has to leave before the end. Timothy gives him a thumbs-up. He responds with a 'What are friends for?' shrug.

The auction raises the best part of seventy thousand pounds.

Timothy's mother hurries from her seat, and approaches Timothy while Roly is still being helped out of his chair.

'Shall I see you again?' she asks.

He sighs.

'I don't think so, Mum,' he says gently.

'I suppose a kiss is out of the question.'

'Oh, what the hell?'

He kisses her on both cheeks, holding his mouth firmly shut, so that he won't smell the stale gin and nicotine breath.

She hurries out, not looking back.

Sniffy approaches.

'Who's she?' he asks.

'Mind your own business.'

'I see. Well, we can only surmise, then. I tried to buy things. I'm afraid they were just too expensive for me.'

'Not a problem.'

'We should meet some time, have a drink.'

'We should. Ah, Dad.'

Timothy hurries away from Sniffy, and repeats his offer of taking his father to the Majestic for lunch.

'It's kind of you, youngest scion of the House of Pickering. But no. The food will be drizzled artistically all over the plate.

296

Little bits of things skulking shyly under other bigger things. I won't be able to find it to eat it, and if I could find it I wouldn't want to eat it. Lasagne today at the Cadogan. All in a lump. Easy.'

Timothy walks with his father to the car.

'Did all right, didn't we, Dad?'

'I suppose so,' says his father. 'I suppose so. I think I'd hoped for more. The vanity of an old man, Timothy. Still, I believe Van Gogh never sold a picture in his lifetime, so we smile on.'

At the car, Timothy says, 'I haven't had a chance to tell you, Dad. I heard about Mum yesterday.'

'You did? Who from?'

'Old boy in the Wig and Mitre. Said he'd known you in the old days.'

'Name of?'

'I've forgotten.'

'Careless.'

'Don't you want to know about her?'

'Not particularly.'

'Oh. Well, I think I should tell you. It may cheer you up. Her plumber ditched her pretty damned pronto.'

'Excellent. That is good news. No, I am pleased to hear that, I admit. Not learned a great deal in my life, but I do have one good piece of advice for women. Don't sleep with plumbers. No good will come of it.'

'She . . . er . . . I got the impression . . . he had the impression . . . because he knew a few people who sort of knew her . . . that things weren't good for her.'

'Oh. What things?'

'Well . . . life. Fortune. He thought she drank. And took drugs. And wasn't in good health. Certainly no oil painting any more. He said.'

'Oh. Well, I'm sorry about all that. I am saddened.'

'Saddened, Dad?'

'Of course. I loved her once.'

'Shall we have a drink at the bar first?'

'I think that would be very nice.'

'Kingsley Amis once said that one of the two most depressing remarks ever made in restaurants was, "Shall we go straight through?"'

'Absolutely. What was the other one?'

'I've forgotten. So, what would you like, Naomi?'

'Campari and soda, please.'

'Excellent choice. I do like my guests to choose drinks I approve of. Campari and soda, please, and . . . do you have a good Sercial Madeira?'

'Of course, sir.'

Naomi has no idea whether her agent has some work proposal to offer, though lunch seems an odd way to approach it, if he has. She knows that he's always liked her, had a soft spot for her, and he is a pretty hard character, with quite a few hard places and not too many soft spots. Melvyn is tall, slightly grizzled, very dry, undoubtedly handsome, somewhat aloof, looks as though he might be an actor, perhaps wishes he was. She thinks the motivation for the lunch might be guilt. He hasn't found her any work lately. But aren't theatrical agents immune from guilt, some above it, some below it?

Anyway, she's determined to make the most of the occasion. Life with her father is simple – delightfully simple, she tells people – but she is going to enjoy her Campari and soda, a glass of white wine, her share of a bottle of red, perhaps even, if things go well, an Armagnac, and maybe she wouldn't be looking forward to all this quite so keenly if she was finding the simplicity quite as delightful as she pretends. Bread and cheese overlooking the river tomorrow . . .

and tomorrow . . . and tomorrow. Unless there really is an offer of work, of course.

'So, how *are* you?'

The 'are' is in italics, with a lot of unspoken words clinging to its frail body, like 'under the circumstances' and 'considering that you were three-quarters round the bloody twist last year'.

'Very good. No, really, *very* good.'

The 'very' is in italics too, but Naomi is painfully aware that not as many silent words are clinging to its coat-tails.

'So the marriage is over.'

'Yes. Yes.'

'I can't pretend to grieve, Naomi.'

'No. Quite.'

'I met him the other day, at a recording of his wretched sitcom pilot. Set in a dental surgery of all places.'

Naomi's blood runs cold. She didn't even know that it had got that far.

'It was about as amusing as the draining of an abscess. It'll flop unless it gets an injection. Of humour. It's called *This Won't Hurt*. Well, I tell you, it will. I put you up for it, of course. He said that he couldn't work with you again.'

'The bastard! He told me he thought he could write funny lines for me now that we weren't together.'

'He's a two-faced little shit of minuscule talent. It'll never go to a series. Which should be good news for him. He told me he half wanted it to fail, he had an idea for a novel which would be a mixture of Waugh and Proust. "Snobbish and very, very long, do you mean?" I suggested. He wasn't pleased. Oh, Lord. Should I be saying this? Do you miss him? Does a part of you still love him?'

'No parts of me love him. My ears, my eyes, my belly button, my toes, all of them are relieved each morning when I wake up in bed alone.'

'Good. That's reassuring. Living with your father, eh?'

'Yes.'

'How does that work?'

'Well, it's quite delightful. Simple, but delightful. We went sailing last summer, to Denmark.'

'Nice little country.'

She dislikes his patronising tone.

'It's not Denmark's fault that it has never invaded and conquered and annexed huge parts of the rest of the world,' she says.

'So, where did you sail to in Denmark?'

Naomi is astonished. Melvyn has never seemed remotely interested in her leisure activities. He's not a man to whom you could show your holiday snaps.

'We sailed right through the Limfjord, which is delightful, then down via an idyllic little island called Samsø, then Copenhagen . . .'

As she talks Naomi is at the helm again, capturing that last extra degree of wind, her father bringing her up a mug of tea, smiling happily, trusting her. She knows that she looks good in her shorts and jaunty yachting cap. She knows that he is proud of her. Melvyn sees suddenly the return of true beauty to her face.

But he has heard enough. She will never get the chance to tell him about Sønderborg and the Kiel Canal.

'Surprisingly good restaurants in Copenhagen,' he says, bringing the conversation onto his second favourite subject. 'Lovely Danish restaurant in the Old Brompton Road. Now, what are you going to have?'

As Naomi is tucking into her rillettes of salmon – creamy, buttery yet also slightly rough – Melvyn says, 'What about Edith?'

'Edith?'

'Your daughter.'

'Oh. Emily.'

Melvyn isn't interested in me. I am not a person who could call her daughter Edith. He would know that if he cared.

'Emily. That's right.' His tone suggests that he is praising her for remembering her daughter's name. Naomi has always liked Melvyn, but he's irritating her today. 'So, what about Emily? Does she enjoy living with her grandfather?'

'She's not with us.'

'Oh. Don't tell me she's with Marcel?'

'Marcel?'

'Proust. The "in memory of sitcoms past" man.'

Quicken up, Naomi. He'll think you've gone dull, down by your river.

'Oh, Colin, no, no, oh, good heavens, no, Melvyn, she's precious. I wouldn't leave her with him.'

'Good. I *was* worried.'

'No, she's with Simon and Francesca, Simon's second wife, but she's very nice, well, Emily likes her, she likes them both, Simon is a bit of a changed man, I have to admit. Erm . . . last summer . . .'

'When you . . .'

'Exactly. Dad wanted me to go sailing with him, I left Emily with them, we went sailing, and we came back, and we all met in London . . .'

Mum, I want to live with Simon and Francesca.

'Are you all right, Naomi?'

'I'm fine, Melvyn, really. Lovely rillettes. Delicious Menetou-Salon. I'm fine. It's just . . . a little painful. She wanted to go and live with them. Not with me. Oh, she loved me. Loves me. But.'

'See plenty of her?'

'Oh, yes. Heaps. It's just that, when I . . .'

'Last summer.'

'Precisely . . . she was a little bit . . . you know . . . well, frightened.'

'I think you were a bit frightening for a time.'

'I think I was. I'm all right, Melvyn. Honestly. Is this what this lunch is all about, to see if I'm all right?'

'No, not exactly.'

The question of what the lunch is all about hangs in the air over the widely spaced, well-filled tables like a cloud that just may grow into a thunderstorm, but may slip harmlessly by. It's a restaurant of the old school, discreet, serious, reliable, ever so slightly dull.

Naomi's whole brill with saffron and tomato butter sauce arrives. It's amazing how a generous, well-cooked dish can cheer a person up. Emily *is* truly happy, and that *is* what truly matters.

'I'm greedy, Melvyn,' she says. 'I love a whole fish, on the bone. I mistrust fillets. There's never enough.'

'You're a good woman to take out to lunch,' says Melvyn. 'I've three women on my books that I won't eat with. Can't bear to see them pushing their food round the plate. But, despite your appetite, or even because of it, you look very good. When you smiled, remembering your sailing holiday, do you know, I'd almost forgotten how lovely you are.'

'Do you think we ought to increase my age range on my Spotlight page, Melvyn? Leave the lower end at twenty-eight, up the top end to forty-five? I've been thinking about it.'

'When does a woman not think about her age?'

What sort of an answer is that?

'So, Naomi, all that business last summer.'

A waiter approaches slowly, smoothly, silently. Melvyn waves him away politely.

'Thank you. I'll pour my own. We're having a rather intimate discussion.'

Are we?

302

'So Naomi, all that business . . .'

'. . . last summer.'

'Just so. Are you . . . ?'

'It's in the past, Melvyn. I mean, I still feel the same about religion, but I'm going to keep it to myself until I find some other way, some better way, of dealing with it. I have no intention of damaging my career.'

'What career, Naomi?'

'I beg your pardon?'

'You have no career.'

The blood drains from Naomi's face. She continues to remove flesh from bone, dip flesh into sauce, and eat, but she tastes nothing.

'I'd have liked to wait till after we'd finished eating, but the conversation keeps tipping me towards the showdown. I can play you on my line no longer. I like you too much for that, Naomi. Always have liked you. Always felt we were a bit more than agent and client. We were friends.'

'I've felt that.'

She hardly has the energy to bring out those three words of one syllable.

'I'm afraid I can represent you no longer.'

At other tables people's conversations are carrying on quite normally. Naomi thinks how strange it is, to be surrounded by people whose worlds are not imploding.

'I see. But surely there might be some work?'

She isn't going to beg, but she doesn't intend to just give up.

'Yes, there might. I'm not saying you should give up hope. But . . . the fact is, Naomi, I have four other actresses on my books whom I am more likely to suggest for the parts I might suggest for you. That's why I think it unfair to keep you on.'

He pours her some more of the St Emilion. She thanks him.

'Why would you suggest the other four first?'

'Because, Naomi, nobody is going to say, "Isn't she the one who pesters us all to become atheists?"'

'There's a black list.'

'Not exactly. Not like that. But it's a gossipy industry, Naomi.'

'You can say that again.'

'I never need to say anything again. Everything I say is known by everyone in the Groucho within hours. It isn't just that. If it was just that I might be able to swing it. It's your sitcoms.'

'You put me up for them.'

'I know. I know. Well, it's only *Get Stuffed*, really. You . . . you weren't good.'

'I didn't have a chance to be good.'

'You know that. I know that. Others don't. They are unable to discriminate between causes. Have a pud. Have something more on me.'

'I couldn't eat a thing. How do you think I could eat after a blow like this? Well, perhaps the pear and frangipane tart. I think I should go on a different tack. Drama. The classics. Theatre.'

'I agree. And for that you need a fresh start, and for that you need a new agent.'

'Will I find a new agent?'

'Not easily.'

'So, this is it?'

'Not necessarily.'

Melvyn leans across the table towards her. Her heart starts to race. She hasn't expected this. She ticks herself off for her naivety.

'There is a way, now that you aren't married.'

Melvyn looks round the restaurant nervously, revealing to anyone who might be watching, though nobody is, that

304

he is about to make a dubious proposition. Naomi is amazed that he doesn't do it more smoothly, and thinks, I don't think he's quite as sophisticated as he thinks he is. I know nothing about his background, he was probably born in a back-to-back in Hunslet.

'You could be my mistress.'

'I can't believe what I'm hearing, Melvyn. I thought better of you. The casting couch. Well, not exactly. What should it be called with an agent? The representing couch?'

'No. Listen. I know it sounds that way.'

'So how else can it sound?'

'The pear and frangipane tart?'

'That's for me. Thank you. That was good timing, wasn't it, just when you're making *me* sound like a tart.'

'That's ridiculous. Listen, Naomi. All that I said to you, about why I can't find you work, is true. It's not a made-up story so that the only way you can work is to sleep with me. Even if you sleep with me, I won't be able to put you up for too much, for the reasons I've given. But I will keep you on my books, and I will try, because . . . I love you, Naomi. No, not the casting couch. Not the representation couch. Not a cynical move. The last ploy of a lonely and disappointed man.'

'Why do it that way?'

'Because I don't think you love me, and I thought that this was a way in which I might have a chance. I realise from your face that I have no chance.'

'I'm afraid not.'

'Have lunch with me again sometime. No strings attached. Please.'

His face begins to crumple. There are tears in his eyes. He pulls himself together, blows his nose on a very elegant, monogrammed handkerchief which was surely made for show and not to be a receptacle for mucus.

305

'Sorry,' he says.

She looks straight into his face and wonders if he is acting. He can read her mind.

'I'm not acting,' he says. 'I can't act. If I could, with my looks, I wouldn't be an agent.'

Tommo picks him up as usual. It's the last of the Pennine Piss-ups.

'Tim,' he says, grabbing him in a warm, affectionate, slightly crippling hug.

'Good to see you, Tommo,' says Timothy.

As usual, Tommo has brought a presentation pack of biscuits.

'One or two new ones,' he says. 'You can't let the grass grow under your feet if you intend to stay a market leader.'

Timothy puts the biscuits on the hall table, where the show fox shouts its absence. To his amazement he is missing the dead birds and animals, he feels a warm retrospective affection for them, the house seems empty without them. When he gets home he'll put the presentation pack with all the other boxes of biscuits, in the second cupboard on the left in the kitchen. Timothy doesn't eat biscuits. He thinks it odd of Tommo to continue to bring biscuits now that number ninety-six is wifeless, but it's the tradition of the Pennine Piss-ups, and Tommo is a great one for tradition.

Tommo sits in the car, cracks his fingers in that way that Timothy hates, and says, as always, 'Now then,' meaning, 'Here we go again. How many of these jaunts is it now, over the years? Twenty, thirty? Of course there'd be far more if Steven didn't live down south. So, this is the last one, eh?'

'Now then,' echoes Timothy, meaning, 'About the twenty-third one, I think. Remember that first one? Goodness, how I hated it. I didn't drink much in those days, my heart was heavy with grief, you meant well but it was agony. I'm an old hand now, sink my pints with the best of them. Funny, really. You're an established man of biscuits, Steven's stinking rich, Dave has greengrocer's shops all over the North of England and in Spain now as well, and here am I giving up my business to work at a bird reserve for the RSPB, and yet I am completely at my ease in the company of the three of you, I no longer feel like a slightly inferior and eccentric being who is only invited out of charity and pity. And of course over the years I have learned, bit by agonising bit, to live with Sam's death, though of course I still find myself wondering what he would be like at the age he is now. I can't pass a cricket ground without wondering if he'd have liked the game. But of course I don't think about this on our piss-ups, so they are genuinely happy moments in my life now. And now they're ending, and I feel sad – not as sad as I did at their outset, but I do have a gentle feeling of enveloping melancholia.' There's no need to say all that. 'Now then' suffices admirably.

Tommo sets off as if calling at number ninety-six had been a pit stop.

'Got one for you,' he says.

Oh, well. Get the joke over early, then we can relax.

'A man walks along a pavement, and he sees a very old man sitting on the pavement looking very sad. "Why are you sitting there looking so sad?" he asks. "I'm ninety-two," says the old man, "and I've married a girl aged twenty-one."'

Here we go.

'"She likes to make love twice before breakfast . . ."'

Almost always sex with old Tommo.

'" . . . once before lunch, twice after tea, once before supper and twice at bedtime." "So why are you so sad?" asks the man. The old man looks at him sadly and says, "I can't remember where I live."'

If only I'd known it was going to have a clean ending I could have enjoyed it, thinks Timothy. He wonders why he's such a prude about jokes. He isn't a prude in bed.

They pick Dave Kent up next. Timothy hears Tommo say, 'Hope your brood aren't so grown-up that they'll scorn the chance to have a few biscuits, Mrs K. One or two new ones this time. If you don't stay ahead of the field, the writing's on the wall.'

Dave explodes into the car, with a gesture that cries, 'Get those foaming pints poured, landlord.' The more prosperous he gets, the bigger the holes in his jeans. He's taken to wearing a gold crucifix dangling above his hairy greengrocer's cleavage.

'Four whole hours away from her,' he announces.

He has hated his wife for fifteen years. The marriage seems to work brilliantly.

'Now then,' says Tommo.

'Now then,' says Dave Kent. 'End of an era, eh, Timothy?'

'Yep,' says Timothy.

'Sad.'

'Yep.'

'Sold the house?'

'Looks like it.'

'New job sorted?'

'Looks like it.'

'Got one for you,' says Tommo.

'Tommo's off,' says Dave complacently.

'Tim's heard it, but it's a corker,' says Tommo. 'A man walks along a pavement . . .'

Once the joke's safely out of the way, Dave says, urgently, 'Ran into Sniffy and Steven last night. I was terrified Steven would let on something about tonight, but he didn't. But Sniffy did say, "Well, you've done a bit of all right for yourself, haven't you?" and Steven got distinctly shirty.'

'He's very very sensitive about his pay-off,' warns Dave.

'Got it,' says Tommo. 'It's sealed lips time.'

As Tommo weaves in and out of the traffic, lapping several sluggards on the ring road, they reflect on Steven's life, on

308

the fact that none of them like him very much, and on the contrasting fact that he is indispensable to the Pennine Piss-ups, which is why Timothy's farewell is being held several weeks before Timothy actually takes his leave of Coningsfield. Steven is up for his mother's funeral. Who knows when he'll be up North again?

'What did he actually do in the aerospace industry?' asks Tommo.

'Not really sure,' says Dave, 'but he was a high flyer.'

'Wish I could be sacked for incompetence and get a million and a half,' says Tommo. 'Though actually I wouldn't. I'd miss the biscuits terribly.'

Tommo doesn't need to remember which number house is Steven's mother's. It's the only one with a red Ferrari in the drive.

He pulls up with a screech of brakes, and begins to get out of the car.

'You don't need to get out,' says Dave. 'He's not deaf.'

'I want to give him some biscuits,' says Tommo.

There's a brief silence in the car after Tommo has left. Timothy can see that Dave is preparing one of his insightful character assessment nuggets. He looks forward to it. He relishes Dave's nuggets.

'I suppose we've known old Tommo for, what is it, very nearly thirty years,' says Dave. 'He's . . .' Dave pauses. Timothy isn't sure whether this is for dramatic effect or because he is choosing his words carefully. '. . . a good sort.'

They hear the Good Sort saying, 'Got some biccies for you, Stevey boy. Thought it might be tactless to stop. Sort of might point up the fact that your mum's snuffed it. Also, shrewd businessman like you, you have a nose for money, rather like to hear how our new lines strike you.'

Steven Venables emerges from the house. He's wearing a dark suit and a black tie.

'Greetings, fellow slummers,' he announces, on getting in the car.

'Black tie!' exclaims Dave. 'I thought the funeral was on Tuesday.'

'I'm having a suitable period of mourning,' says Steven. 'I'm quite interested in Eastern religions. They show more respect for the dead over there.'

'We're all sad about your mum, Steven,' says Tommo, swinging right into Garsley Hill Road at about forty miles an hour.

'Thanks.'

'Got one for you. The boys have heard it, but it's a corker. A man walks along a pavement . . .'

Up, up they roar, into the dark, windswept hills. It's a shame that the last Pennine Piss-up should be in the dark, but the views over the stern slopes aren't the point, and there's a kind of glamour about growling between the bare winter hedges, the headlights picking out a startled owl, an oak tree starkly beautiful without its clothes, a cottage brightly lit against the gloom. As they climb, they sing the old rugby songs. Timothy knows the tricks now, the silent bits, and is no longer caught out, but somehow the singing doesn't seem quite the same. It's as if they feel that perhaps they are a year or two too old for rugby songs now.

Their first stop is no longer the Mill House in Bugginsby Far Bottom. This is a private house now. The pub has been defeated by the breathalyser and cheap supermarket beer. It's still called the Mill House, though.

'Do you know,' says Timothy, as they reflect on this, 'I couldn't buy a house that I knew had been a pub. It would be filled for me with the ghosts of drinkers past, their faces accusing me of spoiling their fun, the distant click of cue against ball on an invisible pool table waking me at midnight.'

'You're too sensitive,' says Tommo. 'Always were.'

Luckily, the Lord Nelson in Osfinklethwaite is still surviving. The landlord with the gammy leg and the hump has died, but his bold-busomed buxom widow soldiers on and has replaced him, for atmosphere, with a parrot. Some say, unkindly, that this is a distinct improvement. The beer is as good as ever, though Tommo confines himself, as always on these occasions, to bottled water.

'Luckily, I'm one of those people who don't need alcohol to relax,' he says, as he often says.

Timothy, though, has learned to hold his beer like a man. He can drink almost pint for pint with Steven. Out come the dominoes. The clack clack of contentment. And yet, somehow, he's aware that it isn't quite the same. Maybe it's just the knowledge that this is their last evening of fives and threes. Steven's dark suit and black tie don't help, nor does the knowledge that he's going back to an empty house. He thinks back to Tommo's joke. A man of ninety-two with a girl of twenty-one. Ninety-two doesn't seem as old as once it did. They're all over forty. Timothy is off to East Anglia. Dave will end up in Spain, for sure. Steven won't go up North any more, making post-modern deconstructionist ironic jokes about slumming it, now that his mother's gone. Tommo will miss them. Sadness clings to the hills this night. Tommo does his best. 'This man rushes to the doctor's, bursts in. He says, "Doctor, doctor, I've got a domino stuck up my arse."'

'Oh, not again, Tommo,' says Timothy.

'Oh, have I told it?' says Tommo, but even this doesn't stop him. 'The doctor says, "Don't you ever knock?"'

The next port of call is a pub they've only found recently, the Dovecote at Burton Kirkby. It isn't perfect, it's a bit smart, and does quite a lot of meals, but they don't actually frown on drinkers and there's a wonderful warm table by the huge open fire. Supermarkets have cheap beer but they don't have huge open fires, yet many landlords replace

311

the fires because they're too lazy. Luckily, not Cyril and Edna, mine hosts at the Dovecote.

The four of them sit and stare at the fire and drink rather more gently than usual. Is this the end of their youth, as well as an era? Somehow, nobody likes to suggest a game of dominoes. Partly, it's that the clack clack of the shuffling between games seems too loud for the diners in this place; even these tough men are not immune to the gentrification of their countryside. Partly, somehow, this evening, the dominoes haven't seemed to matter, the play at the Lord Nelson has been just slightly listless. Only slightly, but it's a warning sign. And the fire is mesmerising. Occasionally, one of them reminds the others of some amusing incident in the past. They laugh, bathing in the safety of what cannot now be changed. Then there is silence again, companionable enough, until the next little spurt of recollection. They have no future. The present is only half real. Only the past remains.

Dave is drinking even faster than usual, spurring himself rather desperately towards enjoyment. Tonight, Timothy doesn't really feel like keeping up. It's all over, it has ended already, and they shouldn't still be here. He does try to keep up, though, because he senses that Steven isn't finding it easy either. He's gone soft, down South, has Steven. All that money has softened him.

For various reasons they all feel that they've had enough, but it's too early to admit defeat. They always go to four pubs. To admit defeat after two would be pathetic.

Their third port of call is the Black Swan at Cold Heptonwick.

'I'd begun to wonder if I'd got it wrong,' says Sniffy, rising from his corner seat like a ghost.

He shows no sign of resentment at his exclusion from their plans. He is affability itself.

Things don't look promising. Timothy fears that this is the

last pint he'll be able to manage tonight. Steven admits utter and total defeat, and goes onto gin and tonics. The conversation has done no better than limp along at the Dovecote. Now, with Sniffy here, even that level may be unattainable.

But a strange thing happens. For the first time in their lives they are pleased to see Sniffy. At least it's an injection of something into the evening, it's a jab at the dying embers with a poker.

They have one more crack at the dominoes. It's not easy. With five of them, one always has to stand down, but suddenly the game is invested with a purpose, the defeat of Steven, the humiliation of the gin and tonics man. They fail to defeat him, but that doesn't matter. The point is in the wanting to.

Timothy does manage another half, because he's worried that if he refuses they may move on to a fourth pub. They don't. Nobody even suggests it. For the first time in its history, the Pennine Piss-up takes place in only three pubs. It is indeed the end of an era.

Notre Dame doesn't stun you with its grandeur. It woos you with its charms. It's a graceful, elegant, feminine cathedral. Suddenly Naomi finds that tears are running down her cheeks. She sniffs and blows her nose. Clive and Antoine look away, pretend not to have noticed anything. But the tears pour, and Naomi knows that they must have seen.

Their days, like Gaul itself, are divided into three parts. In the mornings, Clive teaches, Antoine paints, and, when called upon, Naomi rides a bicycle across his canvases. In the afternoons, they show her corners of Paris, some famous, some obscure. Today it's the turn of the famous. And in the evenings, they eat and drink and talk. How could they not talk, in St-Germain-des-Prés? Conversation is the area's legacy.

Clive and Antoine have an apartment on the top floor

of a six-storey, relatively modern building in the Rue St Benoît. 'You see. Their hands are everywhere. Even your street is named after a saint,' Naomi had commented on arrival.

From the apartment it's but a short walk to Les Deux Magots and the Café de Flore, where Jean-Paul Sartre and Simone de Beauvoir so famously talked and talked. And talked. Naomi has not read Sartre or de Beauvoir. She wishes she had, but she knows that wishes have no value, and so she also wishes that she didn't wish that she had.

Often, and especially when money was short, the three of them ate and drank at home. On other evenings they wandered to one of the cafés. Occasionally they ate in the sober, traditional, comforting Brasserie Lipp, where many intellectuals have sampled the sauerkraut and the carafes of Morgon.

There is a plaque on the wall, almost directly below the apartment. It tells that the poet Léo Larguier (1878–1950) lived there for thirty years. Tonight, as they pass it, Naomi is deeply moved by the thought that this poet of whom she has never heard is commemorated in this way, half a century after his death. Her emotions are very close to the surface today. She fears that she may cry again before the evening is over.

In the buzzing Café de Flore she is pleased that her French is not good. She can believe that every conversation at every table is brilliant.

She sips her Ricard. She never drinks Ricard except in France. In her drinking habits she is a chameleon.

She knows that 'the boys', as she calls them, want to talk to her about her tears in Notre Dame. She knows also that there is another subject that must be broached sooner or later. She decides that it is the safer one to broach.

'I remember when the Tomlinsons were staying with us,' she says. 'They stayed and stayed and stayed. At last they said that they were going. We saw them off. Do you remember, Clive?'

314

'Oh, my goodness, yes. Oh, it was dreadful. English embarrassment at its worst, Antoine.'

Clive and Naomi smile and shudder at the same time. They are briefly transported from the Boulevard St-Germain to the Lower Cragley Road.

'What happened?'

For a moment, neither of them hears Antoine.

'Oh,' says Naomi. 'They left, after breakfast, after what seemed like three weeks, and we all danced round the table in the dining room, well, not Dad, obviously, but Mum and me and Clive, even Julian. We danced round the table with our arms raised in the air, chanting, "They've gone. They've gone." And they came back. Mr Tomlinson had forgotten his glasses. They came back and they saw us.'

'Wonderful.'

'I know, but we were too embarrassed to find it wonderful.'

Naomi takes a tiny sip of her Ricard. She is trying to make it last.

'It served them right. And perhaps you did a favour to their future hosts.'

'I know. I know. And I don't think I'd be embarrassed these days.'

'Your story, of course, had a point to it, Naomi,' says Antoine, 'and the answer is no, no, no. No, you are not outstaying your welcome. No, we don't want you to go. And no, when that time comes, we won't tell you.'

'Then how will I know when it comes? How do I know it hasn't come now?'

'Because you can see that our joy in your company is very, very real.'

'Time to eat,' announces Clive.

He signals to a waiter, who comes immediately. People do, to Clive. He pays. He handles all money matters in his life with Antoine.

They wander back past the apartment, and turn left into the Rue Jacob. Naomi loves this street, with its little galleries and antique shops and art shops.

They are going to one of their very favourite restaurants tonight, a tiny bistro right opposite the Hotel d'Angleterre, where Hemingway stayed. How many ghosts there are in this city. It's hard sometimes not to feel like a ghost oneself.

Clive is in jeans and an avant-garde shirt, Antoine sober in corduroy. Naomi has tried not to look conspicuously pretty, in black trousers and a pale cream top. She has failed.

Everyone knows them in the restaurant. Clive and Antoine have been irregular regulars for years, and Naomi has been with them now for almost three months. Her father pretends that he is sorry that she has gone, but deep down, well though they got on, he is happy, because he has his History of Ancient Greece to finish. Already, 'the English actress' is accepted in the restaurant almost as fully as 'the artist and his rear-gunner'.

The subject of Naomi's tears hangs over the table like an invisible chandelier, but first there is ordering to be done. Naomi chooses snails and the *pot au feu de canard*. The waitress seems extremely pleased, almost thrilled, by her choice. Clive plumps, as they say in the restaurant reviews, for black pudding with apples and the sea bass en papillote. The waitress nods her approval. Antoine, the Frenchman, makes the most conservative choice, chestnut soup and *entrecôte au poivre*. The waitress shows no reaction.

Then there is the wine to be examined, sniffed, sipped, approved.

Now Antoine looks at Clive. He feels that he can't raise the subject, but Clive is her brother, after all.

'Naomi?' says Clive very gently. 'We couldn't help noticing that you were crying in Notre Dame. Were you . . . ? Are you . . . ? No. Let me put it more simply. Why were you crying?'

'Not because I was realising that I was wrong not to believe. Just because . . . I thought of the amazing faith that built all the world's great cathedrals. You don't have to believe to appreciate the beauty. You don't have to believe to admire the piety and faith of people through the ages. Their faith was glorious, magnificent, awesome, like their cathedrals. I cried because I thought of all the workers who died during the building of the cathedrals. I thought of all the poor people who gave what they couldn't afford to the Church. I thought of all those people who were terrified of hell. The fact that science seems to me to make it certain that their faith was misplaced doesn't diminish it in my eyes at all, it actually gives it a heroic quality. I cried for all these things. I cried at the way their faith was manipulated for political and national . . .'

She sees the worry that Clive can't quite hide. Is she in danger of going over the edge again? She breaks off in mid-sentence, and smiles. 'Sorry. I promised not to ride my hobby horse while I was with you, didn't I?' She meets Clive's eyes and holds the gaze, and he suddenly has complete faith in her future. It's an exhilarating moment for him.

'I think Dad hopes that I'll be cured while I'm here,' she says, 'but I don't think that my condition is a disease. Sorry. Enough said. What shall we do tomorrow?'

But Antoine doesn't take the opportunity to change the subject.

'The awe of the atheist,' he says. 'I think that's wonderful, Naomi. That was very moving to see. You don't believe a word of it, yet you gaze devoutly.'

The food arrives. They clink glasses with deep affection, and eat in silence for a few moments. Naomi gazes at the love posters on the walls of this intimate, secret place. They were painted by Yves Saint Laurent and presented to the mother of the present owner at Christmas and New Year. Naomi suddenly realises that 'the boys' have chosen this

317

restaurant this evening for a reason. They are going to discuss her love life, or rather, its absence.

But Clive also is not yet ready to change the subject.

'The awe of the atheist,' he says. 'What a wonderful subject that would be for you, Antoine, if you weren't obsessed with containing order and disorder together in every canvas. What a theme. To show, in one human face, the appreciation of the art, how the person is moved by the art, and yet how at the same time they do not believe in this art that they admire. To show God as a fiction, but a fiction that stirs the innermost heart. If only you would paint something like that, Antoine. If only you weren't so rigid.'

'And now who is riding his hobby horse?' says Antoine.

There is a very brief pause.

'Changing the subject,' says Clive firmly, 'we have to discuss my sister's life.'

'Do we really? Why can't she just live it?'

'Because she isn't living it.'

'I'm happy here,' protests Naomi.

'Oh, yes. Happy. We do nice things. Of course you're happy. Nice trips round a great city. Nice meals. Helping Antoine with his work.'

'Indispensable.'

'No, Antoine, I'm not indispensable. Anyone else could ride that bike.'

'Not as you do. Somehow, you instinctively invest a meaning even to the random part of the picture, a form that cannot quite be described as a form but is nevertheless not entirely formless.'

'Then maybe I will destroy the whole point.'

'This is irrelevant,' says Clive. 'We have to think of the future.'

'Why can't we just live in the present?' complains Naomi. 'For tonight, at least. This is so lovely.'

318

'You simply cannot remain a gooseberry with two shirt-lifters for ever.'

'I don't understand this phrase, Clive,' says Antoine.

'Really? It just means that you and I—'

'I understand shirt-lifters. What is this gooseberry?'

'Oh. It's a single person who tags along with a couple.'

'Why is it called a gooseberry?'

'I don't know, actually. Do you know, Naomi?'

'Not a clue, I'm ashamed to say. Sometimes I wonder if I really do have an enquiring mind.'

'I've heard of the raspberry. That's a rude noise, no?'

'Yes.'

'Are there other berries whose significance in British culture I should know about? What, for instance, is a logan-berry? A bum-boy making a rude noise in bed between two lesbians?'

'Antoine, stop being silly. Why are you being so silly?'

'Because if we're sensible and force Naomi to consider what she is going to do with the rest of her life, she will realise that eventually she has to leave, and I don't want her to leave. These last many weeks, what a delight. Those days Emily spent here, once more at peace in the love of her mother, giving and, even more difficult, accepting love. What a privilege it was to witness it.'

Naomi feels tears pricking at her eyes again. She fights them.

Emily had visited for a week. Naomi had told Clive and Antoine that Emily was very happy in her own company, would wander through the streets, maybe even hire a bicycle and brave the Parisian traffic. She wasn't a loner, she did have friends, but she was a free spirit and she loved to drift with her thoughts and dreams. In the event she clung to Naomi's side, not out of timidity, not in an irritating or regressive way, but as if she was trying to make up for all the days they had spent apart. And, in an age full of eating disorders, her appetite had been a joy to see.

'We can't be selfish, Antoine,' rebukes Clive. Despite the way the two of them dress, it is Clive who is the realist. 'Naomi, do you ever want to act again?'

'If it was worthwhile. If I could do good things. Preferably things not written by Colin Coppinger.'

'Might you try to find another agent?'

'One day, perhaps.'

'Do you want a new man in your life?'

'What man would take me?'

'Seventeen that I know of, in St-Germain-des-Prés. There's a waiter in the Brasserie Lipp whose intensity frightens me.'

'Oh, dear. How awful. No, I don't think I do want a new man in my life. I feel so very happy like this, so serene, so safe.'

'"Serene" I can accept, but "safe"! You shouldn't even consider doing "safe", Naomi.'

'I don't have a lot of respect for most of the men I meet.'

'Ok, not a new man. How about an old man?' asks Clive. 'How about . . . Timothy, was it?'

'He'll be married. He's the marrying kind.'

'He may not be.'

'He believes in God.'

'He may not now.'

'I don't think so. He had it pretty bad.'

'You spoke just now of your respect for faith,' says Antoine gently. 'Surely now that you're almost – can you really be in your forties? – surely you're mature enough not to let religious feelings get in the way of more personal matters? Or are you still . . . just a little bit obsessed, perhaps?'

Naomi doesn't reply at first. She seems a long way off. The reassurance that Clive felt just a few minutes ago turns out not to be proof against anxiety. Perhaps, because of what

320

has happened, and because of his love, he will never again be free from the need for reassurance.

Reassurance comes the moment Naomi speaks.

'It's funny,' she says. 'I think of Timothy as if he was the great love of my life, but we only ever spent three nights together. Over twenty years ago now, but I remember every moment as if it were yesterday. Particularly the second night.'

She catches the knowing look that Antoine and Clive exchange with each other. She feels herself blushing.

'She's blushing,' says Antoine. 'Is there anything prettier in this world than a pretty English girl blushing?'

'Oh, do shut up!' cries Naomi, in such a loud voice that everyone in the restaurant turns to look at her, and the waitress, who is clearing their plates, almost drops them.

'He was such a child in some ways – awkward, gawky – but I think now that he was also adult beyond his years. When he played Romeo, he wasn't terribly good but he had repose, so it sort of worked. Even when he took the applause, he wasn't a bit embarrassed, and I'd expected that he would be.'

Their main courses arrive.

'M'm. That looks lovely,' says Naomi of her dish. 'Succulent, unshowy, nourishing.' But even the *pot au feu de canard* doesn't divert her from the subject of Timothy. 'When I last saw him, after the recording of an episode of *Get Stuffed*, he was so passionate, so loyal to his father, at the time I was disconcerted, I thought I was in love with Colin, but, later, you know, I . . . well, enough said, let's eat.'

She takes a mouthful. Normally she has the most graceful and natural of table manners, but now she can't even wait till she's finished the mouthful before she speaks of Timothy again.

'You're right, Clive,' she says through a mouthful of duck. 'I'll have to go and try to find him. I know where he lives.'

Antoine sighs.

'You know what you've done, don't you, you stupid man?' he asks.

'Made sure that my sister tries to start living her own life again.'

'Well, yes, there is that. But you've just lost me the best cyclist I've ever had or am ever likely to have.'

Liam is very pleased to be asked to help his father with his move.

Timothy is moving into a furnished, rented cottage, two up, two down, in a row of what were once fishermen's cottages and are now the homes of struggling artisans or the second homes of Londoners seeking the simple, organic dream. So he isn't taking any furniture, just the bulk of his books, his meagre record collection, his unimpressive array of clothes, which includes just one and a half suits – where did those trousers end up? – the pumice stone that reminds him of his Auntie May Treadwell, a few photographs of wild places and of friends who never quite managed to be wild, the barely usable toaster that he made in woodwork at Coningsfield Grammar, the framed front page of the programme for *Romeo and Juliet*, a photo of his father in a rather cheap frame, his camera and binoculars and alarm clock and batteries, his father's masterly group of three Icelandic puffins, the English-Finnish dictionary he found on a bus – may as well take it, you never know, the reserve might be visited by a very beautiful, long-legged blonde twitcher from Helsinki, it's a bit of a long shot but you'd be really pissed off if it happened and you'd thrown the dictionary away – and his complete collection of old medicine tins. He couldn't remember at exactly what stage of his adolescence he had decided that as an aid to having a personality he'd collect these tins, but he had discovered very soon that he wasn't the collector type. The larger of the tins had once contained Compound Bismuth Lozenges and was now home to his spare euro coins. The other tin announced that it contained 'The "Allenburys" Throat Pastilles: Menthol, Rhatany and Cocaine', which sounded a bit more exciting than the eighty euros in filthy germ-infested notes that huddled inside it now. Last, and probably least, he takes a really rather awful painting, mercifully in need of cleaning, which, had it been cleaned, would have shown a rather weedy monarch of some distinctly unprepossessing glen.

Yesterday he had gone with Liam to the municipal tip, and had thrown away many other things, including a slim volume entitled *Great Recipes of Doncaster*, which he had picked up for a snip at a car boot sale and which he now knew he would never use, all his videos of *Nappy Ever After*, *Cobblers in Koblenz* and *Get Stuffed* – he couldn't bear to watch Naomi in them now – and all the photos of his two weddings.

'Are you sure, Dad?'

'Absolutely, Liam. Sorry.'

'No, I've no problem with it.'

'It's not meant as an insult to your mum or Hannah, Liam, it's just . . . over.'

'OK. Cool.'

He had tossed these things into the skip one at a time, with carefree wristy flicks, as if throwing a frisbee or sending ducks and drakes skimming over the water. Liam had been embarrassed, had tried to look as if he wasn't with this strange man. Timothy had felt a great surge of liberation, of sloughing off dead skins, of freeing himself from failed relationships, of greeting the future with open arms. Afterwards there had come the inevitable reaction, the fear, the emptiness, the memory of Sam, the sharp, almost unbearable desire for Naomi.

It's a morning of bright sunshine and sharp showers. Liam

323

at sixteen has grown tall and, though not handsome, has a quirky attraction about him, which, Maggie has told Timothy in a letter, 'is standing him in good stead'. He seems to Timothy to be a reassuringly normal kid. His ambition is to be an industrial chemist, or an international surf boarder. Timothy has worried that the task of helping him load and unload will be tedious to the growing boy, but in fact he is clearly delighted to help his dad.

'Thank you for doing this,' Timothy says. 'It'd be very depressing on my own.'

'That's OK,' says Liam. 'I can't believe how few records you have. It's pathetic, Dad.'

'I know. Several movements in popular music culture have passed me by completely.'

'You've got quite a lot of books, though.'

'Not compared to some people.'

'I'd never read a book if I didn't have to. Books are boring.'

Timothy stops and looks at Liam gravely.

'I once heard Tim Henman say that on television,' he says. 'You know. The tennis player. I thought, "No, Tim, books contain all the magic of thought and imagination that great minds think up. If you can't find anything stimulating or interesting in any book ever written, I'm afraid it's you that's boring." Say that you aren't bookish, as unfortunately seems to be the case with you, but don't ever say, in my presence, that books are boring.'

Liam looks at him, stunned by this attack. Then he gives a really friendly, uncomplicated, freckly smile and says, 'Sorry, Dad.'

He continues loading the car in silence for a while, then says, 'Dad? About books. I was just, you know, being obnoxious really, cos it's what kids do. If we aren't obnoxious to our parents, who will be? I don't mean it. I might read a book one day, when I've left school.'

He picks up a particularly heavy suitcase, making light of it, pleased to show his manliness.

'I'm not a yob, Dad,' he says. 'I like antiques. Like this suitcase. In fact, you could put the car and its contents on the *Antiques Road Show* as a job lot.'

Timothy grimaces.

'I know. I know. But this is a new start, Liam. A new Timothy will emerge, brighter, trendier, smarter.'

'You ought to leave this picture, then. It's terrible.'

'Dreadful.'

'Probably a silly question, but why are you taking it, then?'

'Not a silly question at all. Your Grampa saved up his pocket money to buy it to hang on his wall because he was planning to run away from home and was gathering a few possessions together. I haven't the heart to abandon it.'

'A bit heavy, I'd have thought. I wasn't going to take anything when I ran away from home.'

'You ran away from home?'

'No, I was going to. I told Mum. I said, "That's it. I've had enough of you." She said, "Hang on a moment. You'll need to eat and do your laundry in your new home. I'll just write you out a few instructions." I looked at the instructions and I thought, "Hell, that's complicated." So I told her I was giving her one last chance.'

He grins infectiously.

There's a moment when Timothy thinks of breaking the silence of the years, but it passes.

'All done, captain,' says Liam. 'Let's get this show on the road.'

Timothy feels that he is being hurried and harried. He wants to wander round the house slowly, on his own, taking a last look at the empty rooms, at the workshop stripped bare, at the kitchen in which, in another century, Roly had made his doorstep sandwiches, and at the old, now badgerless office where Naomi had given him the news that had blighted his life. He wants to imagine that he is saying farewell to his old home in a book. He wants to indulge in purple passages as he wanders for the last time along the passages which are, actually, almost purple. What deliciously conflicting emotions . . .

'Come on, Dad. Don't want to be unloading in the dark.'

'Right. Right.'

They're off. The loaded elderly Ford estate car is not a responsive beast, but they make reasonable progress towards the motorway.

'Sorry to rush you back there, Dad,' says Liam. 'I thought it best.'

Timothy looks at Liam in amazement.

'Well, got to be a painful day for you, forced to be, so I thought, get it over. Maybe I was wrong, but I think farewells are fucking awful.'

'Well . . . thanks, Liam.'

'I can't fucking stand them.'

'Well, no, they are difficult. Liam, on the question of . . . oh, Lord, I suddenly feel so old . . . but on the question of . . . bad language, don't get me wrong, I'm no prude and there are far worse things in life, but I find it basically very boring and depressing and . . . I don't want to sound as if I'm cross with you, you're helping and it's great and, as I said, this would have been very depressing for me on my own, but . . . I just don't think the F word, while not exactly a hanging offence, I just don't think it's a word dads and sons should be using in their conversations with each other. All right?'

'Absolutely. I just thought I'd test my boundaries. Isn't that what kids do?'

'Do you test your boundaries with . . . your mother?' Timothy wants to say 'Maggie', but finds he can't.

'Yeah. She just gives way. No contest. Disappointing, really.'

'I should spend more time with you.'

'Up to you. Wish you would.'

Liam reaches for a CD.

'Don't know this one. What is it? Rock? Rap?'

'Not exactly.'

'OK, let's try it.'

By the time they have listened to both sides of the Jake Thackeray CD, they are halfway to East Anglia.

When they get there, Timothy parks on the gravel opposite the row of terraced cottages. Hostile gulls shriek at them. A cat looks at them in disgust and walks very slowly away. The air is salty. Across the marshes the sails of a fine windmill are not turning. Liam looks at the house and says, 'Christ, it's tiny,' but after he has unpacked, and as they set off to the Fishermen's Arms for a well-earned meal, he looks back at it and says, 'Actually, it's quite cool, Dad.'

'My boy, Liam,' says Timothy to two grizzled regulars seated on bar stools. He introduces them to Liam. 'Scrubber Nantwich, Mickey Fudge.' Liam shakes hands with them and tries to hide his amazement at how sociable his father is being. They order fish and chips and Timothy decides that there's no harm in letting Liam have a beer on this auspicious day.

Things are going so well, in this lively and cheery, low-ceilinged boozer, that Timothy suddenly realises that this is the moment. Miss it, and Sam's death will be a black hole between father and son for ever.

They move to a far alcove, and in its privacy Timothy dives head first into the cold water of remembered death, says what he's wanted to say for more than a decade.

'Do you often think of Sam?'

'It's funny, Dad. One of my friends asked me the other

day, "Do you ever think of your brother who died?" and I said, "What the fuck do you—" Oh, sorry, Dad.'

'No, no. I accept it in reported speech.'

God, that makes me sound pompous.

'But I did say it. I said, "What the fuck do you think I am? Of course I . . . er . . . fucking do." Well, I was pretty angry.'

'You were fucking right to be angry.'

It's Liam's turn to look at his father in amazement.

'Dad!'

'I threw that one in. You can have it. You deserve it.'

'Thanks, Dad.'

'Not a problem. So what do you think when you think about him?'

'Very straightforward thoughts, Dad. I miss him. I imagine what he'd be like. The way I imagine him, he's great, and I just miss him so much. And I just think, you know, he had no life. And . . . sometimes I feel a bit angry, well, very angry, sort of for him, but most of the time I just . . . no, I just miss him.'

Liam takes a sip of his beer and looks at his glass as if rebuking it for the strange taste of its contents.

'You don't . . .' Timothy isn't sure if he should continue, if this next question is perhaps a question too far. 'You don't . . . ever feel guilty that . . . you know . . . you have a life and he doesn't?'

'No. I know you all think I must be . . . I don't know, I'm not that good with words . . . haunted. Because you never ever mention anything about it, which makes it a bit difficult for me. I mean, I'm sad, of course, sometimes, no, often, but why should I feel guilty? None of it was my fault.'

'No, no. Quite. Well, good. That's good.'

'I may not be good with words and reading and that, but I do think. I mean, if you're given a brain, you've got to.

And what I think is, it brings home to me how lucky I am to have a life. I'm not going to screw it up, Dad. I'm going to f—I'm going to live it to the full.'

Timothy feels that a great weight has been taken off his shoulders. What a fool he has been not to mention the subject for so long. Yes, he feels good. A little frightened about his new life, but . . . lifted by his son, encouraged, able to face it a little more bravely than he had expected.

The fish and chips arrive, and with them there comes to Timothy a slight feeling of disappointment. It isn't because of the fish and chips. They look good. It's because of his conversation with Liam. It's been almost too easy. For the second time that day, he feels as if he's been cheated of a big dramatic scene.

Naomi walks slowly up the long, wide hill. The bronzed, slender legs of the sailor are gone, replaced by lumps of weary lead. She's very nervous. A tiny part of her wants to turn back before she gets to number ninety-six, where, almost a quarter of a century ago, she told Timothy that she was breaking it off with him.

Workmen are removing the flower beds from the centre of the dual carriageway. It's the first stage of the vastly expensive Coningsfield Supertram project. Naomi can just remember her Uncle Spencer holding her on his shoulders to watch the very last tram pass by in the sixties, before the tramlines were removed, also at vast expense, to be replaced by flower beds. A spasm of anger at the way the country is run passes through her, and this, by giving her concerns outside her own life, calms her just a bit.

Number ninety-six looks smaller than she remembers. The board announcing that it's a taxidermist's has gone. The garden looks naked without it. Naomi feels a quick flutter of relief, soon overtaken by fear. She crunches up the path, rings the doorbell, listens to the silence. She rings again, waits, peers through the frosted glass, raps the knocker quite violently, waits again, peers through the frosted glass again. She can see what looks like a small pile of mail on the floor. The house is utterly silent. The house is dead. She peers through the window of the lounge. The room is bare. The room on the other side of the front door, the room never used, is equally bare.

Timothy has gone.

She turns away, goes to the garden gate, looks back. The windows of the house stare at her impassively, emptily. She shudders.

She walks up the steps to the front door of number ninety-four. She has a vague recollection that it used to be some kind of small hotel. It's a health centre now.

She goes in, approaches the reception desk.

'Can I help you?' asks a crisp receptionist crisply.

'I'm actually looking for Timothy Pickering. He lived next door with his father. They were taxidermists. He seems to have gone.'

'I'm afraid I can't help you,' says the receptionist. 'They weren't our patients.'

'Oh. I mean, I just wondered, as they were neighbours, if you knew ... um ... where they've gone or anything.'

'I'm afraid not. As I say, they weren't our patients.' She calls out to a woman at a desk. 'Gwenda? Do we know anything about the people at number ninety-six?'

Gwenda looks up, frowns, shakes her head.

'I'm afraid not,' she says. 'They weren't our patients.'

Naomi senses an undercurrent, a subtext of, 'And, since they didn't have the courtesy to use us, we wouldn't bloody well tell you even if we did know,' but she is in a heightened state, and may be imagining this.

She walks back up the hill, past the staring windows of

330

number ninety-six, and walks up the path, past rows of rather sickly hydrangeas, to the front door of number ninety-eight. She presses the bell. An asinine jingle rings out, utterly inappropriate to this faded Victorian villa.

A pale, tense woman with a scarf round her hair opens the door as if expecting to be hit on the head with a blunt instrument and robbed.

'Yes?'

'Oh, hello. My name's Naomi Walls.'

'I see,' says the woman, but her tone of voice says, 'It's all very well for you to say that. Where's your proof?'

'I used to know Timothy Pickering, who lived next door. We knew each other at the grammar school.'

The woman thaws slightly at the mention of the grammar school.

'He's moved.'

Still alive, then, from the sound of it. Naomi relaxes just a bit.

'Went last week.'

'Last week!'

The nearness of it devastates her.

'I think somebody's bought it, and is going to do it up before moving in.'

'Do you . . .' Somehow she knows, before she asks it, that nothing will come of this. '. . . happen to know where he's gone?'

The woman shakes her head.

'I'm afraid not. I think I did hear something about "down South", but I couldn't be sure.'

'He hasn't left a forwarding address or anything?'

'No. Hubby has spoken to him once or twice.' She looks round nervously, then lowers her voice, as if fearing that hubby might be listening from behind a hydrangea. 'Hubby's not much of a one for small talk. Not much of a one for big

331

talk, come to that. Puts people off. We weren't close with him. And, anyway, we've only been here nine years. I'm sorry I can't be more help.'

'That's all right. Thank you, anyway.'

She sets off down the garden path.

'The Post Office'll know,' calls out the woman. 'He'll have left a forwarding address there.'

'Thank you,' says Naomi, 'but I'm wondering if he has. There seems to be some mail on the floor. It'd be just like him to forget to.'

She smiles at the woman, though she doesn't feel like smiling, and sets off, but before she reaches the gate the woman calls out again.

'Don't I know you?'

Naomi stops, turns round, smiles just slightly coquettishly, rather cheered by this.

'You might,' she says. 'I used to—'

'Don't prompt me,' says the woman urgently. 'I like to try and remember.' She lowers her voice again. 'I'm terrified of Alzheimer's.'

The woman creases her brow in thought, and Naomi stands there, being observed, being studied, feeling rather awkward. She hopes that it will be *Cobblers in Koblenz* that the woman remembers, not *Nappy Ever After* or *Get Stuffed*.

'Got it,' says the woman triumphantly. 'Didn't you used to work on the wet fish counter at Morrisons in Staveley Road?'

PART EIGHT

They Say You Should Never Go Back
2003–2004

Timothy sits, as he has sat for the last four lunchtimes, at a little circular window table in the Amalfi restaurant in Old Compton Street. It is a cheery place, the Amalfi, still as cheery as it was twenty-five years ago, and he doesn't feel that there are many places of which that is true.

He is aware of the chatter and the laughter, but it does not touch his cold skin. He is thinking only of her, and of the days and nights when his skin was not so cold.

He orders spaghetti carbonara and saltimbocca alla romana. If Naomi was with him he wouldn't be ordering the veal. But of course she is not with him. She has not been with him for twenty-five years.

Lively background music is playing. He doesn't know what it is. He never knows what the music is. The Italian waitress approaches. He would like to ask her what the music is, he wants to understand about music, live his lost youth, catch up with the world, but he is ashamed to admit that he doesn't know. She will think he has no street cred.

The waitress is pretty, which does not stir him. He uses her, though, to map his fading memory of Naomi. A little taller than the waitress. A little slimmer, or no longer so?

335

Hair much lighter, or does she colour it now? What a useless map this is going to be. Nose longer, not quite as flared. Deliciously straight, in fact, though if it had been flared he would be thinking of it as deliciously flared. The waitress is talking to him. He has no idea what she is saying. In fact, he resents the interruption.

'Sorry?' he says, trying not to sound irritated.

'Would you like another glass of the Montepulciano?'

Better not. Drink solves nothing.

'Why not?'

As he hears himself say it he winces, winces at his lack of self-control, winces at his characteristic choice of words. Not a ringing, life-enhancing, 'Yes, please,' but 'Why not?' He feels that recently he has largely conquered his negativity, so it's a disappointment to hear himself saying, 'Why not?' He calls the waitress back, flashes his best smile at her – his smile, perhaps because he has not used it enough, packs considerable power – and says, with enthusiasm, 'A large one, please.' And then when she has gone, he curses himself, because he doesn't want a large one. Big things, little things, nothing in life is easy for Timothy. Except his new job. He's so happy in his new job. What would Naomi think of it? Warden in a bird reserve. Perfect for a man of reserve. He can hear her saying it.

Every week he scans the *Radio Times*, buys the *Stage*, reads the reviews in the *Sunday Times*, never finds her name. People in the Fishermen's Arms tell him that he should Google her, but he doesn't know what that means. He still hasn't got a computer. He's frightened of having one, because he knows that he would fall victim to it. He's frightened of Googling her, because he is uncertain what will happen if he does find her. This way, hunting for her, there is still hope.

His wine arrives. Its size dismays him. He takes a large sip so that there will not be such a fearsome amount left in the glass.

He's on his annual holiday. The birds have nested, but the public are still visiting, so it's not yet time to begin the major works that will have to be carried out this winter if global warming and rising sea waters are not to overwhelm his new-found paradise.

He came to the Amalfi on Monday, on the first day of his week's holiday in London, drawn by the memory of the three meals they had here twenty-five years ago. It was amazing to find that in a changing world it still existed. It was amazing to find how little it had changed.

And on Monday, as he tried to remember how he had felt on that oh so short long weekend, it had occurred to him that she might also be drawn back one day to this place, and they would meet again at last and collapse into each other's arms. So on Tuesday he had thought how awful it would be if she came the day after he'd been there, so he had come again, and in doing so had condemned himself to come every day of his holiday. He knows that it's stupid, but he's caught in a trap now, he's like a man who can't stop doing the lottery for fear that the numbers he has chosen every week will come up the moment he stops.

He likes the Amalfi, the food is good and generous, the prices are reasonable, it's reassuringly busy. When one is in the Amalfi, the world seems a pleasant place. Timothy thinks that is no mean achievement.

There are four small round window tables, all close together like all the tables in this crowded little place. He hasn't sat at the same table on all five visits. He isn't entirely a creature of habit.

From the table he is sitting at today (pedants may be interested to know that it's the second-most easterly of the four) his view comprises four buildings on the opposite side of Old Compton Street. They are part of a terrace of four-storey buildings.

On his right is an amusement arcade called Play2win, It's painted a dull blue and has large windows with nothing in them. A sign announces that people under eighteen may not enter. Flashing lights on various game machines strive to tempt the punters in. Timothy is not tempted.

Next to it is a secretive building, painted black. A sign announces that this is *www.januslondon.com*, purveyors of erotica to Consenting Adults. Its black blankness deters the timid. Here too, a sign informs those under eighteen that they are not allowed to enter. Another notice sternly announces, '*Warning. Persons passing beyond this notice will find material on display which they may consider indecent.*' Timothy is tempted, but does not dare.

Next to this is the Vintage House. It describes itself as '*The Malt Whisky Centre*'. Its windows, unsurprisingly, are full of malt whiskies. A sign warns – you've guessed it – that persons under eighteen are not permitted to enter. Timothy has no wish to enter. He can't handle spirits.

On the extreme left of his field of vision is the Patisserie Valerie, its windows full of luscious cakes. At last there is an establishment that persons under eighteen may enter. Timothy thinks it not surprising that some young people cause trouble. People are maturing physically at younger and younger ages, there are these varied, exciting pleasures and temptations, and the only one they are legally permitted to have is cake. He finds it hard not to enter the Patisserie Valerie. Like many men who have been brought up puritanically, he has a secret weakness for cake.

There is no point, he feels, in pretending that this is one of the world's great views. It cannot in all honesty compare with the panorama of Florence spread out below the Piazzale Michelangiolo. It begins to pall slightly after five lunches – with two more to come, for he cannot give up now until he has to go back to work, or he will spend the rest of his wretched life wondering if she had gone there on the Saturday or the Sunday – for it has begun to seem unnatural that she is avoiding this delightful place day after day – and he will have to endure the view every day, because it's imperative that he sit at a window seat, in case she passes by and doesn't enter. It is, however, a very comforting view, for it speaks eloquently of human weakness, catering as it does for those who like a little flutter, for those with unusual sexual wants, for those with a taste for strong liquor and for those with a weakness for cakes. Indeed, he hopes as he watches that he will see some gambling alcoholic pervert with a sweet tooth enter all four establishments in turn.

He wants to get up and go, free himself from this obsessive pattern, but he can't. He is waiting eagerly for three things – spaghetti carbonara, saltimbocca alla romana, and Naomi.

The first of the three arrives. It's fair to assume that in due course in this efficient restaurant the second will also arrive. It's madness to hope that the third will. Madness.

Yet Timothy does not believe that he is mad.

The door opens, a woman aged about forty-two enters, and it's not her. He hates her for her non-Naominess. He hates her for reminding him that Naomi will now be forty-two. He hates her for reminding him that he is forty-two. He gives her a cool stare, which he feels she richly deserves, and turns away to scan the road once more.

What's this? What's this? Is it . . . ? It can't be.

It is.

No, not Naomi. Sniffy Arkwright. Sniffy Arkwright looking longingly at the stern, ungiving frontage of *www.januslondon.com*. Those splay feet and those blubbery lips are unmistakable.

Timothy isn't surprised to see Sniffy sniffing around like this. Sniffy lives on the outside, looking in. He longs to go out and say to him, 'Sniffy, don't stand there sniffing around like that. You're looking so obvious. You might as well be carrying a sandwich board stating, *"Respectable Member of Society Ashamed to be Seen Entering Sex Shop"*. Go in.'

Proust had his madeleines. Timothy has the unlikely vehicle of Sniffy Arkwright to jump-start his remembrances of things past. In his uncertainty in Old Compton Street Sniffy seems to have brought the North of England with him. The memories come in waves. Pennine Piss-ups. Roly's sandwiches. Driving past L'Ancresse. Oh, God, the curlew. Some humiliations grow even more unbearable with the passage of time. He doesn't want to think of all this, of Steven Venables whom he no longer sees, of Dave Kent whom he sees all too rarely, of Tommo and his jokes, which he had dreaded so much and which he would welcome now, of a past life that he has shed all too easily, as if it had never happened, as if it had all been time wasted. Twenty-five years of Naomiless desert. It was worth more than that. It deserves more generous sentiments.

Suddenly Sniffy plucks up his courage and enters the sex emporium. Timothy is pleased to see him go. Now maybe the tide of memories will ebb. Think East Anglia. Think now. But to think now is to think, 'When?' and 'How?' When will I see Naomi? How can I see her?

He finishes his spaghetti carbonara, lifts his glass to take a sip of wine and finds to his astonishment that it's empty. He's horrified to hear himself ordering another glass.

'A large one?'

'Why not?'

Shit.

His wine arrives. He's a little dismayed to find that the large glasses no longer look dismayingly large.

The saltimbocca soon follows. He eats it slowly, savouring every mouthful, taking some mouthfuls of the tender meat with a little bit of sage, some without. Naomi used to say that he ate too fast. Naomi, Naomi, Naomi. Will she ever see that he has learned to eat slowly?

Sniffy must have been at the play, seen his Romeo, seen her Juliet. Suddenly Timothy realises a dreadful truth. That night, when he had given the best performance of his life, Naomi had too. He has watched every show she's been in, and she has never been quite as good again, never again tapped into that magic. His heart swims with pity for her. She needs him. Oh, Naomi. Come to eat. Step inside. What's keeping you, my darling?

Sniffy emerges, clutching a shopping bag. What erotica are in it? Timothy will never know.

Sniffy scuttles along the pavement like a guilty toad, and when he feels he is far enough away from Januslondon, he crosses the road and turns back towards the Amalfi. Timothy's heart almost stops. He couldn't bear to discuss Naomi with this man. (Sniffy may actually know something about her? That fear again?)

But Sniffy passes on his way, and Timothy's terror subsides. He finishes his saltimbocca. Twelve youngish people are sitting not far behind him. The noise level is rising. Their laughter is loud and a little desperate, as if they believe that the world may end tomorrow. Timothy is so happy that they are there. It cloaks him in anonymity. He is an island of silence in a sea of noise. He is the eye of the storm. He is the centre of the roulette wheel.

The restaurant is beginning to empty, soon the young people will leave. Naomi isn't coming, and suddenly he feels very lost and desperately lonely in the midst of all these people. He wishes now that Sniffy Arkwright *had* come in.

He has to get outside. He can feel claustrophobia coming on. He asks for his bill.

Hurry. Hurry. He doesn't feel so good. The panic comes

341

in waves, the sweat begins to form on his forehead, and as he sweats he feels deathly cold. But the waitress comes, and he pays, adding an excessively generous tip. This makes him feel good, even though he knows that he is doing it so that she will like him and will be kind to him tomorrow. But he has long ago given up worrying about motives. A good action is a good action, whatever the motive.

He staggers out into the street. He breathes in a great lungful of London air, and almost retches. It tastes of stress, sweat and petrol.

He feels slightly exhilarated. He's not going to faint, and that is a minor triumph. He tries to walk in a straight line, loses his balance as he turns a corner, finds himself lurching to the left. If he had lurched to the right he would have been in danger of falling into the path of the traffic, but he lurches to the left and faces only a lesser danger – the French House. The door of the pub opens as he tumbles towards it. He regains his balance and enters, trying to make it look as if this is what he had always intended to do.

A pub is the last place he should be going to. He could leave now. Nobody knows him here. He could pretend to be looking for a friend, and leave when he doesn't find him. But he doesn't want to leave. He has not lived enough. This afternoon he will live a little.

A beautiful, buxom barmaid beams alliteratively at him, and her smile enters his mouth and goes right down through his body to his genitals, warming and exciting him.

He orders a pint of bitter. She tells him that they only serve halves. He is relieved and disappointed. He collapses in ungainly fashion onto a bar stool. The man on the next stool turns to him and says, 'I know three different rain dances.' That's the thing about drinking. There's always somebody more drunk than you.

Timothy doesn't want to talk to this man. He has no desire

to hear about one rain dance, let alone three. It rains too often in Coningsfield. He's absolutely fed up with rain. Nor does he like dancing much. He has no rhythm. He needs to shut this man up and dredges up a moment of inspiration – rare, to be honest.

'I've not been lucky with women,' he says confidentially.

The man turns away, appalled at the prospect of the revelations that will follow.

'It's true, though,' says Timothy silently to himself.

He decides to tell the barmaid about Naomi, in the hope that sharing her may relieve some of the pain of his intensity. Here, at this three-cornered little bar, with the walls plastered with photographs of celebrities who have drunk here, he will tell, for the very first time, the story of the three most exciting days in all his life.

He will tell her silently, of course, because he knows that there is no reason for her to be interested, and besides she is busy.

'We were only seventeen. We were Romeo and Juliet in the school play. Our art master virtually instructed us to fall in love, yet the world was surprised and appalled when we did. We knew so little. We left Coningsfield as brave lovers, Romeo and Juliet still. But in London we became Timothy and Naomi again, provincial hicks. We booked a double room in a hotel in Earls Court. I can't even remember what it was called. I've been back a few times, wandered round where I thought it was, but I can't find it.'

'How fascinating!' He invents a response for the barmaid. 'Perhaps it's been pulled down.'

'Possibly. I was so embarrassed booking in. She said, "Names?" and I went brick red as I said, "Mr and Mrs Pickering." "You *are* married, are you?" she asked. "This is a respectable house." She had a parrot. It looked at us and it knew. "Oh, yes," I said. "We're on our honeymoon." The parrot said, "Pull

343

the other one." "You aren't under age, are you?" persisted the landlady. "We're both nineteen," said Naomi. The parrot said, "Yes, and I'm the Archbishop of Canterbury." The landlady shrugged and said, "It doesn't know what it's saying. It's only a bird. Only I had to ask because it's illegal under the licensing laws. Payment in advance, please."

'That night we kissed and kissed, we sailed on a sea of saliva, and I . . . I couldn't do it. Naomi said it was natural, I was nervous, she was nervous, we were embarrassed in case the people in the next room could hear, we knew they would be able to because the soundproofing was crap, we could hear their bed creaking, every creak was a dagger in my side. I didn't think anybody ever failed to get it up. Gregory Peck, Bob Dylan, Kevin Keegan, the Duke of Edinburgh, I'd never heard of any of them saying, "I'm sorry, darling. I must have been overworking recently."'

'Another half?'

'The next day . . .' Then he realises that this is actually the barmaid, talking, in real life.

'Oh. Better had.'

He's beginning to feel very cosy here, sitting at a little three-sided bar in the middle of Soho on a late autumn afternoon surrounded by people who all look . . . unusual . . . not distinguished exactly, but . . . out of the ordinary. He feels that he's part of a clique, an elite.

He resumes his silent story.

'The next day, we wandered round London, saw the sights, ate in the Amalfi just round the corner, and all the time I was thinking, "Oh, Lord. Night is approaching." Anyway, when it came, no problem. We made love for England.'

'Nice to be patriotic.'

'I can't begin to describe how wonderfully beautiful Naomi was with no clothes on. I mean, I'm sure that you're beautiful with no clothes on too.'

'Thank you.'

'Not that I'll ever know.'

'Shame.'

No. No, Timothy. Don't start fantasising about the barmaid. Respect her. Not that she'll ever know, but you are not what you seem. On the surface you may appear to be a hopeless lonely man comforting himself with onanistic fantasies about every attractive woman he sees, but deep down you're a fine man, a good man, with so much to give, and you know now that the only person you can ever give it to is Naomi.

'In the morning, I . . . I was frightened . . . she wanted me to go down on her and it just seemed . . . such an odd thing to do. You'll laugh at me, but I had to pluck up my courage to do it, but, do you know, it was wonderful. She came in my mouth, and . . . it was just so . . . so very friendly, so intimate and yet . . . exotic . . . just the most incredibly exciting thing. But afterwards . . . afterwards I couldn't talk about it, not to anybody, not even to her, and I felt ashamed as well as proud, which is ridiculous, and . . . it was religion, you see, I was very religious, well, even she was pretty religious. Isn't it extraordinary, dear lovely afternoon barmaid, that I am saying all these things to you silently and you have no idea – for all you know I might be trying to remember the Blackburn Rovers team of 1974? Full of secrets as well as information, faces.'

The barmaid is looking at him again, and he wonders if she can sense something of what he is saying to her inside his head. The thing is . . . it's strange . . . but she's getting prettier and prettier by the half-pint. Any more would be unwise.

'Same again, please.'

Well, he's in the middle of a story. He has to finish it, to explain why it all ended so badly. He has to share what he now sees as his terrible stupidity. He cannot carry the burden of that knowledge on his own any longer.

'Well, anyway, that morning at breakfast, the sun was shining and I was feeling pretty good about things, but also rather uneasy. I suddenly thought that everyone in the breakfast room could see what we'd been doing. And I realised that it was a sin. I mean, I don't think that now, of course, not at all, but I did then, even though of course it hadn't stopped me. And this woman came over to us, big woman, looked quite old, probably not more than sixty, I realise now. I was cutting round the edge of my second egg – they were good breakfasts, I'll give them that – I was going round and round getting nearer to the yolk, which I always eat last, and I saw her face, and I thought, we're going to be publicly abused as fornicators, and my knife slipped and broke the yolk before I was ready, which I hated, always have, still do, and she looked me straight in the eye, and spoke in a voice like a very aristocratic foghorn, and she said, "You look like racing folk. I've a dead cert in the two forty-five at Redcar." Well, I almost fainted from relief, but I knew then . . . I knew then . . . I couldn't do it again until we were married, I just couldn't, and I didn't, and of course we never were married. I mean, it seems so stupid now, even in 1978 lots of people would have thought it stupid, but there it is. I just wanted to get home. I hated that I'd lied to my dad. I wanted it all to be over. But of course, we had to see it through. It would have been awful to go back with our tails between our legs. But the next night, that was difficult. Second night, three climaxes. Third night, anticlimax. Horrid.'

The pub has become a ship of fools now, maybe even the *Mary Celeste*. They are adrift on this Sargasso Sea of an afternoon, these lost souls and he. Hello! The wind must be getting up, the ship is pitching and tossing on the increasing swell, he's afraid, he's sweating, it's so cold, his sweat is frozen, there's ice on the rigging, the deck is coming up to meet him, all is darkness, all is nothing.

He comes round to find himself lying on the floor. The kind barmaid is bending over him. She looks very concerned. Even her cleavage manages to look concerned.

The sweat pours off him.

'I'll be all right now,' he says. He tries to smile, but the smile congeals even as he smiles it, like rain turning to ice on cold soil.

They help him into a chair at one of the wooden tables in the little back room.

'I'm fine,' he says. 'Just a warse of glorter . . . glass of water, and I'll be fine. I've had too much and I . . . I've done this sort of thing before, and . . . I'll be fine.'

He sits and sips, sits and sips, sits and sips. The colour begins to come back to his cheeks. The evening crowd start to pour in, thrusting, eager, full of themselves. The afternoon people take their cue and melt away like ghosts, back to their lonelinesses.

Timothy thanks the barmaid, and wants to kiss her, but doesn't, and there isn't any point anyway because she isn't Naomi, and he too goes back to his loneliness. The fun is over. His room in the Travel Lodge awaits him.

Tonight, with luck, he will be too drunk to have the dream. He dreads his recurring nightmare. He has never felt able to mention it to anybody, not to Naomi, not to Maggie, not to Hannah, not to his father. His dream is like the attacks of terrorists. They don't have to happen very often for the fear to be perpetual.

When, two and a half days later, on a dark, dreary Sunday evening, he drives in the dark along mainly flat roads back to his terrace house on the East Anglian coast, he reflects upon the ridiculous week that he has just so senselessly imposed on himself, and he knows that he must seek Naomi out, Google her, whatever that is, go to something called Face Reunited or Book of Tubes or Your Friends or something that they have on the mysterious Internet, get in touch with the actors' union, be logical, be a man.

His little house is smaller than ever and smells of emptiness and damp. He's left it out in the rain, and it's shrunk. The front door leads straight into what is almost too small to be called a lounge, but that's what it is. 'Well, I don't need a big living room,' he thinks wryly. 'I don't do much living.' 'Until now,' he adds.

On the floor, swept to one side by the door as he opens it, is the post that has accumulated over the last week. So little. How meagre the world's interest in him has been.

He picks the post up, takes it through to the second, equally small room, which would be a cosy dining room if he ever had guests, puts the mail down on the table, goes into the tiny kitchen, makes himself a cup of tea, realises that he has no milk, pours the tea down the sink, makes himself a cup of coffee, takes it through into the unused dining room, sits at the table, and stares at his sad little bundle of mail.

This is his great new life, his new start, his wonderful job with live birds after a lifetime of dead ones, but on this cold Sunday evening there is such a feeling of loneliness in him that he wishes he could let go of his manliness and cry. Manliness? He's no man. He had the dream again last night. He hasn't had it much since he began this job, but he had it last night.

He begins to work his way miserably through the unutterable dreariness of his post. He's offered the chance of booking a cruise to the Caribbean which will be amazing value. He's told of a giant carpet sale, and is unaware that, when he thinks how useless a giant carpet will be in this tiny house, he is echoing a thought that Naomi had in Narcissus Road. He's invited to a seminar on inheritance tax in Ipswich. He's sent photographs of a boy with a horrendous harelip in the hope that it will move him to pity. It moves him to despair that he cannot afford to help in any meaningful way.

There's a letter dictated by his father. He made one pound twenty the other day at fives and threes, playing for twenty pence up and down the crib board. He sounds delighted. Timothy pulls himself together. His life is not too bad. Oh, why did he go to London for his week's holiday, and not to Coningsfield, to bring some brief sunshine into his dad's life? Well, he knows why. Because in London there was the faintest of chances that he would run into Naomi.

And, right at the bottom of the pile, there's a letter in a white envelope, a letter with his address handwritten, in a hand that he doesn't recognise, the hand not of a child but of an adult with childish writing. This one looks as if it might at least be vaguely interesting. He takes a sip of the acrid black coffee, longing to open the letter, but happy to hang onto the moment of longing, because, if this letter disappoints, there will be nothing left for him except to set his alarm and go to bed. And maybe have the dream again.

At first the letter disappoints him. It's from Sniffy Arkwright, of all people. But, as he reads it, his disappointment is slowly replaced by anticipation, which grows slowly into an excitement which will keep him awake, and happily awake, half the night.

Dear Timothy

I imagine this letter will come as a great surprise, as I have never written to you before. But I ran into Tommo the other day, he was his usual self, brimming with health, full of fun, told me a joke about a nun and a combine harvester which I didn't understand, and I suddenly had an amazing thought – hope you didn't faint when you read that!! – and I asked Tommo for your address, and he phoned me with it that very night. He sends his love, incidentally.

Next July it will be twenty-five years since our year left Coningsfield Grammar to make our various ways in the world, and I thought that it would be a good idea to mark the occasion by having a reunion. I happened to meet Dave Kent in the supermarket – he was prodding the fruit and when he saw me he said, 'These are disgusting. They say that they're ripe and ready to eat. They'll never ripen. They'll go bad before they're ready to eat. They've been picked too soon and kept in cold storage for too long. What kind of a pathetic spiritless nation of shoppers are we that we accept this crap?' I said, 'I completely agree with you, Dave, but I want to talk to you about an amazing idea I've had. Shall we have a cup of tea in the café?' He said, 'Fuck that. Let's have a pint in the Builders' Arms.' So we did.

Well, he thought my idea was great, and the upshot was that we got in touch with John Parkin. I don't know if you knew him at school, but he's with Bertram Gould, and they are just about the most respected firm of solicitors in Coningsfield. I knew that he'd be good on the details, and so it's proved. He was also happy to give us his services free, which wasn't bad as he normally gets two hundred and twenty pounds an hour. I wish I did. I mean, he wasn't even clever. (Don't tell him I said that!)

He's drafted a letter which we've sent out to all one hundred and ninety-six people who left school that year. The school think it's a great idea and were happy to give us access to the last addresses that they had, although of course some people may have moved and not told the school. However, in his letter John has asked people to let us know the addresses of anyone they are still in contact with, so this should help us to get in touch with the vast majority.

You and I were always quite close . . .

What?

. . . so I didn't want you to just get a circular, I wanted to write to you personally. I do hope you will be able to come. John has suggested that Coningsfield residents should offer beds to 'out-of-towners', though he himself can't as his wife suffers with her nerves. (I'd suffer with my nerves if I was married to John – don't tell him I said that either!!) Timothy, I've had a word with my old man and with Mother . . .

My old man and Mother? That doesn't sound very Coningsfield Grammar.

. . . and we would feel privileged to be able to offer you a bed for the night. Or nights. Why not make a bit of a break of it, lots of catching up to do.

He is amazed to find that Sniffy, in his forties, is still living with his parents. But then none of them ever knew much about him. None of them ever asked him much about himself. No, let's face it, none of them ever asked him anything about himself.

The proposed date is July the eighteenth, exactly twenty-five years on from the end of our last term, and John is busy getting quotes from possible venues. We'll do it in style. Three-course dinner and a band. Do you remember Rick Ferrensby? He had a group called 'The Ricking Slickers' and he'll know who are the coolest people we can get within budget. It's going to be a great night in the old town.

I do hope you can come, and please do think of my offer of a bed.

With kind regards,
Yours sincerely,

Your old chum
Peregrine Arkwright.

Peregrine! No wonder he didn't object to being called Sniffy. And no wonder he always seemed a bit of a loner. How could anybody call on his mother and say, 'Oh hello, Mrs Arkwright. Can your Peregrine come out to play?'

Naomi. She will get an invitation. She will come.

He leaps at the thought. She will come. There's no need for him to Google and do all those other difficult, mysterious things, chase her up, show his hand, risk the possibility of humilating rejection. Unwise to show her just how much he cares until he's had a chance to test the waters. Much better.

What if she doesn't come? Well, if she doesn't, then he will search her out.

But she will.

Timothy doesn't feel ready for bed yet. The letter could not have transformed his view of his house more if he'd been an estate agent. Small? It's compact. It's bijou. It's cosy. His little terrace flint house is so cosy, he wants to just sit in his favourite armchair, sip a malt whisky with the same amount of water, and reflect on the loveliness of life. Then he will go to bed and make love to Naomi as she has never been loved before and certainly not by that bastard Colin.

All that long, raw, grey winter, all through the bursting daffodil days on the slope of the lane up to the church that he has never even been inside, all through the slow, unchanging months on the timeless marshes where the seasons make no difference, all through the laying and hatching of the delicate little reed buntings' eggs in the reeds that sway in the breeze with the precision of sailors in a storm, Timothy feels that he is in suspended animation. Time moves in three dimensions. There's the normal Greenwich

Mean Time, moving just a bit faster now than it did when he was younger, speeding him on his way to old age and death, using up his life much more quickly than he would have wished. There's East Anglian Scrooge Time, meaner even than Greenwich Time, letting out its countless seconds, its millions of minutes, its long hours so slowly that July the eighteenth seems almost at times to be like the spring tides beyond the shingle that protects the reserve, receding, then approaching, then receding, then coming just a little closer. And the third dimension is his very own special time, Timothy Time, which doesn't move at all, so that he seems suspended, inanimate, trapped in the aspic of the moment.

Somehow, by arrangement between the three dimensions, the hours do pass. He busies himself with his work. It's a successful breeding season. Young avocets abound in the lagoons. There's a bit of a baby boom for the booming bitterns in the reeds. The marsh harriers rear two young successfully. May gives way to June, June to July.

The nearer the great day approaches, the more its greatness recedes. There are so many reasons why Naomi will not come. There are so many reasons why, if she does come, he will wish that she hadn't. At times he feels that he's insane, obsessed, yet his hope is so great that he can't abandon it for a moment, it's with him as he works, it's with him as he eats, it's with him as he sleeps, it's with him as he dreams. And in his anxiety he's beginning to dream the dream more often. It's as if he's terrified that he's unworthy of Naomi.

And now July the seventeenth has arrived at last, and he sets off towards the North in his trusty, rusty, old estate car. It's a car that should smell of Labrador, but doesn't. He has reached the stage of his life when he feels he ought to have a dog, and his choice would be a Labrador. It's inconceivable to him that Naomi could dislike dogs, but she might prefer other breeds to Labradors, which, it has to be admitted,

353

do smell and often pinch the cheese off the table. He can't have a Labrador, until he knows that Naomi likes Labradors, or until – he can hardly bear to articulate the thought to himself – he has lost all hope of her.

How dreary the motorway, how banal the fields, how long the miles, how unwelcoming the service stations, how ugly the bridges, how aggressive the drivers, how smelly the diesel, how huge the juggernauts, how slow the hours.

He's going to stay with Tommo and his wife and boys.

It'll be cramped, and you'll have to share a bathroom, and don't look under the bed, but we'll make you very welcome. Do come the day before. Let's make a bit of a thing of it.
   P.S. Got a corker for you. Hope you haven't heard it!

Dear Peregrine,
I would love to take you up on your kind offer, but unfortunately I can't. Tommo's my closest friend, and he would be hurt if I stayed anywhere else. However, I really look forward to seeing you again and having a jaw about old times.

A jaw about old times! What got into his use of language when he thought of Sniffy?

'Coningsfield Welcomes Careful Drivers'.

As he passes the sign he smiles at the thought of Tommo's driving on those Pennine Piss-ups.

'You are Entering a Nuclear-Free Zone'.

He hopes the Russians and the North Koreans know about this.

'Avoid Congestion, Share A Car'.

What a recipe for social disaster.

At last he reaches the end of Derwentwater Road, and turns into it.

Two police cars and an ambulance are parked very close

to Tommo's house. As he gets closer, he sees to his horror that they are actually outside Tommo's house. His heart starts thumping. Somehow, he knows already.

He pulls up a couple of houses away. He gets out of his car with great reluctance, and walks slowly along the pavement. A mountainous policeman is standing outside the house, his great feet plonked solidly on the fake Yorkshire stone.

'I'm afraid you can't go in there, sir,' he says.

'What's happened?' asks Timothy.

'I'm afraid I'm not at liberty to reveal that,' says the policeman stolidly. He doesn't *look* afraid.

Tommo's wife rushes down the drive, and at that terrible moment, even at that terrible moment, Timothy is horrified to find that he can't remember her name.

'Oh, Timothy,' she says. 'Oh, Timothy.'

She collapses onto his chest, this woman whose name he's forgotten and who has never before even pecked his cheek.

'Oh, Timothy,' she cries. 'I came home. I'd been shopping, getting things for breakfast. Your breakfast,' she sobs bitterly, 'because we don't do breakfast, not any more, not really. But I thought you might want some, with your having come such a long way. And there he was, at the top of the stairs. He's hanged himself.'

Timothy strokes the top of her hair and feels absolutely helpless. He can think of no words that are adequate for such a moment. He feels that his head is sinking to his feet, the way it does after too much drink.

'I'm really sorry,' sobs Tommo's wife, 'but I think you're going to have to try to find somewhere else to stay.'

Timothy pulls up in Coniston Crescent, wipes his moist eyes, then switches on his mobile, and has a problem dialling Dave Kent's number, so much are his fingers shaking.

He finds it difficult to break the dreadful news. Dave is shocked into silence. He asks Dave if he can stay with him, but Dave tells him that he has a full house already. He arranges to meet Dave for a drink at the Mulberry in half an hour, and phones Sniffy. His mother answers the phone.

'Peregrine is still at work,' she explains in an unexpectedly cut-glass voice. 'They work him so hard.'

Once more Timothy finds it difficult to be a messenger of death.

'I am *so* sorry,' says Mrs Arkwright. 'That is *so* terrible. Did he have children?'

'Two boys.'

'That is *so* tragic.'

'Um . . . the thing is . . .' Timothy finds the gear change difficult. 'Um, Sni— Peregrine did rather invite me to stay.'

Rather? What's going on, Timothy? Why does your speech go strange whenever you think of Sniffy?

'But I felt . . . I mean, it was wonderfully kind of him . . . and of you and Mr Arkwright . . . but I felt I ought to stay with Tommo because he was my best friend. But now . . . um . . . I mean, it's very hard to invite myself. And if it isn't convenient . . .'

'Do come. We would be *so* delighted. Peregrine will be *so* thrilled. He's always talking about you.'

Really? Good God.

'We *deplore* the reason, but we will be delighted about the visit. Hamish is *dying* to meet you. But I've just thought. Will the celebrations still take place? People will be *so* disappointed if they don't. Peregrine will be devastated.'

Timothy hasn't thought of that. He phones John Parkin.

'He's with a client,' says his secretary snootily.

'It is rather urgent,' explains Timothy. 'It's about the big reunion tomorrow night. There's been a suicide.'

'Oh, dear.' Her tone suggests that she means, 'How very

356

inconsiderate.' 'I'm just accessing his diary. He has a small window at half past four.'

'Thank you.'

He parks in the almost empty car park of the Mulberry, and enters the cavernous pub, quiet in the afternoon except for four tattooed men playing pool and a Polish couple snogging under the extractor fan.

When Dave Kent enters, they find themselves hugging each other. They take their pints to a far corner.

'Poor old Tommo,' says Timothy, 'and what a dreadful thing for his wife to come home to find.'

He still can't remember her Christian name.

'He must have been pretty desperate to expose her to that,' says Dave.

'I know. That's what's so awful. But why? Why, Dave? And why today of all days? To cast a shadow over the event? Could he be that bitter about something? And about what? Anyway, I don't see how it can have been premeditated or surely he wouldn't have invited me to stay?'

'Well,' says Dave, 'I don't think it can be coincidence that he just happens to do it the day before. Maybe he was dreading it. I mean, the drink issue would have been a problem.'

'What do you mean?'

'Well, how would he have explained not drinking at such an event? To say it was because he was driving wouldn't make sense. It would be so easy to get a taxi. He might have thought that people would discover his secret, and he was so ashamed of it, as we know.'

'I'm sorry, Dave. I'm not with you.'

Dave Kent stares at him in amazement.

'Well, you knew he was an alcoholic?'

'No.'

'He could never touch another drop in his life. That's why

he always drove on our piss-ups and never drank. That's why he never drank at work. He thought nobody knew, but of course everybody did. They put two and two together.'

'Except me.'

'Yes, except you. You do have a slightly naive streak, Timothy.'

'Oh, my God. Poor old Tommo. But he was always the life and soul of the party.'

'Exactly.'

'You mean . . . because really he didn't want to be part of the party?'

'Sort of, yep. I think he felt a complete and utter failure.'

'But he was very successful.'

'Well, to a degree. I mean, you've gone away, you wouldn't know, but they've laid a few off. They haven't kept up with the market. They're perceived as old-fashioned. There are rumours that they'll fail. Who knows how bad things are? Who knows what trouble he's in personally? And Mandy's an expensive woman.'

Mandy!

'Another thing about Tommo. He hated biscuits.'

'What?'

'Well, he always wanted to be a gynaecologist.'

'I thought that was half a joke, because he liked women's bodies.'

'Don't we all? But no. I think he really wanted to be a doctor, any kind of doctor. I think he wanted to hear people say, "Good morning, doctor," and "Ask Tommo what he thinks. He'll know. He's a doctor." Nobody ever said, "Ask Tommo what he thinks. He'll know. He's in biscuits." He was a disappointed man.'

'But he was always handing out tins of biscuits.'

'Well, there you are. What was it Shakespeare said?'

'Me thinks he doth hand out tins of biscuits too much?'

They feel rather ashamed about laughing.

They find that they have finished their pints. There's just time for one more before visiting John Parkin. They shouldn't, but they're shaken, so they do.

While Dave Kent is buying the drinks, Timothy studiously avoids looking at the long legs of the Polish girl, whose skimpy dress is almost up to her crotch as she and her partner continue to be entwined. Today he may see Naomi. Today is not a day for fantasy.

He thinks about Naomi for the first time since the terrible discovery. His stomach sinks into a pit of tension.

'Cheers, Timothy,' says Dave, raising his glass rather glumly. 'My God, just look at those Poles. Have they no respect for the decorum of English pub life? Isn't darts good enough for them?'

'How do we actually know they're Poles?' asks Timothy.

'They broke off briefly from kissing to take a drink. I saw their bone structure.'

They discuss Tommo's death, and whether they should cancel the reunion. They discuss Tommo's life, and whether they could have done more to help him. But how do you help someone whose whole life is based on a strategy of concealing the fact that he has problems?

Dave tells him that Steven Venables has been sacked from the railways, and has received another substantial pay-off in reward for his failure.

'To get paid off by three different forms of transport takes some doing,' he says.

'He's a hero of our times,' says Timothy.

Dave seems to know everything, and Timothy feels that he knows almost nothing. He wants to ask Dave if he knows whether Naomi is coming, but he daren't.

They drive off to see John Parkin in Timothy's car. There's a space in the reserved parking area outside the grand but gloomy Victorian offices, and this stroke of luck enables them to arrive five minutes early.

John Parkin makes them wait eight minutes, even though nobody emerges from his office during that time.

His office smells of dust and dignity. It's very dark.

'He does have a small window,' whispers Timothy behind his hand. There's something about John Parkin that impels him to be childish. Dave glares at him, because he feels it too, and he wants to giggle. They both want to giggle. It's not only John Parkin's humourlessness that brings this out, it's the tension. They have a terrible tale to tell, and they just mustn't giggle as they tell it.

They tell him the bad news. He goes white.

'Poor old Tommo,' he says. 'But what a time to do it.'

'I know. Utterly selfish,' says Timothy drily, but John Parkin clearly fails to detect his tone. He remembers John Parkin now. Hoity-toity even at school. So lacking in humour that he was the only person called Parkin never to be referred to as Ginger throughout his whole schooldays. Born to be a solicitor. He imagines the midwife coming up to Mrs Parkin's bedside and saying, 'It's a solicitor. Isn't that wonderful? You've got a bonny bouncing little solicitor, Mrs Parkin.' This is awful. He's in danger of giggling again. Oh, Tommo. My poor poor Tommo. The giggles are banished by a wave of compassion and sorrow.

'The thing is,' says Dave, 'do we cancel out of respect?'

'We can't,' says John Parkin. 'One girl has come all the way from New Zealand. Besides which, we've paid a hefty deposit to the Balmoral.'

Timothy suspects that the deposit weighs more heavily on John Parkin than the plight of the girl who has come all the way from New Zealand.

They decide that it's not feasible to cancel. Too many people have travelled too far. Too many people are looking forward to it too much. And, besides, there *is* the question of the deposit.

They discuss the option of saying nothing to anyone about Tommo, just having one less chair and one less place setting at one of the tables.

'I'm sorry, but I just don't think that's respectful,' says Timothy. 'We have to announce it. It's an inconvenient and awkward thing to do, and it'll be a very difficult emotional lurch for everyone, especially those who knew him, but I think it's unavoidable. Somebody will have found out, and by the end of the evening everybody will know.'

'At what stage do we announce it?' asks Dave.

'Either the beginning of the meal or the end,' says Timothy. 'No other possibilities.'

'The beginning, I think,' says John Parkin. 'It'll be too much of a shock at the end.'

'I agree,' says Dave. 'Besides, things'll be too raucous by the end. Respect will be too difficult to achieve.'

'Do you really think so?' John Parkin is shocked. 'It's the Grammar School, not some comprehensive.'

'Well, I hope it will,' says Dave.

'And who will make the announcement?' asks Timothy.

'I think I should,' says John Parkin, colouring slightly. 'I am the main organiser. I am—'

He stops in mid-stream. He realises that whatever he says next will sound like boasting.

'True,' says Timothy, 'but you didn't really know him. It would be extraordinarily difficult for you to strike the right note. Very difficult for anybody, but I knew him well. I'm prepared to volunteer.'

They can see all too clearly, in John Parkin's face, his struggle between self-importance and cowardice. Cowardice wins.

'Thank you, Timothy. Very much appreciated,' he says.

Timothy drives back to the Mulberry, drops Dave off beside his car, and sets off towards . . . Peregrine's.

This is definitely not a day for nicknames.

Peregrine and his parents live in a big Georgian house at the foot of the moors. Huge, rusting gates lead onto a long drive, bordered by massive rhododendrons. The drive emerges onto a gravelled area with a statue of a Greek god in the middle. Half his prick has fallen off. It seems symbolic. In front of the gravelled area is a large lawn, only a small segment of which has been mown.

Timothy feels as if he's playing a bit part in a low-budget production of *Brideshead Revisited*. He doesn't wish to make the thing even more downmarket, so he parks his dirty estate car round the side.

He crunches round to the front of the house, acutely conscious of the inelegance of his scruffy overnight bag.

He climbs the front steps, between two stern lions, one of whom has lost three-quarters of his tail. He pulls the bell, and hears a faint somnolence which sounds half a mile away.

It's a while before the door is opened, giving Timothy time to note the decrepit state of the window frames.

At last he hears the sound of approaching asthma. A frail, elderly man in blazer and grey flannels opens the door, which squeals its annoyance at being disturbed. An absence of WD40 replaces Sniffy in Timothy's remembrance of things past.

'Hello,' enthuses the old man, who has hanging jowls, deep-set eyes and straggly white hair carefully arranged to hide as much of his baldness as possible. 'You must be Timothy. I'm Hamish Arkwright. Welcome to Green Acres. Let me take your things.'

'No, no. I'm fine.'

Timothy clings onto his things . . . well, his thing. The plural is inaccurate. He doesn't want Peregrine's father to defile his upper-class hands by contact with his germ-infested bag.

'Peregrine is still at work, I'm afraid. Wednesday is their late evening.'

Timothy realises that he has no idea what Peregrine does.

'I'll show you to your room, and then we'll take tea.'

Hamish has a struggle climbing the stairs. It occurs to Timothy that he is falling apart at much the same rate as his house. He follows slowly in the elderly man's wake.

Timothy's room is large, cold, damp and shabby. He unpacks listlessly, washes perfunctorily, and goes downstairs reluctantly.

The drawing room is also large, cold, damp and shabby. No hint of July penetrates it. The house has seen better days and so has Lavinia Arkwright. But there is still a certain elegance about her, a lined and slightly haggard beauty. She looks . . . no, not glamorous, which might have moved Timothy, but as if she must once have been glamorous, which moves him far more.

She is, however, distinctly more sprightly than her husband, as so many elderly women seem to be. She pours the Lapsang Souchong with a steady hand, and cuts the Battenberg cake with mathematical precision.

'Battenberg is a family tradition,' she announces.

There's a large brown stain in one corner of the moulded ceiling of the drawing room which is decorated in a medley of dark and light greens. Two sections of the wallpaper are peeling slightly from the top, and there are significant cracks in the ceiling.

Timothy senses that both Hamish and Lavinia are shrinking as they enter old age, and he feels unnecessarily large and extremely inelegant as he sips his Lapsang Souchong and eats his Battenberg cake daintily with a tiny fork. He's certain that he will drop at best crumbs, at worst the complete contents of his cup, onto the threadbare Wilton, which looks as though it might fall to bits if cleaned once more.

'We are *so* pleased to get a chance to talk to you,' says Lavinia.

'You've been such a good friend to Peregrine,' says Hamish.

'*Such* a good friend,' echoes Lavinia.

What??

'Peregrine is not blessed with a plethora of close friends,' says Hamish.

'We blame ourselves sometimes,' says Lavinia. 'We should have pushed him. But he *so* enjoyed his outings with you and your chums.'

Timothy tries not to look too blank. What outings are these?

'Your trips to Pennine hostelries,' explains Hamish.

'He'd come home *so* excited,' exclaims Lavinia. 'He's not supposed to get excited, it brings on his insomnia, but it was good to see.'

'We used to stay up late, just to see the smile on his face,' says Hamish. 'So . . . may we say . . . thank you.'

'Thank you,' echoes Lavinia.

Timothy has believed that he has made great strides in overcoming embarrassment in recent years, but he doubts if he has ever felt as embarrassed as this. Shame at the gang's treatment of Sni— Peregrine, he cannot think of him as Sniffy under this decrepit roof. Guilt at their casual cruelty. Even as he accepts a second cup – 'It's delicious' – and a second slice – 'I shouldn't' – he longs to say, 'I am unworthy of your hospitality. Please let me leave.'

But maybe tonight, belatedly, he can begin to make amends.

'Lavinia and I have decided to reveal something to you, Timothy,' says Hamish.

'Before Peregrine gets home,' says Lavinia.

364

Timothy can hear his Spode cup rattling daintily in its saucer. He is trembling.

'We have felt . . . we still feel . . . a certain guilt over Peregrine. A certain shame,' says Hamish.

Good Lord. We are united in shame and guilt. *What* a strange tea.

'I was in business,' says Hamish. 'You are not in business, I understand.'

'No. I'm in wildlife preservation.'

'Splendid. How splendid. In business, Timothy, the best of us have our ups and . . . um . . .'

'. . . downs,' contributes Lavinia unnecessarily.

'We were blessed with two sons. Peregrine, whom you know, and Marmaduke, whom I don't know if you know.'

'No. I don't know him.'

'Though no doubt Peregrine has often spoken of him.'

Never mentioned him.

'Often.'

'Marmaduke is the elder by some eight years, and at the time of the need for his education to commence, things were very buoyant in the world of foam.'

'Foam is the line Hamish is in,' contributes Lavinia, again unnecessarily. 'Was in, I should say.'

'I see.'

'Very buoyant. We put Marmaduke down for Eton, and we sent him there. He's no genius, but he's found a very good position at the Foreign Office.'

'Almost entirely due to going to Eton,' adds Lavinia.

'Almost entirely. By the time Peregrine was to take up his educational cudgels, the world of foam had become very difficult. I made an error or two of judgement . . .'

'I think it was three, actually,' says Lavinia. '*So* easily done.'

Hamish gives her as dirty a look as he can manage without ceasing to be a gentleman.

'I also made a rather unwise investment. To cut a long story short, I lost a lot of money. I could not afford to send Peregrine to Eton. More tea?'

'Thank you. It's delicious.'

Oh, I said that last time. Damn.

'I think I should make it clear at this point that we had realised that it was unlikely that Peregrine would be the sort to go on to university. We had a choice – let's be frank – between selling Green Acres, the family home to five generations of Arkwrights, or of abandoning private education for Peregrine, and settling for Coningsfield Grammar, which had a fine reputation and indeed was and is a fine school, as witnessed by its production of alumni such as yourself. We also did persuade ouselves that it might be an advantage for him, a shy boy, to be in the company of girls.'

'Although, in the event, he seems not to have garnered much from this opportunity.'

'No. Sadly. Peregrine has never glittered socially. Which is why we value your kindness to him so much.'

'Have another slice of Battenberg cake.'

It'd stick in my gullet.

'Thank you. It's delicious.'

Oh, I said that about the tea. Damn.

How the minutes drag as he waits for Peregrine to arrive home. Timothy is left on his own with a pile of back numbers of *Country Life*. He seizes them eagerly, hoping they will help him forget about his treatment of Peregrine. He looks at the frontispieces, golden girls, English roses, either with a Labrador or on a horse. None of them can hold a candle to Naomi. Naomi. Naomi. Why didn't he have the courage to ask John Parkin if she was coming?

Supposing she doesn't want him any more.

Supposing he doesn't want her any more.

Supposing she doesn't come.

He won't know whether she would have wanted him any more.

He won't know whether he would have wanted her any more.

He puts the magazines down. They have helped him to escape one torture, only to plunge him into another.

'Timothy!'

Peregrine's pleasure sends Timothy back into paroxysms of shame.

Timothy finds dinner a grisly affair, all the more so because it's clear that none of the others do.

The four of them are seated at a table that is too large for four, in a dining room that is too large for the table. Even in July the room is cold. They eat off Minton plates, one of which, the one used by Lavinia, is chipped. The cauliflower soup, grey cottage pie and rhubarb fool are unworthy of the plates. They drink thin Bulgarian claret. Peregrine reminisces about their trips to the Pennines, leaving out only the fact that he always gatecrashed them halfway through. This is so excruciating for Timothy that he is actually relieved when the subject turns to Tommo's suicide.

And all the while the pressure is building. In twenty-one hours' time he will know whether Naomi has come.

After dinner, Hamish and Lavinia retire to bed.

'We usually go early,' says Lavinia, 'but tonight we thought we might go even earlier.'

'You and Peregrine will have so much to talk about,' says Hamish.

Peregrine finds some port, and the two of them sit at either side of the empty fireplace, dwarfed by the drawing room, like a squire and his visitor after a good day on the river.

'It's so good to see you,' says Peregrine.

Timothy can think of several replies, but not one of them can be made. He wants to apologise for his behaviour over the years, but he feels that this would serve no purpose. Peregrine may well be in denial over the truth of their 'Pennine Piss-ups'. He may have persuaded himself that he really was invited to them, that he was part of their secret club.

He also wants to ask him what he bought at Janus London, but that line of conversation is closed to him too.

They discuss Tommo yet again, and Peregrine echoes the words they have all used. 'Poor old Tommo.'

Timothy at last thinks of a subject that it is permissible for him to raise.

'Do you know, Peregrine, I've never actually known what it is you do for a living,' he says.

'Oh, not much,' says Peregrine. 'I'm not much of a chap, you know. I'm a chemist.'

'Oh! What sort of a chemist?'

'A "Can I help you, madam?" sort of a chemist. I work in a chemist's shop over in Dingelton. I got the job twenty-three years ago, and I've stayed there ever since. Pathetic, isn't it?'

Yes.

'No!! Of course it isn't.'

'I've no responsibility and that suits me. It's a job well within my powers. I do it well and I get on well with the customers and they like me.'

'Well, that's great.'

'Another drop?'

'Thank you.'

'I shouldn't, but I'll keep you company. Cheers.'

'Cheers.'

'Not bad port.'

'No.'

'I was thinking, Timothy, the other day . . . it would probably strike you as sad . . . it probably is sad . . . but it doesn't seem too sad to me so if it isn't too sad to me I suppose you'd

368

say it isn't sad . . . but in my career . . . I say, listen to me, "career", hardly a career . . . but, as I say, in my career, I must have said to . . . oh, easily a thousand customers, maybe more than a thousand, I mean I'm not talking about a thousand different people, though I suppose over the years it might be, but well over a thousand people counting every time I've spoken to them and some of them I've said it to quite regularly . . . I've said, "Anything for the weekend, sir?" and in all that time . . . I mean, I have a little laugh with some of them over it, I think they think I'm a bit bold . . . in all that time I have had, in my possession, every time I've gone out, in my pocket, "something for the weekend". And I've never ever used it, not once, ever. Is that sad or is that sad?'

At first Timothy doesn't realise that Peregrine has finished.

'Are you sorry you've never used it?' he asks.

Peregrine reflects.

'On the whole, no,' he says. 'I think I'd be scared stiff. Oh. "Stiff". How very inappropriate!'

They have a little laugh over that.

This is his last chance to ask Peregrine what he bought at Janus London, but he can't.

'Another drop?'

'Thank you.'

'I shouldn't, but I'll keep you company. Cheers.'

'Cheers.

'Nice port.'

'Yes.'

'You must be looking forward to seeing Naomi.'

Timothy's insides seem to rush up right into his throat. He can hardly speak.

'Is she coming?'

'Well, I hope so. That's the whole point of it.'

'What on earth can you mean?'

'I can see how right you two are for each other. I always

have. You should have married each other. I wondered how I could help you, and I thought, if we laid on a big reunion, you'd meet.'

'All this was your idea?'

'I told you it was.'

'I know, but . . .'

'You didn't believe me.'

'No. Sorry. Well . . . my God . . . thank you. And it was all for . . . us?'

'Yes.'

'And you say, she's coming?'

'Well, she's accepted. We weren't sure of her address, so we sent it to the address we had, and we sent another one care of the BBC, we put "Naomi Walls, star, *Get Stuffed*" and apparently that went to someone who used to be her agent, and they sent it on to her, and she wrote and said, yes, she was coming.'

Timothy lets out a huge sigh.

'But why . . . why should you do all that?'

'You've always been so kind to me.'

Does he really believe that? Perhaps he does.

'But . . . I mean . . . since you've never ever . . . you know . . . done it, I'm amazed that you're so . . . you know . . . generous about us.'

'I like to see people happy. It's probably the greatest pleasure I get in life.'

Timothy shakes his head very slowly several times, then smiles.

'Thank you, Peregrine,' he says.

'No probs. So, tomorrow, the big day.'

'Absolutely.'

'Best get to bed.'

'Be stupid not to.'

'Drop more port?'

'Thanks.'

'I shouldn't, but I'll keep you company. Cheers.'

'Cheers.'

'Wonderful port.'

'Wonderful.'

A hundred and thirty-one old Coningsfieldians stand in a room not quite big enough, in a hotel not quite good enough, drinking sparkling white wine not quite cold enough, under a huge chandelier not quite clean enough.

Timothy surveys the room, and the sight of this tightly packed throng, every one of whom is aged forty-three or forty-four, strikes him as bizarre.

The organisers had decided that there should be no dress code, formality wasn't the Coningsfieldian way. So a hundred and thirty people have thought hard about what image they wish to convey. Only Peregrine, so recently deSniffified, hasn't. He has no sense of what he should look like, or indeed of what he does look like, which is lucky, because, if he did, he wouldn't go anywhere. He is wearing a striped shirt with a white collar, a brown cardigan with buttons, a tweed jacket with leather patches on the elbows, and grey flannel trousers not quite immaculate enough around the crotch.

There are men in dark suits, men in light suits, men in jacket and tie, men in jacket and open-neck shirt, men in jeans and open-neck shirt, and one man, determined not to look forty-three, in jeans and T-shirt. He does succeed, though, in not looking forty-three. He looks fifty-two.

There are sensible women with good legs in short dresses, sensible women with bad legs in long dresses, modest women with good legs in long dresses, and deluded women with bad legs in short dresses. There are also many women in trousers.

The buzz of conversation is deafening. Men are talking to women whose names they can't remember. Others are talking to women whom they suddenly wish they'd married. Some people are trying to sound modest as they relate how well they've done. Others are trying to keep the conversation more general to avoid revealing how badly they've done. One man is deeply aware that he has lost more hair than anyone else in the room. Some women are saying how well their children are doing. Others are trying not to speak of their offspring. Several women are convinced that Sally Lever has had a facelift.

Timothy isn't interested in any of this. He is only interested in one thing.

And then he catches sight of her. She's here. She's come. His knees almost buckle, his heart hammers, his throat goes dry, he feels sick, he can barely breathe, this is almost as terrible as it's wonderful. She's here. She's come. In a few moments . . . in a few moments, what? In a few moments his life will change for the better, to an unimaginable degree, for ever. Or it will change for the worse, to an unimaginable degree, for ever. He wants to rush over to her, part the crowds like the Red Sea. He also wants to delay the moment, to still have hope.

He has to delay. He can't approach her while she's talking to that cow who once nipped his prick so viciously in geography.

They all have name tags. If he wasn't in love with Naomi he could pretend to be short-sighted and use looking at their names as an excuse for getting quite close to several breasts.

'Timothy Pickering! I thought so. I'm Sally Lever. Well, Sally Mackintosh now. You were in our confirmation class.'

'That's right.'

'You look great.'

'Thank you. It's the outdoor life.' Then, ever so slightly late, 'And so do you.'

'It must be all my indoor exercise.'

Her eyes meet his as she says this. Her face, whether lifted or not, is smooth, lovely, warm. Her teeth are extremely white. She's making advances. Now, today, of all times, I could pull. Whoever Mackintosh is, he's not made her happy. Whoever Mackintosh is, he's not giving her what she wants.

The irony of it. To be propositioned by a mature and lovely woman at this of all moments. For Sally Lever is lovely. With the help, perhaps, of a little of Mackintosh's money, she has grown into her body and her features. She is barely recognisable as the gawky girl of the confirmation classes.

Naomi is no longer with Bitch-Woman. He's waited for this moment for so many years. He must go to her. He must find out.

He finds it difficult to snub Sally's heart-warming, unwelcome advances.

'It's great to see you, Sally,' he says. 'Really great. I do hope we'll be at the same table. But I have someone I just must see.'

She looks disappointed. Women don't often look disappointed when he walks away from them. She is trying not to look dumbfounded. Rejection is a rare visitor to her life.

Timothy thinks that, in his turmoil of ecstasy and fear over Naomi, he must be giving out something sexual, some male scent. He must be Timothy of the Testosterones, on this amazing day.

And indeed he is finding it difficult not to get an erection as he struggles through the throng. He sees Steven Venables over to his right and waves. Steven, one of the richest failures in the history of economics, raises his hand in a gesture both cool and arrogant.

He is almost halfway to Naomi when he is buttonholed by a man whose name begins with R who played the priest in *Romeo and Juliet* and already looks old enough to play it without make-up. He can't squeeze by without a few words. Perhaps if he uses very short replies he can get away quickly. He wishes he could remember the man's name, though. Why is he alone not wearing his name tag? Roger? Robert? Ronald? Reggie?

'Hello, Timothy.'

'Hello.'

'How are you?'

'Fine. You?'

'Fine.'

'Great.'

'Married?'

'Divorced. You?'

'Yep. Me too. That's life, eh?'

'Seems like it.'

This could go on for ever. He touches Rory/Robin/Roy lightly, affectionately, sympathetically on the shoulder, as one divorced man to another, and moves on. The moment he's gone he remembers the man's name. It's Andy.

'Oh, thanks!' He has coincided with a waiter bearing more lukewarm fizz. The waiters are having a real struggle to get through the throng.

Not far to go now. Oh, the excitement, the fear, the hope.

But why isn't she struggling across the room towards *him*? The thought punches him in the solar plexus.

Next there's Amanda Carmichael's fearsome bosom to negotiate. Just as he's squeezing past she turns, and he feels the whole formidable structure as it slides squelchily across his chest. All traces of his erection subside.

Almost there. My goodness, she looks lovely. She's kept her figure and her face has matured into a sensitive, elegant warmth. It's a face that could keep the cold winds at bay for forty years at least. He's overwhelmed by love. He's really worried that he will pass out from the emotion, and, on a more mundane level, that he will begin to sweat and smell in this crowded, overheated room.

He hesitates. He is a man on the edge of a cliff, who can't

decide whether it's safe to jump. There's a pain in his chest. His breath hurts. His tongue is stuck to the roof of his mouth. He won't be able to speak.

She isn't looking towards him. Why doesn't she turn to look at him? Why isn't she hunting him out, her eyes hungry for him? He is conscious that, at this moment he has longed for, at this moment of all moments, his prick is a tiny shrivelled thing. Hope is draining from him.

She's talking to a man he doesn't recognise. Supposing she doesn't feel for him any of what he feels for her. Supposing she's still with Colin. Well, he could get her off Colin. But supposing she's married for a third time, to someone really nice. Supposing she got engaged yesterday. It would be just his luck. No. That's defeatist. He's not particularly unlucky. He knows people much less lucky than himself. Peregrine, for instance. (He will never think of him as Sniffy again, that much at least he can do by way of recompense.)

The moment has come. He can hesitate no longer. He squeezes between two men who have never heard of the Atkins Diet, and, just as he gets to her, she turns, she has been aware of his movements all along. She turns, and in her face there is – he cannot believe it – not even politeness, just coolness, wariness, even anger. His smile dies, and for a moment he thinks that his heart has died too.

'Hello, Timothy,' she says.

He senses that she is having to try hard to be even this polite.

'Hello, Naomi. It's wonderful to see you,' he says, his voice faltering.

'Is it?' She says this almost icily, her words are almost as cold as the blood that's congealing into ice in his veins.

'Of course it is.' He hasn't intended to come out with it, but something is wrong, and he can't afford to tiptoe round it. 'I've longed for this moment for years. Oh, Naomi, I love you so much.'

He can't believe that he has been so direct. Nor can he believe her reply, and the savagery with which it's delivered.

'Pity about yesterday, then, wouldn't you say?'

'Yesterday?'

'Don't pretend you don't know what I'm talking about.'

'I don't. I haven't the faintest idea what you're talking about.'

'You'll have to do better than that.'

This is a nightmare. Only one thing of real significance happened yesterday.

'I had nothing to do with Tommo's death,' he says.

'Tommo's death?'

She hardly knew Tommo, but she is shocked.

'Oh, my God. Oh, I'm so sorry, Timothy.'

Her hand reaches out as if to touch him, it's a gesture he remembers, it's a touch of the old Naomi, but then she pulls the hand away.

'No, I really am sorry,' she says again.

'Thank you. Thank you, Naomi,' he says, 'but why are you so angry with me?'

'I'm not angry really,' she says. 'I'm just . . .' She looks him full in the face for the first time, and he can see the pain in her eyes. 'I'm just . . . really disappointed. Really sad.'

She turns away, plunges into the crowd, is lost to him.

How does he survive the next half-hour, as his life disintegrates around him, as his perplexity grabs him by the throat and shakes him till he can hardly breathe? Well, he didn't think he could live on after Sam's death, but he did. We make noises, we make social noises, we continue to put one leg in front of the other, we do go on, we survive, most of us, it's called life. Except in Tommo's case. Tommo!

This reunion is turning out to be a nightmare.

He manages to swallow some more sparkling wine, even though it's making him acid. He's even able to eat, and indeed appears to enjoy, a miniature Yorkshire pudding. The minutes pass. He contrives to avoid Sally Lever, because he knows that, if he were to speak to her, he would make dangerous suggestions, in his misery. They could take a bedroom, just for an hour, and he could pour his anger and his . . . don't go there, Timothy.

A gavel is banged, silence falls in part of the room, there are cries of 'ssh', and the silence passes across the room like a ripple of wind over the water. Sentences that might have been important are cut off throughout the gathering. 'I'm living in the south of.' 'I really like your.' 'Isn't your brother a?' 'Let's meet in.'

John Parkin, swelling with pride like a turkey about to make love, addresses the assembly.

'Ladies and gentlemen, old Coningsfieldians all, dinner is served.'

Timothy, shattered, bewildered, destroyed, finds that he is moving, moving out of the Sandringham Room of the Balmoral Hotel, down the wide, carpeted stairs of the Balmoral Hotel, across the busy foyer of the Balmoral Hotel, where five back-packers are arguing furiously with a snooty receptionist, and into the Windsor Room of the Balmoral Hotel. How can it be that he is managing to move all this way, when he is no better than a living corpse? It appears that his legs still work and are moving quite independently of his thought processes. Or is he just being pushed along, a piece of flotsam on a human tide?

Anyway, he's there, at his table, and . . . oh, my God, Peregrine has put him next to Naomi. And there Peregrine is, at the far side of their round table, smiling his benediction upon them, his face flushed and sweaty from all his excessive layers of clothes.

There is another bang of another gavel, or of the same gavel – Timothy doesn't know or care how the provision of gavels works – and here is John Parkin again in all his pomp and in these dire circumstances.

'Ladies and gentlemen, Old Coningsfieldians all . . .'

Yes, you did that bit before.

'What a pleasure it is to welcome you to the Balmoral Hotel today for this splendid, and I believe unprecedented, reunion. It has been a great pleasure for me to do my bit to get this great event organised, and to ensure that no less than a hundred and thirty-one of us are sitting down here today to enjoy the . . . er . . .' A humorous tone enters his voice like a mouse creeping into a cold cellar. '. . . the roast beef of Old Coningsfield.' If this is a joke, nobody recognises it as such. 'But first, there is an announcement to be made. I call upon Timothy Pickering.'

Those splendid independent muscles of Timothy's do their bit again. His backside rises from his chair, his back straightens, he finds that he is on his feet, and there is a deep, expectant hush in the crowded room. Not a word is spoken at any of the round tables, everyone is looking at him, and he has no idea what to say.

They say that as you are drowning your whole life passes in front of you. It is of course impossible to verify this by interviewing the drowned. However, Timothy is drowning now, and he will be able to bear witness to its truth. So much flashes past. His dead son. His living son. His blind father. Naomi in bed with him in Earls Court. And, in that flash, he knows that he must rise to the occasion with dignity, slough off his despair, be a man.

'Thank you, John,' he says. 'Ladies and gentlemen, I have a sombre announcement to make. Sometimes a dinner starts with grace. I dislike this, as I don't believe in God.'

He looks down and sees a flicker of surprise on Naomi's face. Well, any reaction is welcome. But still . . . he is at a table beside Naomi, it's a dream come true, and it's awful. No. Concentrate, Timothy.

'I dislike the assumption that it is only through our faith that we may be thankful for what we are about to receive, and that those who do not believe must therefore be assumed not to be thankful. I am thankful to so many people – my dear father, my good friends, the farmers and the wine-makers who made the produce, the lorry drivers who delivered it, the chefs who cooked it, the waiters and waitresses who served it. So many, and more.

'And I am thankful to be here today, because one of our number, who should also be here today, is not. It is my burden to have to tell you what a few of you may already know, but which will come as a terrible shock to the rest of you. Thomas Bentley, always known to everyone including his parents as Tommo, died yesterday, and I'm afraid he died tragically, by his own hand. Many of us remember his good spirits, his jokes, his vitality. They have helped to ease our lives, but the tragedy is that they couldn't help to ease his own life.

'I won't use that old cliché that we must enjoy the rest of the evening because it's what he would have wanted. Sadly, it turns out that we knew so little of what was going on in his mind that we cannot possibly know what he would have wanted. However, many of us have come a long way tonight, many of us have not seen each other for a long time, and life must go on. A great deal of work has been put into making this evening a success, and I must particularly single out Peregrine Arkwright, whose initial idea it was. Unfortunately, in cases like Tommo's, the funeral cannot be held quickly. Many of you, therefore, will have gone back to your homes and will be unable to attend it. In a moment I am going to ask you to observe a minute's silence out of respect for Tommo. Please observe this as intensely as you can, whether you knew him or not, so that, without guilt or shame, we can enjoy the evening and reaffirm to each other the beauty of existence and the good fortune we have from our favoured place in that existence. Ladies and gentlemen, will you please stand and remember Thomas Bentley in silence.'

Everyone stands. The silence is intense. Timothy counts the seconds in his head.

'Thank you,' he says after what has seemed to him like a very long minute.

There is applause, uncertain at first, then more confident, but still sombre. Then, with a buzz of astonishment and shock, the old Coningsfieldians sit.

Naomi turns to Timothy, and says, with great sadness, 'You did that so well. So well.' Then she turns away.

Timothy is even more confused now.

Peregrine looks across at him, anxious, bewildered.

Timothy shrugs and tries to smile.

He finds the terrine as easy to eat as minced face flannel. Naomi continues in conversation with the man on her other side. Timothy tries to talk to the woman on his left, whom he doesn't know, but he can think of nothing interesting to say. She is soon bored, and turns to the man on her left. There are only eleven people at the table, thanks to Tommo's absence, and Timothy now has nobody to whom he can speak, and across the table Peregrine, in awkward conversation with an angular woman, is still casting mystified glances in his direction. It's bad enough that his evening is ruined, but he doesn't want Peregrine's to sink with it.

He decides that he must do something. He turns to Naomi.

'Excuse me,' he says. 'I must speak to you.'

'Certainly,' says Naomi coolly, with a practised social smile that is like a knife in his belly. 'The moment this nice man has finished his fascinating story.'

The nice man's story is as long as it's fascinating, but at last Naomi turns to him.

'You have something you wish to say, Timothy?'

The cold formality of her words is terrible.

'Yes. Yes, I do. You said something about yesterday. I have no idea what you meant by it. I have longed for this day, as I said, for many, many years, and I think you owe me, if only for the memory of those three nights in Earls Court, especially the second one, the courtesy of listening to what I have to say.'

'All right,' agrees Naomi reluctantly.

Timothy describes his journey. The main course arrives, the slightly overdone roast beef of Old Coningsfield, as he tells her about his arrival at Tommo's, his meeting with Dave Kent, their trip to John Parkin's, and his embarrassing experiences at Peregrine's slowly collapsing ancestral home.

She listens in complete silence. He doesn't know what she is thinking.

'Are you denying that you spent yesterday afternoon in bed with my friend Isobel?' she asks in a quiet but determined voice.

Different emotions come at Timothy like arrows from all angles. Anger at Isobel. Relief, overwhelming relief at discovering what this has all been about. But also, disappointment, sharp disappointment, that Naomi believed the story.

'Your friend is a cow, Naomi,' he says in a low voice. 'More wine?'

She shakes her head.

He pours her more wine.

'Your friend is a complete and utter bitch who is eaten up with jealousy and envy. She grabbed my prick and hurt it quite savagely during a geography lesson on glacial moraines. She hates me because you . . .' He is on the point of saying 'love me', but he changes the tense at the last moment. '. . . loved me.'

She doesn't speak. There is a look of horror on her face, but he doesn't know whether she is horrified because she believes he is lying or because she realises that she has believed Isobel's lie or simply because she realises how wrong she has been about Isobel. Does she believe him? He has to put it to the test.

'Shall we go and confront her?' he asks.

She nods miserably.

It's quite a long walk to Isobel's table. People hold out their hands to Timothy, to shake his hand and congratulate him on his speech, so that it becomes a bit of a triumphal procession, which makes him blush. He doesn't want their praise. It's a slur on his integrity, on the depth of his feelings for Tommo. And it's difficult for Naomi, who wants only to hurry to Isobel and confront her. He wants to ignore their outstretched hands, but his sense of social propriety is too strong.

At last there is only space between them and Isobel's table. They approach her with the gravity of Mafia hitmen. She turns a deathly white, then a dull, blotched red. Her guilt shrieks at them. The misery in her face embarrasses Timothy. It reminds him of what he had felt when faced with his mother. He feels violated by the woman's sickness. He needs to turn away before he becomes contaminated or, worse, sympathetic.

He says nothing.

All Naomi says is, 'I shan't be back tonight, Isobel.'

On their way back to their table, Naomi tries to slip her hand into his. She is surprised when his hand refuses hers, pulls itself away. So is he. He hasn't planned this.

At the table Naomi says, 'I'm so sorry, Timothy. So very, very sorry.'

'I can't believe you believed her,' he says, and he turns away.

What am I doing? he thinks. What is my body doing? This is not what I want to do. This is not what I ought to do. This is very stupid. What fool said that? This could cost me the happiness of the rest of my life.

But he is hurt. And he turns away.

During the lemon meringue pie, Naomi turns to him, and says, 'I'm so sorry, Timothy. Really. I knew that the Timothy I knew wouldn't contemplate such a thing, but how was I to know whether you had changed or not. And I haven't seen Isobel for over twenty years. I haven't had a moment to find out what she's like. I was a child last time I saw her.'

'Oh, that's all right,' he says. 'I understand, and it's all forgotten.'

But it isn't. He's stubborn. And he turns away again. The woman on his left has escaped from him. He has no one else to talk to. But his face is set.

Naomi talks to the man on her right with a vitality that is artificial and assumed, but it may grow into something more natural as the evening progresses. This is very dangerous.

But Timothy is stubborn.

After the meal, as they make their way back to the Sandringham Room where the band has begun playing, Peregrine asks Timothy what's wrong. He gives a swift precis.

'That's ridiculous,' says Peregrine. 'You spoke beautifully about Tommo's problems. Why create a problem? Life's hard enough.'

This is unanswerable, so Timothy doesn't answer it. He now wishes to speak to Naomi, but he doesn't know how to.

Rick Ferrensby, asked to find a good band within the budget, has succeeded in half his task. 'The Ricking Slickers' are well within the budget. Reunited for the first time in eleven years, they are naturally a bit rusty at first. And, all right, even when the rust wears off they aren't actually terribly good, they never were, they only thought they were, but they are Coningsfieldian, Old Coningsfieldians, 'less of the "Old" if you don't mind', and as the evening goes on they rediscover some of the basic principles of musicianship, and they choose good numbers for people to dance to, and they are very amiable, and it all works quite satisfactorily.

About half an hour into the dancing, Timothy sees Naomi dancing with Steven Venables, and he knows that this nonsense must stop.

Steven is rich, and lonely, and arrogant, and she cared enough for him to go to bed with him once. Steven is surely dangerous?

It is at that moment, when he watches Naomi with Steven and knows that there is no danger, that Timothy understands that Naomi loves him as much as he loves her, and all nonsense must stop. So he goes over to them, and he smiles at Naomi, and she smiles back, and she drifts gently away from Steven, it's as if he wasn't there. In the end, after all the agonising, it's as simple as that, they are together, as one, and she can feel his prick hardening against her thigh, and Peregrine, watching from the edge of a floor he hasn't dared to step onto, can imagine Timothy's prick hardening against her thigh – he knows only too well what hardening feels like though he has to imagine the 'against her thigh' bit – and he feels only happiness for them, and looks forward to going back home to do whatever the thing he bought at Janus London enables him to do.

As they dance, Naomi puts her face very close to Timothy's ear, and says, 'I was amazed by that grace of yours. So you don't believe in God any more.'

'No.'

'Was it . . . ?' She stops. She wishes she hadn't started. She doesn't want to mention Sam's death this evening.

'Sam's death? No, funnily enough, it wasn't. I had doubts, perhaps I had some doubts even before that, but . . . I believed that you should fight against doubts.'

'And you needed to believe that Sam's death was to some end? That it wasn't utterly pointless.'

'Yes.'

'But it was. Pointless.'

'Yes.'

'Oh, Timothy. I wish I'd been with you, to help you.'

'I wouldn't have had Sam if you had, and his brief life was good. And I wouldn't have had Liam, or you Emily.'

They dance round and round, to the accompaniment of the occasional wrong notes from the Ricking Slickers. Tonight, at last, there will be no wrong notes from Timothy or Naomi.

And Timothy, bending close to her ear, tells her about his doubts, his visit to the church in Seville, the skylark, his belief in the inefficacy of prayer, and the revelation that a life without faith, without expressible meaning, could still be a wonderful thing. He holds her, feels her, turns her, caresses her, kisses her, tells her, and they move as one, their faces almost touching, the rest of the world invisible.

And Peregrine, watching them mouthing what he assumes to be endearments, dreams that one day he might bend his mouth to some woman's ears and murmur, 'You are so beautiful, my dear,' or 'I want to rip your clothes off your body,' or 'I want to squeeze your nipple very firmly but gently with my teeth,' or whatever it is men say – he hasn't the faintest clue what they say – when they whisper into women's ears.

But Timothy is mouthing none of these things.

'The Victorians were terrified of uncertainty,' he is saying. 'But there is nothing wrong with uncertainty. It's a natural state. The real menace is incorrect and unjustified certainty. That's what I'm terrified of, and I really am terrified. There's a lot of it about.'

The Ricking Slickers are playing, and singing, a song they wrote themselves. It's called 'My Baby ain't a Baby any More'.

'I'm so pleased,' says Naomi. 'It would still have been all right if you believed. But it's so much better this way. For me it's one of the greatest things in life, agreeing with people. And to agree with you . . . Oh, Timothy.'

Now, as the floor begins to thin, they start to dance with energy and excitement. Naomi has natural grace. Timothy has none. It doesn't matter. They are together in more important things than rhythm.

Some people are very drunk, a few are sick, more than one liaison is established which should not be established, on and on they dance, and all the while Peregrine watches.

Now the floor is crowded again, the evening is ending, the Ricking Slickers rise to a crescendo, the room is full of happiness and regret. Happiness that the evening has happened, regret that it is ending. Timothy and Naomi, at last, have no regrets.

And, when at last the dancing is over, Peregrine says that Naomi can come back to Green Acres and share Timothy's room, his parents won't mind and, if they do mind, what does it matter, he's not a child – as the Slickers said, their baby's not a baby any more. And Timothy thinks, 'Yes, you are, but I won't say "no".'

So they go back in a taxi in the barely dark summer's night. And, out of respect for Peregrine, and to a lesser extent for the driver, Timothy and Naomi do no more than hold hands in the taxi, gently tracing the shapes of each other's fingers. During the last few hours of the party they forgot to drink, so they are relatively sober, and Peregrine has been so wrapped up in their events that he has also forgotten to drink very much.

Timothy asks about Colin and Naomi says, 'Who?' and he says, 'Oh, good.' He asks her about her family. She tells him that Clive is still happy with Antoine, who is becoming fashionable, that Julian has now experienced five broken engagements, and that her father has just had his History of Ancient Greece, all nine hundred and eighty-three pages of it, rejected for the first time, but not, she believes, for the last time. And he tells her about his blind father and about the visit of his mother to the auction house. And Peregrine laps up every single word.

It's a long ride, but for Peregrine it ends too quickly. Timothy and Naomi, though, cannot arrive soon enough.

By the time they get to Green Acres, the first faint light is creeping over the north-eastern horizon. The three of them walk up the wide staircase together, then Peregrine smiles shyly and whispers, 'Well, you know the way.' He hugs Timothy with sudden, brief intensity, almost breaking three ribs, kisses Naomi with exquisite clumsiness, and is gone.

Timothy and Naomi walk with light tread along the wide corridor, floorboards creaking, and suddenly Timothy isn't sure if he does know the way. Very, very gently he opens a huge door, and yes, thank goodness, it's his room.

The heavy, faded velvet curtains are not drawn. He goes to the window to draw them, then decides not to. He wants the dawn to creep over Naomi's body.

They undress each other with slow solemnity. Timothy gasps at Naomi's beauty. He cannot believe that he has, at the end of it all, won the love of the most beautiful woman in the world. (Whisper it not to him, ever, that, lovely though she is, Naomi is not more beautiful than many of the lovely women who grace our undeserving planet.)

As Timothy enters Naomi, it is as if twenty-five years of frustration pass away, and yet there is still, beneath the ecstasy, a touch of frustration. He wishes to possess her beauty, and it is impossible to possess another person's beauty. Her loveliness hurts him as well as thrills him. But oh, that orgasm. Oh, the pleasure, and oh, the pleasure of feeling the other's pleasure.

The dawn spreads across the room. Timothy gazes at his lover in the freshness of the summer's morning, and now for a few moments he feels nothing but pleasure, no sense of anticlimax, no shame, no weariness.

This time Naomi goes on top of him and looks down at him with a smile such as he has only dreamt about, and it's as though he's holding her aloft in triumph on his prick. The frail old house seems to shake.

The sun rises, the weather wouldn't dare to be cloudy today. Its rays creep slowly across the slightly lumpy wallpaper, which is threatening to come off the bulging, tired walls of their bedroom. It continues its slow progress, until it shines directly onto the lovers' bed.

It would be nice to say that they make love again, ecstatically, their bodies golden in the sun's rays, their emotions soaring as they realise that this golden sunrise is but a metaphor for the golden dawn of their love and life together. But it is not so. They are in a deep, exhausted sleep. The sunrise passes them by entirely.

In the morning the table is laid for breakfast, the domed dishes are on silver trays on the antique sideboard; the bacon and the sausages and the kidneys are not of the highest standard, the eggs are not free range or organic, lack of money may affect the substance of things, but it cannot be allowed to affect the appearance of things.

Hamish is wearing very bold check trousers, a bright red shirt, and a cravat. His knobbly gouty feet may be in slippers, but he wants to look dashing for Timothy.

Peregrine enters the room at twenty to eleven. He looks pale.

'I thought you were working,' says Hamish.

'I told them I wouldn't be in. I'm not indispensable, you know.'

'Perhaps unwise of you to demonstrate it,' says his father.

'They aren't going to sack me, Father. I'm popular there.'

'Oh, good. Nice night?'

'Very. Er . . . Father . . . ?'

Lavinia enters with fresh coffee.

'Ah. Mother too. I can tell you both at once. Um . . . Timothy has . . . um . . . a lady friend. He loves her and . . . she loves him.'

'What a rare and satisfactory state of affairs.'

'Um . . . she had nowhere to stay last night. So . . . um . . . I invited her back.'

Lavinia is shocked.

'But where on earth did you put her?' she exclaims. 'None of the other beds are aired.'

'I put her with Timothy, of course.'

Hamish and Lavinia look at their son in shock, but not, it turns out, in horror.

Lavinia says, 'Oh, thank heavens for that. I'd never have forgiven you if she'd got pneumonia from damp sheets.'

Timothy creeps in, shamefacedly, at a quarter past eleven.

'Naomi's still asleep,' he says.

He tucks into the – it must be admitted – lukewarm bacon, eggs, sausages, kidneys and mushrooms, on this the hungriest, most beautiful morning of his life. Hamish and Lavinia are leaving him to it, but Peregrine sits at the far side of the table, spreading marmalade onto toast and smiling. Timothy has no idea what to say to him. Besides, he is too hungry for words.

Naomi arrives at ten to twelve. The day is warm, even hot, the breakfast is not. But Lavinia brings fresh coffee and a beaming smile.

'How are our young lovers this morning?' she enquires.

Timothy blushes and finds that he cannot speak.

'He's so cruel, Mrs Arkwright,' says Naomi.

'Lavinia, please.'

'So cruel, Lavinia. I woke up and he'd gone. Can you imagine that? For a moment, maybe less than half a minute, but it was terrible . . . I thought that it had all been a dream.'

'Men have a lot to learn,' says Lavinia.

When his mother has gone, Peregrine looks very embarrassed, turns to Naomi, and says, 'I went to bed without washing my cheek where you had kissed me. And I haven't washed it this morning either.'

'I'm not sure I wish to know that,' says Naomi gently.

None of them have the energy or the desire to leave the breakfast table, but it's half past twelve and Timothy and Naomi must go.

Timothy finds Hamish, holds out his hand to him, and says, 'I must apologise to you, sir. I think we have abused your hospitality.'

Hamish gives his strangely crooked smile and says, 'Don't bother your head about it in the slightest, old boy. I'm thrilled, to be honest. Thrilled to see you both so happy. Thrilled to see my boy so happy. And thrilled above all, my dear chap, because . . .' He lowers his voice, in case Peregrine is within earshot, '. . . perhaps for the first time in his life, my beloved younger son has done something spirited and really rather brave.'

PART NINE

Wide Skies

2008

A narrow street off Leicester Square. A narrow red doorway. A narrow staircase. She climbs the staircase slowly, round the corner with the sad flowers, up more narrow stairs, onto a narrow landing. A glass door leads from the communal stairway to the agency. She rings the bell.

Naomi was very surprised, a few days ago, when her old friend Glenda rang and said, 'I spoke to Daphne the other day about you. She's prepared to meet you.' A few weeks before that, Glenda had rung her, depressed after the break-up of a lesbian relationship and after being cast as a midwife for the fourth time in her career, and had suggested they meet. Glenda had tried to get Naomi to start a relationship with her. Naomi had explained that she was very happy with Timothy. Glenda had asked her if she'd be interested in returning to acting. Naomi had said, 'I might be.' Glenda had said that she would try to get Naomi a meeting with her agent, the formidable Daphne Hayloft, portrayed under various names including Deirdre Barnstorm, Denise Hayrick, Dandy Glassroof and Davina Lofthouse by actors who had turned novelist and hadn't quite enough imagination for the job.

It was easy to say, 'I might be,' but now that she is actually here, she wonders if she should be. Does she really want to return to acting? She has told Timothy that she's seeing her friend Rosie for lunch. It's true. She is. She hasn't lied. But she hasn't told him that she's also seeing Daphne. She has committed the sin of omission, and she feels very bad about it.

The bleakness of the staircase has left her utterly unprepared for the opulence of Daphne's warm, florid office. It overflows with paintings and posters and *objets d'art* sent by grateful clients. There are fresh flowers in abundance, and there are books everywhere.

Daphne has a reputation. She eats critics for breakfast. She has supposedly had affairs with four top theatrical and television producers. She is a large lady, as large as her stairs are narrow, and she is wearing a great flowing dress which emphasises her size.

'I have a lot of time for Glenda,' she says in her booming voice, when the polite preliminaries are over. 'And she speaks highly of you as a friend and an actress.'

'We were in *Nappy Ever After* together.'

'Don't boast about it, darling. That show on its own sunk five careers to my knowledge. I'm a busy woman, Naomi. I don't waste time. So, one or two questions. Are you serious about this?'

'I think so.'

'You think so? You can't think you want to act. It's a disease.'

'I'm trying to be honest, Miss Hayloft.'

'Oh, Daphne, please. I read that I'm formidable, but you must never believe the papers. I'm a pussycat. An absolute pussycat. I'm an absolute darling, darling. Aren't I, Clare?'

'Oh, yes, Daphne,' says her pale assistant hurriedly, in an irritatingly low voice.

'You're trying to be honest?' says Daphne. 'How unusual. How refreshing. Come on then. Sock it to me.'

There are theatre bills, posters and signed photographs of stars everywhere. Copies of *Spotlight* litter Daphne's great desk like breeze blocks carelessly unloaded. The room is seriously overheated. Naomi finds it difficult to summon up the energy to sock it to Daphne.

'I really think I want to try again,' she says, choosing her words with precision. 'I've always wanted to be an actress. I'm extremely happy with the new man in my life, but he has his work and in a way it's his identity and I think I would like to have an identity again too. He goes off to work in the morning and I just live for his return in the evening. I think he'll be very supportive.'

'Are there any more where he comes from?'

She doesn't tell Daphne that she has tried to become a painter, gone to classes in Norwich, found that she has no talent for it.

'What does he do, your supportive wonder man?'

'He's the warden of a bird reserve in East Anglia.'

This is a conversation stopper even to a woman as loquacious as Daphne.

'Children?'

'Not by him and grown up.'

'Good. That's a relief, anyway. Now, darling, let's put this honesty of yours to the test. Is there anything you won't do?'

'Filth.'

'Good gracious. It's the only thing some of my clients will do. And how do you define "filth"?'

Naomi has no problem with that one. She's thought a lot about it.

'Indecency without artistic purpose.'

'Nudity?'

'I should be so lucky.'

Daphne's pale, lanky assistant – unspoken job description, must be in the shadow of the great woman at all times – stands up unobtrusively, slinks over to Naomi and asks her, in an irritatingly soft voice, little more than a whisper, if she'd like anything to drink.

Suddenly Naomi sees traps everywhere. She can't decide between builders' tea – subtext, I'm commercial – or chamomile – subtext, I'd like to do more drama. She eliminates water – subtext, I'm cheap. She goes for black coffee – subtext, I have no trouble with my nerves. It suddenly seems that she really does want to be taken on.

'Are you prepared to do commercials?'

'Yes, in general, though there might be a few products I'd refuse to endorse.'

'One can't be too choosy, darling. Now, darling, are you prepared to give your all? Would you mind, for instance, being called back off your honeymoon? What would the Bird Man of East Anglia say?'

'It's a bit hypothetical. We aren't even engaged yet. But, well, I suppose I would. I'm a professional.'

The pale assistant slides in apologetically, and puts a mug of black coffee in front of Naomi.

Daphne leans forward and, in a much lower voice, asks, 'Now, darling, is there anything you'd like to tell me?'

Naomi hesitates, but only for a moment. She developed secretive trends once. Never again. And she doesn't know how much this woman knows.

'Well, yes. I'm a passionate atheist. I still want to convert everyone I meet. But I don't do it. I became a real pain on *Get Stuffed*. I know now it can't be done that way.'

'How can it be done?'

'I'm still searching.'

'Right, darling,' says Daphne decisively. 'I can't promise

you anything. It's tough out there. It's especially tough for actresses. It's even tougher for older actresses. Male bloody writers. On paper you've very little chance. But I'm prepared to give it a try. There's something about you.'

Naomi is dismayed.

'I've something to tell you,' she says. Her voice comes out all weak and wispy. She's hating this.

She had thought a lot about it on the train, decided on the train that she would see how he reacted, and, if he was really upset, she would phone Daphne and call it all off. It would have been so easy if Daphne had turned her down, but to turn down the opportunity herself, that was difficult.

He sits at the wooden kitchen table which, like Naomi at this moment, is distressed.

'Oh?'

'I didn't just see Rosie.'

'Oh?'

'I saw . . . a woman called Daphne Hayloft.'

'Good Lord!'

'She's a theatrical agent.'

He closes his eyes for a few seconds. She knows that dismay is surging through him. She knows that he must have been wondering if this moment would come one day.

'And?' he asks quietly.

'She's prepared to take me on.'

His elbows are plonked on the table, and he rests his cheeks against his clenched hands for a moment. She aches to see him suffering so, but she knows now, in a flash of uneasy self-knowledge, that she has not lost all ambition.

'I thought I'd like to give it one last try,' she says. She is aware that her voice sounds feeble. She is aware that he is seeing the possibility of his whole happy ordered life being destroyed, her away for long periods, him eating his lonely suppers and coming back from the pub to an empty house every night, just like he used to do.

She's on the verge of saying that she won't do it, when at last he speaks.

'Sorry,' he says. 'Sorry. I should be enthusing. I do, deep down.'

Does he mean it?

'Perhaps I shouldn't say this,' he says, 'but I will. Every time I've seen you perform, on television, in the theatre, as Cleopatra—'

'You saw that?'

'Yes.'

'Why didn't you come round afterwards?'

'I was with Maggie. It was difficult.'

'You didn't like it.'

'I did. I just . . . I just think, Naomi, I've never seen you be as good as you were as Juliet.'

'I see.'

'No, don't go all hurt and silly. I know you can be that good again. That's why I don't mind the lonely suppers, coming back from the pub to an empty house. It'll be worth it, I mean it.'

But does he? Or is he being clever, playing a subtle game?

No. He's direct and straightforward and simple. In the best sense. He is.

She must believe it.

She loves him more than anything in the world. Her love is far more important than her career, her ambition, her self-satisfaction. She's on the verge of saying that she won't do it. But she doesn't.

'Let's get married,' he says.

She's often hoped he would say this. She'd often thought of suggesting it herself. But there had seemed to be no hurry, perhaps not any need. They were happy. What difference would a piece of paper make?

398

Why is he saying it now? Is it part of a plan to change her mind about her return to acting?

No. He isn't like that.

Ask him.

'Why are you saying that now, Timothy?'

He shrugs.

'Don't you want to?'

'Oh, Timothy, yes.'

They kiss. The kiss is very enjoyable, but it solves nothing.

'No, but . . . and I do, of course I do, it's about time, but . . . why *are* you saying it now?'

'I don't know why I said it really,' he says. 'Oh, don't think I don't trust you.' Only Timothy can fall back on a double negative to express such a positive thought. 'I suppose . . . I suppose I just think, if things are going to change, if we're going to have the strength to survive the change, 'cause I don't think it's going to be easy, though it's great, marriage might give us . . . I don't know . . . strength . . . confidence. Anyway, I think a marriage would be fun.'

So they open a bottle of wine, and sit at the kitchen table – it's still distressed, but they aren't – and, in a mood of quiet excitement, plan their wedding. Naomi assumes that Timothy will want a quiet wedding after his two fairly massive ones, but he says no, it's the biggest day of his life, and he wants it to be as big as they can make it, which in any case will not be very big. Registry office, of course, and then a marquee in the grounds of the Fishermen's Arms.

'Quite a lot of people will be very happy to see us married,' he says. 'And you will look so lovely, can't waste that.'

'But a marquee?' she says. 'Do we know enough people to fill a marquee?'

'They have small marquees,' he says.

They begin to make a list of all the people they'd like to

invite. It's not a very long list – thirty-three people in all – but the amazing thing about it is that they actually want every one of the thirty-three to come.

How many people can say that about their wedding list?

The phone is ringing. Timothy has come back for his lunch – couscous with herbs and vegetables – and Naomi is down the garden hanging clothes on the rotary clothesline.

Timothy calls out the words that Naomi has never expected to hear again.

'It's your agent.'

Her heart flutters. She walks towards the house, slowly, trying to feel calm, but she is ridiculously excited.

It has been five weeks since that interview in the upstairs room off Leicester Square.

She picks up the phone.

'Hello.'

She tries to sound confident.

'I have Daphne for you,' says the girl with the soft voice.

'Naomi?' booms Daphne.

'Yes.'

'How are you, darling?'

'Fine.'

'Good. Well, I've got you an audition, Peter Glint. He couldn't direct traffic, but he casts well. Forty-three-year-old lesbian masseuse. Right up your street, darling.'

What does she mean by that?

'Well, it's a bit higher up than chiropody.'

'What?'

'I played a chiropodist in *Cobblers in Koblenz*.'

'So you did. You weren't bad in that.'

Naomi doesn't like the tone of voice, which suggests that, had she gone on, Daphne would have said, 'unlike in everything else'.

'What is it – a sitcom?'

'Drama, darling. New series.'

'Is the masseuse to be a regular character?'

'Not regular, but she may figure from time to time. Probably depends how she goes down. And on whom.'

'I beg your pardon?'

'Only joking. I'll email you the details of time and place.'

'Thanks. And thank you, Daphne.'

'Fingers crossed.'

She turns to Timothy.

'I've got an audition.'

'I'm pleased for you,' he says. 'Not delighted. I like having you here. But pleased.'

They eat their couscous in silence. It will lie very lightly on their stomachs. She just hopes that those four words, 'I've got an audition,' will lie equally lightly.

He gets up to go back to work. She has a pit in her stomach.

He kisses her.

'I'll miss you if you get work, because I love you,' he says, 'but we've been into all that, and I meant what I said.'

Did he mean it? Does he mean it now? How can one ever be sure?

He leaves. Whatever he's feeling, he'll work it off through exercise. They are in the middle of carefully enlarging one of the scrapes, making room for the increasing number of avocets.

Naomi goes to the computer, opens it up, checks on her emails.

The audition is in St Peter's Church Hall, 48 Cromarty Street, EC1. It is at 3.30. next Friday.

Her wedding day.

She starts an email, then deletes it, then starts it again, then deletes it again. She feels that she must find the courage to speak to Daphne in person.

But what is she going to say?

There's only one thing she can say.

'Could I speak to Daphne, please? It's Naomi.'

'She's on the other line. Will you hold?'

'I'll hold.'

She can hear Daphne.

'The money's dreadful, darling, but it can never do you any harm to have been in a Stoppard . . . Excellent. I'll tell Bunty.'

Naomi is so conscious of the marshes beyond the house, the wide skies, the cries of the wild birds, the distant low rumble of the breakers. The world in which people tell things to Bunty seems so far away and so unreal, yet in fact all worlds, if they exist, are equally real.

'Naomi.'

'Hello, Daphne. That audition, it's my wedding day.'

'Oh. Can't you change it?'

'Well, hardly.'

'I recall asking you if you'd be prepared to come back from your honeymoon. You assured me you would.'

'That's a bit different from the actual wedding day. Everyone's invited. The marquee's hired.'

Naomi knows, the moment she has uttered it, that it's a big mistake to mention the marquee.

'Oh, well, if you've booked the marquee . . .'

'It's a big day in my life, Daphne. The biggest. Can't I go some other day?'

'Well, I'll try, of course.'

Daphne tries, but it's no use. She soon rings back.

'Sorry,' she says. 'They've got all the leads. They're only down in London for that day to finalise the minor characters.'

'I'll think about it,' says Naomi.

'You do that small thing, darling.'

Naomi sits in the garden, looks at the streaked sky, and

402

thinks. How is she going to get good work, really good parts, at her time of life, and with her record? How good is she really? Is she good enough? Timothy was right not to like her Cleopatra. He believes she could be as good as she had been as Juliet. So why hasn't she ever been as good again? Because she no longer acted instinctively, she thought too much, and the thoughts got in the way, and the magic didn't happen. Can it ever happen again, or is Timothy's faith misplaced? Is it a life she really wants to lead, if she isn't special? All the waiting for the phone to ring. All those directors and producers and casting directors asking her to do trivial scenes five times, now do it a little differently, try feeling hurt, try being Welsh, thank you, that was lovely, there's the lift, press 'down' and go down, down, down into obscurity. The waiting, the recalls, the rejections, it wasn't that they didn't like you, they loved you, you were brilliant, it was just that unfortunately you were too tall, too short, too blonde, too dark, too strong, too weak, not right with Philip Quilt who's already cast (the bastard), and then occasionally when you did get the part, it was so small, so clichéd. The long hours, the egotistical star, the draughty rehearsal room, the venomous critics, the inevitable biscuits, the meals on location, the spreading waistline, the delays, the repetitions, the inhospitable towns, the phone calls home at night, going out of the bar into the cold street so that he doesn't hear the laughter and think she's having a good time, and then, after all that, after all the discomforts and difficulties and deprivations, the instant oblivion of the piece.

She rings Daphne again.

'I'm sorry, Daphne. I've discovered I don't want to do it enough. I didn't know when I saw you. I do now. Thank you for getting the audition for me. Thank you for thinking that I had something about me. I'll remember that. But, no, it's not for me any more.'

'I see,' booms Daphne Hayloft. 'Well, darling, I hope it's a really nice marquee.'

When Timothy comes home, he's tired. She tells him straight away.

'I'm not doing it. I'm not going back into acting.'

She expects her beloved to be delighted, but that would be too easy. He goes very quiet, has that sullen look that she doesn't see very often these days, she liked it once when he was young, she thought it sexy, not now, now it's just sullen.

'I don't want you not to do it because I don't want you to,' he says.

The triple negative, when she has been so positive, makes Naomi snap.

'I'm not doing it for you,' she screams. 'I'm doing it for us.'

She pushes him, across the floor of their tiny lounge, shoves him into the diminutive settee, and says, firmly, 'Now listen.'

She tells him all the details of the life she would have been letting herself in for. She tells him how long she has waited for him and how much she enjoys being with him, and how happy she is to give up her tiny, probably unrealistic ambition. She tells him that if he doesn't make love to her there and then on the carpet and to hell with whether it's Scotchguarded or not, she will hate him for ever.

What's a poor chap to do? He obliges.

And, as he's obliging, Scrubber Nantwich pops his head round the door, to see if they feel like popping to the pub, sees Timothy obliging, sees Naomi being obliged, decides for himself that they don't feel like popping to the pub, and pops out again.

'M'm.'

He smiles.

There's love in his smile.

'M'm,' he repeats.

William has come a long way on his journey through life, and especially on his journey with Naomi, but he still has his inborn horror of gushing. It's a beautiful photograph, the bride openly, uninhibitedly radiant, and so very lovely in a delicate mauve outfit, with a little gold fascinator on her head, and the groom, uncharacteristically smart in his dark green suit with a spectacular gold tie and matching hand-kerchief, fighting a losing battle against his own radiance. It's a photograph, Naomi feels, that deserves more comment than it has received.

And now William speaks again.

'M'm,' he says.

Timothy and Naomi have gone round to the ugly red-brick house to have a bit of supper and show their wedding photographs to their two elderly fathers. Well, to show them to William and describe them to Roly.

It's a pity that Roly can't see the photograph. He would say more than 'M'm.'

And in describing the photograph to Roly, William finds the words that he lacks when considering it himself.

'It's a picture of such simple happiness, Roly. I wish you could see how lovely my daughter is in her joy.'

'I can see her, William. I can see her as she came to number ninety-six on that fateful day. She will be changed, of course.'

'Changed less than you could imagine.'

'I imagine so. I've seen women who were twenty grow attractively into their forties and fifties. In particular I recall Stephanie Tattersall. I had her behind the bike sheds.'

It's lucky that he can't see the open mouths of William, Timothy and Naomi. They're like a nest of thrushes.

'And, by Jove, I recall seeing her, not quite so clearly, my sight was going, coming out of the Odeon twenty-five years later. And if she hadn't been with that hairy Spanish woman she fell in love with, I'd have had a damned good go at having her again. Anyway, enough of that. I don't know where all that came from. I'd forgotten all about her. All I'm saying is, I can map the changes through my memories.'

'And your boy, Roly, there's such a comical look on his face. He's like a man who cannot believe his luck, who feels so happy that he's embarrassed for the world to see it. He feels it might be tactless to show how ecstatic he is.'

'That's my boy.'

They move on to the next photo.

'This is Timothy and Naomi with the best man. What was his name again, Timothy?'

'Peregrine.'

'He wore the silliest smile all day. He made . . . not a very good speech, but . . . charming. His face, Roly, is narrow, his lips verge on flabbiness, his chin is eager to shrink from life's bustle. It's not a face you can imagine a woman wanting to kiss, but it's an utterly amiable face, and you don't get many of those to the pound in this world.'

The next picture is of Peregrine with his parents.

'You may wonder why we invited them,' says Timothy.

'Being Timothy's best man was just about the greatest thing in Peregrine's life,' says Naomi. 'We wanted his parents to witness it. They were so proud of him. We knew they would be.'

'Also,' says Timothy, 'we felt we owed them something. We shagged so violently in their crumbling pile that I'm sure we dislodged several tiles.'

'Timothy! You're as bad as your father,' says Naomi. 'Two dirty old retired taxidermists.'

Timothy looks shocked, but Roly smirks contentedly.

The next picture is of the two dads, arm in arm, smiling, William shyly, Roly effusively.

It was Naomi's idea that the two men should share the ugly house beside the river. Timothy had wondered if they would quarrel and fall out with each other, but they haven't. William has a natural talent as a carer, and Roly has the sense to be happy to be cared for. Their evenings are a joy to them both. Every evening, William reads out loud a section of his History of Ancient Greece. No one else will ever read it. Seven publishers have told him, with varying degrees of kindness, that it's very good but breaks no new ground and is, in essence, both splendid and unsaleable. And to Roly the history of this astonishing nation, its city states, its battles, its ambitions, its philosophies, its drama festivals, is a revelation. Within a few weeks William will have got to the end of the story, and Roly has told him that, when that day comes, he must start at the beginning again. 'I can't possibly remember it all, dear Carer Supreme. Let it be our Forth Bridge that we are painting in the evening of our great journey through life together, my friend.'

After the two dads comes a snap of Clive and Antoine. William had never even considered the possibility that his book would not be published. Its rejections were, at first, a terrible shock. Antoine, on the other hand, has always believed that his works will be rejected. His occasional sales have surprised him. And now . . . 'Somehow, subtly, standing there on the hotel lawn with his . . . um . . . with my son, and without any effort, any show, he oozes affluence,' William tells Roly. Antoine has become fashionable, suddenly. His unsaleable works now fetch thousands of euros. Clive doesn't need to teach English any more, and does so only occasionally when some handsome Parisian youth appeals. He doesn't have sex with them, he is utterly faithful to Antoine, but he likes to have them around. 'Why spend the day with ugliness when you don't have to?' Naomi is just a little shocked by this political incorrectness.

The moussaka in the oven is smelling increasingly mellow. They hurry through the remaining photos.

Julian and Sarah. They did have a bit of a row round about twenty past ten in the evening, during the dancing, but he arrived for the wedding with her, and he left after it still with her, and that was the first time any of them could remember such an amazing thing happening.

'This time, do you think?' William asks Clive and Naomi.

'I'd be surprised, I'm afraid,' says Clive. 'I think his arteries are clogged by discontent.'

Naomi knows that she is the only woman for her elder brother. She doesn't think that the attraction he feels for her is sexual – he has certainly never given any indication that it is, and she doesn't like the thought that it might be. That evening, on her third wedding day, her perfect day, she sensed that Julian was both happy for her and unhappy, that he resented losing what he'd never had and could never have.

'Unfortunately, life is a court case to Julian,' she says now. 'Julian Walls versus the world.'

They pass quickly over the photo of the lads from the bird reserve, one of whom looks like a bittern in his brown suit. It was a great day out for them, and their affection for Timothy and Naomi was heart-warming. But the moussaka smells almost ready.

Then there are the friends, the new gang of four, the new secret club, Peregrine admitted at last in place of poor Tommo, the four of them smiling like overgrown lads.

There's Steven Venables, with his houses in Marlow and Marbella and bored, bored, bored. His smile is thin, cool, perpetual.

There's Dave Kent, also quite rich in his own right. He's

not known for making thoughtful remarks. His wife has divorced him after twenty-one years of hostility, and he's missing her. He told Timothy, in his cups, that he had a girlfriend but it wasn't the same. Timothy asked him what she was like, and received one of Dave's penetrating portraits. 'She has red hair,' he had said. Later, in even more of his cups, he had confessed, 'My memory's not good. It worries me. I've made all my money out of vegetables. They've been my life. I don't want to end up as one.'

And there's Peregrine, standing tall beside his new chums, oozing pride, awash with the joy of membership. One cannot see into the future, but it's an orchestra to a handbell that they will never go out on another piss-up together, especially now that Peregrine is a member. But that doesn't matter. To be part of it is the point, even if there is no it to be part of.

'This one I do wish I could see,' says Roly. 'These two I've hardly seen. Hard to imagine them now.'

He is speaking of Liam and Emily. Emily and Liam. The grandchildren. Emily is twenty-three now, and Liam twenty-two. What a lovely picture of them both, together and happy on this great day. Oh, my, oh, my. Smiling together. Lovely kids. A credit to . . . ?

When they discussed who they are a credit to, Naomi said, 'I think they are a credit to themselves.'

They've slept together. They haven't made any secret of that. They like each other. But. But but but.

Liam is so sporty, so impatient, ants in his pants, finger up his nose, can't sit in a chair for ten minutes without scratching his arse. Skateboarding, surfing, cycling, climbing, sailing, running. Emily, pale, almost ghostly, reading, sketching, painting, dreaming, strolling, watching, thinking. Emily's legs are longer than her mother's, and just a touch too thin, but she is beautiful enough to be a model. On the surface she's a worrier, but Naomi believes that deep down she's quite serene. Liam's chunky legs are pitted with scars from his innumerable accidents. On the surface he's placid, but Timothy suspects that deep down, in the depths of his ocean, the waters churn.

William places this photograph on top of the pile very gently, almost reverently, and then there is a moment of silence. Are they all thinking the same thing? Are they thinking of the one who isn't there, who would have been in his twenties now, whose absence will live on for ever as one age that he would have been succeeds another? Are they thinking that it would be wonderful if Liam and Emily married? Or are they knowing that it wouldn't work, that those very different pairs of legs should be wrapped round someone else in the love affair of life? Or are they thinking, let's not worry whether they'll marry or not, I just want them to be happy, I just want the world to remain good enough for them to enjoy?

Then there's the gang from the Fishermen's Arms. Timothy and Naomi have made new friends in the narrow back bar of the pub, fondly referred to in the area as Wally's Back Passage. They're all there, smiling. Scrubber Nantwich, and Mrs Scrubber, Charlie Purkiss, Mickey Fudge and his new girlfriend Hayley, Fred and Norma Langridge, Odd Pedersen the Danish painter, and mine hosts, Wally and Linda Cartwright, licensed to preside over some cheery chat and help people escape and enjoy each others' company in the only real pub left in a ten-mile radius.

Hurry. Hurry. That food's ready.

There's a nice picture of Naomi's acting friends. Rosie, wife of the cuckoo clockmaker in *Cobblers in Koblenz*, wife of a leading member of the cast of *EastEnders* in real life. Glenda, the midwife in *Nappy Ever After*, disappointed that she keeps getting cast as midwives, disappointed that Naomi has given up 'the profession', and, above all, disappointed that Naomi shows no lesbian tendencies and is throwing herself away on a man.

Simon, Naomi's first husband, and his second wife Francesca. Peace was made a long while ago. They have been so good to Emily, it was only right to invite them.

There are other photos, lots of them, but they are all of the same people in different combinations and at various stages of the evening. They can look at those later. The moussaka beckons.

William enjoys cooking for Roly and has become extremely proud of his efforts. His occasional comments give him away. 'We only do free range.' 'We've gone all organic now.' 'We don't eat threatened species of fish.' Naomi found it hard to hide her smile when this man, who couldn't even boil an egg when he was married, told her, 'I think I've just about got my suppliers sorted out now.' Oh, how she wished that it was possible for her to believe in God, so that she could imagine her mother looking down on this, her mother's surprise, yet it wouldn't work, for it would be surprise mixed with regret – 'He never did that for me.'

And every dish, of course, was easy for a blind man to eat. William never lost sight of that.

'Do you know,' Roly says, as he slowly eats his delicious moussaka, 'I think I'm the luckiest man alive, to be cooked things like this moussaka every night.'

'Come on, you can't say that,' says William. 'I'm luckier than you. I have the joy of cooking a meal every night for a man who enjoys his food. Besides, I have my sight. Come off it, Roly.'

'I don't feel that I'm unlucky to be blind,' says Roly. 'I had my sight. I can remember what the world looks like. I'm so sorry for those who were born blind. Never to know what things look like. Never to know if what they imagine bears any resemblance to what is. How terrible. But I can picture everything. In my world people don't age. In my world hair doesn't go grey. In my world paint doesn't peel.'

There's a moment's silence. Timothy and Naomi are happy to eat and drink, and smile, and watch the light fade, and hold each other's hands, and wait for the next bout of verbal jousting.

'I most definitely am luckier than you,' says Roly. 'I get a marvellous story read to me every evening.'

'I'm much luckier than you,' protests William. 'I have an audience for a work that I wrote. I get the joy of authorship, the gratification of giving pleasure, every evening.'

'I get the pleasure of it without having had to write a word.'

'I enjoyed writing it. Every word. What a privilege to be able to do that.'

As the two men eat, they are both pondering their next move.

'My wife was a lovely woman,' says William. 'Yours – don't take offence, but you told me so – was a bitch.'

'Precisely,' cries Roly triumphantly. 'So I've spent the rest of my life being glad she left me. And you've spent the rest of your life being sad that you lost yours. No contest, old boy.'

Summer fades into autumn. In a deep tunnel near Geneva, a machine called the Hadron Collider is attempting to replicate the Big Bang that scientists believe created the world. Some scientists thought that this attempt was so dangerous that, the day they switched it on, the world would end at eight thirty-one in the morning. It didn't. Timothy and Naomi wonder how these people must have felt at eight thirty-two that morning. What's it like to be proved so comprehensively wrong?

412

'I have to wonder,' says Naomi that morning, 'how, in the face of such activity by legions of top scientists, any educated person, and particularly the person chosen as vice-presidential candidate for one of the two major parties in the greatest democracy on earth, can still believe in Creationism.'

Timothy shakes his head. He knows that the bee is still there in Naomi's bonnet. There cannot be complete peace, in Naomi's life, and therefore in his, until the bee is released. That night – and it's no coincidence, it must be connected to his worries – he has the dream. He knows that, one day, he will have to tell Naomi about the dream. Maybe that is the only way in which he can free himself from it.

Then comes Remembrance Day. The ninetieth anniversary of the end of the most horrific of all wars.

They've been to the Fishermen's Arms for a couple of drinks. There's been a good crowd in Wally's Back Passage. On the way home they've bought fish and chips, and eaten them as they've walked. It's not something they do very often, and they're feeling mellow. Naomi switches the television on. It's the Festival of Remembrance from the Albert Hall. A clergyman is praying for peace. She switches the television off and turns to Timothy.

'I can't believe it,' she says. 'I just can't believe it. Hold me.'

Timothy holds her tight, kisses the top of her head.

She moves away, puts a match to the fire, sits down.

'I don't want to be a bore about this,' she says. 'I don't want to be an extreme person. I did that once, and it doesn't work. But am I going mad, and is it just me, but is the act of praying to God for peace ninety years after he had failed to stop four years of appalling slaughter ridiculous, or is it ridiculous?'

'I have to say I agree with you, it's ridiculous. I'll make some cocoa.'

413

'That'll calm her. Give her cocoa.'

'I didn't mean it like that.'

'I know.'

She follows him into the tiny kitchen.

'They'll say that God gave us free will and if we choose to slaughter each other, that's not his fault,' he says.

'Even if we often do it in his name.'

'Yes.'

'But if God gave us free will, this means that he can't interfere, and if he didn't interfere in the First World War, what would ever lead him to interfere? So, if he is not going to interfere, what is the point of praying to him? Am I stupid? I just don't get it.'

'You're not stupid.'

'But all the millions who believe aren't stupid either.'

'Perhaps they need to believe.'

'But we don't believe and we don't feel that our lives are futile. We have purposes galore.'

He hands her her cocoa.

'Why do people need to believe in a life after death?' she says. 'What's frightening about dying? What can be awful about nothing, unless we have an exaggerated view of our own importance?'

'I agree with you, Naomi. I just don't see that there's any point in our going on and on arguing about it. Especially since I agree. I suggest we enjoy our cocoa and go to bed.'

'Darby and Joan.'

'Romeo and Juliet.'

'Long time ago. I don't believe, Timothy, that if nobody believed in God – oh, dear, I'm catching your negatives, that won't do – oh, no, there's another one – I do believe that if everybody didn't believe in God, they would not behave any worse than they do now. Oh, no, so many negatives, and I feel so positive. I've heard religious people arguing that

414

we should care more about the starving billions in the Third World, and I agree. Atheists care just as much, but have no platform. I know. I know. Bee in bonnet. Got something to show you.'

Naomi puts her mug down on one of the RSPB coasters, and goes upstairs. She returns with the photograph of the impossibly handsome young man.

'You still have it,' he says.

'I still have it.'

'You've been hiding it.'

'I know you don't like it. It's not my secret lover, Timothy.'

'Well, I know that. It was taken a hundred years ago.'

'Ninety-four. Just before the beginning of the Great War. It's my Great-Great-Uncle Thomas. He died at Mons. He died for his country, at the age of nineteen, with his life before him. He was a member of that last generation ever to believe that there's something noble in war. He died five minutes into his first battle.'

Timothy has gone very white.

'Why didn't you tell me?' he asks.

She answers his question, but she doesn't see how disturbed he is. She's too busy examining Thomas's youthful, radiant yet solemn face, the face of a patriot exalted by the fact that he is about to do his duty for his country.

'I didn't want to seem to be boasting of him, and how brave he was. It's just something private, that I never wanted to share with Simon or Colin, and I would have shared it with you happily once we were married, but I sort of . . . well, I've been so happy these last months that I forgot about it, and that's the truth. He was blown to pieces. Not one part of him was ever found. I've kept his picture as a reminder to myself never to waste one second of the privilege of life. I know. That sounds so goody—'

She sees that Timothy is crying, that he has crumpled in

415

on himself, as if he is imploding, just as he had when she had told him she was leaving him. He is gripping his mug of cocoa as if he expects it to explode if he doesn't. His knuckles are white. She sees him pull himself together. She sees that this isn't easy for him.

'Sorry,' he says. 'This is silly.'

'Darling! What's wrong?'

'He was so brave, and I'm a coward. I get a dream. A recurring nightmare. I can't believe we've both made a secret of something, and both our secrets are connected with the First World War. I . . . I get this dream. Regularly. Quite often. I've never . . . never told anyone.'

Naomi sits beside him on the shabby settee and whispers, 'Tell me, sweetheart.'

'There's not much to tell. It's not much of a dream. It's just that it's . . . very vivid. I'm in the trenches. We're ordered to go over the top. I can't. I'm not brave enough. My legs won't move. The sergeant points his gun at me. I'm stuck. I couldn't go if I wanted to. My legs are so heavy, the mud is so sticky, I make feeble efforts. He raises his gun to shoot me. I wake up, streaming with sweat. You've seen me like that.'

'Why didn't you tell me?'

'Didn't want you to know what a coward I am.'

'It's a dream, Timothy.'

'I think about it by day sometimes. Would I have gone over the top? Would I have been brave enough?'

'You might well have been. You don't know. I think you would have been.'

'Then why do I get the dream?'

'I don't know.'

'It's pathetic, isn't it?'

'No. You can't help having a dream. Oh, Timothy, you should have told me. It's no good bottling a thing like that up. Oh, darling.'

'It's not just the dream,' he says. 'One day I was walking by the sea, near Whitby. It was rough, there was a gale blowing. I thought how dreadful it would be if somebody was drowning and I had to jump in and I wondered whether I'd dare. I walked away. Walked away from it, Naomi.'

'Don't be silly. There wasn't any it to walk away from.'

'Supposing the house was on fire and you were inside it and I had to rescue you, would I? Could I?'

'Oh, Timothy,' she says. 'You can't torment yourself with the hypothetical.'

He stands up, blows his nose, squares his shoulders.

'Sorry,' he says. 'Anyway, I've told you about my dream. End of story. But you talk of not fearing death, and clearly I do.'

'Fearing a rain of bullets in a stinking muddy field criss-crossed by barbed wire at the age of eighteen is pretty natural.'

'I'm not eighteen.'

'You are in your dream.'

'You're going to tell me that your Great-Great-Great . . . how many greats?'

'Two.'

'. . . Uncle Thomas wrote a last letter, before he went into battle, saying how scared he was.'

'No. I'm sure he was scared, but he didn't have any choice, and there aren't any letters, and I expect if he'd had the benefit of history and knew what it was going to be like he'd have been as scared as you. Timothy, you can't spend your life worrying about something that hasn't happened to you and luckily for you will never happen to you. Now stop it.'

He finishes his cocoa, which has gone cold and lumpy.

'I suppose millions probably share my fears,' he says. 'I suppose millions wonder how they would have coped, when tested. I suppose that's why football crowds stand so quietly,

417

and natural rebels wear poppies, ninety years after it happened.'

She nods.

'I should have told you about Great-Great-Uncle Thomas, and you should have told me about the dream. We shouldn't have secrets.'

She sits him down on the shabby settee, she sits beside him, and she begins to tell him all about the things that have happened to her since the day she told him she couldn't marry him.

She tells him about her conversations about death with her mother and Emily, about marching down Oxford Street with sandwich boards, driving to Clodsbury at over a hundred miles per hour, waking up in hospital, living with her father, sailing with her father, going up to Coningsfield and finding him gone.

He tells her about the day of Sam's death, and Hannah going off with Mr Finch, who upped and came, and being embarrassed to talk to his father in the home for the blind, and auctioning off his father's works, and his mother turning up.

Some of these things they had told each other before, but now they tell them in detail and in sequence. Eventually they fall asleep in each other's arms, on the shabby settee, and the fire dies, and they wake up cold but happy, and they go to bed at half past four in the morning.

Timothy goes straight to sleep, his breathing regular and unhurried. She puts her lips to his shoulder, and kisses his skin so softly that he would not have felt it if he had been awake, and she whispers, 'Goodnight, my good, good man.'

On Remembrance Day itself, three men, the last three allied survivors of the Great War, lead the parade at the Cenotaph.

They are aged a hundred and twelve, a hundred and ten and a hundred and eight. Naomi watches alone, Timothy, at work, observes the two-minute silence. Thousands of gulls don't.

That afternoon, Timothy has an idea. But he won't mention it to Naomi until the time is right.

The opportunity comes two days later. It's the most lovely winter's day, a cool breeze, bright sunshine, fluffy clouds, and the air as pure as space.

The trusty, rusty estate car is laden. Timothy has been buying supplies. Naomi has gone with him. She just loves being with him. On an impulse he turns off the main road, drives down to the staithe, parks beside the creek. They walk slowly along the path, past a man with an enormous lens and a huge tripod. On their right are reed beds and marshes. On their left, the tide licks at the glistening mud. They listen to the wind moaning in the rigging of the few boats that have not been laid up for the winter. The halyards sing as they flap into the masts. Gulls complain and argue. Geese fly back to their salty lodgings in a perfect V, noisily discussing their day. A heron lazes towards a line of pines. An oystercatcher pipes, bubbles and trills. The winter sunset smells of woodsmoke and toasted teacake. Timothy turns to Naomi and says, 'I know what you could do.'

She doesn't say, 'About what?' She knows.

'You can't play their games. You can't preach. You can't lecture. You can't badger and bully. All you can do is tell our story and hope.'

'Hope what? To change the world?'

'That's not in your gift, darling.'

Naomi smiles.

'What are you smiling at?'

'Nothing.'

They have sworn to tell each other everything, but some things are too small to tell, too silly. She has smiled because she has been thinking how different Timothy's East Anglian 'darling' is to Daphne's London one.

'How can I tell our story? How can I tell your story?'

'We shared enough of our stories the night before last. Of course you can.'

So what will I achieve by telling it?'

'I don't know. Maybe nothing. You'll enjoy it. I'll enjoy it. I'll be proud of you. Somebody may publish it. Somebody, somewhere may think about what you say.'

'That isn't much.'

'I'm sorry, my love. I think it's all you can do. And words, Naomi, words are quite wonderful. Who could not want to spend their days with them?'

The magnificence of the sunset fades rapidly. The wind drops with the dusk, as it so often does. An elderly little fishing boat putters and splutters back to port. On the few yachts the halyards are stilled, the rigging is silent. Even the gulls sleep. One last shrill cry comes from a wading bird, out towards the open water, and then it's night.

'I'll have a go,' says Naomi.

She watches the space where the window is, longing for first light. But you can never see the first light. One moment it is utterly dark. The next moment, the outline of the window is faintly clear.

She can't believe how long the night is, and how quietly Timothy sleeps. There are no trenches in his head tonight.

At last the faintest of lights fills the tiny room. She can see the oak beam in the middle of the curved, cracked ceiling. She is able to put on her slippers and tiptoe out of the room without waking him.

She goes down the narrow staircase, fills the kettle,

switches it on, curses its noisiness, makes herself a cup of tea. She climbs the stairs slowly, passes their bedroom door, enters the guest bedroom, where Julian has slept with Sarah, Clive with Antoine, Emily with Liam. There's just room for the computer in the corner, her computer, which Timothy doesn't use. He doesn't need to. She is his link to the world.

She switches it on. It's not in the first flush. It doesn't like the cold. She has learned not to hurry it.

At last she senses that it's ready to respond. She clicks onto Microsoft Word. After just a bit of teasing, it provides her with a blank page. Thrillingly blank. Terrifyingly blank.

She types one word – 'Novel'.

What is she thinking of? This is no novel.

She deletes it, types 'BOOK', clicks on 'Save'. She is given a list of places to choose from. She opts for 'Desktop'.

There it is, on the desktop, the single, exciting word, 'Book'.

She clicks on the word and the page comes up, 'BOOK'. Truly remarkable, still, to Naomi, although one day, and soon, this process will be regarded as primitive.

So far so good. But now comes the first tricky bit, the first potential crisis. The first word. The first sentence. The first paragraph.

It takes courage to begin. It's like diving off the top board.

She begins.

She hears Timothy's alarm go, hears him stir, hears him go for a pee. As he returns she calls out.

'Timothy. Come and look.'

He bends to enter the little room without cracking his head.

'What is it?'

'I've begun. I think it might be going to be all right. Have a look.'

He bends down beside her, squints at the screen – soon he'll need glasses – and reads.

Three mighty obstacles threaten the burgeoning love of childhood sweethearts Timothy Pickering and Naomi Walls. They are Steven Venables, a dead curlew, and God.

Author's Note

All the locations described in Old Compton Street, Peru, Paris, Seville and Guernsey are real and, I hope, accurate. All other locations, including those in Coningsfield, the Pennines and East Anglia, are imagined.

The unnamed German travel agent, for whom I have a soft spot, is real, as is the speech made at the funeral by the Peruvian lady. There are elements of the late and sadly missed Father John Medcalf, a wonderful man, in Father Paul, though his conversation on his sexual activities is, I am glad to say, entirely fictional. All other characters and events are fictional.